Vagabond Thirty-Four Vagabond Thirty-Fo

A Woman's War against Progress

by Allan Cameron

Vagabond Voices
Glasgow

First published on 2 October 2023 by
Vagabond Voices Publishing Ltd.,
Glasgow,
Scotland.

ISBN 978-1-913212-35-3

Printed and bound in Poland

Cover design by Mark Mechan

Typeset by Park Productions

The author acknowledges subsidy towards the writing of this book from Creative Scotland

ALBA | CHRUTHACHAIL

For further information on Vagabond Voices, see the website,
www.vagabondvoices.co.uk

Contents

Author's Preface

The last thing a long novel needs is a long introduction, so I want to be as brief as possible. The idea for *A Woman's War against Progress* was suggested by a programme on Radio Four which discussed the fate of the reindeer-herders of Tuva (a Russian federal republic), whose way of life has been destroyed since the fall of the Soviet Union. We tend to ignore the evidence that the various iterations of progress appear to have caused more misery than the ways of life they replaced – clearly this is the case for the Tuva, but it is even more so in the case of the native peoples of North America and Australia.

I didn't want to do an ethnographic study of this people and preferred to invent an archetypal linguistic minority that could represent the many minorities around the world. My trips to the Baltic States have taught me that the forests for these countries exercise a particular fascination on some of their citizens, and probably do so in Russia and many other Eastern European countries as well. I personally am a corrupted "civilised" person with absolutely no desire to go into the forest and commune with nature, but the idea of trying to imagine such cultures attracted me and I certainly believe that we "civilised" peoples have been amongst the most brutal and vicious in the history of humanity – although we rarely think so in spite of the undeniable evidence. It promised to be an excellent conceit to develop a novel not only about small cultures but also about the follies of empire, symbolised by the old-Etonian Edwin Perkins and his ghastly theories on race.

Not that Russia was the worst of the Empires, and the Tsarist crimes against minorities – brutal as they were – were nothing compared the behaviours of European states in Africa and the East, or Europeans in North America and Australia. This less extreme setting was perfect for developing more nuanced ideas about how minority languages and cultures interact with the dominant ones. Russia also provided a varied historical background for this story in which I was assisted by my female protagonist, Rahväema, whose life was a gradual corruption caused by the increasing influence of "civilisation" on her thinking, but mitigated by her gradual drift towards a more universal outlook as her successes started to falter. In fact the whole book is intentionally built upon her character and her narration. She has a degree of integrity, but she is not an entirely reliable narrator, as she herself suggests arguing that such a thing is impossible particularly for a political activist.

This novel has a serious purpose, but I have to admit that it was a pleasure to write: I was able to invent proverbs, mythologies and social practices for my fictional people, the Surelikud. I plundered Estonian for Surelik words, and at least one word was taken from Scottish Gaelic, which also sits in the background along with my studies into Slovenian in Italy. When trying to find a voice for the Scribe, I listened to a whole series of speeches by Tony Blair; who else could represent modernity, its banalities and its discontents so well?

The novel's serious purpose does not go as far as trying to convince the reader of any particular ideology. Instead I want the reader to think about the problems we face by approaching them from a completely different angle. I don't agree with everything Rahväema says, of course, and in any case, she is not averse to a degree of self-criticism. I am not a nostalgic for a past I cannot know, but I am trying to demonstrate how completely dysfunctional and mendacious our own societies are.

Finally I want to say that everything that follows this page is the novel and therefore completely fictional. Sometimes I treat historical characters a little cruelly with no firm evidence. Suspend disbelief and find your own way through this forest of words and imaginings by a writer with no experience of the forest!

A Woman's War against Progress

by Rahväema Ranavutavskaya

translated by
Voorapoiss Perkinsov and David Perkins

The Translators' Preface

The author, Rahväema, always wanted an English translation of her memoir, not knowing just how difficult this can be. She would have assumed that as English is a widely spoken language, there would be a translation but it would be translated from a Russian translation and not the Surelik original. She would unquestionably have been much happier with how this book eventually came to be published in English. It has been the joint effort for some years of two elderly half-brothers: Voorapoiss Perkinsov, the author's son by my father, whom she often refers to in the book but never by name, and myself, David Perkins, a "legitimate" English son of the same father.

I was the youngest of the family by far, born in 1948, and cannot remember having loved or even liked my father, who luckily was often absent, but whose return I always dreaded. Although he never served in the armed forces, he ran his house, when he was present, with military zeal. All the children had to make their beds and tidy their rooms before breakfast, and then stand to attention in a line on the landing, while he carried out his inspection. He was exactly as Rahväema describes him in this memoir. As I came of age in the sixties, we were always set on a course whose collision was inevitable as neither of us were willing to take evasive action.

I had vaguely known that I had a half-brother in Russia, and I set about trying to trace him, which was not easy during the Cold War, particularly in its colder moments. I established a correspondence in English during the seventies, and finally met him in the Gorbachev years, and it was like meeting an old friend. We have a lot in common: our father's physiognomy which was unfortunate, a belief in humanity, a love of reading, a dislike of the limelight and committees, and a disdain for our parents.

He also convinced me of the importance of the Surelikud, of whom I knew nothing. It is ironic that he, Rahväema's rejected son, is now the one who continues to support her approach to the campaign. He doesn't believe in "virtual languages", which at best could take on the stunted growth of a liturgical language, and at worst become a playground for bureaucrats and academics. For him a language is only sustained by a language community who live that language daily – unconsciously.

Although we are very close and spend time together at least once a year, and are in constant contact with each other, this translation did on occasion test our friendship. Unsurprisingly he was more sensitive to the original Surelik text and I to the translated one, the English that had to take its place. I probably haven't been able to match the full poetic force of Rahväema's dictated prose, or even her quirkiness and humour, not to mention the intentionally chaotic structure that got on the scribe's nerves. The fact is that, before her, Surelik had no prose literature but it did have a prolific poetic tradition whose oral authorship is often unknown.

While writing this preface to the English edition, I have consulted my brother at every stage, and there is one thing that he is very keen to underscore. Since the publication of this memoir in its original Surelik text shortly before her death, he has reassessed his view of his mother and her role. He already knew that they shared many ideas when it came to the language, but he now understands her behaviour precisely because of the memoir itself. He now feels that she made the right choice in abandoning him. It is much better to have been brought up by a loving aunt than by an embittered mother who in every act of cherishing him would have felt that she was sacrificing herself and the language that she loved. Guilt

4

and compassion are worthless and little more than a false declaration of virtue, if they fail to change not only the actions of whoever experiences those emotions but also the heart that wanted to obstruct that change.

David Perkins, March 2019, Goring-on-Thames

A Woman's War against Progress

In the autumn of 1916, I came out of the forest and abandoned the peace known only to those who know neither gods nor devils. And I came to a sophisticated and technologically advanced world where men dressed with unsurpassed elegance, although any pre-war beaus in the capital would have considered them to be rustics from a far-off province, which was more or less what they were.

And when I came from the wood, I left behind the knowledge and wisdom of the Surelikud, which was only one of the many forms of knowledge and wisdom that inhabited the wood. Ours was both an understanding of the wood and an understanding that the varieties of life in the wood understood the wood in different and barely communicable ways, and yet those understandings fed off each other in spite of their mutual opaqueness. Even where there was conflict, it was understood as the inevitable result of how the wood lived and breathed together.

The Surelikud moved through the wood in two ways: either in silence or with laughter and song. The latter was never loud because the wood is not hard of hearing, and it announced our friendly intentions. Sometimes we halted to pick berries and natter, and sometimes we argued – to the amusement of the trees. But when we moved in silence, the whole wood stiffened, particularly the other animals. The trees spectated and said to each other, "Who will win today, the cunning Surelikud or the strong-limbed boar?" The trees were the first to hear the silence of the Surelikud, but it was the hearts of the flighted birds and sharp-sensed deer and the strong-limbed boar that quickened.

"The Surelikud are a devious animal," thought the trees, "and deviousness counts more than strength. They hunt together like a single beast, and they laugh and sing and chatter like divided souls, but they always love the wood, and take only according to measured and contingent needs, as do all the varieties of life that live within our kingdom."

But it is not of the knowledge and wisdom of the Surelikud and the wood that I wish to speak in this book, but of the greedy knowledge of the self-appointed civilised world – the treeless world – which I have strived throughout my life to master in the cause of the dwindling Surelikud and their increasingly threatened forest lands. That I should call it "theirs" and not "ours" is evidence of how I have become imbued with the culture I fought against, and my achievements on behalf of that cause have been patchy. Inevitably, I would say.

Of my life before my arrival in Väikelinn I will say little, because it was the better part of me which I have since sealed in a box to protect it from the person I became in order to protect our Surelik way of life from others. In short, this is the tale of how I was corrupted by my own struggle to protect the Surelikud, even though it came from a generous impulse. And I dictate it not to justify myself but to describe the desperate fate of my people.

Who knows which language you're reading this in? There are only about sixty thousand of the true Surelikud of the forest left, and if numbers continue to fall there will be none in a generation or two. Maybe our descendents will speak in the language of the Triers who fought so hard for something that melted away like the spring snow, or in the language of the Noisy Musics and the Little Noisy Musics who share a language and the belief that everything can be bought and sold, even the land and the rivers. Some day perhaps even the air itself.

Now I stand and dictate this memoir to a young Surelik woman who can write in the Surelik language, but doesn't know it as a Surelik should. To know this language you don't have to write it; you have to speak it and think it as you travel alone through the forest which has its own language that you have to listen to. The forest language must be akin to the Surelik language for surely they must have gradually come into existence together through a silent dialogue of languid incomprehension. What would be the point of the Surelikud, if there were no forest left? No point. Our language is structured like the branches of a tree, which intertwine and cannot be distinguished one from the other.

The Surelik my scribe normally writes contains many words I've never heard amongst the Surelik peoples. These words either describe things you cannot see or the useless things the Triers and the Noisy Musics rely on greatly. I will make sure that she will not type or record any of these words in this memoir.

Let me make it clear: a language comes out of its people, and its people are anchored by their language. It joins the generations of a people together and when that continuity is broken either by the imposition of another language or a sudden metamorphosis within the language itself, then that people ceases to exist, and either it is subsumed into a greater language or it reinvents itself as a new people. The Surelikud of the Forest are the pure Surelikud; you could say the only Surelikud. They live the Surelik life and hold to the Surelik culture. The Surelikud of the plain are half Surelik and half Trier. Neither birds of the forest nor beasts that walk the forest floor. They speak the language of the Triers often perfectly, and their Surelik is corrupted by their words and, worse, their way of thinking. I was born in the forest, and am therefore a true Surelik. I remained in the forest until I was almost sixteen, when I moved to the Surelik settlements on the plain. During my life I have lived amongst them often and more often amongst the Triers themselves, but always I have remained a Surelik of the forest, or like to think so.

The Triers and the Noisy Musics say that we're superstitious – and maybe we are, but they who believe that they'll live in another world after death are surely more so. We believe in the spirits of the rivers and the forest, which we try to placate, but they believe in life everlasting. As we own nothing in this life, how could we believe that we own an existence in another? We are no different from the birds, the beasts and the trees. We die to make room for others who should grow stronger and taller.

Who are these Noisy Musics? Well, a few years before the rule of the most powerful Triers fell and the Noisy Musics took control of the planet, the Triers' elders, a group of stubborn old men who always said the same things, gave in and allowed their young people to listen to the noisy music of their sworn enemy, as the young loved it so much. At the time I lived amongst the Triers, using my wits in a more liberal regime and observing a society in transition, so deep was my desire to find out how I could exploit it to further the Surelik cause. When the noisy music started in the bars and places where people congregated, it drove me away. The voices of the Noisy Musics were coarse and sharp and greedy for life. It turned out that Noisy Musics, when they did eventually come, were much worse than their music, but that's another story.

The Triers tried too hard, because they thought that history is a malleable thing, and that good can be achieved through sacrifice, which in part is true, whereas the Noisy Musics thought that good could be achieved by greed or rather all the various conflicting greeds finding a magical equilibrium in which all would prosper, but in reality all the greeds compounded and expanded exponentially and this is why every week another tract of forest is bought by a mining company belonging to the Wall-Builders. Who they bought it from I do not know. Not from us, we can be sure of that.

The Wall-Builders do not live far beyond our forest, and they are as busy as bees. Their cities grow out of the ground like mushrooms, whose subtle, wiry roots appear incapable of bringing sustenance to such ambitious buildings that stretch to the sky. We know them here for their love of digging deep into the ground and taking what the ground contains. The areas where they dig are fenced off and no one can travel there, but we know that they've dried the rivers and crushed and chewed the land into piles of useless dirt where neither plant nor animal can flourish. There are ruins of a mine from the Great Caesars' times, and some people say that the Wall-Builders' mines will meet the same end: they will be subsumed into the forest and the buildings will be repainted with a layer of green foliage. They've not understood that the scale is quite different now and the damage not always reversible. Still the buzzing of the Wall-Builders brings no joy, and they're not so different from the Triers and the Noisy Musics, but they drink less and work harder. One day they will own this blasted and poisoned planet. They will own its husk. Or maybe they'll save it, if given a chance.

My scribe has asked me why I use such terms as the Triers, the Noisy Musics and the Wall-Builders, when there are words for these peoples in Surelik, but these are new words, soulless words half-borrowed and half-cobbled together – as cumbersome as the cultures they indicate. To use such words is to contaminate ourselves and our language. Before the alien words were coined, everyone who was not Surelik was called Surnudhinget. We did not discriminate, and this was right and proper. That I call them Triers and Noisy Musics is my own compromise with modernity, and once I would have thought that this was going too far.

Write this down. I want them to know of our little disputes, which will be instructive. My dear scribe, you've been half-corrupted by progress but you're still part of the story. You've got to write down everything I say, even if I'm talking to you! Except when I tell you not to.

I should perhaps introduce my scribe, who is carrying out an essential role in this whole exercise. She is more than ten centimetres taller than I am. Ten centimetres? What is that to the decades of experience that make me her superior? This is why she is seated beside me at her computer and I dictate to her my extraordinary life and adventures and fame, which of course she envies, as is quite natural for a bureaucrat of her stamp. We struggle against each other, which is also inevitable, and her respect is mixed with enmity.

And yet we are also friends – of a kind – for how could we embark on such a grand project as this, if there were not a bond of loyalty. Not so much loyalty to each other, as to our cause. So she is punctilious in transcribing my words even when I humiliate her, for humiliate her I must if I am to instruct her on how this battle must be fought. Of course she won't follow my teachings; she is too wrapped up in her world of things to understand the importance of quiet, of reflection and of abstinence.

Where was I? The Triers and the Noisy Musics. I prefer the Triers; though they're barely aware of our presence, they are nevertheless our neighbours. We know them and have learnt to deal with them. The Surelikud in the plain are no longer real Surelikud. That's the problem: the Surelikud who settle have to integrate with the big burly neighbour who surrounds us completely. The Triers have no give. They're the rock and we're the river. We survive only by keeping on the move. If we settle, then we become little more than exotic Triers to be put on display and patted on the back.

We can only breathe in the forest, which is ours. It doesn't change us, because we don't try to change it. It knows our smell and relaxes. We've lived together for as long as it can remember.

But yes, I prefer the Triers. What they try to do is often well intentioned. They tried to make us equal, not realising that we are already equal. Every organism is equal, because each is a necessary part of the whole. We Surelikud never thought that a man is more important because he rode in a fancy carriage and claimed to own a valley and two mountains. Possibly fat and out of breath, such a man would never feel the world around him, the world we're all part of, a world that's half rotting and half exploding with luxuriance. Life is a balance and if you take too much away from the earth, you upset that balance.

Yes, I prefer the Triers, because they retain at best something of what it is to be human. They know how to suffer, so they know the meaning of joy. If you lose that essential truth, you lose your humanity.

This has happened to the Noisy Musics. They think that happiness, whatever that is, is their right because they've paid for it with the money they love so much. They don't understand that joy is an occasional gift of nature which comes to those who don't seek it out voraciously, and that contentment comes with calmness of the soul and an inability to despair.

You say, my dear scribe, that I cannot know, not having visited the land of the Noisy Musics. But I have heard it in their music. They scream with desire and wallow in their tears. Their pain can be felt thousands of miles away.

I've never been lonely, but often I've felt the need to be alone. That is the way of our people. We meet and we say what we have to say - and no more. We move in small groups or even alone, as I often did.

I have never believed in the essentiality of art and literature. I'm only having my story written down because I'm not dying alone, as our culture is dying with me. Until now I've had no need to record a beautiful thought or experience, because I knew that - just as the moon changes and then changes back - one of us who comes after would think or experience it again. There was no need to grasp and conserve what one day would blossom and ripen on another tree.

This memoir contains periods in which I left my Surelik homeland and lived amongst the language of the Triers. I learnt it, yes, but initially had no intention of becoming one of them, and sometimes I pretended not to understand a word they said. They would speak to me in their rounded, musical, manly tongue and I paid them no heed, and nearly always they would leave me in peace – eventually, for on many occasions they persisted for a period of time that was clearly more tiresome to them than it was for me. As they grew increasingly agitated, I was warmed by a malicious peacefulness.

Occasionally I was arrested by the uniformed men of the Militsiya, as they called it. They would switch between shouting angrily and scoffing haughtily, and were capable of shoving and slapping me, but I was still calmer. I was for them both a threat and an absurd irrelevance. Usually they would let me go, but once they registered me and gave me a card with a woman's face on it. I was told that she resembled me very closely.

Dostoyevsky said that everyone has secrets they don't admit to themselves. How grand of him to know us all so well when discoursing on our inability to know or admit! I am the exception to his rule, along with many others – including himself, I think. I analyse myself mercilessly, cruelly, because I have to if I want to get to where I want to get to. But don't think that you'll get such things in the pages of this memoir. If that is why you bought this book, you'll be disappointed. This is even truer for foreign readers, who should not purchase the haverings of an unknown leader of an unknown people, unless they want to know more about humanity in its wider and more varied circumstances, though it is united by that aptly named human condition we can never properly define.

I'll be selective. I say this unashamedly, for this is how we manage to explain the truth as we see it: I'll do this by selecting the events and arguments that fashion a convincing image of that truth. We think through a process of categorisation and selection; we have to, because what we know, half know or mistakenly believe we know – those three restless, unstable clouds that drift in the endless space of our minds – are too vast and amorphous to be taken comprehensively into account. I don't select to defend myself, though there must be a little bit of that, but to defend the cause that has driven my life since the death of my first husband, Pyotr Sergeyevich.

And you may ask, "What exactly was that cause?"

A very good question, and I cannot find a satisfactory answer because my own perception of it has changed over the many decades of my struggle. My enemies have changed. Sometimes I'm nostalgic about my old ones. One oppressive progress was replaced by an even more oppressive one. So oppressive that it poisons the soul and reduces humanity to a domestic animal who exists and consumes as instructed by subtle messages even the messenger doesn't understand. It is the society of multi-coloured greyness, the market in which change is conformist and dialogue formatted on a single voice.

Some people say that I'm like that: an imperious and controlling voice that leaves no room for dissidence, doubt or even nuance. They could not be further from the truth; my mind is full of dissidence, doubt and nuance, but the leader of the weakest people in the world, who has never gone unchallenged, must feign self-assurance and certainty, and today's young candidates, who have formed a queue awaiting my death, have to understand that they cannot stand up to a powerful and hostile world and remain stuttering, indecisive supplicants. I have to advance like an empress who has neither army nor police force, neither judiciary nor parliament, just the West Siberian Surelik Cultural Committee, the impoverished capitalist offshoot of what had for a short while been an Autonomous Surelik Republic, whose task was to rubber-stamp decisions taken elsewhere. But it did have better offices!

I advance armed only with my self-confidence, which is the bastard child of my suffering and loss, and of course my wit, which comes with my Surelik blood, our language and our stories. These things can only take you so far, and my removal could have harmed the Surelikud's destiny. That may sound arrogant, but I am the Surelik people, I have traded my soul in order to be theirs, and I will live on in their hearts, and this memoir will help to achieve this.

And yet I write of course for the Surelikud, but also for the foreigner to whom I plead their case. Now the powerful

15

peoples of the world – the Noisy Musics, the Triers, the Wall-Builders and even the many other countries that believe themselves to be powerful but aren't – face two enemies more powerful than they are.

Where are these new empires? you ask. What kind of peoples are they? Ah, can't you see that their territory almost covers the planet. They share the same territory and engage in a symbiotic struggle between each other.

No idea? The first of course is Nature, once relaxed and tolerant of humanity's voracity. Now it is riled, and its polluted sinews have stirred, and both the powerful and the weak will shudder under its furious, reverberant blows. And the second empire belongs to mechanisation and chemical manipulation, which have become a drugged, metallic monster to replace the humanity who created it – or rather to merge with humanity, making it more mechanic and itself more human in a soulless manner.

If the powerful peoples of the world wish to make peace with these new empires, they will have to come to the Surelikud and learn our ways, for they cannot defeat the new empires with tanks and aeroplanes. They must learn humility and with that, the knowledge of when to retreat, when to negotiate and when to accept their own powerlessness. In other words, they need to regain their humanity.

But I must tell my story in my own tongue and my own way, keeping my various readers in mind, as I'm in danger of running ahead of myself. Before setting off on that narrative, I want to clarify one more thing: my life since I took up my struggle has been an enormous personal effort. I am a paradox: born of a long line of semi-nomads wandering the forest at will and engaging now and then with the townships on the edge of empire, I have taken on the arduous task of defending with all my strength that beautifully feckless and harmless way of life. I have subjected myself to a spartan regime of discipline and study so that others could let their bodies wander where their souls' whims wished to take them. I analysed our oppressors' impenetrable and once to me incomprehensible societies so that all that was familiar to my childhood could to some extent survive. Though battered and buffeted, the Surelik way has survived, and today it is still recognisable, but I, one of the last true Surelikud, am no longer a true Surelik – merely its paladin! Such a degradation.

Until quite recent times, I would still lose myself in the familiar intricacies of the forest, sometimes for weeks on end, but I would not recognise the smells that lurk beneath the canopy: had it changed or had I? I fear that it was the latter; my nostrils had been desensitised by the sickly odours of the modern world which manufactures words to play with the wants of domesticated human beings held in pens and driven by persuaders electronically integrated into their needs for such artefacts and contraptions I could never have imagined or conjured up from intellect. The hidden hands are few but they rummage everywhere.

I did not plan to make this terrible admission in the opening pages. Imperious and controlling indeed! I am a woman who has kept her emotions in place and paid the price. But don't tell me that I don't have them; it's more that I no longer have any use for them. They have become an unnecessary luxury, and in the past our people had a sensible suspicion of luxuries.

And I suppose that readers, or at least readers with less subtle minds, will ask why I didn't abandon this life and re-immerse myself in the true life of a Surelik. There are decisions which, once taken, cannot be reversed for many reasons: there is the desire to see what can be achieved, as abandonment would leave unanswered the question of how it could have turned out. Life is an experiment. Choose your experiment, and you choose your life. And how little thought you give to it. Life is governed, in spite of all those dull philosophers, by whim and not reason. Then along come some decisions which involve the sacrifices of others, so those who decided for them have to take responsibility for the first act. You cannot abandon the others along with the cause, because Man is a moral animal. I learnt that from the Triers, because only amongst corruption can "morality" have meaning. Our morality is innate, but if it is generally followed, it becomes invisible.

Finally and most significantly, you cannot unlearn corruption: progress takes you down a road – down a steep slope – and only the very strong can find their way back. It would have required more strength than the considerable strength I had displayed in pursuing my aims for all those years. Perhaps I lacked that extra strength required or perhaps I knew that I was more useful in this forum of intentional miscommunication where I could use dishonourable discourse to defend the honour of a passive and pacifist people surrounded and misused. And only I – in all this world – could do this!

I was born in 1900 and ushered into a new century whose calculation and very existence was unknown to those I lived amongst. I was born into one of the smallest worlds imaginable, consisting of my parents, my sister, my uncle, my grandmother and four or five other families. I also had a much older sister. Later the old people told me that at that time there were no police, magistrates, schools or other appendages of the state amongst the Surelikud of the Forest, even though we were supposedly subjects of the Great Caesar. Even the Surelikud who lived on the plain didn't have much of those things.

Had any Triers passed by and seen my sister and me at play, they would have marvelled at our happiness amongst such poverty, but poverty is not easy to gauge. Our bellies were filled and our lives were rich. We may have lacked many things, but we didn't know that such things existed. Ignorance can also be a source of contentment. We all lived the same life, and what I remember most is the lack of urgency in our society. Our chores took the time they needed, and we could suspend them at will. We were never short of time, and in a way we were ignorant of that as well. Our life was not without conflict, but such as there was was resolved if not amicably, at least by argument and custom. I remember that my father argued with my uncle, and they came to blows, but nothing like the fights I've seen outside taverns frequented by the Triers, which could flare up for the slightest thing. I believe the reason for this was that although we had very little, we lacked nothing. What we lacked were the stresses and strains which arise from deprivation amongst plenty, the circulation of money which carries with it both power and vulnerability for those who have it, and we lacked something for which we had no name, but I would later discover that it was progress and progress is a faith in nothing particular except the goodness and necessity of all changes. Over my long life I have seen many terrible acts carried out in the name of progress. It seems that the further progress progresses, the greater the harm it inflicts.

The forest is feared and perceived as secretive and wasteful by civilised peoples who live on land that supposedly belongs to them rather than to the trees whose legal claim is much stronger and argued by the deepness of their roots which sink into the earth they never abandon and always protect. In such societies, people escape to woods because they're outcasts. They have lost everything and seek refuge in the anonymity of trees, where they gradually die, not only because they don't know how to survive in that alien environment but mainly because they pine for the community that has spurned them. Occasionally they are drawn back by some voyeuristic urge to spy on the people they still belong to, but always from the protection of the trees. And this the community take as a sign of the outcast's malign nature, of one who is plotting against them, possibly in league with the evil spirits of the wood – for how could the outcast survive there without their permission.

But we Surelikud – the true Surelikud who are born in the forest – return to the forest as a place where we can be ourselves and, above all, a place where we can understand our existence and its purpose – because a purpose it most certainly does have. For our proverb says, "The tree is both a welcome and a refuge to those whom the world has spurned." However the Surnudhinget will never understand this parental nature of the forest.

When I moved to the plain, I was advised to become a Christian. It was a practical decision which concerned the problem of living amongst the Triers and the converted Surelikud. To the Surelikud of the forest, Christianity and Islam looked more or less the same. Both those religions suggest an ethical coherence, but in practice they fall far below their good intentions. They're constantly at war – either with each other or amongst themselves. I believe that it's their desire to convert that has made them who they are. The Surelikud have never wanted to change or subsume any other people, so the Forest Surelikud have never gone to war. When someone else's war comes close, we simply move on – we melt away deeper into the forest where no one troubles us.

Before I could be baptised, I had to be instructed. It was a large, bearded priest who took on this task. His breath had a sweet, tangy smell often suffused with that of beer, and his presence was threatening. One day he launched himself at me furiously but his girth and his lack of agility impeded him. If I had once fallen into his heavy grasp, I could never have freed myself. I ran tipping a chair behind me, which increased his anger. We played cat and mouse for what felt like several eternities and terror had sharpened my wits. Eventually he collapsed in a chair, and I noticed that he was out of breath. "Why bother with a dirty little savage from the forest," he muttered to himself. I left the room.

Nonetheless I continued to attend his lessons, and he never bothered me again. I needed the baptism and the indoctrination to get the necessary papers. But I never did. The revolution came, and the priest – a hated figure for the Surelikud, it turned out – fled for safety elsewhere, possibly disrobing himself of his profession as he went. At that time, half a continent was reinventing itself on a daily basis.

His instructions were both intriguing and bizarre. A core

of their beliefs had some value, in my opinion. All these religions they invented are both lies and truths. Perhaps the whole truth we can never bring into focus is like Frankenstein's monster: one religion is the head, another the torso and another the legs. All have been sewn together in a clumsy manner. The universe is in the hands of a benign monster who can hardly walk. No wonder he can't keep control, no wonder he can't save us from ourselves – from our own obsessive behaviour; no wonder he can't reveal his purpose, because He's not sure of it himself. He weeps as he staggers forward.

We Surelikud, let me say, have a more subtle approach. For us Nature is the start and end of our universe, and Nature is the great sculptor who with its random acts reveals its unconscious mind.

I like this reference to the unconscious, such a modernist thing for a Surelik woman to say, and it's more suggestive of a deist God than a theist One. In our folklore, we have godlike spirits which are suggestive of both: Valmistaya who created the land and the forest, and Kōblus. They were always friends and walked in the forest together. Everywhere they went, the animals, the birds and the humans would suspend their constant search for food so that they could listen to the wind and catch those understandings each could interpret in their own particular way in accordance with their natures and senses.

Then came the Triers, forever in search of progress and modernity, carrying diseases belonging to the peoples to their west. We translate progress as "stuff" – an incomprehensible narcotic. Commodities. Things to stimulate whims and desires in far-off foreign lands. They started to cut down the forest which infuriated Valmistaya who turned to Kōblus for support. His anger only grew when Kōblus, who liked to ponder things at length often without arriving at any clear decision, said in his placid, matter-of-fact voice, "What can they do? Their populations are increasing and some are starving. Can you

21

compare trees to humans, who are – you'll agree, I'm sure – the animals closest to us, your greatest achievement so far."

"What?" replied Valmistaya, "Do humans eat wood? Are they some kind of beetle? The odd tree cut down to build a hut, I can accept, but if they continue to cut down the trees with their current avidity, there will be nothing left of the forest which is home to so many birds, animals and insects."

Kōblus took on a meditative air which suggested great wisdom, but he was in a panic because he had never thought of this. He liked his promenades in the forest just as much as Valmistaya did, but he disliked losing arguments. It was inevitable that the two most powerful forces in the universe would clash and one of the titans would emerge victorious. If I were a teller of war stories, I would tell of the ensuing battle and describe each blow and each parry after a detailed appraisal of the contestants' armour and weapons. I would examine their tactics and state of mind but ... but as I am a peace-loving Surelik and care little for such things, I will ignore such trivialities and immediately reveal the result: Kōblus defeated Valmistaya, and the Triers continued to cut the wood, but as Kōblus had been disingenuous and even deceived himself, he was no longer the same Kōblus. Moreover we are the products of our habits and relationships, and without his companion it was no longer a pleasure to wander in the forest, nor did he take interest in being good, but only in appearing to be good. He had been civilised.

My short experience of the regime of the Great Caesar up close, taught me that the Triers were then driven by a sense of guilt – by the idea that in that difficult world they had made for themselves, their behaviour would decide whether what they would encounter in the next world would be even worse. They were crushed between the horrors of this world and potential ones of the next; you could say that the former was the state and the latter the church, both with its own tough morality which appeared to conflict with the other's, but in truth they were the two pillars of a single machine for manipulating human psychology.

The Tryers used to have two souls, one European and the other Asian. They thought that their better one was European, but they were mistaken. The Asian is in their roots and is more varied, tolerant, simple and transparent whilst the European is the arrogant drunk, the aggressor, the hypocrite and the self-propagandist who proclaims his innate superiority even as he descends to wars and genocide. Maybe what I've said about two souls is true of all the Christian peoples, and the rest is just a version of Slavophilia that I picked up somewhere on my travels.

It takes half a lifetime to fully learn life's most important lesson: the unimportance of our own lives. It takes the same period to sense the significance of all lives – the great teaming and tender mass of humanity which lives on and holds the universe in its mind. This is difficult for the self-sufficient Surelikud to understand, and without the harassment of the Triers we would never have learnt it. They introduced us to the concept of tragedy. And that has both enriched and saddened me.

The first revolution came around six months after I moved to the plain, and the second in the autumn another half year later; news of the first reached us belatedly but we were used to that and accepted it with a shrug of the shoulders, unaware of what it meant. News of the second revolution came more quickly and by the middle of the following year things were changing fast and a year later, faster still. With rumours of another war or wars, new regiments were being recruited. And they even wanted one for the Surelikud! Something that the Great Caesar had never thought of. I had known a young man for some time; in fact he courted me, but I was unconvinced. He seemed unreliable, lazy and fun-seeking, and such a man was no use for a Surelik girl with hardly a kopeck in her purse. No use at all, but I liked to chat to him and laugh at his silliness and flattery. When, one summer day, I heard shouting and the sound of a military band – something I'd always feared or at least considered to be no concern of mine – I wandered in its direction for some reason still cannot understand. On reaching Väikelinn's central square, I hardly had time to take it all in before a soldier came cantering towards me on what I thought was a very fine horse. As he did so, an officer shouted at him to come back, but was ignored. Only when the soldier skilfully swerved round to a halt right in front of me, did I realise that it was my Pyotr. He smiled from on high his open and innocent smile: "I've even got a horse, and we've been training for weeks. What do you think of it? You wouldn't marry a peasant, but I bet that you'd marry a soldier." And his argument was not entirely unfounded.

He looked so good in his uniform. Who cared which regime he was fighting for, he was a handsome young man and I suppose that I loved him? I didn't really love him; I loved the idea of him as I perceived it – and perhaps it was simply what he was trying to communicate to others – and to me in particular. He was full of himself, and that was deeply attractive and reassuring, and by joining with him, I was sharing his narcissism. I belonged to him and he, I thought, belonged to me. I must have picked up this romanticism from the Triers, for we Surelikud have always been a practical people. It must have been the new regime's picture houses which very occasionally showed a silent film that told of wars with the rich countries and the old landowners. In the foreground, there was always a love story in which the man often died. If not, then it was the woman. Heroism always brought their downfall and immortalised them. After watching one of those films, part of me longed for a war in which he could die a heroic death and come home in that beautiful uniform splattered with blood. I would weep and hurl myself on his lifeless body uncaring of the blood stains. I would kiss him on his muddied face and scream. The other young women would envy me, but come over and hug me, identifying themselves with tragedy, because for that brief moment I symbolised tragic pure love. That's where the daydream ended, as there was nowhere else for it to go. In a film, it just would just say, THE END, but in a daydream, reality would knock at the door and the other part of me remembered that I didn't want him dead, no matter how heroic the death.

The Triers' army was very clever with the uniform for the Surelik cavalry. There were only ever two thousand of them, even at the height of the Civil War. They managed to combine the uniform with some elements of our national dress, which is mainly an invention of the plain. Everything was changing, so why couldn't we. We had never been a military nation, and could never have been a match for the Triers or the Muslim tribes. When war came to our region, our traditional response was that drift deeper into the forest. Nor were we an equestrian people. Horses are useless in the forest, where one man can be as strong as twenty or two hundred, especially if he knows his way around. Still, he looked good on horseback, and I loved him as only a young woman can.

She's smiling; of course she's smiling. My stupid scribe is smiling because, she says, I'm still in love with Pyotr. We have worked together for all these years, and still she doesn't know me. Or maybe she does!

In films and novels, weddings are grand affairs, but during a civil war in one of the poorest parts of a poor nation, the grandness was only in our hearts. Pyotr loved me, of that I have never had any doubt, but he too perhaps loved the idea of me. Those strong feelings carried us through the shambles of our wedding. I had no one, not even the vile priest who would have undoubtedly come to anything where there was the chance of free beer. But he had fled. The church wouldn't marry us, as Pyotr's mother wanted, more because of his politics than my incomplete conversion to Christianity. We had a civil marriage, which the new regime smiled upon, and it was followed by a party. Pyotr had demonstrated unexpected organisational skills: using his meagre savings mixed with a loan from a wealthier friend, he had hired a hall and ordered food and drink - not sufficient to requirement, it turned out, but he couldn't have known. Most of the wedding guests were soldiers in the Red Army and drifters who had learnt of the food and drink. There were young women but insufficient, mainly Pyotr's relations, and they were consequently in demand. Once they'd had their food and drink, the drifters' attention turned to the women who were more inclined to the men in uniform, and their fathers weren't happy with either group given the ephemeral nature of their presence in Väikelinn. With such tensions, the subsequent brawl was only to be expected. I was no expert at the time, and could not have commented on its inevitability. The drifters turned out to be more than a match for the soldiers, and Pyotr attempted to stand up, but I grabbed him by the arm and pulled him back. He kindly gave in, though I felt that custom quite possibly required his intervention. I had no wish for him to come to our wedding bed with a broken nose and a black eye.

At such a time, a bride should have been in tears that her special day was ruined, but what meaning did it have for me? I was the outsider at the centre of something bigger than anything I'd experienced, and enjoyed it for what it was. I was told later - but I can't remember by whom - that it was only a slight exaggeration of a typical Triers' wedding, the ritual having been spiced up by the times, the soldiers and the drifters. The veracity of such assertions in a vast nation is never to be trusted. It was a lesson in the complex differences that run through such a society, and I loved the spectacle as long as I and Pyotr stayed out of it. In fact I felt slightly flattered at such exuberance at an event which supposedly celebrated my marriage, my life, though it also filled the empty stomachs of those who were keeping away from wars by moving around. And I surely felt more than that - almost certainly a sense of belonging to something new. Perhaps these passionate Triers were not such demons after all and I would be one of them eventually. At that time, I thought it my duty to support my husband in every way, not only because he was about to face the dangers of war for a cause and no apparent personal gain.

The brawl soon played itself out, once the fathers got involved and the mothers had no choice but to pacify the storm. There were hugs and handshakes, laughter and smiles, while a certain euphoria hung in the air, as happens after a difficult hunt or some other great exertion. One of the soldiers shouted, "Great wedding, Pyotr, why did you miss the fun?" My youthful Pyotr blushed with embarrassment, and I squeezed his hand. Men amongst men.

After our wedding night, Pyotr rose and went to the front door, and being a lazy fellow like many of the Surelikud who live on the plain, he went no further and stood in the doorway urinating as high in the air as he could as though revealing to all the perfect duality of his equipment. I say "urinating", from a word borrowed from the Triers' language to make it sound so unrespectable by trying to be respectable, but I should have said, he peed, he pissed, he pished, he slashed, he slished, and he whooped with joy as the cold air from the plain enveloped his body. He did all this not entirely out of laziness, but also to communicate an important philosophical point to all his neighbours: we are just an animal, and we have all the animal functions. We are an ape that has language – that is the ability to speak and to understand the speech of others, if they speak one of our own languages. That is no small thing, and now in my old age I find this ability so much more marvellous and bewildering than I did at the time. And at that time, I just laughed and told him he was a holy fool, too like the Triers' with their crazy ideas about how to change the world. And then I beckoned him back to bed.

If we had known what the future had kept in store for us, we would have laughed less. We were like month-old lambs at play in the field, happy enough with the warmth of spring and unconscious of the fence whose significance was that other powers had harsh plans for them. Language should give us the ability to reason, but however much we try, we are still blown along on the currents of history which have no hands or head or will of their own, but resemble more closely the forces of winds and tides. And yet we have to reason, just as the snake has to slip through the grass and the tiger has to seek its prey. And I eventually chose to use my reason to obstruct the irrationality of reason, which often goes under that foolish and misleading term, "Progress".

I'll say nothing more about the following three weeks up until his departure with the regiment, other than that they were amongst the happiest of my life. He was a solicitous husband and from the distance of my advancing years I would now define him as little more than a lad entirely ignorant of life and what it held in store for him. On the day of his departure, he got up with great determination and revealed little of his feelings. He fussed around with this military kit and dismantled his rifle as he had been trained to do, checking each component. He ate little for his lunch, and after minimal displays of affection he mounted his horse as though playing that part in one of those silent films. He rode away with his head held high and barely turned it towards me for one last farewell. I watched him leave the smallholding until he disappeared into the outskirts of Väikelinn, where the regiment was meeting.

For more than a year, I'd known the plain, the settlements, the fields in the distance, and the cartloads of produce or manure that helped produce the produce – all that great traffic of stuff to grow and stuff to eat. The needy land was always there and kept them on the go. At the time, this was to me slightly mysterious but also irrelevant and strangely threatening, because the government would probably want to cut down more of the forest and turn the violated land over to agriculture. That too is what they call progress.

I now believe that the lands of the Triers and the Noisy Musics are very similar, because in each they would drive further either to the east or to the west, and as they went, they would grab the land hungrily, desperately, greedily. The Triers are slightly better because they struggle and are uncertain, constantly looking for foreign approbation, but the Noisy Musics are flabby with plenitude and are certain about everything, particularly their own lies and their position in the world. Their desire to control the land, and all there is in it, knows no boundaries – it covers the whole sphere of the earth, even where the earth is only baking sand or permafrost, with barely a footstep for miles around. I have to be honest and admit that, while greed is rare amongst the Surelikud, a degree of envy there must have been because we have a saying: "The trees in the Tuva lands are always higher than our own."

Never did I think when I married the gallant and uniformed Pyotr Sergeyevich that I too would become a slave to the land and the seasons, seeding the earth and waiting for its unpredictable beneficence. I became a farmer's wife or should I say, a farmer, as he was away at the war and when he came back briefly, he had little interest in the crops and the animals. In spite of my upbringing, I came to know the land – to love it a little and respect its reluctant abundance, its allure to life and ephemeral freshness, its maternal generosity to all that grows from its fertile womb, and its prodigal, promiscuous and undiscerning bounty. It would like to make room for everything, if only man would leave it alone.

And if man left it alone for some time, it would return to forest, its most natural consort and helpmate.

The land was made for the trees, which climb with masculine arrogance towards the sky, but as the masculine always contains something of the feminine just as the feminine always contains something of the masculine, they crowd around and create a nurturing home for birds and insects. The land was made for the trees, and progress – human progress – is the unnatural force that tries so hard to break apart that sacred union. The land was made for the trees, which protect the land from greedy hands that would dig deeper and deeper into its flesh to extract not only the nutrients that belong to the trees and the plants, but also the toxins the earth has so carefully and judiciously hidden away where they can do no harm.

Progress abhors an obstructed view. An empty landscape is transparent, and staring at its expanse man can feel that he owns it, knows it and can use it as though it were his own body.

Progress is driven not by curiosity, as some believe, but by a fear of not being able to understand and thus the need to control. It is a search for faith, rather than knowledge which is both deeper and therefore more uncertain. Ignorance is the companion of certainty.

Progress fails to take into account the inability of humans to understand fully the world they have been thrown into, which is the greatest gift they receive from Nature.

Towards the end of the Civil War, Pyotr came home happy and exhausted. Now the end was in sight, he started to think of the future – ours and the nation's, which seemed to include us Surelikud without it even noticing us, except when they wanted soldiers. He took me by the hand and led me to our bed, but he wasn't in any hurry to make love; he wanted to chat about his plans and his hopes – and about how everything was going so well. He had taken off his jacket and thrown it on the floor, but kept his boots on – a picture of unfocused energy.

I wasn't for giving into his dreams. The animals would always be there, as would the hungry earth. Dirty work and sometimes of little benefit. Soldiers can dream when victories are coming fast, and the moments of greatest suffering are in the past, but a peasant just has to work. A forest Surelik could dream for half a day, for that matter, but that was no longer who I was.

"Why do you fight in their wars?" I asked unkindly, after all he'd been through.

"This one is different. This one is not about conquest but changing the world for the better."

"A walk in the woods is enough to rediscover the only benign face there is ever likely to be. Triers struggle ceaselessly to expand their borders, but this brings their people no respite, only further wars and miseries. You give to the future, but the future will only repay with unhappiness. The future is fickle and jealous of its rule. You'll see. Besides you've given them enough; let someone else fight for the future."

As he sat motionless on the bed, Pyotr didn't seem angry or upset at my words. He appeared to ponder them, as though he suddenly didn't know what to do with his life. His optimism had clearly been an effort, like that of the ant moving across the floor in a laborious zig-zag, pausing every now and then for no discernible reason, as it appeared to be unaware of its exposed position. And in flash he crushed it under his boot, which he rotated to make sure of his purpose.

"*Why* did you do that?" I asked him.

"Do what?"

"Kill the ant."

He looked at me in bafflement, and I realised that it hadn't been a conscious gesture.

"It's not as though a single ant is an infestation," I said, making no attempt to hide my disapproval.

"And in the forest what would you do in the case of an infestation?"

"In the forest we always move on, so we never care about any guests, whatever their number. Only settlement encourages the proprietorial – carving out a sterile and controlled environment."

He tussled my hair and laughed happily: "You crazy woman, you crazy Surelik woman."

"You're half Surelik yourself," I replied.

"Don't I know it! My mother always said, 'Make sure that you marry one of us, a Surelik – better to get one from the forest; they work harder and they always make you laugh."

And he laughed again.

The scribe renews her condescending smile, and claims that she was right all along. And I am about to dictate the first of my stories, or what I would like to call parables:

The Parable of the Visitor

He came in the day, just after noon when the sun was high and the air was bright. He was around thirty, his skin dark and his eyes black – no one has skin as dark as that in our lands, so he must have been a foreigner, thought the Surelik woman who filled the doorway with her distrust.

He spoke our language well, but with a slight accent which added to his attraction. He carried with him an unknown history and provided no credible explanation. He was lean – wiry is the word. He didn't look ill, even though his cheeks were sunken, and his dark brown skin warmed by the sun perhaps concealed the ravages of hunger.

"Do you have food for a starving man?" he asked bluntly but with a lively smile. From the beginning he appeared to have a plan, and would have known that the Surelik peasants had rules about hospitality. A hungry man should never pass your door still a hungry man, but it was spring, there was little food in the house and her husband and two sons were working in the fields.

She sighed and looked at him again. He was surely a lazy good-for-nothing who would take food from good hardworking people. He smiled knowingly and must have caught her thoughts along with the odours in her breath, "Look at the birds of the air: do they sow the fields, do they reap its bounty and gather it into their barns? Yet God feeds them. Are you not much better than they?"

"Enough of that in this house," she said as she ladled some stew into a bowl for him. He talks like a priest, she thought, but I never saw a priest go hungry. I never saw a priest without a neat little paunch and a troubled countenance. Only a stupid priest would go hungry and this one is a sharp as a knife – and as dangerous.

"Eat and be away with you," she smiled back as she placed his plate on the table.

He didn't talk; he ate. And he did this slowly and with relish. He was absorbed by the pleasure of it.

When only the juices remained, he broke off a piece of bread, as though a man about his business, and chased that liquid around the plate, mopping it up and raising the dripping bread to his mouth.

Once the plate was clean, he lifted his eyes and smiled the impish expression of a boy in a man's body. "You wouldn't have a little more for a man who hasn't eaten for a week?"

"A week! Who do you take me for? A day perhaps."

"How disbelieving you are! How unwilling to perceive the wondrous nature of the world we live in."

"That'll be because of all the toil and trouble we face. You can wander around this wondrous world smiling at dumb peasants; we're tied to this little piece of land, and every day it's a fight to survive. You can just leave and take your wonderment with you. I have things to do."

"Now this house," he said, apparently changing tack, "is blessed."

"Blessedly cold in winter and blessedly hot in summer with a blessedly leaky roof whenever it rains and whatever the season."

"You need to look beyond yourself and your land ..."

"... at the big house, you mean. At the banquets and carriages, their bedrooms and hallways, their paintings and statues. And like you, they can travel the land, but in finer style. They don't have to beg a bowl of stew from a busy family, because they take our food from us every day of our lives, and they don't even have to ask."

"Did you ever hear the story that Jesus sometimes travels the land dressed a poor vagrant begging a bowl of soup, and every house that offers him one is blessed? Surely you must have heard that one."

"No, I never did, and I would have laughed merrily if I had. That's one of the few joys left: laughing at the folly of humankind."

"My dear daughter, I have come just in time, and I see that the devil's work has been done before me. For I am Jesus Christ your Saviour and have come to bless your house, and bring peace and prosperity."

At this the woman flew into a rage and pushed the false Jesus to the door. He could feel the strength in her arms, as she said, "Would Jesus play such a foolish and unkind trick to test out our people in such an uneven way, without a thought about the season? Is it harvest time when the animals are fat? Does he know what food is or isn't in the house? And on this spin of the dice, is eternity to be decided?"

"He knows everything. I know everything."

"Do you now? Do you know that I'm about to give you a very large kick up the backside? Do you know that?"

He looked concerned, surprised, but also a little titillated by the challenge. "Are you a Christian," he said, "to say such things?"

"I am, but we've only been Christians here for a hundred years, since Great Caesar's men came and cut the trees and made us work the land, and the priests came with them."

"Only a hundred years," he said in a soulful, priestly voice.

"Why are you so surprised if you know everything, and Jesus would never set about his food in that gluttonous fashion you did. That was human hunger and a human empty belly."

"There isn't a Christian bone in you." Now he was getting angry.

"More than you, you blasphemous imposter, you charlatan. I was brought up in the Orthodox faith; I know the stories. I don't go to church often, but I hold Jesus dear because he didn't judge and said we shouldn't judge. We still keep some of our pagan ways, but we're Christian enough to know that you do too much judging."

Chameleon-like, he changed again, adopting a more pliant and pleading tone, clearly forgetting his claim to be the son of God about his business – and there was a gleam in his eye.

"Now you've fed a hungry man, would you show him the same kindness by lying with him on that bed of straw? Clean straw, so inviting to a man who has been sleeping on the ground and lying in the mud – a man who has come out of a long winter and felt many a chill wind but never the warmth of a female embrace."

"Well, you're a dirty chancer, if there ever was one," she said, but didn't object as he slowly undid the buttons on her coarse peasant blouse and revealed her still youthful chest. "But there'll be no time for sleeping on this straw. You're more of a devil than a saint," she added but he gave no sign of objecting to how she had redefined him.

He made love to her as she'd never been made love to before, but she'd only ever known her husband's lovemaking. Once if was over, she lost no time in pushing the Jesus imposter out of bed, and he dressed with even greater speed. He too now thought of practicalities, and the appearance of an angry husband was one of them. He had too many identities to ever be content with a single one again. He'd taken all he could possibly take, but she slipped him another piece of bread as he left.

When he was about a hundred metres from the house, she came out into the spring air and shouted, "Away with you, you fraud and beggar, and never but never come back to this village again." He turned with a frightened look, and then hurried on his way.

She turned back into the house and smiled to herself. She didn't know what her smile looked like, as there were no mirrors in the house, but she felt its warmth.

That evening she would light the stove in spite of the better weather, and she would send her sons into the other room, and she would hold her husband close. She would be more loving to her sons, and she would light a candle to all the lost souls who only worked through life and never knew a single day dissimilar from another.

They say that you can learn how to live from a saint, and how not to live from a devil, but you can only really learn how to live in this harsh and restrictive world from a man who is neither saint nor devil – though perhaps a little closer to a devil. And from that day on, the house was slightly more blessed than it had been in the past.

*

This scribe of mine doesn't understand her job. She's complaining about the parable – she says that it makes me look odd, that I'll look like someone trying to be God almighty and this is a Christian country. Well, I never did get baptised, but I did get those stories. The Prodigal Son and so on. Parables upon parables, they threw at me. Why shouldn't the Surelikud have their own? I'm not creating a religion; we've had none for as long as anyone can remember. And, dear scribe, there are many more of these to come.

I am telling these parables not to lay down a law, but to deny it. Civilised men are lazy and prefer not to think things out, so they have religions to tell them how to live, and these religions wouldn't do too bad a job, if they were followed, but they aren't. Civilised men value the letter and not the spirit: they count the fingers drumming on the table and not the heart beats in their chests. They believe in order to belong and not to act. They claim to be peaceful and go to war.

I am less ambitious, and more conscious of our limitations – by which I mean not of our talents, which are potentially enormous in every human being, but of our ability to do good in a world ruled by criminals.

We should try to do our best in as much as we can understand what that is, but we should never consider ourselves to be a good woman or man. Such delusions are crippling and restrict our vision. If we want to be good – and that is a difficult choice – we need to consider our every act, and this could inevitably shorten or devastate our lives.

The precise outcomes of our actions can never, even then,

be predicted but experience can teach us to guess, and for some time that could work quite well. But if conditions change as they eventually will – and today they change frequently – then our experience is useless and our intellect essential.

Our actions may be neutral or even benign, if our behaviour patterns belong to the few, but deleterious if they belong to the many. Or in other words, if a few people are doing something (such as skiving off work), this could be useful (as a warning to the boss or manager or commissar that the workforce is restless and they must mend their ways, which they rarely do), but if everyone in the country did it suddenly and together for a long period with no particular purpose in mind other than having a rest, then everyone would starve.

A good society not only tolerates a variety of behavioural patterns, it also encourages them in the knowledge that this releases the diverse creativity of its citizens and enhances collective diversity.

Pyotr and I had one more conversation of note before he left. It was a few days later when he told me of his comrade-in-arms, Nikolai, who found a Polish lover when the Triers' army was pushing the Polish army back from the Triers' lands. At that time she had no problem with his actions or those of his fellow soldiers. They seemed to be not only in love but also well-suited to each other. He was smitten and could not speak of anything else; so much so that Pyotr and the others never stopped teasing him and pretending to play a violin whenever he started off. But when the Triers reached the Polish lands and the orders from above were to continue their advance until they took Warsaw, her attitude changed. She left him and then three days later as they continued to push further into enemy territory, she reappeared and stabbed him to death.

"And what did you do to her?" I said.

"Nothing. But not for the want of trying. When she reappeared, she said that she couldn't live without him and enticed him into the woods. Some time had passed before we began to think that something might have happened. New orders to advance had arrived, so we had little time, but it was sufficient to find his body in the woods. She had knifed him in the stomach so that death did not come instantly. If we'd got our hands on her, ..." Pyotr looked at me.

"I don't want to know," I told him firmly. "She had her reasons."

"And we had ours."

"That is the idiocy of war. People murder others they have no personal quarrel with, and they do it for a flag and piece of land. What senseless slaughter. They wanted to occupy land that was not theirs, and then we – or should I say 'the Triers' – invaded theirs. Both armies were equally culpable and responsible for the bloodshed. Tragically this woman killed someone she loved. That is nationalism for you."

"You're just a silly girl. That is not how it works. And if that's how you feel, why did you marry a soldier?"

"How right you are! I was certainly silly to love that uniform and not understand what it meant. I never thought that this war would be so bloody and go on for so long. How silly not to read the irrefutable symbolism of civilisation. I'm just a savage from the forest."

"So you fell in love with my uniform and not my wit – and not my handsome face?"

"I had already fallen in love with them," I smiled, "but I didn't trust them. For some reason I did trust your uniform. That was my undeniable silliness. I worry about what this war has done to you. Once you would have put a sparrow back in its nest, and stroked its neck. Now you can kill a human being and yearn to exchange one cruelty with another."

"Don't you worry about me, Rahväema; I haven't changed. And I don't think that I would have put a sparrow back on its branch." It was clear, however, that he was pleased with the substance of my reply.

"What would you have done then?"

"Nothing."

"Better treatment than you meted out to the ant, I suppose."

"The ant? Come on, you're not still holding that against me. An ant!"

I smiled at him coquettishly as though to say that I was only teasing him. Which I was, but teasing carries its own instructions which often cannot be expressed in other ways.

When Pyotr Sergeyevich Ilusadev next returned, he had started a little war of his own: he had wanted to set up a Surelik Republic, free from all control of the Triers. With his own brand of socialism. When did Pyotr become such a serious boy? I asked myself. I married a funny chancer, and the army returned him to me as a small-town Lenin. Somehow he had two hundred men, mainly Surelikud along with some other discontents who never tired of fighting – or were so tired of fighting they couldn't think what else to do. For the Red Army, he was a deserter and rebel, and they'd sent out a detachment to quell his insurrection. A backwater event that would never figure in the history of the Civil War, but it stands out as a uniquely tragic event in the history of the Surelikud, although at the time few knew that it was taking place, even in Väikelinn.

"You see, we sent them packing," Pyotr shouted to me, as he sat proudly in his saddle and gave no sign of wanting to come down to my level.

"And they'll be back, only in a greater number – and angrier," I shouted across the distance that divided us. How different he was from when he first rode up to me in his uniform. He sat so easily in the saddle, you would think that he'd spent his whole life there. He looked distant and proud; no longer a lad, now completely a man and a Trier. I felt that never again could there be laughter in his voice.

"We'll fight them off again. We know our own land," he said in a softer voice, looking like Napoleon.

"No, you know their land and their ways. The Surelikud

were never a violent people, but you don't want a Surelik society; you want a little Trier Republic independent of the big Trier Republic; you want a republic of your own. Whilst you were away killing for that Big Republic, you learnt to think like them – you were infected by their desire to dominate."

"Nonsense, woman!"

"'Nonsense, woman' was never the way a Surelik man spoke to a Surelik woman. You have proved my point."

"Nonsense, woman," he spat with exasperation whilst his horse snorted as though it were of the same opinion, and drew a little closer to emphasise his irritation, "I've learnt that this Trier regime is worse than the last one."

"What foolish things you say! Have you no memory? Have so many years gone by? The Triers in the old regime treated us no differently than they treated the deer in the forest and fish in the river. No, I tell a lie. They treated them better – as they were a resource to be conserved, whilst if they could have annihilated us, they would have."

"They could have."

"No, they did try, but we disappeared into the forest, which they feared like the next world they believed in so strongly. In the end they gave up, and used us for our labour when they could, but they still perceived us as animals. On the plain, we became their pack horses.

"The problem with the new Triers is not their brutality, but their so-called humanity. They see us as humans, and as they consider themselves to be the humans with the best possible ideas, they want us to speak their language, go to their schools, follow their new religion based on the balded, bearded, plump-faced man, and become just like them, and they've certainly succeeded with you."

"They're right to think that women are foolish."

"No, that's the old Triers; the new ones want equality."

"Old ones, new ones, they're all the same. A people doesn't just change from one day to the next. They may change what they believe and the flag that they wave, but they act in accordance with their deep-rooted customs which change slowly, if at all."

In those days I knew little about politics, nor did I care. Great events had occurred around me, but I had just got on with my life. We didn't pay rent to the big house, and that was an improvement, but that happened before I even lifted a hoe. So when he talked of insurrections suppressed and how the authorities had broken their promise to bring back elections to the workers' assemblies at the end of the Civil War, I barely listened. Later I would realise that this was the brutal treatment of the Kronstadt rebellion and the pointless death on either side as soldiers and seaman who once fought together now fought against each other. Pyotr too was probably not that interested, until they arrested twenty soldiers in his own regiment and had them shot. It turned him. He not only discovered his anger after so much warfare, he also found the charisma to enrage others and lead them into a dangerous and reckless campaign, but then what was one more to men so hardened by warfare they couldn't remember peace and how it worked. Having confused me even more, he rode away. He came not to hold me or joke with me, but to explain. He had the good heart of a foolish man, and yet he was no longer himself. After he'd left, I couldn't make sense of any of it, but I did understand that no hero's death awaited, no wailing women to be my chorus. If I were to weep, it would be inside myself.

That night of broken sleep, I got out of bed, went to the window and thought of Petya and where he might be. Whether he was still alive. And the cold windless night held all that uncertainty in its soulless stillness, as though this was all there really was: not love and passion, not pain and suffering, not kindness and ferocity, but only this sterile emptiness which was our past and would be our future. The cosiness of the other oceanic reality – the forest – seemed much further away than it really was. It seemed to belong to another epoch, to a distant and unreachable past. It was the only element in which I could swim, and here on the farm I was a fish swept up on the beach desperately hoping for another wave to carry me back home.

And then I heard a sound, a ghostly sound that spoke of speed and more distance, of unknown places that almost drew me to them as much as the forest. The attraction of the unknown against the attraction of the familiar. That sound didn't have the warmth of humanity or the musicality of bird-song or the subtle humour of the wind whistling its Delphic message through the foliage; instead it had the metallic blunt-ness of machinery. It spoke of man conquering nature, and therefore conquering himself.

The train whistle underscored my solitude, and yet made it less oppressive. It awakened me and I sensed that out there at and between its departure and arrival, a new world was stirring and it would not be friendly. Then I saw the train itself, travelling at an unnatural speed – urgent and anxious, full of importance and lacking any understanding of its real destination. Arms, munitions, refugees, soldiers – foodstuffs perhaps or hopefully – rushing towards intended and unin-tended outcomes: an uncertainty very different from the still, diaphanous, timeless uncertainty of the night, both weight-less and ponderous. It too was wakened by that brutish force which pierced the incomprehensible substance of the night like a bullet through human flesh.

Now the war was practically over, did death visit less often? Possibly but was it worth the stress, the fear, the dislocation? The Triers would gloat, "We suffered. Yes, we suffered deeply, but we showed those Whites, those lackeys of the cruel, idiot Great Caesar. We cleared them out and found some hope. Ragged hope, we'll willingly admit."

That was fine for the Triers, who were a tough lot – and given to such philosophical musings. We Surelikud, a peaceful people, well-trained in the servitude that grasps freedom with both hands by simply refusing to resist. And continuing on our merry way, so distant is our hope of any retaliation. We are exonerated from honour, and that is a form of freedom.

I returned to my routine of brute labour and the weeks flowed into each other. The only thing I learnt during this period was that this was not how I wanted to spend my life. I had no idea what I should do, so I continued. Perhaps I could have got used to it, but this would not be my destiny. That was the one thing I could be sure of, even if I learnt little else. I was a woman in limbo, a very busy one. But I had my distractions, the most delightful of whom was a little girl called Tatyana Ivanovna. She lived on the next farm and came round to see me. She said that she wanted to do some odd jobs, but it was clear that she mainly wanted to chat. About anything that came into her head. It was a benign and very instructive interrogation; for instance she once asked, "What does the calf drink, if you take all its milk?"

"Well, I let it have all its milk when it's very little," and I thought that this would be the end of it.

"What do you mean by when it's very little? How long would that be?"

"About three months. So the calf is big and strong," I said, lengthening the period so that it looked more respectable and failing to mention that I eked it out with the addition of water and ground oats.

"And what happens then? Do you take all of it?"

"Not at all. We couldn't have that, could we?" I lied.

"Then how much do you take?"

"Well, we share it out evenly. Half for the calf, and half for me."

"That's not very fair if the cow made the milk for the calf."

Children are supposed to give in long before this, I thought to myself, but such a bright child needed to know the truth. "The problem is that the cow cost my husband a lot of money, and he pays off the money for the cow, because I sell most of the milk. Do you understand now?"

"No. He didn't pay the money to the cow; he must have paid it to someone else. That's not the cow's fault."

I was beginning to feel that the child must have been sent away from all the other houses, and now she had worked her way round to me. "You're right, it's not the cow's fault. That's just the way it is."

"And at some stage you take all the milk, don't you?"

"Well, you're a clever child. But it's just the way it is."

"Then the way it is is wrong, isn't it?"

"I suppose it is."

"Is it the government? My uncle doesn't like the new government."

"Not especially. This has been the way for a very long time. From before the time the Triers had their big, big nation."

"That would be before my mum was born then."

"Even longer than that. Perhaps before your great great grandfather was born."

"That's a lot of cows that have been having their milk stolen."

By this stage, she had won my heart and made me laugh, and everything she said was in perfect but slightly pedantic Surelik. She was one of those children with an ear for the way adults speak.

Another time, she asked, "So where has your husband gone? Has he left you? My aunt was left by her husband during the revolution, and she has five children. My mum is always complaining about him. She says that he was a lazy ..." She laughed and said, "I think that it's a word we're not supposed to say."

"Probably not. But no, my husband hasn't left me. He went to fight against the enemy."

"Who are they?"

"The Whites," I lied.

"The Whites? I've heard of them. I think that my uncle likes them. He keeps saying that he doesn't like the 'new lot'. No, he definitely doesn't like them."

"Tanya dear, you shouldn't go around telling everyone what other people think, especially *not* your family. You might get them in trouble."

44

"Why would that be? He's entitled to his own opinion, isn't he?"

And so it went on. Delightful as she was as a child, I probably wouldn't have mentioned her if she hadn't become an important part of my story later in life. But that was how she was as a child.

Eighteen months after Pyotr left, a militiaman knocked at my door. He was a thin elderly man with one of those grim faces officials often had, as though the weight of all the State's troubles were on their shoulders.

"Are you Rahväema Ranavutavskaya Ilusadeva

"Why do you ask?

"Are you Rahväema Ranavutavskaya, the wife of Pyotr Sergeyevich Ilusadev, veteran of the Civil War awarded the Order of the Red Banner for his part in the defence of Vladivostok before it fell to the flag of the Rising Sun?"

"Was. I was his wife, but I haven't seen Pyotr for two years," I exaggerated because I thought it wise and besides his last visit was momentary and possibly no one noticed.

"Legally you're still his wife. No divorce was recorded, so legally you're still married."

"So? I'm not looking for another man. They're far too much trouble these days."

"I have some bad news. Or perhaps not bad news, but I am legally bound to notify you. I'm afraid that your husband has been arrested."

He looked at me blankly. This man with a grim face was only interested in the law.

"Well, I'm not pleased to hear that. What did he do to be arrested?"

"He is accused of banditry and despoliation."

"What's despoliation?"

The man who loved the law looked uncertain. "It goes with banditry," he said.

"Doesn't the Order of the Red Banner get a little dispensation?"

45

The Bureaucrat of the People looked horrified: "These are very serious charges."

"Where will I find him?"

A tall man with a large belly, a large dog and very probably a large ego entered the room. His uniform was clean; that no dust was clinging to it was an achievement in itself. He looked around and saw me – one seamless action. He asked me what my business was, but he had apparently already decided that it was not enough to justify my presence there.

"It's my husband; he's in one of your cells."

"I know the case. The revolutionary government does not ..." – he paused to let me consider the significance of the place wherefrom the wisdom and finality he was about to enunciate had originated – "... tolerate banditry and petty bourgeois individualism."

"I'm not justifying his actions. I'm pleading for clemency. He fought in the Red Army throughout the Civil War."

"Clemency is out of the question. We have to discourage banditry and economic subversion."

He turned to one of the soldiers and instructed him with no more than a nod of the head. He started to walk out of the room but turned again to say, "But get her out of here first."

The soldiers rushed me out of the building. Their action was not rough, but it was unquestioning and not open to appeal. Once we were outside and they released their grip, one of them looked at me with what amounted to a silent apology.

As I walked away, I heard shots and my husband was never seen or heard of again. After that I never felt the same about the Triers' new republic. They had tried so hard, and this was what they had ended up with.

And then still walking away from the Militsiya building, I saw a man leaning against a wall. He wore remarkably smart clothes, which even the well-off avoided at the time, and besides there weren't many of them. Foreign clothes perhaps. European, I thought, but of an expensive cut and cloth. He was relaxed, but in a malicious manner, and when I came closer to him, he pushed himself away from the wall and asked confidentially in Surelik, "How are you, Rahväema?"

"Do I know you? Will you tell me how you know my name?" in my confusion I replied with two questions without wanting the answers.

"Strictly speaking the answer is no on both counts."

"Why then should I waste my time with you? And how come you can speak Surelik?"

"So many questions from a young woman! A Surelik woman at that!"

"Should a Surelik woman be more submissive then? I think not. You may speak the language perfectly, but you know nothing about the Surelikud."

"I'm something of a linguist," he announced proudly, "I can divulge that."

"Then what do you want of me?"

"I want nothing for myself. I merely want to help you – give you some very good advice, absolutely free of charge and to no personal benefit of my own. You're probably too young and silly to take it, but I'll give you the chance."

I said nothing but looked him straight in the eye. I didn't trust him, and in spite of his regular features, I found him ugly. His voice was wheedling, and his insouciance and self-importance repelled me.

Tired of my silence, he continued, "A stubborn young woman, I see. I won't take offence, as you've just lost your husband – your estranged husband."

I remembered the existence of the Cheka, the government spies everyone feared. And they had recently opened an office in Väikelinn. He must have been one of them.

"Whatever he was to you," he continued again ignoring my stare, "he is dead and you can do nothing for him now. But you can do something for yourself: go back to the police station and tell the man you've just spoken to that you know all the names of Ilusadev's fellow conspirators, some of whom are still on the run. For this you'll be paid and, what's more, you'll be hired to acquire more information. This will take you into the heart of power, where you can use your influence to change things for the better, for I can see that you're a selfless and sensitive young woman, and would like to do good."

"Go to hell," I said simply, my only sensible contribution to this shameful conversation.

He smiled bitterly and I felt his anger: "Why are you defending them? These are your husband's murderers, are they not? Who corrupted him? He was a valued hero of the Civil War and had everything going for him?"

"You think?"

"Of course I do. You cannot deny it."

"I do. I do deny it. If anything, he was the one who recruited them, and he had his reasons, I'm sure of that."

"Well, I'll keep this conversation to myself, though you have shown yourself to be a subversive who kept the company of some of the most dangerous subversives in the country."

"The most naive ones, you mean. You must be a government spy; you talk like one."

He looked a little piqued, a little offended, and sneered, "I'm not a spy. I have no need to spy. I have other business."

"Well good day, whoever you are."

I started to walk away but remembered the question I'd been wanting to ask: "And what is *your* name?"

"Kurat," he replied unbothered whether I knew or not.

"Kurat? Just Kurat? No other names."

"None at all. Kurat will always do, and you'll be seeing me again."

"I hope not."

Now the scribe is saying that this passage has to go, but unfortunately for her, she doesn't make the decisions. Her argument is that Kurat has never been part of Surelik thinking.

She's right of course. And yet the world is complex, and we all influence each other. I will say more of this later, but what

I will say now is that there are many ways of telling a story and representing reality.

Now, stay quiet, scribe. I need peace to think where to pick up the thread of my story. And go back over things. I haven't finished all the story of Pyotr Sergeyevich Ilusadev yet – and he deserves more than this.

So he was gone. Never to return, if I may venture to take the rhetorical risk of a repetition, and I do because of my frustration that I cannot possibly explain to the reader the impossible gap that had opened up in my life. It's true that I hadn't spent that much time with him; the war had had more of his company than I had. Perhaps for that very reason I idealised him still and hadn't got to know him fully or as fully as we can ever know another human.

A few weeks after Pyotr's execution, a soldier came – I do not know whether he was a friend or following orders, because all he did was say, "These are for you," and touched his *budenovka* before returning from where he came. The parcel contained a few of Pyotr's possessions and a strange letter from him in which he apologised for being a bad husband, which was not his fault, and that he had always known that it would end badly; even though he pushed away the superstitious part of his nature, it stubbornly remained. I will insert here this part of his letter which I have always kept:

After our first skirmish with our ex-comrades of the Red Army, whom we successfully repulsed at the cost of a few wounds, I slept like a man renewed, and dreamt of my Surelik Republic – a peaceful nation and friendly to its neighbours great and small. I was its leader – elected by the assemblies and beloved of all the Surelikud. And then I woke to the laughter of jackals who rampaged raucously across the empty plain, knowingly in their malign and clownish role. And a chill wind brought their message of a harsh and cruel world where dreams are places we escape to but never arrive at. And then I knew two important things: that we were destined to be killed by our enemies and no such republic would ever exist even though we were now obliged to carry on fighting for it, and that I am a true Surelik after all because a Surelik listens to the voices of nature, however harsh they may be. And I thought of you, as I do again within the walls of this cell and I know with the same certitude that I shall never hold you again. Please believe that my love will survive me and travel with you always. I wish you a long and productive life, and as long as you live, part of me will also live on.

No, I don't still love him. I don't hanker after him or imagine his fine body. I'm an old woman now, ancient in fact. When I was in my early seventies, I started to think about him, but for another reason. I thought that if he hadn't died, I would have continued to play the part of a peasant woman. Every day would have been too busy for a forest Surelik, and I would have aged quickly, perhaps with a gaggle of children around me. And almost certainly Pyotr would have brought laughter into my life, even though yet more terrible events awaited people who lived in the lands of the Triers, and would have affected our children.

After his death, I started to think more deeply about our society and where it was going. Perhaps I wanted to know what had driven him, but more probably I started with my pain and the fat man with his fat dog. No wonder Kurat was waiting for me after the Militsiya threw me out of their building. Settled people live with evil day-to-day and consequently have to believe in the devil. Otherwise they would have to think less of human beings, and that is a sad place to be. My life hasn't just been about struggling to save a language and a culture; it has also been about trying to retain my stubborn belief in the innate goodness of humanity. Kurat has always been a little like the devil. I don't hold with the concept, but I understand why the Triers do, even in the period when atheism was the official credo. And they are the better for it.

After my husband's death, things had quietened down so much that the general and his train found time to come and assess our little insurrection, and I would have known nothing of it had another official not come to my door and announced that the general wished to speak with the rebel's wife. I had no choice but to go with him, and was led onto his train and into his luxurious apartment – a claustrophobic environment that a Surelik of the forest always distrusts. He rose from behind a mahogany desk and was still wearing his long leather coat which was open and flapped about. He was a tallish, wiry man with quick intelligent eyes behind his pince-nez, but also a coolness that brought a chill to the heart – the coolness of a man who knew how to get his way. He came round the desk in a genial manner and a leather-gloved hand shook mine gently, while he very correctly stated his name and rank, which of course I knew. And I said nothing. Then he returned to his seat and left me standing. Always always businesslike, and surely always with a purpose.

"So what do you think of our revolution?" he said whilst looking at a sheet of paper, and after a pause, "Comrade Rahväema Ilusadeva?", having eventually found my name on it.

"I don't concern myself with such things," I lied. Since Pyotr's death I had started to catch up with everything he'd believed in.

"You are not interested." I sensed a little suppressed outrage in his voice. Mine was not the correct answer, and he continued, "What kind of person could sit by and watch such a human tragedy unfolding and the greatness of our times, and not be moved?"

"A Surelik," I answered, "a Surelik of the forest, for that is where I grew up."

For some reason he liked this reply and smiled. It was a courteous, intelligent smile, and of course he knew all about the Surelikud. Being an intellectual, he immediately wished to show the depth of his knowledge. "An Ugro-Finnic language," he said, smiling once more and warming to his subject. He said many things about us, some I didn't know of, and some I discovered later were untrue, for an intellectual's vanity always takes them too far. They do not understand that even the finest mind has its limits, and as for the general, however much anthropology on the Surelikud he'd read, he could never really have known what it was to be a Surelik.

I sensibly waited for the powerful man to finish his lecture, and then said, "You must understand that we have never been interested in warfare, and this is particularly true of the Surelikud of the forest. My husband was an exception, but then he was half-Trier."

The general's smile disappeared, and he quite possibly didn't like the implication that his survey of Surelik language and culture could have left something out. Equally he could have been uneasy with the suggestion that the Trier half of my dead husband may have been his downfall. The general stood up once more and once more semi-circumnavigated the desk as wide as a plain. There he stopped and with his measured and purposeful manner removed his pince-nez and carefully placed it on the desk. Then he approached me with the professional air of a doctor approaching a patient requiring a medical examination, and suddenly he pushed me back, quite hard and too hard for my light frame so that I was up against the carriage wall a good two seconds before him, and that gave me time to duck and evade him. Although infinitely fitter, trimmer and lighter on his feet than the clumsy priest, he made no attempt to chase me. He simply walked back to his desk, lifted his pince-nez and replaced it just as carefully on his nose.

Now the floodgates opened, though a little prudence remained, thank the God of the Triers: "Do you think that I would do that with the general of the army that shot my husband – a good man guilty of believing in the promises made by all your band. No wonder a simple Surelik doesn't worry her head with such matters." I was paraphrasing my husband, which seemed appropriate in the circumstances, and the now seated general stared at me with a lopsided smile that didn't know what it was doing. "Do you think that I would be here, if I hadn't been summoned? Do you think that I would have listened humbly to your lecture on a people you know nothing about and never will, if I didn't fear your power? But even a woman – and a Surelik at that – can reach the moment when her dignity rebels."

"Enough of that. Enough said. Quite enough," he snarled. "We summoned you, comrade, as you like to define it, because crimes have to be investigated fully. To do less would be irresponsible."

"And rape is part of the investigation or investigative techniques?"

He sat up stiffly and perhaps his face turned a little red. We all of us believe that we're fundamentally good people. A minor defect here or there, of course, but fundamentally good. "Not rape! I simply misread the signals."

"Signals?" I responded but neither of us wanted to continue the conversation, which had dangers for us both – very different ones, and the stakes for me were much higher.

He rose and in more chivalric mode waved me to the door and said, "I'll show you out, Comrade Ilusadeva." We walked down a corridor in awkward silence before, always wanting the last word, he added, "And for the record, comrade, we genuinely do believe in the equality of all human beings, and thus being a woman, a Surelik or both makes no difference to us."

"Very good. My husband believed that as well, and let's hope that he was right," I responded more measuredly.

Before stepping out of the train, there was a reception manned by staff officers – confident young men greatly in awe of the general. He majestically waved to me and ordered, "Give some provisions to Comrade Ilusadeva!"

"That won't be necessary," came my instinctive retort, "I have quite enough on our own land. I have no children and my husband is dead. Now it's my land, I suppose." I saw that the young men were furious and the general, taken completely by surprise, was lost for words. Sensing danger and perhaps retaining my Surelik belief that no unkindness is justified, I threw in the means to get out of the impasse: "Of course, I'm indebted to the state for having gifted it to us."

The general, looking untypically human in his relief, grasped my hand with both of his, and shaking it with some firmness cried, "This is what we're here for. This is what we have all suffered for. And innocents have been killed. The price has been very high, but we can now move forward and one day I hope that people will consider the price was worth it. What do you think, Comrade Ilusadeva?"

I wasn't convinced, but for some reason I nodded, and the young men, noting their general's warmth, which may have been uncommon, stepped forward and shook my hand as well, more formally and less rhetorically.

I left a little shamefaced about the final charade, but also a little triumphant. I had entered the train, insulted the general and amazingly walked free. For a Surelik that's like winning the Battle of Borodino, which nobody did. I had decided not to mention Kronstadt as that would have been like sending a troop of ill-trained soldiers against a well-equipped and war-hardened battalion, but I had recognised the man Pyotr spoke of. Had he not suppressed so cruelly the Baltic Fortress, the cavalrymen in my husband's regiment would not have rebelled, nor eventually would have Pyotr and his men who from two hundred strong ended up as two dozen hiding in the woods. So much for the Surelik Republic that never was. And inside that glove of the finest soft leather there was *stalin*,[1] and from now I shall call him the Leather Glove and his nemesis the Moustache. He was the better of the two, but the other was one of the worst criminals to walk this earth and, no doubt, both of them were better men before the Revolution, for power corrupts and war brutalises.

---

1   Rahväema used the Russian word for steel (translator's note).

I decided that I would gift the land to the community and give away my husband's things – his tools and farming equipment. The house was already state-owned and would be allocated to someone else. Having completed these procedures, I went into the forest and wandered like the elk from one clearing to another in search of my own kind, as the proverb says. But it wasn't my own kind that I found. I wandered on my own and enjoyed the solitude, as I thought of all that had happened on the Surelik plain – Surelik mostly in name, as they lived like all the other Triers. Occasionally I met someone, but not anyone I knew or even someone who knew someone I knew. Most of the Surelikud had gone far deeper into the forest when the Revolution came, and as the revolution had turned into a long war, they would have become quite used to their new routes and now showed little sign of wanting to return closer to the plain. They would have missed the little luxuries they exchanged for meat, berries and mushrooms, but the disruption had left little room for barter and there was the danger of getting involved in the Triers' conflict. The huts in the clearings were often empty and nature was regaining what little had been stolen from her. Then I came across some huts and in them I found white soldiers on the run, still in their ragged uniforms because they had nothing else. Initially I feared them, but when I saw how listless and beaten they were, I knew that they were no danger.

I thought then that the new Triers were not much better than the old. They spoke of progress, but all they did was constrain and discipline people's lives. They registered, taught, ordered, drilled, called up, threw away, marshalled, coaxed, commanded, promised, sneered, neglected and finally registered once more. And these victorious rebels could have been almost as brutal and unbending in their suppression of rebellion as the Whites had been. But they weren't. They won because they were less brutal at that stage, and offered hope for something better. And yet these shattered souls wore uniforms that once had shone, as the foreign funders of the

Whites had fattened their bellies. Were they the same men? In defeat, they had become human or at least more human.

And those who set out to free the world without a care for themselves, are now – in victory – less human or, like Pyotr Ilusadev, dead because they rebelled against the rebels. They do not ask themselves why people continue to rebel not for restoration but for that promised change, undelivered and enveloped in a fog of rhetoric so ugly in its empty grandeur, it dulls the mind. They dismiss dissidence with silly epithets: petty-bourgeois deviationists, bandits, infantile oppositionists, and the like. Such words are so much easier than listening, understanding or – the unthinkable – learning from others. Nevertheless these had to be difficult times coming out of disorder in which few luxuries could be afforded, and perhaps listening to others was one of them.

When I met those Whites, I realised that they were as certain of their fate as my dear Petya must have been when he and the last of his band were holed up in the forest. At least, Pyotr would have learnt a few tips from his mother about how to live in the forest, but these men knew nothing and I had to teach them from scratch about its hidden bounty. The men who might once have commanded my execution now listened to me as children to an adult. They were exaggeratedly thankful for the simple ways that could help them, which required very little of me. There's nothing sorrier than a defeated army – even one that caused so much suffering and evil as the Whites did. They think of all their suffering and the dead, and understand so many things the victorious army can't quite grasp. To some extent that army turned the Red Army or at least its high command into something resembling itself, and that was one of its greatest crimes. Nobody even remembered that one of the first things the new regime did was to abolish the death penalty – and I thought of Petya again.

One young man, tall but gaunt in his rags, spoke like one of the aristocrats – I now could tell, my knowledge of the Triers' tongue being almost perfect. His name was Andrei

Alexeyevich Belsky, and he seemed to seek out my company more than the others. He once told me, when seated by a tree and near to tears, that he still couldn't believe that the rabble he'd seen in 1917 had eventually won. Turning to me with his pleading eyes, the only part of him that didn't have difficulty in communicating, he said, "Was it our fault that we lost? Was it military incompetence or were we in the wrong? The peasants had to choose and ultimately they chose for the other side." His men understood things better; they knew the answer but this man couldn't get it and that made him more pitiable but also more irritating. It was as though he thought that I could provide the truth in the same way as I could teach him how to snare an animal or look for mushrooms. That was the remarkable thing of those years: a man whose father would have owned vast estates and riches, and a man who even in his youth ordered men of all ages without any sense that this was less than his entitlement, was now reduced to dependency on a Surelik woman of the forest. No one could overstate the degree of change that had occurred. But also what had failed to change. I had been barely in time to see the fag end of the world governed by the Great Caesar.

Never could Belsky understand that they were the ones who executed without mercy, whose fierceness would brutalise a nation and leave its stain on later generations. Of course, others were to blame for the crimes to come; no one is exonerated by someone else's previous deeds, but it started here with a ruthless attempt to strangle the new republic. And it failed for two reasons – that terrifying ferocity itself and the vastness of the Triers' lands. When ferocity crushed resistance in one place, lack of resources sparked off even more in another. Too many fires and too little water.

I thought of my Surelik childhood in the forest and it seemed so distant and so ideal – though at the time, I had taken it for normality. No one in the Triers' many lands would have envied us, but in truth we lived in what they called paradise.

One day a man wandered into the clearing. His name was Halvatud – and it was the only name he ever admitted to. He walked like a broken reed – an existence that was held in existence by a thread, and yet he lived as though he had the strength and energy of a boxer at the height of his career – and did so by using improvised motions of his limbs that appeared to defy the actual laws of mechanics. He was supposed to have the assistance of a stick, and in fact he did carry one, but never used it. Or rather he didn't use it to assist his walking, but did use it as a decoration and a means to emphasise his arguments. Perhaps he only carried it to remind us that he should have been using it but wasn't – that he was defying gravity through sheer willpower.

His method, however concocted, must have increased the curvature of his spine. He had a short withered left leg and a hunched right shoulder, as though nature had designed one to counterbalance the other. To walk on the withered leg, the other leg had to leap a little to minimise the weight that would fall on its companion. As he moved through life by an act of will, that will became so powerful that it swept aside all bitterness over the destiny that had been inflicted on him, and also found room for love and wisdom.

He said that he had been waiting several years for me to appear, and that he was going to be my disciple but not my epigone.

I asked him if he had taken me for Jesus Christ.

"There are some differences," he replied.

"Yes of course, I'm a woman and haven't invented a religion."

"Those differences are minimal," he introduced me to his way of thinking – both commonsensical and utterly bizarre. "Women are too sensible to go around inventing religions. Can you think of one example? Though I can tell you that there was once the sterile puritanism of the Shakers. The difference here is that I'll be your only disciple, and one who will often infuriate you. You haven't called me; I have called myself and I'll stick to you like a thick coat on a winter's day: however

58

much I'll raise you blood pressure and however much my nag-
ging will make you skin prickle with sweat and exasperation,
you'll never take me off, let alone discard me."

"You've got the wrong woman: no one pushes me around
or threatens me."

"I have no intention of pushing you around. My job will
be to keep you on course – that difficult course you've chosen
for yourself. 'Both hands have to be cupped if you're to drink
from stream.' We need to work together."

"You take a lot on yourself, and speak with great confidence,
whereas I haven't made any decisions yet. And I don't remember ever speaking to anyone of my plans or my desires."

"Well, if it is great confidence, it is the strange confidence of
one who has suffered and of one who can claim to belong to
all Surelikud, both those of the plain and those of the forest,
because I was brought up in both. My parents were together
long enough to conceive me, and my mother was disgusted
by my broken frame. She could not hold me and could not
speak in my presence. When I was ten years old, I escaped my
mother who lived on the plain – I should say that I left her,
because my leaving was something she was quite indifferent
to and possibly greeted with satisfaction – and I went into the
forest where the people welcomed me and marvelled that such
a skeletal monstrosity could continue to walk. I became one of
them but never lost my understanding and liking for the ways
of the plain. Once you've known the beguiling amenities of
the plain, it is difficult to find the forest wholly comfortable.
That has always been the problem. And I mixed with the
Shennakhud, the oral historians who carry our collective
histories and wisdoms in their heads, and I learnt from them.
That is why I now wish to tell you the story of the great Surelik
warrior Võitleja."

"Oh leave me alone! I come from the forest and have heard
those stories over and over again. I know all the Shennakhud
and you've got nothing new for me."

"Yes, yes, we've all heard about his feats during the battle

59

against the Muurahvas, and how he raided their clearings and stole their women. We all know of his strength and courage and how he could fight off the enemy ten, twenty or even fifty at a time, and how he eventually died, as all great warriors do at the lake of death, but most people, including yourself, don't know the full circumstances of his death."

"Well you're the maddest madman I ever came across, but I'll let you speak. It had better be entertaining – at least as entertaining as the words of the Shennakhud," I laughed because he was already entertaining me, and there was a bright intelligence in his smiling eyes.

"Võitleja was visited by a black swan shortly before he died, but what are less known are the circumstances of his death. He was fighting against the Muurahvas, our fiercest enemies of the time, even though they were a very similar people who have apparently disappeared. Or, more probably, the two peoples merged as did their related languages. The location and the extent of these wars are of course unknown, but time has attributed them with epic proportions. Perhaps they were even fewer than we are now.

"Võitleja and his Surelik hordes were driven by the Muurahvas into the waters of Lake Surmajärv, and he was fighting with water up to his knees, when he saw a black swan. This far we all know the story, but I can tell you more. Võitleja's immediate reaction to the bird, who passed unperturbed amongst the warriors' cruel blows that reddened the waters of that lake that fed on the blood of courageous men, was to pause in wonder at her beauty, the silkiness of her feathers and the haughty manner in which she stared at him alone. It was the moment in which he understood all things, including the pointless belligerence of his life. It was a moment in which joy mixed with regret. It was a moment which for him seemed to last forever, but only just long enough for a Muurahva's sword to run through his gut. Võitleja fell to his knees and splashed around in the waters. The black swan swam gently around him, disdainfully inspecting the gravity of his wound. Being a warrior and forgetting all that had been revealed, anger and revenge took hold, and finding unnatural reserves of strength, he rose out of the water with the sole intention of beheading the bird. But it was his head that was severed by his human foe, and it fell into the lake never to be found. The two parts of his body travelled to the next world without the wisdom he'd rejected, and so the black swan gifted it to the Surelik people who since then have never gone to war."

"That was amusing, I'll grant you that, but you've made it all up."

"We are some remnant of the past, we Surelikud, we scattered mortals, thoughtful in a sea of busy peoples. Our wisdom is different, and it's in the telling – not the exact historical truth. Remember this if you ever have to narrate the story of your own life."

"Be quiet, you fool; why would I ever want to write my autobiography? A little Surelik women from the forest? You're teasing me, are you not?"

"The greatest truths come from a fool's mouth. Remember that too," and the gentle cripple lifted my hand and kissed it. The absurdity of the scene silenced me and he was already making his slow and purposeful way out of the clearing before I could shout, "That's a great deal of remembering you've left me to do." But he didn't turn as he had nothing else to say.

So our relationship was born. I wouldn't say that he convinced me that day, and I never did call on him in the biblical sense or any other. He kept calling himself and turning up at critical moments. As the decades passed, I came to welcome his appearances more and more, just as I dreaded Kurat's. The importance he would have in my life was as yet unknown to me, and I took him for a fool, a joker, a chancer, an eccentric or a wise man. Perhaps he was all of these things or none of them. No, wise he was most assuredly, and good. The only way a wise man can be good is if he is unaware of his own wisdom. After many decades I came to understand this, and now that he has met such a brutal, pointless and casual death, I start to realise that there is much I still don't understand about him. I took him for granted, like a gift from the Triers' heaven. Not that *he* ever believed in any of that stuff.

Kurat and Halvatud – what strange men! You see what oddities you come across when you mix with the civilised. Such creatures are engendered by the infected, polluted exhalations of the struggle for stuff, for reputation and for the elusive leisure they all yearn for – a struggle that is fought with physical violence, lies and silken words. This is what I thought at the time, and yet I knew very little about what civilisation was; I only knew its outer ripples.

My life with the White soldiers continued. I was useful to them and felt quite safe, and they respected me as people do when they have no idea how to survive in an alien environment.

The Parable of the Fishermen and the Film Crew

In the late twenties there was a famous film director and an even more famous actor who went to Sakhalin where they wanted to make a film about primitive Siberians and how the Soviets plus Electricity were coming to improve their lives. They chose the Oroks and first they filmed the hunters, which took them into the forests and onto the rugged snow-covered heights. They felt like men fighting the elements and winning. Their faces became tanned and the lungs filled with the freshness of the air. Healthiness exuded from the pores of their skin, and they felt that after this adventure they could take on anything.

Next they had to film the fishermen, and they went out in one of their traditional fishing boats. It was the largest they could find – at eight metres from stern to prow, with a cabin on it to shelter from the elements. There were eight fishermen on board, and when the wind was weak or coming from the wrong direction, they could move the boat slowly with oars. They left from the fishing port, and the boat moved briskly under a steady breeze and a friendly sun. The famous actor was thinking about how good this would look in his autobiography, and the director was preparing the text to be read, while the cameraman was setting up his equipment. Modern men with modern ways recording for posterity the less-than-modern ways of a small fishing community, it was enough to make them feel proud.

By the time they had everything ready on this floating object uncoupled from any fixed point on the earth's surface, the breeze had strengthened and the boat was leaning over. This didn't seem to bother them too much and it could have provided a dramatic element they hadn't thought of. The director went over to the famous actor, and gave him the ethnographic text he had to read. The famous actor was bored, and so he started to quibble about the text with the director, who looked at him in silence barely concealing his irritation. The famous actor was mainly there for his face and his voice, as well as his fame of course. So absorbed were they with their disagreement that they didn't notice the changing weather, even when they found themselves struggling to keep themselves upright on the deck. Suddenly it came, the first powerful gust of wind that pushed the boat so far over that some seawater splashed over the gunnel onto the deck – as a warning which triggered the fisherman into action. They rushed to undo some ropes, and it appeared that they wanted to furl the sails. This gust had knocked over the camera, which was saved by a fisherman who handed it to the cameraman with a look of distaste, as it had distracted him from his work. One of the men – the captain perhaps – was standing with an axe, and the camera crew couldn't understand why. Then, just as the fishermen were beginning to bring the sail down, another still more powerful gust hit the boat, and the captain – we'll call him that – did a very peculiar thing, he cut two stays on the windward side, the mast cracked, the sail and mast fell into the sea, and the boat partially righted itself, but the broken mast was still attached to its stump by some of the wood that had bent rather than snapped. He then leapt up onto higher deck and cut the mast free of the boat. The boat righted itself completely but the sea was now rough, and that spray had soaked them through to their skins was quite unbearable.

This did not deter the famous actor who walked up to the captain and demanded to know what he thought he was doing. How would they get back to port in time for supper? They had been promised a return no later than six o'clock. The captain ignored him and possibly didn't even hear him, because he was shouting orders in his own language, staring in various directions along the boat possibly to ascertain whether there was further damage and looking to the sky in search of signs of a possible improvement or further deterioration in the weather. The famous actor then attempted to grab the captain's arm, and tried to shout his disapproval through the wind and spray, but the captain merely moved him quickly to one side, as he might have done with a sack of potatoes someone had carelessly left on deck. It was an instinctive action he was barely conscious of. The famous actor felt the strength of those hands and decided that it would be better to find someone else who was more sensible than the captain-like person. He found a fisherman who appeared to be fiddling around with an oar, which the famous actor took to be another act of ineptitude, though he in concert with his fellow fishermen was trying to manoeuvre the boat into the right direction to sit out the storm. As the famous actor was continuously asking why the captain had delivered their only means of getting home that evening into the sea, and showed no signs of giving up, the fisherman finally turned to him and, moving the flat of his hand to signify a boat keeling over, said, "To save our lives..." and then with a sarcastic smile, "and your picnic hamper." Just as words were rising from the famous actor's diaphragm to express his contempt for such impudence, a wave shook the boat, spoilt his delivery which was about to demonstrate the full force of his artistic prowess and landed his arse on the deck where it and the rest of him started to slip in the direction of the sea on part of the boat where there was no gunnel. Undoubtedly that would have been his destination if the fisherman hadn't grabbed his forearm as he went careering by. This split-second manoeuvre saved the famous actor's life but unfortunately required the oar to be released and it was lost to the sea. At this point, the fisherman lost his temper and shouted at the bedraggled and terrified actor to join his friends in the cabin and stay out of his way.

There was more bad news when he got to the cabin. Once the camera had been restored to the cameraman, the cameraman did not learn the lesson and failed to secure his equipment in a safe place, so with the second gust of wind the camera finally got to the place it clearly was very keen to get to and that was the bottom of the ocean. The cameraman was dejected, but the director was weeping. "I can't see us being back at the hotel for supper," said the famous actor. "Just as well that I brought the hamper."

"The hamper!" wailed the director. "Are you crazy? You're talking about a hamper, and we're all going to drown."

"Oh I don't know about that. I know that the fishermen don't appear to be very competent sailors, and I can't get a sensible answer to my perfectly reasonable enquiries," said the famous actor who had apparently forgotten all about his recent brush with death. "And there's a rather good bottle of ..."

"Enough, enough!" wailed the director, and the cameraman stayed quiet and reflected on the idiocy of his two companions.

That night all three slept remarkably well, given the circumstances. The first to wake was the director. The sea was now almost flat calm, so different from when he went to sleep on a bench, a metamorphosis so absolute that relief was mixed with a strange anxiety over the sea's unstable and alien nature. It was as if the water in the night had been made of a different substance. The boat's movement was slight, and bright sunlight was coming through the cabin windows. Before he went to sleep, he had noticed that the fishermen were still busying around, so when he went out on deck he expected them to be asleep as well. But they weren't. They had improvised a small sail on a mast that was about a quarter of the original one. It was catching the slight wind, but how much forward movement it was achieving was difficult to say, and the sea was laid out like a fresh, clean table cloth – invitingly. What most surprised him was that six of the men were rowing, the captain was steering, and another one was doing some carpentry whose purpose was not immediately comprehensible. Making coffins, the director joked to himself. He was hungry and light-headed, but glad to be alive. The crew didn't seem frightened. Concerned and focused, yes, but he felt that this was part of their lives. And this was all charmingly pleasant after the fright of the previous evening.

He had decided to leave them in peace. The film crew *sans* camera were now little more than ballast. Unfortunately the famous actor was now up and about. Suddenly there was a histrionic blast of anger, "My hamper!" Then he appeared red in the face, "Somebody has stolen my hamper."

"Perhaps it went overboard. Quite a few things have," the director ventured with little hope of placating such indignation. The actor's voice, which could have carried from one mountaintop to another, still got louder, and the director took hold of his convenient forearm with his weak grip, but the owner of the forearm shook it free immediately and his irritation increased. "They may well have been up all night," the director pleaded, "there is no particular rush."

"Oh yes there is, I want my breakfast."

Eventually the man who was building or repairing something came across. "Is there a problem?"

"My hamper, comrade, my hamper! It appears to have gone missing."

"Oh it'll be over here," said the fisherman who only released information in small doses.

Still complaining, the famous actor followed him and the director followed them both out of curiosity.

There was a small hold, and the fisherman opened the hatch to reveal a number of victuals, but it mainly consisted salted fish and bread that looked as though it had to be soaked in water before it could be eaten. "During the night, we collected together every scrap of food on board, and we've calculated how much each person can eat in a day."

The consequent eruption, though not of Pompeian proportions, was sufficient to oblige the captain to abandon the helm and deal with the furore. He listened briefly to the fisherman explaining the situation in their language. All the time he seemed preoccupied and exasperated. Then he turned and went back to work. The fisherman stood there with an untypical smile which in the circumstances the actor and director also found to be incongruous. Speaking in the Triers' language and opening his arms as though to say that if they didn't like what he was about to say, it was nothing to do with him, the fisherman explained through his lingering smile, "He says that it'll take ten days to get to land, if we catch the current going north, and so we have enough food if we ration it carefully. If you don't like it, we could always feed you to the fish and then everyone else would have a larger ration."

Surprisingly for a man who could get upset over the absence of minor luxuries, the famous actor took this *fait accompli* with what appeared to be a degree of *sang-froid* though not yet *esprit de corps*. Troubled, he said in a quiet and subdued voice, "We need to have a meeting." The director's heart sank like a leadline at the suggestion. No good would come of this, he knew as someone who had already observed that normal social relations had been inverted, and the fishermen were the only experts who could get them out of their predicament, and for the moment all their great store of culture and education was useless.

In the cabin, the cameraman was happily reading a book, and greeted the other two with a smile and other pleasantries.

He took to the idea of a "meeting" with the same enthusiasm as the director did, but he couldn't resist the famous actor for long.

"They have stolen my food," came the stentorian voice which had already obliged the cameraman to take the minutes.

"Requisitioned is the word, I think," said the director.

"Which is entirely acceptable in an emergency," the cameraman confirmed, sensing that he had an ally.

"And wish to share it out amongst themselves," the actor ignored their irrelevant and irreverent comments.

"Not amongst themselves, but amongst us all. That's what he said," the director corrected.

"Isn't that socialism?" queried the cameraman. "It appears that the fisherman got to that idea long before us. What do you think, comrade actor?"

The famous actor thought to himself that this really was a difficult time for a man of his artistic sensitivities. The world had been taken over by upstarts and ignoramuses. And such a man occasionally had to adopt the most byzantine arguments to justify what had once been considered mere common sense. "No, socialism isn't just that..."

"You mean that it's also assemblies and electricity."

"No, I mean that socialism acknowledges that not everyone is at the same level of enlightenment. We all want everyone to progress in that direction, but sadly not everyone has the education, intelligence, maturity or, in a nutshell, wit, as do more enlightened persons like ourselves."

"Count me out, I'm just a cameraman."

"Not at all, it is a most honourable calling," said the famous actor through gritted teeth.

"Bullshit," said the cameraman, throwing the notebook with only three lines of minutes across the room. "This is complete bullshit. We're relying on those people to get us to land safely. I think they'll do it, and we certainly can't."

After his kind remark on the status of cameramen, these words seemed coarse and peevish to the famous actor. "Do you have any idea of what was in that hamper?" And he listed the items many of which showed a preference for Viticultural names. The director started to laugh and then he couldn't stop. The cameraman joined in. The famous actor was mortified, but given the laughter showed no sign of abating, he too, in spite of himself, found his lips beginning to twitch. And then amazingly he burst out into laughter that was louder and more uproarious than theirs. "I suppose," he said with difficulty through his laughter, "that we'll just have to sit tight until we get to land."

"And then," said the director with equal difficulty, "you can report them to the authorities for theft of a hamper."

"Should I minute that?" asked the cameraman to more hoots of laughter.

"We'll write a play about this experience," the actor said, limp with jocularity.

"A comedy, you mean?" said the cameraman.

"A tragedy for me," corrected the actor.

"... and for your hamper," the director added. They laughed and laughed away their fears, their anger and their stress. The commotion was such that a fisherman put his head around the door, and peered at the three who immediately went silent. He said nothing, but his face expressed his perplexity before he was gone. Then the film crew sniggered to each other like conspiratorial children – for the moment happy children. And the good ship limped on with its crew of fishermen and its cargo of fools – or temporary fools we should call them. The crew and the cargo had little to do with each other. One lot worked to assuage their apprehensions, and the other loaded theirs with the boredom of the journey and the dullness of the ever-changing sea. They got to land in eight days, and the food was shared out with scrupulous fairness. On the seventh the captain had a bad accident that damaged his back. On reaching land he was stretchered off, and one of the crew, his brother apparently, was in tears. And on that land, everything changed back. The film crew started to command and the fishermen adopted once more their diffident obedience, and were clearly pleased to see the last of their cargo. The famous actor didn't report the theft of a hamper, though he did think about it. And its contents still haunted him for several months after that.

*

Scribe, don't force me to gloss this one. It's pretty obvious. She says that a parable should have a moral to it. Well, I have reinvented the parable, and use it not to provide a moral, but to pose a question. And what question is that? she asks. Well, more than one but principally one that still troubles me: are human beings naturally an egalitarian species or a hierarchical one? They can be both, as history tells us, but as a Surelik, I feel that nature made us like the fishermen and not the camera crew. But the Noisy Musics and the Little Noisy Musics strongly believe that man developed from the ape because he wanted to go to market, and naturally all we want to do is get richer than everyone else. I'm not civilised enough to comment on that.

For some time I lived with those dregs of a White army and was able to observe how their relationships developed. The young aristocratic officer, Andrei Alexeyevich, wanted to maintain a semblance of military discipline in spite of the lack of an army and, what's more, the lack of pay for these condemned men who quite possibly had not been wholly convinced about why they had been fighting on that side. They probably moved from one war to another, and eventually found it difficult to think of another way of spending their lives. They'd backed the wrong horse, but for them it may have been no more than that: a bet. They became increasingly sullen in his presence, and he too was aware of it. I didn't know how it would end, but I was sure that it would end badly and possibly put my own life in danger. I decided to leave, but the difficulty of the decision was one of the reasons for wasting so much time. I was obliged either to go deeper into the forest in search of my community or return to the plain, where so many terrible memories remained. As with the lives of most human beings, particularly those who have touched civilisation only lightly, mine has been full of such momentous decisions. If I had chosen differently, my life would have been so very different. Is there regret? Stupidly there is, because the life I have carved out has been so unique and quite unimaginable at the time. I once hoped that it would be more significant, but it has not been insignificant. I've had my minor victories and one very important one, but the great turnaround in our fortunes would not be lasting. Both paths – south and further into the forest or north and into the plain – held their dangers. The vastness of the southern option meant that successful location of my people was not guaranteed. Northwards was more dangerous, but I was a little hooked – not on the farming of course but on the ideas of change that flowed and eddied there, and perhaps even that damned language of the Triers. So much written down, and so much devalued by doing just that. So much to learn and so much to unlearn. This must be the endless dilemma of a minority people, but sharpened by the dramas of the time. The proverb says, "He who travels alone is always in good company," but I think that after my short stay in Väikelinn I was less convinced by this Surelik truism.

I followed the advice of a White soldier and left without saying a single goodbye. To my surprise, Andrei Alexeyevich Belsky would reappear in my life where I would have least expected him. Like the chameleon, he would change without changing and belong to what essentially he had always been: a man with a strong allegiance to order. I knew that this time Väikelinn would not impress. I'd heard of other places, much larger and more complex, and I was drawn. For us Väikelinn belonged to the land of the Triers, but for the Triers Väikelinn belonged to the land of the Surelikud – I speak of cultural judgements here, because obviously they believed that it all belonged to them, even the deepest forest where my relations were at that moment eating and chatting in a little clearing they'd just made and where no Trier had ever stepped. So many threads, so many lives, so much chaos and so much order vainly struggling to prevail.

To survive in the civilised world, you have to plan. In the forest, you take from nature's larder only what you need not because of any innate moral superiority but because you know that this same larder will be equally well stocked the next day and the next week. Seasonal changes exist, but these are in the diet. The food is always there. So once I was close to the edge of the forest, I did something I'd never done before: I set a large number of snares to catch small mammals and birds, so that I could sell them in the town. The country was still short of food, and much was taken away for the cities. I had to come in at night and starting with a few people I knew, I would distribute my goods, which also included mushrooms, berries, bark and leaves with special properties. By the end of the night most of the food was sold, and I never met my buyers. They simply left their money with my friends. It was not a great deal of money, as I had only taken what I could carry in my sack, but it was enough to live on for a month. Even in a socialist economy, particularly after fairly recent reforms, money did help things along. Such things were not strictly speaking illegal, but it could have looked bad if it was done in the light of day, and I didn't want to draw attention to myself.

I knew there was a professor of linguistics who was a Surelik speaker and had set up an institution to promote Surelik literacy. Given that the language had never been a written one, this was a huge task, but one that had been undertaken successfully with several other minority languages in the lands of the Triers. I had to seek her out, as I had decided that I needed a proper education in the Triers' language. When I met her, I was pleased to find that she was no more than fifteen years older than me, and was very informal in her manner, as many people were in those early years of the regime. Vera Golikasova Talunikovich, this was her name, sat me down in her office, and told me all about her life whilst making sure to ask me about mine, thus collecting more information than I probably wanted to give. She had been brought up in the capital, but her parents were both Surelik speakers and spoke it at home. She was impressed with my Surelik and even more with my command of the Triers' language.

"You speak it so well for someone who has just come in from the forest," she said, apparently believing my lie, which was probably pointless in a small town, though I still thought it big, because my imagination struggled to conceive of anything much bigger. "I need you because we have no speakers from the forest - people who grew up as monoglots and have a wide knowledge of taxonomy." Of course, I didn't know such words as "monoglot" and "polyglot" in either language. She seemed to switch continually between the two. "I want you to work as what is called a lexicographer," she said in the Trier tongue. "You'll work with trained lexicographers, and you will help in writing the first Surelik vocabulary and then the first Surelik-Trier dictionary."

How can I tell you this part of the story? Most people would say that it takes a dull dog to be a lexicographer, but they would be wrong. This was one of the most exciting of my many metiers. Oftentimes I now hear someone say a word I coined. I admire my handiwork and savour the moment. I reflect on possible expansions and diminutions in their meanings or on a nuance that has developed over the many intervening decades. I may find that nuance elegant or misleading, just as we reflect on how our children turn out in adulthood.

As she had suggested, they started off on the flora and fauna which they were ignorant about. They barely knew the words in the Triers' language, let alone Surelik. They were bemused, and unashamed of their lack of knowledge of the countryside and the forest - such vile and base things for them. This turned me into a useful oddity who was mixing in a circle that wasn't properly mine, and this was probably an extra incentive for acquiring their culture, though now I realise that many of them weren't that cultured. Vera Golikasova, or Verochka as I shall always remember her, was true to her word, and every other day we met for my instruction. She was as erudite as she was transparent and so, when the dark days came, I was sure that she wouldn't last for long but actually that wasn't the cause of her untimely death. It came during the relative tolerance of the war years during which she volunteered to lift the wounded from the battlefield. Fifty-seven of them she had dragged back to safety before a sniper's bullet inevitably took her from this world along with all her intelligence, sacrifice and sense of duty so typical of that generation.

I know that the reader is getting bored, so I must try harder. After all, this is... well, this is lexicography, and I bet that even if you have heard of it, you've never given it a second thought, except perhaps to complain about an entry in a dictionary which is incorrect in your opinion. This is not about war and it's not about love or sex or gratuitous violence. It is merely about the cogs, levers and minute mechanisms of what we use to communicate with each other. We can do it, so why does it matter? Just as we don't have to know how a car works in order to drive it. Maybe, but that belief would make you a philistine. A car is made up of precision components that are increasingly standardised, but languages are made up of components that are far from precise, though they manage to communicate remarkably well and much better in a literate society. I don't believe that illiterate societies are inferior and they are certainly no less skilled, as I argue elsewhere in this dictation, but here I'll admit that the written and the printed word store information and that information will degrade if we let the words run wild as they can do in illiterate society to no great cost.

So I had to ask myself many questions. "What is a word?" You think you know that but the word "bookshop" is one word: it could easily be "book shop" or "book-shop". That is a banal example, and the problem is much greater when no written form exists.[2] Normally this wouldn't be much of a problem because there is already an established convention. "What if there isn't a word?" This will have you clicking your tongues and saying, "Of course, this is just a savage, rudimentary language with little vocabulary." Not at all. As we were to discover, Surelik proved to have a massive vocabulary, nor was it devoid of technological innovations. For instance, from the early days of the European war, we had a word for plane. In fact we have several, some were borrowed like "avion" and some were improvised, as perhaps all words originally were, like "lendavasi" [which means "flying thing"]. In the end we made up our own, "masinlind" [which means "machine bird"]. The way this agglutination works in a language is almost entirely arbitrary and varies from language to language, but always it affects the way we perceive our languages. In other words, the graphic and the orthographic presentation of our languages refashions the ways in which we interpret them and use them. Of course, every language is deficient, even the widely spoken languages of the Triers, the Wall-Builders and the Noisy Musics. "Is every word to take part?" This is a fascinating question and its difficulties will not have been immediately apparent to the reader. I have already mentioned loan words, which mainly come from the Triers' language, but also from the Wall-Builders' and some of the other small minority languages in the region. Some of the loan words from the Triers' language were themselves borrowed from other European languages, including Latin and Ancient Greek. Inevitably this divided us between the purists who wanted to coin new words to replace them and conservatives who felt that once a word has entered the language, it would be very

---

2   In this translation, we have adapted the example to the English language. In the original, Rahväema use the Surelik word for "toad-snare".

artificial to ban them. In the end a sensible compromise was reached, and those words that had a degree of currency were kept. And finally, "What is the Surelik language?" Again this is not an uncommon problem, but it is usually resolved over long periods of time, which was not possible in our century - a century that found it hard not to meddle in everything, driven by a strange belief that there was always a best way of doing things. Surelik is spoken over a large area, and no one appears to know all the dialects. There are the Surelikud of the north-west who have integrated very successfully into the Triers' lands and have many loan words. They were a prosperous farming people of land-owning peasants, and always kept aloof from us savages as they would see it. Still, they are quite definitely Surelikud, whatever they say.

This, you can imagine, was for me exciting and opened all kinds of openings to this other world, while convincing me that I was doing something significant for my own community through a medium I had never really thought of throughout my childhood: the written word. Of course I was vaguely aware that there was such a thing, and during the very occasional presence of the authorities of the Great Caesar, there was a great deal of the printed word being waved around - in a language we could not read because we could not speak it. Our incomprehension of both their spoken and written language was our greatest weapon, though when they left there was always the menace of their return, but for us the real age of fear was yet to come. There was however also the irony that to save our language we had make use of an adapted version of their alphabet.

And later I would use our marvellous invention to write many books on various subjects: Surelik grammar, Surelik history, Surelik cuisine, Surelik politics and pretty much Surelik anything. I wrote books in both Surelik and the language of the Triers', the latter mainly to make a bit more money.

"Why then are you dictating this book?" asks the scribe quite reasonably. Well, I'm dictating it as a compromise between the old days in which a person like me would produce an oral text to be memorised and handed down, obviously to be changed from one generation to another, and modernity which requires the printed word – the almost indelible printed word, which is undermined only by its own rigidity as it cannot keep up with the evolution of its language. I am dictating it because it seemed like a good idea at the time. I hadn't thought of her interruptions, and question now whether spontaneity can ever be found in the printed word. But I am also a stubborn person, and I will continue in this manner which is itself an evolving one. In fact, the more I think about it, this is the right way to do it. Counterintuitively I realise that this collaborative process, however awkward, puts me even more at the centre of this text, and that is exactly where I want to be. This, more than anything else I have written, is my legacy. It will be more honest and less coherent, for coherence is always a managed afterthought.

It could be said that happiness is keeping busy, but there is another reason why I now feel that this was the happiest time of my adult life, if we exclude my ephemeral weeks as a newly-wed: there was also the sense of being part of a new, rational and kindlier world in which everyone counted; looking back there were dark clouds on the horizon but the sun was still shining. After the terrible wars and famines, which affected the Surelikud much less than most, it seemed uncharitable to hold the young and struggling republic to an impossible standard when it was doing so much with the best intentions. Had I forgiven their treatment of Pyotr? Not really, but life went on and I had to admit that war is always an obscenity, which was why we avoided it as much as we could. Now of course, much greater crimes have come and gone, overshadowing the civil war.

In those months and years, I learnt the exhilaration of creativity. Think of it, a new literate language was being hammered out in our foundry. In place of heavy tools and the sound of machinery, we used the tools of the intellect: pen, paper, reference works, lists, notes and in the background an intense and imposing silence occasionally broken by whispers as colleagues questioned and replied to each other. We had our criteria, our guidelines and our aims, but we applied them with considerable autonomy given the lack of resources and time. My career advanced as many colleagues moved on to more important positions, mainly at the Ministry of Minority Peoples, but at this stage uninterested in a political career, I remained in the foundry of our language's literary future where the real work was done and within a couple of years I was the most qualified person after Verochka who also showed no signs of leaving.

At some stage Verochka came to my desk and told me that a strange man was insisting that he had to talk to me. Mystified as to who it could be, I asked for more information. "He has a disability and carries a stick that he never uses," she told me and no sooner were the words out of her mouth than Halvatud came into the room unbidden. Smiling, he lifted his stick and waved it with an absurd flourish. And he continued to process across the room, navigating the desks carefully but always keeping his eyes on me as though he thought that I might escape. Verochka didn't seem to mind and, on seeing that I had recognised him, discreetly moved away.

"Which wind has blown you this way?" I said not without a hint of irritation.

"You!" he replied.

"Me? I know that you believe in being called, but I never called you."

"Yes you, Rahväemarmas.[3] I have matters to discuss with you. Important matters."

"I'm no longer in the forest, Halvatud..."

"... more's the pity."

"... and I am a busy woman now, Halvatud, so if you must

---

3   Rahväemarmas: suffix *armas* is a term of affection.

say something, then get it on with it."

He only seemed mildly offended and, reviving his smile perhaps with a little effort, he said crisply, "Have you ever thought of getting remarried?"

"Is this a proposal? You're crazier than I thought you were."

"No, dear Rahväema, why would a bright young woman like you want to marry a cripple like me, who is held to this life by a gossamer thread?"

"Don't flannel me, Halvatud, and don't waste my time."

"Answer my question then."

"Your question? Oh that. Of course not, I'm quite happy as I am and have no need of some stupid man to be my partner for life. We Surelik women are of independent mind, and the last one, poor man, brought only sadness and solitude. Now I have my work, my colleagues, my routine, which is almost as good as starting to walk on a bright spring morning in the forest. And it's every day of the year."

"I thought as much. And I'm pleased to hear it."

"So good of you to take such an interest."

"And one more thing," he grinned, "stay away from foreigners."

"Why foreigners? Few come this way, but they'll always be welcome to me."

"Okay," he continued, "you're quite right about that. I'll have to be more specific: stay away from the Little Noisy Musics."

"Little chance of one of them turning up here."

"Any permutation is possible even in the desert or on the frozen polar wastes."

"Or the forest."

"The forest is the place of the greatest variety, not the least."

"You get around for a man with a stick," I said.

"And you'll have noted that I never use it." With that he turned around and left without a backward glance. I felt that I had been a little harsh, and sensed that there was something inexplicably good about that man. And then I forgot his every word.

The years passed uneventfully and happily – unconsciously happy years as I have already said – and Verochka came to my room, when I was now her deputy. It was 1926, and she was still her brisk and friendly self: "Rahväema, I have news for you – I have news for everyone, but I'll tell you first."

"Good news?"

"Maybe, but more likely not. They're proposing this reform as a desire to take the minority languages more seriously, so they're demanding that all the language administrations move to the capital. I see it as an attempt to deprive communities of their intellectuals, and switch the allegiances of those intellectuals towards the centre. Already we are far too distant from our base." She used the political language of the time, but her fears were well-founded.

There was no question of not moving with the others. My work was my life, and my mind was drawn back to the night after I saw Pyotr for the last time – and to the train that bewitched me with its speed and purpose. I had thought about its destination, which could have been anywhere but surely sooner or later it would have been the capital; everything led to the capital. The capital was the centre of everything that moved in the Triers' lands.

The city, ah the city! Listen, my readers, my friends, my fellow Surelikud, and of course my foreign readers, for I want these words to be translated into the languages of the Triers and the Noisy Musics which shall carry them far and wide like the winds of the sullen plains. The city is a monster; it's an anthill and a universe. It's a republic of ideas and conflicts, and it is as dependent and abandoned as an abused and impoverished widow – fragile and old before her time. It is energy and exhausted infertility, and if it weren't for the exuberance of the peasant populations that sustain it, it would die in a matter of years.

A monster I called it, and rightly so, for it and its downtrodden poor are the force that drain the land and the forest of their natural cycles. It crushes the city-dweller and it crushes the peasant, and yet it may be the answer to the problems it has caused.

All this I understand only after many decades. When I first stepped onto the city streets, I could only stare in dismay at the scale of man's achievements. The monumental and the mass. And where to start: a place that offers everything, offers nothing. It confuses and bewilders. How do you choose from all that stuff? And yet it is also exhilarating, especially at first sight.

Later I would learn that other societies considered that city to be lacking in goods and services, but they could not have imagined the life of the Surelikud.

The buildings rose up brick by brick and stone by stone, always interconnecting to make a whole as though conjured up by magic. But magic it was not: each brick, each stone, each pane of glass was placed by a man working long hours for little reward. The foundations of these temples to pride were made of peasants' bones and crushed lives. The children who grew up to be the next generation of labourers hadn't known the albeit limited freedom and love of the peasant family, as these lives were crushed not only by greed but also by the clock – the harshest whip to strike a Trier's back.

But at the time I saw nothing but the beauty – the sullen, self-contented beauty of solid facades which now enclosed varied and cramped lives within their hidden grasp. They sprang from history and distant ways of thinking, and were designed for other uses, but this in no way lessened the power and intellect of their collective statement. I was dizzy with delight, as though I had landed in another world, more studied and geometric than the ones I'd previously known. It appeared to have been made for giants, and yet the humans who walked in their shadows looked like humans in their variety and zest for the little things of life, not the great, the grand and the overstated.

At the time these buildings and their apartments were overcrowded with the grandchildren, great grandchildren and even distant descendents of the workers whose bones they'd ground to dust. Imperfect justice had been achieved at the cost of some limitations on personal privacy. Misery had been shared out more equitably, and for many that was an improvement.

Things started well enough. The offices looked good, though not up to the standards of Europe and the lands of the Noisy Musics. Certainly they were better than the draughty rooms we'd had in the Surelik lands.

It was Verochka who again introduced me to another important man in my life – the man who was to be my second husband. He was a tall man with a prominent nose and small eyes – not a handsome man, but his healthy skin and his air of sufferance, as though he only tolerated us because for some reason he happened to be standing in front of us. Vera was cool with him, which was unusual, but I found him interesting – there's no question of that – and particularly after he had started to speak. He spoke initially in Surelik, but only the niceties of saying hello and asking how I was in a voice that gave no suggestion that he cared a damn. I was to find out later that this was all the Surelik he knew though he told everyone he was fluent. He switched then to the language of the Triers and the pronunciation was no better, but he could make himself understood – more or less. I had never seen such a human being in my life. He was like a strange animal that had wandered into the forest. It happened occasionally: some exotic beast had escaped or been released, and it made straight for the cover of the forest – to wander relatively safe but lonely for the rest of its life. And mistaking his aloofness for disorientation, I felt compassion for this lost animal amid so many beasts similar to each other. He was beautifully dressed and his gestures expressed confidence but it was very contained. There was something about him that was both relaxed and impatient. He wanted something and he wanted it quick. Any kind of administrative delay would make him furious, as I was to find out.

Fortunately for him, Verochka was not keen on administrative delays. Her approach was to get everything done in the simplest and quickest manner, because she was short of time and ambitious to do as much as she could for our language. We took him to the room where we talked with such visitors, and foreigners in those days were not such an unusual occurrence. He fitted the armchair around his body very nicely, and with one knee over the other, he took out a pipe and started to press tobacco into it. The whole process consumed a great deal of time, and Verochka tried to press ahead with business, but he had no intention of being hurried or indeed being slowed down. He truly was the strangest of strange animals. Only when the first smoke billowed out of his thin-lipped mouth did he start to speak and answered one of Verochka's questions. I was right to say that he was an impatient man, but he knew that provoking other people's impatience was an effective negotiating tool.

It turned out that the man had some strange theory that some people had descended from the Surelikud. According to him, a "science" of history and genetics had apparently proved this link. I was unconvinced as he looked more like the Triers than the Surelikud, and let's face it, the Surelikud are a bastard people. And I had no problem with that. I liked it, in fact. It was our culture that I cared about, and by that I meant not just our language, myths, poetry and song, but also the way we lived in the forest – as much an integral part of it as the birch trees and the tigers, which today are also in danger of extinction. He talked on and on in his atrocious Trier language, but even if he'd spoken in the purest Surelik we wouldn't have understood, so unlikely were his theories, which paradoxically brought out the best in him. He wanted us to believe so much that for a short while he threw aside his aloofness and, spent pipe in hand, he leaned forward and suddenly became animated. This was the force that had driven him eastwards, unlike the hordes of political tourists who traipsed the Triers' lands in search of a utopia that had failed to blossom. No, this man was a one-off with his own crazy beliefs and not the slightest interest in what interested so many. For instance the statistics for the first five-year plan were of no interest to him, but the Surelik use of the locative case could have him leaping out his chair and shouting, "Yes, at last, the final piece in the jigsaw!"

But I run ahead of myself, these wonders of the gentleman who visited that day were yet to come. He laid out his theories, which we dismissed, and hinted that he wanted to use our precious resources to get to the Surelik lands so that he could prove his strongly held beliefs – strongly held in advance of hard evidence was hardly a scientific approach. Once he started on his second pipe, Verochka had had enough and said that they would think about how they could help. We could reconvene once his ideas were clearer. In the meantime, we had to get back to work. He seemed upset beyond measure – far beyond what you'd expect from a grown man. Clearly the foreigner was not used to not getting his way, and was willing to show it. I would have given in but Verochka pushed him out of the room forcefully and then out of the building, always agreeing with him as they went, much as you would do with an awkward child.

By then I had developed a taste for the theatre. Yes I, the girl from the forest, had from the start developed quite a few tastes for what civilisation can provide. Of course, thirty or forty Surelikud sitting round a fire in the evening with four or five shacks standing guard behind us while a poet declaimed one of the epic adventures of Võitleja could be such a moving experience, and perhaps it still is, but when I was young it was an integral part of a whole. No nostalgia involved. It was itself, the only way it could be. But when you've been in a comfortable theatre and no forest wind is chilling your back – which didn't bother me before because that's what the forest wind did – and some fine actors have come on stage and recited their lines in the Triers' language so cleverly, you could not fail to be impressed. They made fun of the government, and the government probably needed a bit of that. Every government needs a bit of that. In 1928 I'd been to see a play by Erdman and liked it, so when I heard that he had a new play called *The Suicide*, I bought a ticket. Everything was exciting about the theatre, even going to the ticket office and when you had the ticket in your hand, you felt exhilaration. This was a moment to long for. This Erdman would find ever crazier tricks to muddle up your mind, so that in the end you didn't know whether you were climbing up the tree or down. Was the government wilfully bad or was it just incompetent? Was there any point in believing anything, or were some people just too flippant for their own good? And so it went on. It was all done by men and women trying to be other men and women entirely different from themselves. No, we never did that in the forest. We could have, I suppose, but we never got round to it. I'm sure that we could have. Then three or four days before the first performance, the GPU went in, shut the theatre down permanently and confiscated all copies of the play they could get their hands on, but fortunately they did not succeed because some survived and the play would eventually be staged decades later when the Birthmark became the leader of the Triers. The poor playwright was sent off into internal exile for two years. He was sent fifty kilometres from the capital, so compared with what would happen later, his punishment was not too severe. At the time it felt terrible. I wept for the man – and for my useless theatre ticket. How could it be bad to make people think? Is it a crime to make us laugh at other people's conceits and follies?

A few days later I spoke about this to Verochka. She was not unsympathetic, but she gave me a lecture, "Rahväema, I don't approve. In fact, I agree with you – in principle at least – but you must understand that it is either this lot or the others: the people of the past, of the time of the Great Caesar. If you're not with our lot, you're with that lot. That's how it is. I know that everything is not right, but we're doing so much. Just look at what we're doing with our language. This Erdman is a very clever young man, but perhaps he should see the big picture. Not just carp from the sidelines."

"Verochka, it's a play! If a regime cannot tolerate a play which will be seen by a few thousand souls, then it has no right to be a regime. To let it be staged would not be a sign of its fragility, but of the solidity of its power, which it has now started to abuse," I replied in that rhetorical form you know so well, my dear scribe. She nods in agreement.

Verochka looked worried. "Rahväemarmas, be careful who you speak to like that. These are difficult times that we have to get through and they may get even worse. But the Moustache won't be around for long. He has a dull brain and sooner or later he'll trip up. Meanwhile we have work to do – important work."

I wouldn't have it. When my blood is up, I don't care what I say or to whom: "Vera, this is where our paths divide. I took you for another." She looked hurt but still concerned. She never complained, but simply looked for the simplest solution to yet another problem.

I was angry with Verochka, but she was right at least in part. I see that now. I was young and saw things as black and white. Oh that's such a cliché. Such an irritating cliché! As irritating as the inescapable truth it represents. Of course it's a cliché because the civilised people must always have been like that: we would like justice, but a little bit of justice is all we'll ever get. And when an injustice happens, we have to ask ourselves, "Is this injustice so bad that I can't tolerate it – that I would turn the world upside down again rather than let it pass? Well, now I come to think about it, maybe not. I've got my own plans. And who knows what's going on there? No smoke without fire." Speaking of clichés, was there ever a cliché more evil than "No smoke without fire". How many innocent people went to the scaffold and all people could do was say: "No smoke without fire."

Yes, she was right, but then so was I. It was intolerable. And you never know exactly when it's the moment to move and when it's the moment to stitch up your lips. "The Moustache won't be around for long." Well she got that wrong. Very wrong. So wrong that a cruel regime ruled for more than two decades. And Verochka died defending it from an even crueller and wholly evil regime. She lived in the world of hard decisions and I in the world of absolutes. She was the hero. The hero was her, not me. I see that now. And who will write her biography? At the very least I must dictate this belated eulogy to her, and my faithful scribe whom I mistreat at every turn will write it down for me and for her.

Verochka – my dear Vera Golikasova Talunikovich – you lived a worthy life in line with your duties to your language, your country, humanity and this splendid planet of ours. And that's why you died unburied in no man's land, and I lived on just as that curséd Kurat predicted I would. You, Verochka, made the right and moral decisions, and they always lead to an early death. Forgotten and possibly reviled in this new Trier regime. But is it so bad to want justice? Let the writers have their say! We wanted justice under the Birthmark, but we ended up with the injustices of the Drunkard, whose dogged blindness in the fog of alcoholism came in the company of hunger.

You see! There I go again, starting the eulogy quite properly with Verochka and ending it with self-justification, which undermines what I'd said, what I'd admitted to. Some confession! Some eulogy. Losing the thread. Well then, let me take it up again.

Verochka, you symbolise for me the many millions of people who sacrificed so much – even at times their own good principles – to build a better land for generations to come. You are the twenty-seven million who would die fighting the canker that came from the West – or not fighting it but trying to find a way through and still being swept away by the contagion. The innocent, the children – who could be more innocent than they – the elderly, the frightened, the partisans, the soldiers. That's you, Verochka, forgotten by all but me – for alone at my age no other colleague could remember you personally even in a land that well remembers those unforgiving years. I build this monument to you and all who were like you. So many, so many that my brain goes dizzy trying to conceive those inconceivable figures. That's why I think of you, because you were there and helped me through those dangerous years and little thanks you got for it.

This monument is unworthy of you, but in the absence of others I present it to you. Let it be taken as the sincerest and most important thing within this autobiography, whose truths are concentrated in those parts that go beyond the paltry minutiae of my life.

Shortly after our argument, she came again this time with a smile not principally for me. She was probably pleased that she could cut two branches with a single blow of her axe. "You remember that strange foreigner? The one who believes that his special race descends from or should I say evolved from the Surelikud. Well, he wants to visit the Surelik lands, and I've been fobbing him off as best I can, which is not easy to do. And I had no inclination to give in until you said those things the other day. Then I had another problem: how to save you from your wonderfully big mouth?"

I must have frowned, because she said, "Hear me out!"

"Well, get on with it."

"I sent in a report to the ministry, in which I said that this foreigner is a great admirer of our new regime and its ideology. And that he was also interested in our enlightened treatment of minorities and I had reassured him about that. So much so that he now wishes to visit the Surelik lands. I then advised them that it would be imprudent to send him without a reliable guide whom I would appoint. They fell for it; they absolutely fell for it. Strange how the distrustful can be persuaded only by the words they want to hear. They're even going to fund the trip!"

"Why should I care?"

"Then it's true what they say about a girl from the forest."

She jabbed me in the ribs. "You – you're going to be the guide. I know that he could bore the jittery jackals to sleep, but you get a trip home and a little time to get over the reduction in your theatre options. What could possibly be better? You probably won't get to the forest you speak of so often, but two months in Väikelinn won't be that bad."

I stood in silence and started to think it through. I don't like being pushed around and initially I wanted to reject the idea. Who knows which decision would have been worse? The trip – I thought to myself – would be good, and I didn't dislike the man as much as she did. The city I'd grown to love in spite of myself now felt a little hostile, and I finally understood that she was doing it all for me. It was true that she had grown up in that environment and she knew it well, while I only thought that I knew it when I didn't. "Alright, I'll go then."

"You won't regret it. And you may even get more than two months. He's an operator that man, and he'd already be there if it weren't for me, stubborn bitch that I am. Still, he won't bother me any more, and you'll be in less danger. Not no danger at all, so keep those vocal cords under control."

So we went. First by train, then in a bus that struggled along every kilometre, and finally in some regional town whose name I forget, a car from Väikelinn took us over the last stretch – a generous allocation of resources due to the importance of my travelling companion, who repaid our nation by complaining all the way. I teased him absent-mindedly for his complaints and his limited knowledge of the Triers' language, and by the end I could even get a smile out of him. The closer we came to the Surelik lands, the more he was dependent on me, something he must have resented at some level.

Suddenly my companion became very attentive, and insisted on my presence at every event that local officials put on for his benefit. It appeared that Verochka's well-intentioned scheming to get me to a safer environment had been too successful in convincing the authorities that this was a genuine and influential supporter of their regime and ideology. In those times they needed all the friends they could get, and the local party was primarily interested in placating their superiors in the capital. And resources were still lacking.

He seemed happy with his treatment, but not surprised. I found him charming and yes, I was flattered that this foreigner courted me so assiduously. He wasn't transparent like Pyotr, and he was never effusive. It was clear that he felt that he had a lot to offer, and I was willing to believe that he had. The local Surelik officials and even those who worked for them did treat me with a kind of respect, though I did also detect a little hostility.

Later in life I would usually be able to sense when something was going to happen, but the sudden turn in his behaviour took me by surprise. We were climbing the stairs of our hotel and close to my room when he grabbed me and tried to kiss me. I pushed him away and he was insulted. "You ungrateful little tart," he said in his laboured Trier language, while occasionally breaking into his own. "You savage from the forest, who do you think you are?" he said stumbling from one grammatical error to another. I almost wanted to laugh, but I was still frightened. I entered my room quickly and having locked the door I sat down to consider my situation. I didn't find him unattractive, but his manner and what he'd said were inexcusable.

The morning brought another surprise: one of the hotel staff appeared at my door and said as he handed over a bunch of flowers, "The strange foreign man insisted that I give you this." His sullenness betrayed his irritation, and as there is no florist in Väikelinn, the man I simply called Edvin must have got someone to go into the woods outside the town and pick them for him. Even then I couldn't see him doing it himself. Once the porter or whoever he was had left, I read the note attached to flowers: "Dear Rahväema, please forgive my boorish behaviour last night. Please come down to the dining room, and I will make it up to you. Edwin."

I was curious, I will admit it. I had left my work and there-fore I had left my life and its purpose behind in the capi-tal. I was in the company of someone I didn't really know and was vaguely attracted to that unknowability. I waited ten minutes and then went down. There he was, and com-pletely unchanged. Still the aloofness, still the contempt for all around him, still the awkward, lanky, slightly uncoordi-nated man he must have always been. He was certainly not the penitent.

"And how are you this fine morning?" he said in almost per-fect Trier, probably because it was one of his stock sentences. I was already quite familiar with his eccentric rhetoric.

I said something short and possibly dismissive, not yet willing to give any ground, even though the Surelikud have survived by giving ground. We're proud of it. It's our way of life.

He smiled – a cool indifferent smile that was hard to read – and, like a man who's going around a business transaction he's well accustomed to, he took out a little box, placing it in front of me without relaxing his grip. One of his fingers touched a metal protrusion and the lid flew open to reveal a ring with cut stones. Gold, apparently. Not that I'd ever seen it in my life, and I'd very rarely heard it mentioned.

Well of course, he went through the rigmarole of a proposal, as I have seen it done in foreign films since then. But he was more businesslike, whereas everything is very emotional in the films. And I said that I didn't know; I wasn't sure; I needed time. My own little rigmarole, or that is how it came out. I was stunned. I suppose that is the only way I can describe it. The "savage from the forest" was now to be his wife, all undertaken with absurd impetuosity.

He greeted my uncertainty not with anger this time, but desperation. He suddenly became a little boy, his eyes shone and a single tear very slowly descended his left cheek. He couldn't live without me. He wasn't good with words even in his own language, he explained.

I don't know to this day whether all of this was completely staged or whether in that moment he really did feel something. Whatever the case, it worked and he got his way. I would be his wife.

I won't go through the business of getting married a second time, most of which I recall only vaguely. We went to the ZAGS offices, or Department of Public Service, with our two witnesses in tow, and Edvin had already reverted to his usual self. He replied to the registrar's questions in the bored tones of an important man responding to a necessary but tiresome bureaucratic procedure, a feature of modernity he was atavistically intolerant of, just as I inherited my love of the forest from the long experience of my forebears. His date of birth, his place of birth, his nationality, whether he had been married and, if so, whether he had been divorced. He never paused or looked uncomfortable beyond his irritation. He lived in the world as if he owned it. The registrar, a pleasant and plump woman in full uniform, smiled benignly and appeared to be genuinely moved by our union. "We're internationalists, you know," she said, glossing over the fact that the regime was quite often distrustful of foreigners and not always without reason.

Perhaps, like others, she thought that Edvin had contacts in high places. Fear makes actors of us all – but not Edvin. Devious he definitely was, but also immune to external pressures. And his deviousness was always in the company of his sense of entitlement, which could not however assist his command of the Triers' language, which stumbled along whilst delivered with the poise of Pushkin reborn.

After the wedding, I asked, "Edvin, Edvin Perkins. Is that your full name?"

"Sir Edwin Perkins," he corrected me stiffly.

"Is Sir your first name then? Not Edvin."

He smiled condescendingly. "Sir just means that my king and country have appreciated the many things I've done for them and they want it to be known publicly. No, you don't have to call me Sir, because now you're my wife."

"So what country do you come from? I don't know why I never asked you before."

"Didn't you know? I'm one of the Little Noisy Musics, the most powerful people in the world. The sun never sets on our empire, and a quarter of the world's population is under our control. I bet that makes you feel good!"

It never did. It made the Triers look quite modest. And of course in that moment I remembered Halvatud's warning.

As we walked away from the Wedding Hall, I recognised a man walking towards us. He was even more smartly dressed than Edwin was, and of course his name was Kurat. "What a fine-looking couple! Freshly married, I hear," he said in the Triers' language.

"And who are you that you know our business," said Sir Edwin in his best Trier.

"One whose business it is to know everyone's business," smiled Kurat speaking perfect Little Noisy Music – my husband would tell me later that Kurat spoke in the dialect of all the best people in his country. This produced a miraculous change in Sir Edwin's behaviour. In fact the next thing he did was to ask Kurat what school he went to. Of course I didn't understand at the time as he too had switched to that language, his native tongue.

To which Kurat apparently replied, "My school was so long ago that I can't remember, and I have a very good memory."

"To me," Sir Edwin opined, "it sounds a bit like Harrow. Yes, I'm sure of it. It's Harrow, isn't it?"

"Actually no, and my name's Kurat. Clearly I'll have to work upon my Etonian," said Kurat, now he was the one looking a little bored. "Rahväema, it's good to see you again," he continued but in Surelik this time. "What a smart idea to marry this dolt. It will take you very far, you know. Get as much out of him as you can, because he's a dishonest bastard.

Lie to him; lie to him all the time. He'll still be telling you more of them himself. He's a charlatan, of course, but aren't they all. He's a charlatan, but not that good at it. Not as smart as he thinks he is."

"Last time you insulted my first husband – or rather his name, because he was dead – and now you insult my second husband. I won't listen to a word you say."

"You should do though, because you're not listening to me just brought you a lot of trouble. It's never a good idea to ignore Kurat, who's the one who encourages you to look after yourself. If everybody took my advice, the world would be a better place, but there are too many people like you. Here's a new word in his language: *sugar daddy*. You'll find out what it means in due course. Screw him for all you can get, and be quick. He has already squandered half his inheritance."

Sir Edwin's ears pricked up at the sound of *sugar daddy*, and he was wondering whether he had misheard when he said, "Is that Surelik he's speaking? Can't be Harrow then, after all."

"Sir Edwin," Kurat must have more or less said, "I hear great things about what you're doing here."

"How do you know my name?"

"It's my... Let's just say that I always do. I like the scam of convincing these people that you admire their ideology. Such a good way to get free travel."

"I don't admire them and never tried to convince them. I was just interested in the Surelik connection. An academic study, you understand. The idea that I would support the Bolshies – really, whatever next. It would ruin my career, you know. You mustn't go around saying such things."

"Ah yes, your career, Sir Edwin! Before you changed the subject, I was saying what a splendid career you've had. Now, I always forget, which university did you go to?"

"Oxford."

"Tut tut, Sir Edwin. Now I recall. Your parents paid to get you into St Andrew's, and you were thrown out in your second term for attempting to kidnap a female student and stabbing a brave young man who was trying to stop you." And your father had already spent a fortune on getting the university to overlook that little incident with the chapel's collection money. Such a fuss about nothing."

"Mr Kurat. Such slander." Edwin looked terrified.

"I'm not criticising you, Sir Edwin; I'm admiring you. Judging people's moral behaviour, now that really isn't my job. By the way, Kurat will do. No 'mister' please, as I find titles so common."

For a little while and quite unusually Edwin's vocal chords seemed to have seized up, and this didn't seem to faze Kurat at all. He just kept staring at my newly-wed husband in state of bemused pleasure. Eventually Edwin pulled himself together and said, "You seem a fine and jolly cove - a bit eccentric perhaps, but we upper-class chaps from the best country in the world go in for a bit of eccentricity. It's our calling card. Would you like to come to dinner with us this evening?"

"This evening on your wedding night? That would be wholly inappropriate, don't you think? But Sir Edwin, I must apprise you of another little eccentricity of mine: I don't do meals of any kind. Never have. Just haven't got round to it, I suppose. Still, I'm sure that we'll meet again, because I believe in you, *Sir* Edwin, and expect great things of you. More great things, I should say."

After that he congratulated me in Surelik again on my fine choice of a husband, and was on his way as one who has always has important business but never stoops to low as to make haste.

Edvin was both flattered and put out.

I won't tire my readers with the inanities of my life with Edwin, as it should be pronounced. The worst thing is that some of those inanities I actually enjoyed. It is terrible to confess these things, and if I were writing this book in my own hand, I would have concealed all this shameful stuff. But here I am - dictating to my scribe, like a confessant of the Triers' religion with her priest. I bare my soul! Like one of the Triers' novels. Except they don't confess inanities and banalities, they go for complex moral dilemmas. But what do you expect of a little Surelik woman who came from the forest when she was sixteen, as innocent and uncivilised as any human being can be? And, I believe, I was then a better person. In my innocence, how could I understand the insincerity of the flattery that was heaped upon us all because of a misapprehension that was of Verochka's making? She was a truthful person, and when a truthful person says a white lie, then who knows what unforeseen outcomes can flow from it. Already quite a few, and none of them good.

Sir Edwin Perkins was a follower of Gobineau and his science of race. I knew nothing about it at the time, but I looked into it later in life and was not surprised by what I found. It explained a great deal. I was part of his professional research perhaps. A sample. One day he said as though paying me a generous compliment, "You'll be pleased to know that my studies are leading towards some quite remarkable conclusions. In fact, it now appears that the Surelikud aren't forbears of the Anglo-Saxons at all, but they are primitive Hungarians, which is almost as good. How about that!"

"Primitive?"

"I understand that it is difficult for you to comprehend such things, but the Hungarians are one of Europe's great nations."

"I'm supposed to take this as a compliment?"

"Yes, really. Like the Beer Cellars, the Viticulturists and of course us, the Little Noisy Musics."

She's off again! The scribe, she's complaining about these names in spite of all my explanations. She says that he couldn't have used the term Little Noisy Musics, because they hadn't started to make their noisy music. Of course. Of course. Does she think that these were his exact words? I have a good memory, but not so good that I can reproduce the exact words used seventy years ago. Besides, she should know by now that we rarely spoke Surelik, so none of these words were actually his, but in his broken version of the language of the Triers. The scribe tells me that this narrative is not worthy of our people. It has no gravitas, no music, no grandeur, no end point or real starting point other than a girl close to womanhood wandering out of the forest. What does she mean? No brothers fighting over the walls of a great city to be. No victorious admiral dying on his victorious ship. No explorer lifting a flag over new found territories, and renaming everything in accordance with his comforting domestic culture which he has carried from afar like some splendid delicate plant which is actually more akin to a ferocious epidemic.

What does she want? And I've completely lost my place in the narrative. We are the Surelikud, not one of those imperial peoples that I have renamed in an act of innocuous revenge. The Triers, the Noisy Musics, the Little Noisy Musics, the Viticulturalists and the Beer Cellars. Even the Beautiful Ceilings had a go at it, and so they get their "silly" name, to use her term. Do we have serried ranks that could go goosestepping courageously into other lands singing bombastic songs and adopting the sullen grimace of steadfastness, which conceals the jostling laughter in which heroes indulge once they've done their dirty job? I think not. We can mutter discontent while hoping not to be heard. We can smile when we'd rather spit. We can agree grudgingly when we'd prefer to scream our disaccord and lift our fists in rage. We do not have our nation or even the lesser status of an autonomous republic.

But we can do many things. We can protest when the time is right and the enemy unsettled – or even just more well-disposed. We can learn. We can write. We can conserve our culture. We can set an example of civility. And we can hope – in a measured way. My story and the story of my people requires no grandeur or gravitas, no propaganda or pretence, no threats or violence, and above all it has no desire to change others other than to soften their harshness and awaken them to the glories of non-intervention. It requires honesty and artfulness, intelligence and intellect, because a small people cannot make a single mistake without paying a very high price, whilst imperial powers can make many – and the greater the empire, the more mistakes can be made and brushed aside in an avalanche of lies. But I do not hate them and I do not envy them. They barely live, in spite of the grandeur of their ambitious schemes. Immensity is dull, except the immense variety to be found in the confined finitude of a small people. There is more variety here, and it is better for the added variety empire also imposes. This is not to excuse empire; it is only to admit that some small benefit can sometimes accrue from it for, as we say, "If it weren't for the torrid wind of the plains, there would be no pleasant breeze to whistle in the forest."

So, having calmed down my scribe, let's continue the story of my relationship with Edwin which, more acute readers will have already guessed, is a very painful process for me to go through. And I don't always come out of it well. Yet it has to be done! Though I'm not going to dwell on my guilt as those classic Trier writers do. Or maybe I am! That's the pleasure of dictation and recital: not even the authors know what's round the corner, just as you cannot know how you'll feel about things in a few days' time – or a few hours' time, if you're a temperamental Trier who has a drink or gambling or romantic or philosophical problem. Okay, I can see the scribe wriggling in her chair, and she has a point. I'll dump the stereotype and say, "if you're a human being who may also not have complete control over his or her drinking and gambling habits". The problem is – and I'm going to be generous to them for once – the Triers are more human than most peoples and they have an excellent habit of running themselves down. Unusual for an empire.

So Edwin was talking about the Hungarians whom he'd chosen possibly on a quite random basis or because he liked Admiral Horthy and couldn't understand why he wasn't a Little Noisy Music. He believed that nations had some kind of genetic identity, which is absurd – especially in Eurasia where nations have been rushing west and back again for as long as ever a tiger strode in the Siberian Forest. If anything can make a nation – and that could be queried – it is a language. Certainly the Surelik language is what defines a Surelik. Of course some people think – and I have been one of them – that a true Surelik has to live in the forest. Whatever you think on that matter, which I still vacillate about, everyone agrees that to be a Surelik you have to speak the language.

So here is Edwin, measuring people's heads and peering at people's noses – and pretending to be very scientific, but I can tell you that he was a man of dreams. There's nothing wrong with that, but his dreams always revolved around him, his nation, his race and his empire or rather his place within it. He wanted other people to share his own high opinion of himself – and hence he was condemned to a lifetime of disappointments, though it has to be admitted that he dealt with his disappointments stoically. The inability of the world to recognise his genius was clearly evidence of gross ineptitude on the part of the world.

He was not without a sense of humour, and once said, "The Little Noisy Musics consider anything they cannot understand to be uncivilised." I was enchanted but discovered later that he found this attitude to be wholly rational and even admirable. When I challenged him, he said, "Yes, I was joking, but wit always contains an element of truth, which it expresses in a forceful but veiled manner." No wonder I sometimes wanted to go back to the forest.

But I didn't.

I got into a routine, and knew that there was something deeply inauthentic about our relationship. He was often away – "on business"[4] he would say – and during those extended

---

4   "on business": italicised English in the original, and it should be remembered that Rahväema developed a good command of English during her marriage to Edwin Perkins.

absences I retained my prestigious position in society, while I was in Väikelinn and to a lesser extent when in the capital.

Since I had started on the lexicography, I had been studying the culture of the Triers and the wider European context to which it belongs, but now I had so much time on my hands, I put in my best years of study. Not just the rational arts of literature and criticism, but also their music, which I much admire, and to a lesser extent, their painting and sculpture. I did this not to obtain an education that they could endorse, but to understand my enemy and how to minimise the hurt they could inflict on us. Or so I keep saying, but actually I was hooked! At the time, I didn't understand many things; for instance, I believed that all the Triers were well-versed in their own cultures and had read all the classic writers, such as Pushkin, Lermontov, Tolstoy, Dostoyevsky, Turgenev and Gogol. People may laugh at my naivety, and I see my dutiful scribe smiling benignly in my direction. No need for condescension as I have no shame about this. Far from it. What concerns me here is what I've lost: by engaging with the Triers' culture, I've watered down my own. My introduction to their civilisation – so-called – deprived me of the purity of my thoughts in my native tongue.

I don't deny that I also gained a great deal. I learnt to reason more deeply, and this did help me in my struggle.

In our own clumsy way, Edwin and I had some interesting conversations that taught me a great deal about his homeland. He was impressive to watch: a complete idiot – such an idiot that he thought he was a genius – who managed to ingratiate anybody when he wanted to – no matter who they were or what their politics. I couldn't argue with that; I even married him. On the other hand he could be incredibly rude when he didn't get what he wanted, but there again he seemed to come out of the contest unscathed. Perhaps he wasn't such a fool or perhaps he had an instinct that told him exactly how far he could go. I have thought about it a great deal, and have found no convincing answer, but I have a few theories. Social animals often have hierarchies which are largely created out of the previous generation's hierarchy, though occasionally they can be overturned. Edwin went to one of those fancy schools of the Little Noisy Musics' and could easily be recognised if not as the leader of the pack, as someone not far behind in the pecking order. The idea of Edwin as an arrogant chimpanzee is an image I now find wholly acceptable.

But it couldn't have been that or not only that. Not everyone from these schools could have been like that. I often thought that it may have been something to do with certitude, which people find attractive. Or reassuring in some way. He spoke with such conviction that he was believed. We know that con-men use this technique and it works beautifully.

And then there was his boyish neediness which I think was shaped like a tank and it just kept coming at you. It felt like you couldn't avoid it. It was overwhelming and unavoidable. Frankly this is the theory I find most convincing, but also the one that is the "least scientific" and the most indebted to a personal hunch. I doubt that many others will share my view.

Edwin put great store by the inventiveness of the Little Noisy Musics, and at the time there was definitely an element of truth. But did all these wonderful inventions, which certainly had potential for improving the way people lived, deliver on their promises? It seems that the very society that was so inventive was incapable of improving the lives of the people who lived there. When I challenged him, he called me a Luddite, and when he had explained the meaning of the word, I asked him a question that had never occurred to him: "If these workers were smashing machinery, they must have found that life had been worsened after the introduction of machinery, whether or not their actions were rational." But then Edwin considered any action he disagreed with to be irrational, and after a moment's reflection he dismissed my query in a blast of raucous laughter.

His answer, when I pressed him further, was that no one can stand in the way of progress. This was the first time that I became aware of the absurdity of this argument - or rather act of faith. So his failure to answer my question suggested another question which I only asked myself: why is it that apparently innocuous inventions can carry with them such devastating outcomes that they can sometimes do more damage than a passing army? I will review a few of them in this memoir, starting with the apparently most innocuous of them all:

The Radio

After the Civil War, things got back to normal - or rather to the normal as it was to be, which was somewhat better than it had been, but that was a low stump to leap over. The priests had gone (except perhaps a few of the better ones who adapted to the new way of things) and the teachers had taken their place - working for the new schools and the adult literacy campaigns.

And some other stuff, which wasn't always that good. The new Trier regime was very keen on modernity: factories, Taylorism, electricity, roads and all the other inventions civilisation had so inventively invented. No doubt some were good but, in my opinion, some were bad and one of the first things was the radio, which I now look on as benign but only because other more noxious inventions have come along and left it in the shadows.

After Pyotr had left for the war and when my solitude became unbearable, I used to go down to a local bar and mix with the drinkers who came in all shapes and sizes: the glum who liked to sit alone in the company of a glass of beer as their sole companion, the nervous who needed a beer or two before they could loosen up, and of course the garrulous who made an entrance in mid sentence, loud and full of a desire to engage and, above all, to perform.

But most important of all was the band, which consisted of four elderly men and occasionally a woman in her mid-forties who would do the singing – in both Surelik and the language of the Triers. I got to know them well, and enjoyed their music. These musicians were varied in their skills, but as musicians often do, they played along together very well and were close friends. Then came the radio. It suddenly appeared like something from another planet, and the world changed without asking our permission. It had been around since the year I was born, but for us it was new. Initially the manager was in love with it. He kept fiddling with it and changing stations, though there weren't that many at the time. And it was a large self-important thing with dials. When the reception was good, we could listen to some excellent music, it's true, but a great deal of it wasn't up to the standard of our band, who were after all live human beings. There were speeches, patriotic songs, news, debates, and public information bulletins. And most of it came from one inconspicuous room to the whole of the Triers' vast nation. We were no longer the producers of our own culture.

For a while the musicians remained – in competition with the new machine that was so deft at defying distance and community. We would listen to the same things and the same versions of events as all the other citizens and all the many peoples of the ex-empire of the weak, feckless and ultimately tragic Great Caesar. We would become acquainted with the voices of a few people – perhaps know them better than some of our own townsfolk – and that joined millions of people together: it felt like they'd become part of our life. Their familiarity made them feel intimate, but of course they weren't. And this inauthentic emotion was shared by all the many listeners across the country, who remained as invisible as they had ever been.

The four ageing musicians were only paid with free beer, and the singer who taught at a local school and also sang at weddings and public events was paid a small sum, which was why she wasn't always booked along with the others. Although they didn't disappear immediately, the manager reduced their hours and monitored the effects on the customers, but they were as taken with the self-important novelty as he was. Suddenly they felt part of something bigger and more powerful. Väikelinn was changing and they thought it was for the better.

I spoke to the singer before they finally left, and she didn't seem to mind, as she certainly would have done if another band had been hired in their place. "You can't stand in the way of progress," she said, and I would never understand why civilised people accept the removal of their agency with such resignation. Are they not supposed to be the thrusting citizens of the modern state who have finally taken their place at the top table? No matter what regime you had at the time, this was the narrative, and the dislocation between the manufactured fantasy and the harsh reality has only got bigger since then. Progress could not be changed any more than the weather, though now the military have developed ways to do just that – progress then is even more refractory than the weather. "But why are people unable to challenge it?" I asked myself, like the child in front of the naked king. Something real had been taken away from us, and replaced with something synthetic which aimed to please everyone, and therefore could only do so in a very shallow manner. It also obstructed the creative activities of hundreds of thousands across the nation.

It is still this submissiveness with which we received the radio that I find most striking about its sudden appearance and its gradual colonisation of the globe. In part it was down to its magical enticement and glamour, along with the seeming impossibility of its very existence which made a god of man and undermined the rules of nature, however much we sophisticatedly allocated its presence to the laws of science which we knew nothing about. And in part it was something darker: capitalism's desperate and extravagant belief that it can overcome all the barriers of distance, geography and topography and rebuild the planet in the image of a market, which it held to be more natural than nature. Our own alternative economy still measured itself against those of other countries and attempted to mimic them rather than playing to our own intuitions and abilities.

Proponents of the radio claim that it brings us together, but it fragments us at the same time that it homogenises us; the poverty and insecurity of most people and many countries contrasts with the absurd wealth and security of others, and the media make us more aware of this. It impoverishes and they can't understand why. When it comes to devices like the radio, the problem is that it is a monologue like, you may say, the one I'm dictating now, but unlike this one it reaches out to every corner of the land – or used to. It is received, but there can be no intelligent reply. It is the tablets of stone that are reinvented on a daily basis in conjunction with a government's contingent propaganda – tablets of stone that become each day as weightless as the ether.

I was of course living in a country that had supposedly abolished capitalism, which in some ways it had, but not in the collective psychology of its leadership which always looked to the economies of its foes for a yardstick, rather than perceiving the unspoilt nature of its principally peasant population as an asset. It didn't ask the important question: if the "free market" devalues and alienates human behaviour, how can a better world be built from its surrogate?

The self-important box set the pattern for future inventions in communications: it didn't only change the world, but kept changing it in a contradictory fashion. First it sprinkled stardust on the few, and then scattered it a little less on many more. Inevitably the Triers decided by the end of the twenties to set up a radio station in Surelik. I'm the last to complain about this – it was more effective in standardising the language than were my efforts at lexicography. Always supposing that standardisation is a good thing.

It had a strange effect on some of the young Surelik men who ran it. They became local celebrities and strutted the planks that acted as pavements alongside the muddy streets of Väikelinn. And naturally others envied them and wanted to emulate their success at being known by people they didn't know, which wasn't always possible in the small world of the Surelikud. In the meantime the Surelikud of the forest knew nothing of any of this, and if they heard some rumour, they would have spat on the ground and marvelled at the idiocy of civilisation.

"What was all that about?" says the scribe with her usual inability to understand anything I try to do. "You're supposed to be telling the story of your life"

"Do you ever pay attention to anything or do you go through life in a vacant dream, as so many have been doing since they invented the television – which we'll get to in good time? What is the title of this book which I had you type on the first page? Don't glare at me like that! It was *A Woman's War against Progress*. This book we're putting together is not just about me. As it will say on the front cover, it's as much about progress as it is about me. More so. These inventions I'll be looking at are the most important protagonists of the twentieth century, whether we like it or not. Everyone seems to think that they're a source of bounty, and something they couldn't do without – unless it has been replaced by something even more addictive. I listen to the radio a lot, and learn from it – and like a book it consists primarily of words. The printing press, which made the book so accessible, is for me the most benign of inventions, but it did not come without a cost. It spread ideas, which was a good, but this only made the powerful crueller and more oppressive – and that process continued to advance as the centuries passed and literacy expanded. It took until 1789 for them to call it progress and cease entirely to look backwards for perfection. But every force produces an equal and opposite force. And printing too spoke to the many who could not reply. It too was a monologue, though initially people often read aloud in company where it could be discussed. I still

106

believe that it was ultimately and overwhelmingly benign because it awoke us to how the world worked – it finally turned us into the conscious animal we'd always potentially been. But then there is the counterargument – the simple realisation that this accumulation of knowledge made possible all those later and most infamous inventions, which include the tank, the bomber and the atom bomb. A paradox that can only be understood by a Surelik autodidact from the forest.

And the scribe describes my words as stubborn nonsense. So be it, and she can go back to her vacant dream.

As Edwin was making no progress with his Surelikud and little with the language of the Triers, we changed places and he started to teach me his language which would prove helpful later in life. Gradually this language became the one we used most often when we were on our own, and as communication improved, so our relationship deteriorated.

We argued over little things and big – but mostly it concerned his disdain for "primitive peoples" like the Surelikud which was much more explicit than the Triers'. And this was in spite of the fact that he'd just discovered that we were the prototype for the Hungarians. Yes, of course, the word "prototype" does imply where he was coming from with his gangling gait and his glaikit eyes. And what, I wondered, would he have thought of primitive peoples who weren't the progenitors of such an exalted lineage, which came in second place after the Anglo-Saxons, and therefore so close to it.

One little habit of his was to insist that Surelik must have a restricted vocabulary. For instance, one day he was mending something with a screwdriver (with little success, it appeared) and suddenly, perhaps as an excuse for abandoning a difficult task, he held it up, waved it about, and said, "I bet you don't have a word for this in Surelik."

Actually I knew that there was, as I had coined it when we were working on the dictionary, but I didn't tell him that. "Kruvikeeraya," I said with a smile. Nor did I tell him that before I'd got involved, we just used the Triers' word for it, and that word performed its task very competently. That's what languages do: they either invent or borrow, but they're never stuck for a word once the need arises.

"Really, I think you're making up." And to be fair, he had only got the tense wrong.

"Look it up in the Surelik-Trier dictionary if you want."

He wasn't happy. He hadn't handed out his daily dose of humiliation, and wasn't to go to leave it there: "You're not telling me that there are no words missing from the Surelik language – which belongs to a people with no experience of civilisation in any form."

"Alright, alright! If you insist that there must be words missing in Surelik, I'll tell you one we don't have: junk! What's junk? Well, things that don't work, of course, but quite a few other things as well. Obsolete things, that is things that don't work as well as newer models or technologies. And things that no self-respecting person would wish to be associated with, even if they were working perfectly but had been superseded. An old person finds things to be junk which differ from those that a middle-aged person or a youth would. Junk also means unfashionable. But these niceties are incomprehensible to the Surelikud of the forest, as we have few possessions. We mend them, mend them and then mend them again. As I'm sure they do where you come from, but probably not to the same extent. Nothing can last forever, but we try our best to institute immortality for objects, even if we don't believe in it for human beings. 'Junk' is a word that's only significant in affluent societies."

He returned to his task, none the wiser, and we continued on our parallel existences not understanding each other and very possibly having ceased to care about that problem.

"I quite like the regime here," he said one day. "It's like a Little Noisy Music boarding school, only it's an entire nation. It works on the basis of fear, violence and the pleasures that can be derived from such things. In boarding schools, it is more orderly than this, because everyone gets a chance to receive pain and then inflict it: the younger children are the victims of persecution by the older children. It would work perfectly if it weren't for a few weak-kneed pusillanimous individuals (he spat) who try to spoil things by refusing to persecute. Such vile do-gooders.

"Here things are a little different: as most of the persecutors end up amongst the victims. This is a terrible inversion of the natural order, but it is perhaps suited to the Triers who haven't yet reached our level of civilisation."

Often I couldn't understand a word Edwin was saying, not because of his mix of the Little Noisy Music language and a troubled version of the Triers', but because he spoke of a world that was entirely alien. The schools sounded like prisons, but he was insanely proud of having been to one because that was where the rich children went, and he always wore its tie. It seems that I'm not the only cruel parent in this world. Much later, when Western culture came our way – including the bizarre Little Noisy Music subsection of it – I started to understand many things and this conversation was no exception. In fact, I realised that Edwin, in his blinkered, dull-witted way, had stumbled on an important truth: he had learnt to be violent in such a school, and to suppress the part of him which was human. But of course he couldn't follow through on his discovery, because looking back from where I am now, I also see a difference: whereas the schools of the Little Noisy Musics survive and prosper from one generation to another, our terrible suffering in the land of the Triers was of course much worse but for a relatively short period, though it didn't feel like that at the time. It was the product of an evil man, but it also resulted from the fragility of the vastness and the exhaustion of a nation pulled in too many directions, invaded by too many foreign armies and dragged through too many traumas.

Life with Edwin was dull. Dull, dull, dull. So dull that I can't think of a way to describe it that isn't dull itself. As far as I could see, he did little work and kept himself topped up with alcohol most of the time. He was a talker, so God knows why he spent four years in a country where he could hardly make himself understood, but then again what he said was of little importance; it was, however, always delivered with utter self-belief. And those were the four years of our union. I think that the reader now understands this, but there is an anecdote I would like to add, because it is both amusing and indicative of how we lived together.

Once a bureaucrat not only has an idea in his head but has decided to open a file and write it down, it then becomes indelible. Thus the Triers, in as much as they were aware of his existence, still seemed to be convinced that he was a great supporter of their regime. During a trip to Moscow, where he was supposed to be consulting the main library (I have no idea if he did), we were invited to a concert. That evening he put on a bow tie and dinner jacket. When the driver came to the hotel and saw Edwin dressed like that, he politely told him, "I'm afraid, comrade, that you cannot attend the recital dressed like that."

"Like what?"

"A capitalist."

"Why a capitalist? I left my top hat and tails in my own country."

"Frankly, that was very wise of you, but the manner in which you're dressed is still a slight problem, comrade. It could be misunderstood."

"Why are you so obsessed with clothes?" Edwin seemed convinced that he could win any argument and was oblivious of the risks in a land where symbolism was everything. Drawing himself up as he always did before uttering something that he considered to be of great intellectual weight, he said, "It's not true that the habit makes the monk or that epaulettes make the officer."

"I think, comrade," said the driver who was no fool, "that they very probably did, but I can assure you that your current clothing does make you a class enemy, however fond you may be of it."

"Why does he keep calling me 'comrade'? I'm a subject of King George and proud of it."

At this stage I had to speak up: "Edwin, get changed. There's no way you're going to the theatre dressed like that. You're not in the land of the Little Noisy Musics now. I'm telling you: get back upstairs to your room and get changed."

He looked at me and he looked at the official, who fortunately saw the funny side of this little scene. And he looked with his pleading little-boy face, but found us both implacable. Then he made his decision and it was the right one: "Well, I say... When in Rome, ... , I suppose. Just to keep you people happy. I was just trying to bring a bit of civilisation to the steppes of this backward nation," he laughed as he sat in a hotel foyer at the centre of a very large city, "a touch of class, I would say. Pearls before swine – before swine, I say." And he went off to get changed, clearly convinced that these potent words had retrieved his self-respect.

The driver, whose patience had been stretched too far, looked at me with a mixture of curiosity and outrage. "You'd better get him in line!" he said before turning to find himself a chair.

"That would not be easy."

"You're his wife," which suggested that I was responsible, "you can find a way. For your own good."

"I'm not an expert on Little Noisy Musics, but I see that you're a complete novice."

"So what should we do?"

"Send him home, preferably without me."

"Is it that bad?"

"I'm afraid that it is." I was telling a complete stranger what I had only just admitted to myself. The instructive part of this conversation is that, contrary to Edwin's stated claim, it is often the minor issues that trigger serious events, whether in statecraft or in our own small lives. It may be that my conversation with the driver for foreign visitors, who in our lands was often an official of a certain rank, set in train the series of incidents that probably would have been inevitable. It hastened them, we might say.

That's enough of Edwin – the dead years. Unfortunately I'll have to narrate one other incident – brutal, life-changing and something I have never publicly revealed.

For some time we had avoided sex – or rather I had. I found him increasingly obnoxious. I don't know why I didn't leave. I didn't want to admit to myself and others that I had made a foolish mistake. I did not want to lose face. But there was something else: that marriage of ours gave me a space for study that I would never have found elsewhere in a land that was working madly to catch up with modernity – the only thing that mattered. And where, pray, is all that modernity and sacrifice now? Sold off for a few kopecks by foreigners to foreigners. If it wasn't for oil, we would be eating our shoes. At the time, it would still have been quite easy to leave my husband, though the Moustache would soon introduce restrictions there too. Anyway I didn't. And that's the unchangeable past.

One night he came in late when I was already in bed, and immediately attacked me without uttering a word. He smelt of wine. A heady, pungent smell that spoke of distant lands and distant ways – not his apparently, but I shall always associate my befoulment with that drink. His sweat stank of arrogance – a smell that pushes its way into the world with the lack of consciousness of a heavy mammal. Stupid, but in no need of intelligence or alertness. He moved methodically as though this were something he did. It was something dangerous that was stronger than himself. It was something so powerful it wanted to conquer the world, so the forced conquering of a small Surelik woman would be as memorable as swatting a fly.

The scribe has just come over and hugged me. Nobody knew. She is my friend, of course she is, even though I'm unkind to her and say things I shouldn't. But she's not going to make me cry. That's not how I do things. That's not how you survive. She says that it is – that it's good to talk these things through. She may be right, but that is not how I do things. If you live with a bad person, you become worse than you were, and if you live with a good person, you become better. It follows just as trees grow leaves after the first glow of spring, as we used to say in Surelik. God knows what they say now? Something about mobile phones, I suspect. As a beeping noise follows the pressing of the on-button, perhaps. We live in such poetic times.

As the wife of a wealthy Little Noisy Music (we should remember that they were the big player at the time), I had started to give myself airs and graces, which is a terrible thing for a forest Surelik to admit to. In such a corner of a distant oblast, you didn't have to be an ambassador or cultural attaché representing the Little Noisy Musics to be feted by local potentates. We went to the opera at the small theatre they'd built in Väikelinn and to the poetry readings, which were generally dull events at which earnest young men and women would sing their praises of the Moustache. But I was there! I – a Surelik woman from the forest who once went around in rags, although I hadn't known they were rags at the time – was mixing with the cream of Surelik society and the wider oblast. My husband, who had been an exotic and ingratiating figure there though in fact he had contempt for everyone, had been able to raise me effortlessly to a position of prominence. I suspect and very much hope that I played my part badly, awkwardly and quite ridiculously without measure or social skills, and that they laughed behind my back. As I know he did. But I eventually started to laugh at him.

How could I assess such a man? I, who had grown up in the forest without books but with so many words I treated with same carelessness a tree experiences when it discards its leaves, could not then appreciate the hubris of the wealthy who display their self-imagined grandeur like they spend their money – or indeed in place of money.

Edwin left the next day, and it was revealed that he had been told to leave the country and his departure had already been planned. Then it turned out that he was a bigamist and the father of several children who lived with his wife in the land of the Little Noisy Musics. This of course was not the reason for his sudden departure. Those were times when we were getting used to not knowing why things happened, and they were going to get worse. So we were never married – legally – but then what is a marriage if not a legal contract as Engels and many bohemians had long argued? News of my new status came to me as something of a relief. However it was a lot for me to take in. Too much.

Regrettably, the rape had led to a pregnancy. This was the low point in my life, though others were to come, which some people might think were worse, because they don't understand that the horrors of life divide into those we know how to deal with and those we don't. Verochka organised things from afar, and I was given research work in Väikelinn which also involved visiting people in the forest. And in this moment of depression, I gradually became aware of something very unexpected: the Surelik of the plain started to think that I was someone important.

It all started with the radio, which I've just been maligning. The Surelik station in Väikelinn decided to interview me about my work on the dictionaries. In truth, I had been away from the work for some time, though I was occasionally doing work with the forest Surelikud, which resulted in both new vocabulary for the dictionaries and anthropological articles. It was the latter that really interested me at the time. I had read some of the works of Franz Boas which since the 1880s had been challenging the pseudo-science of men like my ex-husband – or perhaps I should say, my never-husband. I had come across him almost by chance, not entirely of course because I was in contact with people interested in this new discipline. The interview was a happy distraction from my many problems, and I went there only partially prepared – but I didn't have to be: I was brimming with things to say. This struck a chord with many people of different ages. Without realising it, my dreams were beginning to take shape. I had never had a plan. I had no idea how to devise one. It is hardly surprising then that my path to leading campaigner would still remain chaotic and driven by chance as well as passion.

Not every Surelik approved of my recent, local fame, if we can call it that. I was at a bar in the centre of town – holding court, one might say – when a large Surelik with a lopsided grin but still a handsome man of around sixty years shouted, "*Prowa*,[5] come here! I want to speak to *prowa*, the lady who speaks for everyone." You could see that he was a hunter; you could see it in his eyes. They call us hunter-gatherers, but that is something very different. This was a Surelik who was never happy with a single kill. If he could've killed a hundred birds in an afternoon, he would have done it. Even if they rotted. Of course he would take them to Väikelinn, which was why he was there, and having cashed in, he was having a fine time lording it in the bars. And he clearly recognised my face from some newspaper article or other. "Come, come my little lady, have no fear. I want a little of the wisdom you spread around so magnanimously. Yes, magnanimously, like a pasha, like a prince – or in your case a princess."

I could see that he'd been drinking one *shtof* after another, and that no good could come of our conversation.[6] But oddly I was drawn to him. Possibly it was that "have no fear" which drew me in, as I wanted to make clear to him that I had never experienced

---

5   *prowa*: the Surelik for "lady"
6   *shtof*: a Russian liquid measure equal to 1.23 litres, but Rahvaema appears to use to mean any glass of alcohol. .

such a thing – though of course I had and fear can make us bolder. People like him have an instinctive understanding of human psychology and use it to manipulate others – everyone they come into contact with. They like a challenge, and perhaps I should have been flattered by his hostility.

I walked up to him and stared at him for a while, summoning up all my haughtiness in spite of the startling mass of his body, hot and sweaty, but not unpleasant. "What is it you want, old man," I stated in an impatient tone.

"Woman, when was it that you left the Surelik forest?"

Surprised by his approach, I spoke without thinking, "At the age of sixteen."

"Ah," he smiled as though everything was now explained and the conversation was as good as over. "So all you knew of Surelik ways was when you were a little lass never far from your mother's skirts."

I felt that I was losing the argument before it had even started. "You may not have noticed that in 1917 things happened, and women are no longer to be scoffed at and treated as though they were children."

He laughed happily and turned to his silent companion seated on a stool, whereas the hunter stood so that he could make use of his stage: "You see what happens when they give women a little education." The other man laughed as though he enjoyed the conversation, but continued to say nothing. "Well, what have we here?" the big man said once he'd turned back towards me and looked me up and down with a discerning eye. "What have we got to do with the revolution? Were we the ones who carried it out? Were we the ones who shook off the oppressor, or just the ones whose oppressor was supplanted by another?"

His companion looked worried by the direction of his argument, and having admired the speaker's courage, I wanted to placate him. "I don't deny that. But progress was closing in on us. Better this one than the other."

"Really? And what did you know of the previous one – apart from what you were told by the next one? Woman, you're tying yourself in knots here. It's not your fault, but you shouldn't put on these airs."

Now anger rose, and the battle lines were clear, but they were the ones he had chosen. I could see that he was right about some things – or at least to pose such questions – and he was attaching those arguments to his frontal attack on who I was and still am. "Who here is putting on airs? And mixing up arguments. Why this absurd hostility?"

"Dear *prowa*, there is no hostility. The problem is that you haven't answered my first question. What could you have known of our ways if you left your homeland so young and tender?"

For a moment I was struck dumb, because I knew where he was going and he had complete control of the situation. I paused for a few seconds, as I thought hard how to release myself from his snake-like grip. But that was all I had, and he'd pulled me away into his world – ruthlessly.

"Of course, you knew nothing. The Surelikud aren't interested in politics or philosophy or religion. How could they be? Because the forest has its own religion. We are all free in the forest – all living things, of which we are just one. We have been given this life to enjoy for as long as we can. Do I hate the wild boar or the fish in the river? Of course not. Of course, of course. No, hear me out. I take only when I need to take, and I enjoy the whole process, as everything should be enjoyed. Every aspect of life, even women." At this stage he slapped my backside, and before I had a moment to gasp my irritation, he continued in full stride. "Take the Triers, do they look happy? Come on, tell me! Of course they aren't, as your hesitation demonstrates. They're not happy, and you know why? Because they fiddle around with all that stuff: politics and religion and philosophy, whatever that is. Which is just an excuse for killing each other. We are better than that. We know our place in the world. It's a modest one, but an excellent one, don't you think? Yes, of course, you cannot deny it. There is still enough of the Surelik in you to understand this. Of course, of course. No good can ever come of playing around with the Triers. They're a broken people like all Europeans. Actually not quite so broken as the other Europeans. But that's where they're going, so why should we get on their train that's going nowhere? Do you really think that a few Surelikud are going to make a difference, when there are millions of those Triers? Fortunately the forest is vast, and its larder is far bigger than the modest needs of the Surelikud."

This was most irritating. He was using my own arguments against me. Had he heard them on the radio? The way he used them felt like a performance. But they carried with them a burdensome truth that I have struggled with ever since. Several times the reader will have heard me mention this overwhelming sense of losing my culture whilst I acquired another, and this realisation I gleaned retrospectively from this very conversation with the boisterous man. It wasn't that I was forgetting things but rather that the new culture raised its own quite justifiable claims on me, because every language and every culture is a vibrant being with its intrinsic beauty that it occupies outside nature and indeed almost all physicality. It is another universe. And once the Triers' culture had established itself in me, it had to have its own demands, whatever my original intentions. This dilemma would haunt me for decades, but eventually I would resolve this contradiction almost satisfactorily, but I will come to that later.

In that moment, I was overwhelmed by what he'd said. I did leave the forest very young. I had been partially subsumed into the Triers' culture. I was taking a lot on myself and speaking as a representative of people who had given me no mandate, and in the forest there were no radios. I didn't consider him to be a Surelik of the forest, because he was clearly in the same limbo as I was. His hypocrisy did not detract from the truth of what he was saying. If even small successes bring with them small disappointments, what could unexpectedly large successes bring? In the fullness of time, I was to find out.

In that moment, I had to deal with him if I were to retain my recently acquired status, and at the same time I was digesting his words and putting together those I would need if I was to reverse the situation.

In that moment, almost spontaneously I looked at him

sharply and asked, "So how much game did you sell in the market today?"

"None of your business," he responded carelessly.

"Alright," I turned to the rest of the room who by now were all spectators, "has anyone any idea how many birds, rabbits and bigger beasts he sold in the market today? I'm talking here of the forest animals he killed and dragged out of the forest on his cart."

There was an amused silence, possibly because he had bought them all a drink. He looked like the expansive type who would do so. "Come on, come on, are you all freemasons in here? Or are you afraid of the big man, even though this little woman is not?"

A small man sitting right at the end of the bar with thick glasses and a disorderly beard spoke up, "I don't know how many, but it was quite a lot! Like you said, birds, rabbits and a wild boar. And he got a pretty price for them."

"So what if I did?" the man said, still unperturbed, "a man has got to make a living. Times have been hard, and I'm feeding hungry mouths. All fresh meat straight from the forest."

"Of course, that was a great act of kindness, but I sense a little inconsistency here in this archetypal Surelik, this champion of the forest and this source of ancient wisdom: did you not say, 'I take only when I need to take, and I enjoy the whole process, as everything should be enjoyed. Every aspect of life, even women.' That last bit was very gallant, I'll grant you that. It's good to know that we woman are to be enjoyed, and therefore have a minor role in the scheme of things." There was laughter and someone whistled, but this was not the place to overdo the new Trier regime's directives on women's rights; I needed to keep to the main line of attack. "So this paragon of Surelik fortitude only takes when he has a need, but at this rate there won't be a living being in the forest except him running around with his gun desperately looking for what's no longer there." The exaggeration was intentional.

"What nonsense, the forest is that vast. Such exaggeration from the little woman. She's trying her best, I'll give her that, but she's in the wrong league here. I said that I take when I need to, and I needed money to pay some bills. What's wrong with that?" He shrugged happily.

"I think that you're the one tying yourself in knots. It's not your fault, but you shouldn't put on these airs. Now consider this, our Surelik chief here won't say a word about politics, but strangely enough he doesn't mind blabbering about how good the old Trier regime was in relation to the one we have now."

He jumped to his feet in horror, and not without good reason, because what he'd said to me and the other man was not for public consumption. "I didn't say the old regime was good, I only ..." Then he lost his temper: "I'll kill you. I'll break your puny back, so I will..."

This was my chance for the *coup de grâce*. I ran up to him, and his large belly was almost level with my chest, well placed for me to prod with my index finger: "Such a big man, such a big, big man that he wants to kill a little woman. What courage, what fortitude! Võitleja reborn. Hurray!" And with each word, I pressed my finger into the softness of his belly. Elegant argumentation had nothing to do with it, and the place was in uproar: loud laughter, banging on tables, incomprehensible shouts. Who knows? He flopped back in his chair, conscious of his defeat.

I turned to go and a last glimmer of fight was left in him: "Where are you going, woman? We're not finished yet."

"Oh yes we are," I said firmly, knowing that any re-engagement was now more dangerous for me than for him, "I have things to do. You stay on here and drink a few *shtofs* to get over it. I'll buy you one, to show no hard feelings."

"Over my dead body," he growled to himself, and some onlookers started to mock him. I'd won in an underhand way, just as he had at the start, but it is the ending that matters. He lost because the spectators had chosen me, not out of any malice they felt towards him, but because they enjoyed the theatre. And my victory had occurred when all eyes were on us.

I left with a good deal of elation and a tiny bit of guilt. I had exploited what he had said in confidence and I had played to the audience. To put it another way, I had all the makings of a good politician. And I had also learnt that you can learn from everyone, including a conceited fool.

Before my pregnancy became visible, something else happened which I think should be recounted in this memoir. It related to the problem that arose in the encounter in the Väikelinn bar I have just described, but it was in some way quite painful. On the other hand, it was chance to get to know Halvatud better.

He appeared as usual unsummoned, and wanted to accompany me on a trip to the forest I had been planning for some time. This was a more ambitious undertaking than any of my previous ones, which hadn't yielded as much information as I wanted. Of course his incapacity could have held us up, and knowing this I dispensed with my two assistants for this trip. Somehow I thought that he would be more useful, and I was right in quite unexpected ways. We reached a clearing with the typical Surelik huts, and I was surprised to see the children running towards us, but it was Halvatud they wanted to see. He smiled and joked with a naturalness that came from a good, quiet and kindly soul. He seemed to be at home. Then the adults came, smiling as they did, and with a businesslike bustle and the joy of those who are witnessing a pleasant but not uncommon event. He introduced me and it seemed that he needed no introduction himself. He gave them a very impressive story of my life, but it failed to impress them. I mentioned my family and some relations, but they shrugged and remained silent.

I think that Halvatud's success, which was based on his previous visits and long-established friendships and acquaintances, upset me and made it difficult for me to work. The more I tried to ingratiate myself, the more I failed to create a rapport. Then I found myself confusing my identity as a Surelik of the forest and my identity as a researcher, as though my desperate desire to belong was quietly subverting my desire to understand. Or to put it less metaphysically, I was losing my self-confidence. It seems that they were not attracted to my vocabulary which consisted of all their words and the ones I'd acquired on the plain and in the city, many of which I'd invented myself. He, on the other hand, moved around in his manner that was both energetic and laborious, and he gathered their news, laughed at their stories and commiserated over their mishaps. He had no desire to impress or ingratiate.

All this, I knew, was an extension of the same paradox I'd encountered with the boisterous man in the Väikelinn bar. My greatest popularity was amongst the Surelikud of the plain, but here I was ignored. Halvatud, born on the plain, was seen as a freak there but feted here. How this pained me. I asked once again about my parents, and no one seemed to know. Later I would hear that they were both dead. I had a sister close to me in age and in my heart, who lived in an industrial city in the Triers' heartlands, and another, much older, who lived in the forest. I asked if the word could be put out and she contacted, which after some resistance, they did. I was shocked to hear later that she was not interested in seeing me.

I continued the work for another couple of weeks, though it was clear that Halvatud was producing much more in terms of quantity and quality. Possibly I wasn't aware of how much this was troubling me. Whatever the case, I eventually did something stupid: I lost my temper and shouted at him in front of almost the entire community, including the children who worshipped him and listened to his stories, particularly his various, invented ones about the exploits of Võitleja. "I'm the one in charge of this project!" I cried. That's all. No more than that, but immediately I knew that I had violated several proscriptions ... I mean norms ... I mean taboos. God damn it, too many words. Words upon words upon words. Suddenly they seemed paltry things. Overused and overblown. Flamboyant and flatulent. I had misplaced my forest language who knows where and placed my progressive language in the forest, which was misplaced indeed. The word I used for "project" meant nothing to them. Why was I in charge, when he was doing all the work? Why had I shouted without good reason? Why was it that I was lording it around? This was the final straw.

Halvatud started to make his way towards me over the few metres that divided us, and everyone waited to see what he would do. When he reached me, he embraced me, which did not help me and probably increased their sympathy for him even further. "Let's talk this over," he said, and we made our way to the edge of the clearing.

"Why do they hate me?" I asked almost in tears.

"They don't hate you," he said. "Perhaps that would be better. They don't understand you. It's not just the way you speak and all the ideas you come up with; it is that they cannot place you. You speak with a perfect accent like them, but your language is alien. The principal reason why they don't warm to you is that they sense that you want to change them ..."

"But that's absurd," I answered angrily. "That's exactly what I don't want to do. I want to protect their way of life."

"Of course, I know that very well, but they don't. Anyway, that's not the point. You want to protect them and explain to them what you've learnt by living with the Triers. But they don't want to be enlightened. They want to carry on as before. So many times they just ignored the Triers and nothing too bad ever happened, because this is a sideshow – an unimportant province. They don't realise that things are changing fast and remoteness will eventually disappear. Not immediately, but in a generation or two. That's no time, and you're absolutely right in your aims, but you need to approach them differently."

"Like you do? But what is it anyway that makes you so attractive to them? That's what I'd like to know. I see no justification for their behaviour."

He looked embarrassed and thought for a while. "I don't talk to them as though I have something to teach them; I talk to them as though I have something to learn from them."

"But you're different. I'm a Surelik of the forest, and I know what a Surelik of the forest knows. I don't have anything to learn from them."

"That's my point. I was born on the plain and escaped to

the forest when I was fourteen. I am weak and dependent. They may kill a bird every now and then, but they would never kill a bird with a broken wing. They would feed it and keep it warm. They were good to me and I took great interest in their lives and their ways. I wanted to be like them. I will always be a postulant for them, and you will always be the clever girl who went off and adopted a whole lot of fancy habits and ideas that belong to the Triers. They distrust you."

I was crushed by this line of thinking, and unfortunately I was almost persuaded by it. "So the man in the bar was right?"

"In some ways he was. But you are still the only person who can fight for these people. What does it matter to you if they love you, ignore you or disdain you?"

"It's fine for you to say that! These are my people."

"They are, in as much as any people can belong to one person – and the only way that they can do this is in some symbolic form. You've thought of yourself as some kind of political activist even when you weren't that active, so this is what it's about. Your place is back there on the frontline: in Väikelinn and the Triers' capital. Come back here as often as you want, but leave your work behind you when you come. Start to listen to them – all individuals of course, but if you listen to enough of them, you'll get an idea of what they're about. And remember, as the man in the bar suggested, your knowledge of them is nearly two decades old. They change; everyone changes. And the last two decades have contained two centuries of history."

"Do you realise what a blow this is for me. It strikes at the very essence of who I am. And now there is nothing I can be but this."

"Rahväema, of course I understand, but don't become so dramatic and rhetorical – you're talking to yourself and you're not on the radio. What are you trying to convince yourself about? It's a blow, but life is made up of hardships. They are our best but most cruel teachers."

"I've met enough hardships in life to understand how some people can hate themselves and feel guilty for things that were either trivial or patently nothing to do with them. They are overcome by evils which for some reason they believe to derive from themselves; this haunts them and belittles them, but they rarely manage keep this at bay with their good works and their attempts at creating friendships which are often repulsed."

"But you don't feel like that, in spite of the evils that have happened to you personally – that keep you awake at night."

"That's correct. I'm as strong after them as I was before – maybe even stronger."

"Why do you think that is?"

"Childhood. I had a good childhood, though for me it was just a childhood like any other. Freud, who was a fool, was right about that at least. It is childhood that makes the adult."

Have patience, reader (if I can have it, surely you can too), the scribe is kicking up a fuss again. She says that I can't just dismiss an important historical figure as a fool like that. Well, she has a point and at the time I'm now talking about, he truly was a living statue of a man forever handing down his pronouncements. Thank you, scribe, I shall moderate my assertion: he was a fool when he claimed that these interesting things he wrote about were scientific facts. Now let me get back to my conversation with Halvatud, and no more interruptions.

Where was I? Well, who cares? You've understood: my education and erudition were meaningless to the forest Surelikud, whilst it was admired by those of the plain, who feel that I had somehow demonstrated how wrong various racist tropes had been. In other words their attitude is mixed: in part a feeling that I had distanced myself from them in some way that is not altogether clear, given that they too are a hybrid, and on the other hand I had put the Surelikud on the map, slightly improved their status and demonstrated that Surelik can produce its own literature and culture.

I was going to leave this episode out. That was my firm intention. The problem is this dictation; now I've started this way I can't change it. The scribe says that I can still cut it, but

125

she doesn't understand. I've said it out loud, and I've heard my own voice. It's an important truth: Rahväema was almost sent packing by her own people in 1933. Halvatud said that this was an essential part of being a political activist, but so is concealing uncomfortable truths. Now that I've revealed this to you, scribe, and anyone who reads this book, I feel that I understand what it was all about a great deal better. It is in the telling that we often find the finer points and lessons of something we have rarely wanted to think about.

What I actually said at the time was that "the mother of the country" had been sent packing, to which Halvatud with his customary wisdom replied, "'Mother of the Country' – is that what you want to be? That's some ambition."

"Was it not you," I blushed at having revealed my secret dream to him, my close companion, "who put that idea in my head and who has been doing little else since we first met? Aren't you, even now, defining my role and telling me where to go?"

And now I have to speak about my son, which will be even more painful to divulge. Another matter entirely. Everyone knows the story – amongst the Surelikud, that is. My son would grow up to be a fine young man, I cannot deny that. In fact, he is something of a rival as an active campaigner for Surelik rights. A timid man in many ways, he was the adviser to our deputy in the regional duma until he retired in 2003. But I could not love him when he was a child; he resembled his father too much. How was I to know that he would grow up into someone very different from both his parents? Physically he was and is like his father, apart from his darker complexion – but he is a modest, mild-mannered intellectual who likes to work in the background. What he thinks of me, I cannot say.

Anyway I could stand it no longer and shortly after his third birthday I took him to my sister's. It was a rare visit to the industrial city where she lived, and she greeted me with her warm heart and made much of the boy. She cooked us a meal and gave me all her news. I would tell you of it if I could remember a single thing, but I don't think that I even listened. She had a relaxed, even sleepy face, and yet she could work at speed and with precision as soon as she set about a task. Her face was wide, but still more European than mine and her eyes described a settled intelligence.

"You know, when you went to the township in the plain," she said in a soft voice as though she were about to say something she'd been thinking of saying for a long time, "we thought that you were leaving for a few months – six at the most. Your father said, 'Let her go. That way she'll see what it's like. Keep her here and it'll become all the more enticing in her head.' And yet you stayed. Many of us have been dragged from the forest by the militsya or hunger – or even by the allure of modernity, as our father thought. But you were different. God knows why you went, but you did and you stayed. And you did so many things. Even though we never understood, we were always very proud of you, and perhaps a little afraid – or distrustful, I suppose. That's a terrible word, but it was because we couldn't understand.

"I think now that you've become a bit of a Trier, in spite of your politics, your speeches and spectacular events. You're the single oak in the tiny grove owned by a wealthy landowner who owns more lands, forests and oaks than he could ever imagine. You're the oak that everyone notices, and the rest of us trees are huddled together in pleasant anonymity."

"There are no landowners now," I said sharply.

"Yes, so they say, but what do we have? Someone's controlling all this, and it's not me or anyone I know. I just get on with life, and that takes up all my time."

"I know, I know, dear sister," I said, and I thought of the boisterous Surelik hunter. "I know that we cannot understand where a decision will lead us. It is not that we don't have agency; it is that we cannot know how our future agency will take us along the sequence of events initiated by our first decision."

"You always were the clever one. Our father used to say that one day you would be one of the elders, but instead off you went and gave the Triers a drubbing."

"Not a drubbing. It's a more complex business when you're the weaker party."

"Oh, I'm sure your right. It must be a lot more complex than someone like me could ever understand."

"What's happened to your Surelik? Do you not speak it often at home?" I asked for some bizarre reason instead of disabusing her of her sense of inferiority. I was also aware that my tone of voice had suddenly become almost official.

"Not much. This is the first time in months."

"But your husband is Surelik, is he not?"

"Yes, but he was never very good at speaking it. Besides we think it better for the children to speak in the Triers' language."

"But don't you care?"

"Not really. I miss the forest. Sometimes. But the world has changed in so many ways since we were children. You know what the Triers keep saying – that a century went by between 1914 and 1924. What happened to your handsome first husband? Before you got this one you didn't like. What was name? Pyotr, I think."

"Yes, Pyotr."

"He was a mild man, and didn't get involved in the fight."

"Only because I was holding his arm, and telling him not to."

"Which means that he listened. That's a good and unusual thing in the Triers' lands."

"So you were at my wedding?"

"Of course."

"I didn't remember," I mentioned casually.

"You had a lot on, and those were heady days, before the real war started. The world had been turned upside down. Perhaps for the better in the long run, but there were some tough years ahead. And you still haven't told me what happened to Pyotr."

"He died. He was shot."

"By the Whites?

"By the Reds. They gave him a medal and then shot him."

"They did that, didn't they?"

"They certainly did."

"No children?"

"We were hardly ever together."

She drew from that well of goodness that was her soul and looked at me with sadness. "You've had your trials. And you were such a beautiful couple," she smiled.

All she and I had in common was our past – our distant childhood which had been one of unbelievable closeness. If ever two souls were one, then we had been them. Every day was measured by her smiles, her gossip (she was a little older) and her natural kindness. We had no mirrors and no real sense of self. We lived through others. It was hard, then, to understand how our experience of the intervening years had created such an unbridgeable chasm. Wasn't she exactly the kind of person I thought I was fighting for?

Why was I surprised? I had been studying hard to encompass the Triers' culture in order to know my enemy, but had ended up being more compromised than she was. She hadn't turned her back on Surelik culture, because she hadn't thought about it. It wasn't relevant to her life. She had a family to bring up in difficult times. It was survival and hard work, whilst still holding onto her humanity.

Finally she said, "Well you've come a long way for a reason, so tell me about yourself and why you've come."

"Ah," I replied, remembering the purpose of the journey and regretting some of my behaviour, "I have this boy, and cannot stand his presence. He reminds me of his devil of a father. A foreign baby with a foreign face. He may have come from my womb, but for me he's an alien presence."

She looked at me with that maddening intuition of hers. "So you want to leave him here? Am I correct?" I could sense the disapproval in her voice.

Off I went with barely another word. What was there to

say? It was the best thing for the boy, and whatever guilt I felt, I had to keep it to myself. She died of cancer shortly after my son graduated from university, and he was devastated. She had taken the love I could have made mine, and she had earnt it. I had lost an opportunity but gained a more important one: the chance to love my people and my culture.

And what did she think of me? Well, it was obvious: she took the boy not for my sake – or not primarily. She must have looked at that fatherless boy with a mother who despised him through no fault of his own, and she didn't even argue with me or attempt to shame me. She took him because of that well which, every time she drew on its water, refilled with more than she had taken.

That's why she died young and I live on. The Triers say that their God takes His own earlier than others. And I must be evil to continue to live on in this world far beyond my allotted span. I suspect that intelligent readers are now thinking that I have secretly and possibly unconsciously converted to the religion of the Triers, but they would be wrong. Not entirely wrong though, as I would like to believe in this God now that I have been tainted by civilisation. It would make sense emotionally, but unfortunately it doesn't make sense to me intellectually. It is a balm for the victims of a crazy global economy that could destroy our planet. In that sense, it is also a soporific.

I was so selfish at that time that I never considered her husband. He too was involved financially and emotionally in the growth of my son, and she must have known that he would agree: a clear sign of a good marriage. She was even true to my unspoken desire that he be brought up with our language. She must have spoken to him in it, otherwise he would never have become the campaigner he eventually would be. When you observe the wideness of human goodness, it seems terrible that this majority has to suffer so much. It is not humanity that brings on catastrophe, but the political systems it unwittingly generates.

In due course I got myself transferred back to the capital with Verochka's assistance. My work was no longer in lexicography but a kind of public relations job which was supposed to raise the profile of the Surelik language, which was difficult because the bureaucrats who hired me had no interest in it. While living there, I came to know one of the finest men I ever encountered in my life. I lack adjectives to describe him – his intelligence, his kindness, his loyalty, his morality and his damnable but equally wonderful unpredictability. If ever there were a man who could demonstrate civilisation's capacity to enhance human potential, it was him, him, him. And they shot him too.

I met him at the Writers' Union. I had been invited by a friend and accepted solely because of my curiosity about the Triers' society and culture. I expected it to be tiresome company and it was. There were many earnest young men, mostly bespectacled, who seemed to be preoccupied with demonstrating their erudition and also – because those were the times – expressing their orthodoxy and loyalty to the regime whose erratic ideas were hard to follow.

But one man remained silent, occasionally nodding his head in agreement or shaking it in disagreement but always with a relaxed smile. He seemed to sit comfortably amongst the tensions of those brutal times, emanating a calmness, a kindly helpfulness, a diligent openness, all of which may be what they call love – the generalised love that is an attitude or approach to others and to the world – another word that the Surelik vocabulary once lacked, because it was, perhaps in a less intense form, an innate part of our society. It is as though progress has not only distributed wealth unevenly but also good and evil, kindness and cruelty, love and hatred. I do not remember those extremes in my childhood.

His name was Osip. A typical European in his looks and bearing. After my experience with Perkins of the Little Noisy Musics, I had wished to avoid such people, but his manner, behaviour and above all his words could only attract me. His narrow face was unremarkable except for his high forehead exaggerated by his slightly receding hairline. He wore expensive spectacles for those spartan days, and the other sign of a little restrained vanity was a well-trimmed moustache along with a bearded chin, also typical of a Western intellectual. He looked like a man who enjoyed drink and company, partly in his case to observe it. When he spoke in a gentle baritone, I felt myself come to life; his words seemed to open up so many possibilities, when most writers were talking and writing to please the censor. The voice and the precision of his sentences combined to inexplicably powerful effect. Their language was not mine, but for him I would have renounced Surelik – I would have renounced everything, and now I cannot understand why I was always so impulsive. Am I the childlike savage? I wish that I were, but I am something else.

During the debate, I stood up and reminded them that in their territories many other languages were spoken. I told them of the forest and of stories and folklore. The regime was ambiguous on such things, and could at times be supportive. Many eyes looked at me with fear – I was going into dangerous territory and they didn't know which way to leap. But he did, and that voice seemed to speak to me directly: "The comrade makes an interesting point, though I cannot say that I have ever heard of the Surelikud and their forest life. Comrades, we clearly have a lot to learn."

He had said very little, and although that little was wrapped up in the strange rhetoric of the times, there was more in it that was hidden than was made plain. I had never heard such immediate and forthright approbation in all the times I had championed my cause amongst the Triers. The others were silent for quite a few seconds before someone found a way to shift the conversation to another subject. Afterwards he glided over, tall and graceful in his movement, and I already expected so much of him.

He fired questions at me and wanted to know everything about the Surelikud. His warmth and tenderness overwhelmed me, and the event ended with his insistence that he would do something, what exactly he wasn't sure. But something needed to be done.

He took me to a bar and by the time we sat down I knew that this man was interested in me - and that very probably he was a man in the habit of being interested in women. He didn't wait for me to ask questions about him but presented me with a slightly formal résumé of who he was: "I am an Odessa Jew, which means that I'm a cosmopolitan Jew. I've learnt from ourselves and I've learnt from others, in particular I've learnt from the Armenians who were the Jews of the Sultan's lands where most of them have been killed. But I only know the ones who, like the Surelikud, live in the Triers' lands. I have travelled there and they have our workers' assemblies which are no longer for workers and possibly aren't even assemblies, but they remain remarkably themselves: you could learn from them. I am a journalist and novelist and a sometime screenwriter; you may've heard of me?" I nodded that I had, which was true, but I hadn't read his work.

"My journalism allows me to travel a great deal, and feeds into my novels. Films too take me to interesting places. Not bad for the son of an Odessa carter." And he stopped there, not mentioning his trips abroad and the translations of his books, for he feared that he could oversell himself and was uncertain of how a Surelik might perceive these things. This showed that he wasn't as adept at reading a woman's thoughts as perhaps he thought he was; I was already his.

So he was a Jew. How much they made of it, this end of the Triers' lands! Both the Triers and Osip himself, though his was a reflex action. He looked like the Triers and the Triers looked like him, and even today after so many terrible things have happened, I find it difficult to comprehend. They spoke the same language, and he more than they had it running in his blood, as though every word of his - written or spoken - came from all the speakers of the Triers' language that had ever lived. You had to be a Westerner to fully understand this division they clung to. He never darkened the door of a synagogue, nor did many of them frequent a church, and yet the labels remained – in his mind and theirs. More in his, I think. And the answer, it gradually became clear, lay in his childhood. Under the Great Caesar, the Jewish intake to gymnasia was restricted, and clever but poor Jews could be pushed aside by less talented Triers and rich Jews. This wound would never quite heal, not that he spoke of it much. Perhaps the only thing Osip despised was self-pity. He loved everyone – all Triers, Jewish and not, all foreigners from every corner of the globe. I'll not call him an internationalist because that makes it sound like some thought-out, theoretical position, when it actually came from the heart. He loved everyone from everywhere, and he loved them mainly because he found them funny.

I awoke in the morning to find the bed empty. I thought at last that I had found my companion for life, and lifted myself from the bed as though I were weightless. In such moments – too few, far too few in a long life – we feel part of an ordered world even in a moment of cruel disorder, as though a relationship really can be an island and for me it briefly was. My lost first love, forgotten. My torturous, unhappy second marriage, forgotten. The callous abandonment of my only son, forgotten. The killings outside, forgotten. My struggle for Surelikud for which I had in part abandoned my son, whom I barely thought of at the time, forgotten. I had the purity of a perfect love. Of course they could come for us at any time, and that would be the end, but the knowledge of that one solid relationship could have sustained me even through twenty years of forced labour. This, at least, is what I thought at the time.

There were only two small rooms, one for him and one for the two children. This should have been comfortable, but for some reason I could barely speak to the children. It was as though that side of life had been cut out of me. The obvious reason which the reader has probably guessed may be correct, but I refuse even now to examine this matter. They were there, and frankly I found their presence an irritant.

The invidious position of women – then even more than now – is nowhere better demonstrated by a woman's change of status through her husband or partner. I had encountered this with Edwin Perkins, but then I had only been tolerated, but once I was with Osip I was courted. Whatever problems were brewing, he was still at that time an internationally recognised author the regime could hold up as an example of literary merit and of their tolerance. His involvement with film made him particularly powerful, as did his contacts with men right at the centre of power. If this was flattering to start with (it was so long ago I cannot confirm), it soon became tedious because of the people who wanted to contact him through me. I, on the other hand, saw this as an opportunity to talk about the Surelikud to people of influence. Lenin spoke of one step forward, two steps back, but he knew nothing about it. For those who campaign for minority languages it is more like half a step forward and four steps back. I argued passionately and unendingly, and I was speaking to deafened ears. Mostly they would agree and agree again, thank me for such interesting information which should be more widely known. And unbelievably they looked as though they really meant it. Only gradually did I realise that I was making no headway. Osip too was more verbal in his support than practical, but then he wasn't practical about anything. And his voice of influence was fading, as an imperceptible change in attitudes gradually mounted up.

I remember in particular a conversation with a heavily built man with very short hair and a restless nature which appeared to impede his concentration. He had an idea for yet another film about the Civil War, which I listened to with the restraint I'd also learnt, having had a view of that war very different from his glorious epic. Then he asked a few desultory questions of me, and I sped down that well-trodden path with my customary alacrity. At some stage, I asked, "Do you know what Surelikud means in Surelik? It's etymology, I mean."

He shook his head, only half interested.

"It means 'mortals', because humans are the only animal that is aware of the inevitability of its own death. What makes us differ as humans is what we do with that knowledge. We Surelikud don't believe in life after death – a belief we consider to be very enlightened, which is why we call all non-Surelik people Surnudhinged which means 'dead minds'..., but perhaps we could translate that as 'dead souls'."

"... like Gogol ..." he interrupted with a little stirring of life in his eyes.

"No, not like Gogol – long before Gogol. But because this inability of the non-Surelik to deal with the reality of death makes it impossible for them to develop their mortal minds or souls. There is some arrogance in this, I admit, for what do we know of all the peoples of the world, but it is certainly true of the Europeans, and perhaps I can speculate that the further away from the Surelikud you are, the more you are a dead soul."

"What nonsense," he laughed, and I laughed too, but inwardly at his inability to understand. The futility of my lobbying was now plain, and I could also see that I was no different from them – feigning interest in their plans and waiting for the opportunity to make my pitch. All of us were wasting our time.

The only course of action seemed to be that I should seek out members of the Surelik community in Moscow: they were the only ones in the world who would care. But before I speak of that, I should mention that Osip was always a pleasant distraction and evidence that life is primarily there in our close relationships, where we can always make a difference. For him, life was always about getting the most out of life, not only for oneself – in fact it can never be just about oneself. He never produced that dictum, but he lived his short life as though it was his instinctive moral guide. After our first night together, he started to make some breakfast, and I, knowing nothing of his habits, translated an old Surelik saying into the language of the Triers: "A thousand steps before you break your fast."

He didn't immediately understand, and then he laughed. "You have to go for a short walk before breakfast? What a bore."

"Or even a long one. The Surelikud aren't good with numbers over fifty."

He laughed again and said, "The Surelikud seem a little too interested in health and fitness for me. I wouldn't last long in that forest."

"No, you wouldn't. You would hate it."

"Right, give me another one. A better one, please."

"How about: 'Move your dwelling often and you'll always know your place in the world.'"

"Oh yes. Then I'm a Surelik. I never stay put, and yet I do, I really do know my place in the world. It's where history is, but also quite often where the fun is. Life is a serious affair that has to be treated light-heartedly. That's my proverb – my own private Osip one. But I like your Surelik one better."

"Yours is also a good one, but sometimes they don't allow you to do either."

His expression changed and then after long pause while he digested what I'd said, he busied himself with the breakfast. Eventually he muttered, "You're right, of course you're right."

When breakfast came, he was bubbling along once more, "Here it is, without one thousand steps. I'm going to arrange work so we can take in this Surelik place. I'm dying to see it, but I'm telling you now: I'm spending no more than half an hour in that forest. Just a quick sniff around the edges of it, and then back to the nearest bar for some strong liquor."

He would be true to his word and I would learn much from that trip, but little that would give me encouragement.

If Osip found Väikelinn a disappointing little town, he gave no sign of it. There it was with its muddy main street and planks on the side that acted as a pavement. There were minor improvements, but nothing that changed the essence of what it was except a new café that looked more suited to the capital. "This'll be where the bigwigs go," said Osip following some instinct and walking in its direction. "We'll do the real bars later." He was working and, typically for one of his trade, he was attracted to the one thing that didn't belong, perhaps because he found it familiar but more likely because he understood its incongruity. We sat down and a well-dressed waitress was prompt in her service, which was uncommon in our society at the time. Osip of course wanted to chat to her and find out as much as he could, but she wouldn't have it. With great politeness, she repeated our order – presumably to take charge of the conversation again – and once I had nodded, she walked away with measured haste.

In garrulous mood, he then delivered a monologue to me on the attractiveness of Väikelinn and his feeling that he was going to enjoy the company of Surelik people – an opinion that appeared to be based on his knowledge of me and the uncommunicative waitress. As he spoke I looked at my surroundings with some interest: there was no doubt that the café, though plain, had been designed with some thought in accordance with the fashions of the period. As I scanned the room, I came to the man sitting at the next table; he was smallish and stout with a stern, slightly jowly face and penetrating eyes that expressed both intelligence and a certain fear of the world. I vaguely remembered him and his name was Ärrituv, but he spoke before I could, "You'll be speaking Russian better than Surelik by now. Quite a change for a girl from the forest. Poor Pyotr will be long forgotten, I dare say." And he said it in Russian to increase the condescension and he said it in a strong Surelik accent just to emphasise his distaste for what he must have seen as treachery or mere arrogance on my part. I must have stunk of the city, when I still thought that I stank of the forest.

Osip broke in while I still struggled with the notion that I had returned to Väikelinn in a form that some – in fact many

- would interpret as offensive for a number of reasons even they probably couldn't fathom. "She often talks of Pyotr," he lied and added more truthfully, "and she's unstinting in her support of the Surelik cause."

"Unstinting is she?" Ärrituv seemed unpersuaded by Osip's defence. "It looks like she's grown very prosperous on unstinting. I should try it myself some time."

Osip never gave in, and he wasn't outraged by the man's spitefulness, in fact he enjoyed it and knew where it came from: "Rahväema has never given up on her Surelik ways. Every morning without fail, a thousand steps; not one more and not one less."

Ärrituv sensed scorn where none was intended and said dismissively, "That's just nonsense from the forest. Nothing to do with us. And does she count them?"

Osip, still smiling broadly, moved on: "I'm here for a film we're making on the Civil War. I could do with a character just like you. Have you ever acted? You have something of the actor about you. Perhaps it's innate."

Ärrituv was suspicious but also unable to dismiss Osip now. "I've never acted. Not really. I do play the accordion at the Surelik Friends of the Revolution get-togethers every month. Most people really enjoy it."

"Well, there we have it. I thought as much and I'll be in touch shortly." Osip shook his hand, which conveniently signified that Ärrituv had to leave, and he did so unsteadily like someone who had suddenly been disoriented.

As he walked away, I whispered to Osip, "That hasn't helped. It'll only make things worse when you don't give Ärrituv a part."

Osip didn't answer but immediately shouted, "Ärrituv, Ärrituv, come back here!" Ärrituv turned, now distressed and slightly angry, but he couldn't stop himself from returning. Just in case...

"Now what?" he said with undisguised surliness, certain of the inevitability of a put-down.

"Ärrituv, forgive me, I forgot to ask for your address," Osip continued with that reliable smile – the one that unfailingly inspires trust. "But I tell you what, why don't we meet at the Red Martyrs Hotel at 10 o'clock tomorrow morning? We can discuss the matter further."

Ärrituv was now transformed. The apologies and expressions of gratitude fell in abundance like fruit from an autumnal tree. He shook my hand warmly and said that it was great to have me back.

We laughed and laughed our way back to the hotel, but my laughter was muted by the realisation that he still hadn't helped. I was worried about Ärrituv himself, I was worried about everyone – most of whom would have thought the same as Ärrituv, but would never have been so explicit. Winning him over wasn't the problem, but Osip who moved his dwelling often would never understand what it is to come from a community like that of the Surelikud.

Osip loved to talk to people – all people without distinction interested him: the young, the old, workmen, officials, the ostracised, leading members of the Communist Party, oppositionists, criminals, policemen, prostitutes and kept men, earnest young people who have given their lives to the cause, those who laugh continuously, those whose sullen faces light up the world in other ways, the judgemental and those who, like him, were tolerant of everything. Humanity works because it is so varied.

Every day an old man sat on a bench near the centre, and Osip was fascinated by him. The man, who was bearded and whose eyes appeared to stare out from the depths of his soul, had some difficulty speaking the language of the Triers, but could make himself understood well enough. "Old man," said Osip, "how come you're always here?"

"What do you want me to do? My legs are not much good, and my daughter brings me here in the morning so that I can see all the people rushing about."

"I don't see much rushing about here, old man. You should see the capital, if that's what you want."

"Well, this is fast enough for me. They say that in the Noisy Musics' capital, everything is on the move, everything is in a hurry, motor cars everywhere. A terrible carry-on, I'm sure. But this is enough for me, quite enough."

"Would you like me to take you for a walk?"

"I'm not a dog, you know."

"Of course not, but I could hold your arm, and we could go to the park, chatting as we go."

"You're very kind, young man ..."

"Not so young."

"Young enough. I'm sure of that. Young enough to die."

"What do you mean by that?" Osip asked sharply, but the old man was unable to find the words to explain, so Osip put out his arm. "Shall we go?"

"No, no, I was saying ... what was I saying? I was saying that you don't want too much excitement at my age. I just sit here and watch, and almost no one sees me. So thank you, young man, for stopping for a chat."

"Do you come from the forest?" Osip asked.

"I did, but it was a long time ago."

"And what have you been doing since?"

"Surviving mostly. Working like a beast, and seeing so many souls go wherever the Triers think they go."

"And have things improved, old man?"

"Not that I can tell, but who am I to judge. I'm just one man with no education and not much life left. I can tell you one thing: this was once a backwater the Triers left alone, but the new lot want their hands on everything. Papers and more papers. Registration of names and residence and you name it. And I'm glad that I had none of that when I was young. Not that it is necessarily a bad thing. I'm just one man with no education, and you ask too many questions of me."

"Are you fearful of the new regime? Do you think that I'm a policeman?"

The old man laughed. "You, a policeman? Don't make me laugh. You look like someone the new lot would like to put in prison."

"Why do you say that?" Osip now looked genuinely perturbed.

"You see, that's another question. And I'm not sure why, not at all. If I were sure, then I would have had a different life, but I'm just an old Surelik from the forest without any education and minding my own business."

"So, you are afraid of the new regime"

"I'm not afraid of these times. At my age no one is going to hurry me on my way. Or rather stand on the fingers of a man who's using them to grasp onto the cliff edge but will never have the strength to pull himself back up. I observe this nonsense, and tell myself that I should never have left the forest, which would be safer even if it were crawling with lions, alligators and all the most dangerous snakes on the planet. And all we've got are bears and the odd tiger," he chortled. "What can you do? Nothing. Even pity is redundant. People just keep their heads down and hope that this sickness will pass. If somebody murders someone else, that's a crime, an immoral act, but if an epidemic or a freak storm occurs and people die, then that's just nature taking its toll, as it always does. But this if different. We Surelikud don't know how to define it. Somebody somewhere – the Moustache perhaps – is committing evil deeds, but it's coming from so far away that it could be coming down from the heavens. It's the local high officials who are most susceptible to the virus – the Spanish flu was less discriminating – and nearly all the Surelik bigwigs on the regional central committee are either dead or in the camps. Who knows? They're gone, that's for sure."

"Well, I wouldn't go around saying too many things like that, even at your age."

"I'm not worried about myself. It's you I'm worried about. I said that you're young enough to die."

Osip was taken aback. "Was that a prophecy?"

"There you go again. I don't know how to prophesy. I cannot

read, but I can see who is suddenly not around anymore, and I think that most of those who suddenly disappear have been shot or sent to the labour camps. One day they're rushing around worrying about little things, and then suddenly their lives are disrupted. They probably never know why. Not the real reason."

"Yes, yes, but why me."

"Well, I don't really know. Just a feeling I have. As I say, I know the faces that aren't here anymore. And yours looks like one of them. I'm just a man with no education..."

At this stage Osip lost his temper with the man and shouted incoherently, whilst the man remained relaxed and even allowed himself a little grin when he reminded Osip of how their conversation had developed, "Why have I told you this? I don't know really. I think that it's because you keep asking me questions." Then Osip gave up and strode away swearing at the stupidity of his interlocutor and revealing just how rattled he was. I ran after him, but it took a long time for him to regain his composure, in which he was aided by a *shtof* of vodka.

Not all was gloom in our backwater, as backwater it still was, whatever the changes of the last fifteen years. As things were going well with the filming, Osip agreed that after the day's shoot we would visit Tatyana, as I'd been wanting to do for some time. But after work, he was tired and was decidedly less keen to fulfil his promise. "So how old is this girl?" he asked with little interest.

"Tanya must have been six or seven when I knew her in 1921 or 22, so she must be around twenty now. She could be married."

"And why is she so important to you?"

"Come on, the man of spontaneity. Do I need to explain? Although I can. She was one of brightest little girls I ever came across. I think that she'll have gone far, even at the age of twenty. Her mother will tell us."

"No, of course, you don't have to explain," he said grudgingly.

He was very open with his time, but also very careful with it. He never really would see the point of Tatyana Ivanovna. "After all, I've foisted a lot of my friends on you."

"Keep foisting. Keep on foisting. I'm the one with time. A bit of lexicography. A bit of teaching. A bit of translation. And even a bit of the job I'm supposed to be doing, if someone could explain what it is. I struggle through, but even now as I glide towards forty, I feel that I haven't even got started. One day, I think that I'll be as busy as you, but in a smaller world."

"Really? And what are you going to be doing that will change the world."

"Not the world, Osya, I don't have the megalomania of a Trier like you. My ambition, and it stuns me that you haven't guessed it already, is to achieve an autonomous republic for the Surelikud."

How he laughed. The car could have gone off the road. Initially I laughed too, but it went on for so long that it became offensive. I stopped laughing and my head became hot and my face flushed, but I didn't know what to say, because every possible retort would have made me look more ridiculous – in his eyes at least. "I've been thinking about the flag," he was having difficulty speaking through his laughter, "it could be a pile of logs. That would look good, wouldn't it? But not too many of them, because with those axes of yours, it must take a man nearly a day to bring a tree down."

"That's because we rarely cut a tree down, and we choose one where they are too close together. We could get a hut out of a single tree. We don't have equipment for cutting large numbers of trees."

"Well exactly. Join the twentieth century and then they'll maybe give you your autonomous republic. But I wouldn't bet on it. You'd need more than a sharper axe to qualify for that."

"Stop the car!" I screamed.

"Come on, Rahväema, don't take it the wrong way. I'm only teasing."

"Stop the car!" I screamed again.

144

And he did, because he thought he could use that slippery tongue of his to charm his way out of the problem. But I was not in the mood. As soon as the car stopped, I jumped out of it before he could grab me, and my intention was to walk to Tanya's mother's house. It was a good three kilometres. He was now out of the car and running after me. He was talking, pleading and arguing, but I cannot remember a word he said because I didn't listen to a single one of them. Occasionally I cursed him in Surelik.

Eventually he ran ahead and blocked my way, but all he could come up with was, "Rahväema, don't be such a child."

"Some children have more sense than adults, Tanya was one such child and you are one such adult."

He had a smile that suggested he still wanted to laugh and had to suppress it. This did not help calm my anger.

"Rahväema, we shouldn't be arguing. We're friends, we're lovers, we should be enjoying ourselves. Who knows what's around the corner?"

I replied in Surelik, which he couldn't understand.

"What are you playing at?"

"I'm waiting for you to listen for a moment," switching back to Russian, "instead of treating me like an object to have fun with. I sick of men. I had enough of them. Never found a good one, just idiots who brought me unhappiness. The first thing that you've got to understand is that my Surelik culture is not some inferior thing that you in your liberal magnanimity accept as some kind of relic from history. It's a living thing that is just as good as your language, even if yours is spoken by hundreds of millions of people. Secondly, your ambition, which is an entirely honourable one, is to establish your own artistic credentials, but mine is to give the Surelik people the dignity of a status that belongs to most people of the world." Then I ended with an unfair and unlikely accusation just to drive the point home: "That is probably something you'll probably never understand."

He looked at me dumbfounded. As though I had transformed

into some entirely different creature, but not one he disliked. "*Razvalyukha!*[7] Rahväema, you're right! I'm such a shit. I'm sorry." This of course was like honey to my ears. I loved him and didn't want to lose him, but there was another strong emotion: standing in that half-alien land on my own, I felt not only quite alone but bereft of my hopes. His laughter had driven home the enormity of my ambition, and it had had its effect. Momentarily at least, I had lost my conviction. The conviction I needed if I was ever to have a chance, however slim, of achieving that aim I'd only confessed to Halvatud.

I looked at him and of course he was utterly likeable, particularly as he now looked like he wanted to burst into tears. As did I, but for very different reasons, which weren't about him but the practical possibilities of an autonomous republic. I would have liked complete independence. An autonomous republic for me was a compromise. I had no idea what I should do. We had to make up; I had gone that far, and I wanted him to understand and not just think that he had understood. This was an encounter between a strong culture and a weak culture, but a weak culture is not intrinsically inferior. It may in fact be superior, because a weak culture has to cohabit and learn from a strong culture, and therefore has a wider range of experiences. It could be said that this relationship resembled that of a man and a woman in our patriarchal societies – our civilised societies. It was even true of our own quite splendid relationship in comparison to many others.

I started by smiling at him: "Osip, you'll have heard of political re-education. It's not a pretty term, but you'll have to have a few lessons not from the full force of the law and the state, but from a diminutive daughter of a diminutive people who inflict no pain on anyone but have committed the terrible crime of taking too long to cut down a tree. We're not Stakhanovites, it's true, but that's because we're too busy being human beings."

---

7   Russian in the original. Развалюх means ...

And he smiled back and danced over, his usual ebullient self again, and I then knew that he wouldn't understand but would only think that he had understood, and what he exactly understood would also be a mystery.

It was a relief for both of us that the argument was over, though there was also that slight irritation with ourselves – a sense that we really had behaved like children or at least what we considered children to be.

We went back to the car and quickly arrived at my old village barely a kilometre outside Väikelinn. A few things were not the same. The road was slightly better, and a large schoolhouse had been built, but my old home and Tanya's were unchanged. If anything hers had slightly deteriorated, which was the first sign that the family could have moved. Her mother and to some extent her father had always kept the modest wooden building clean and freshly painted. As we got close, we could hear that there was a couple in the building. And they were having an argument. A vicious one.

A man shouted, "Woman, why do you ask these questions?"

And then a calmer, young woman's voice said, "Because I need the answers."

Then there was the sound of someone hitting another person, and she said, "You bastard."

"Knock on the door!" I commanded Osip.

"I don't think that it's your friend's family."

"I said knock on the door."

He clearly decided that then was not the moment for disobedience, but you could see that he didn't want to.

Suddenly it went silent in the house. Then the man said, "Go and see who's there. I hope that it's not the militsya." After what seemed to me a long wait, the door suddenly opened. "What do you want?"

Osip spoke quietly and a little nervously, "Were you living here about fifteen years ago?"

"What if I was? It's none of your business."

"Tatyana, don't you remember me," I said.

She looked at me for a couple of seconds before recognising her childhood friend and then her expression changed: "Rahväema, what are you doing here?" And in less than a moment, she was hugging and kissing me. "What are you doing here? I thought that you lived in the big city."

"We're here... Well, let's say we're here for various reasons. But one thing I had to do was come and see you. How are you doing?"

"I'm married," and then in a lower voice, "as you can see," with nod to indoors. Then she walked back into the house, and spoke in a loud voice, "Do you remember Rahväema, the woman I was always talking about? Well, she's here with her husband or friend – I don't really know. This is wonderful, you know. I'm really excited. Can they come in?"

"If they must," came the male voice.

She returned and I noticed that one of her eyes was swelling and turning darker already. "Please come in," and then in a lower voice, "he's grumpy but he's fine. He really is."

I went in and Osip reluctantly followed. There was a forty-year-old man standing in the middle of the room and hostility seemed to emanate from him as though this was the fuel that got him up in the morning. However it didn't look as though it were directed at us, but rather at everyone and everything. The two things I remember most about him were that he always spoke with authority, as though he were commanding a small and unruly platoon, and he had bad teeth for a man of his age.

"I'm a mother you know," Tatyana said and it wasn't clear whether she was pleased with this or not. Possibly both. She smiled weakly and was clearly beginning to lose the verve that had gripped her the moment she saw me.

"Oh Tanya, so much news. Are you happy?"

"Of course," she said, pushing the words out as though they had the whole weight of her soul on them. "Would you like to see him?"

"Of course," I said more brightly than her.

She took me into one of the back rooms. It was a small room

with almost no furniture. A child was asleep, and he was at least two years old. Possibly three.

"He's cute, isn't he?" A look of happiness did cross her face as she looked down on her son. Someone else emerged from that physiognomy – someone who should have been close to me but I had abandoned.

"He certainly is," I stated enthusiastically, even though I'd lost all enthusiasm for children.

"He keeps me going, and my one terror is that something could happen to him."

"Where are your parents?"

"My mother died of cancer five years ago, and the militsya arrested my father about two years ago. He must be in the camps. The terrible things is that I think my husband reported him to the authorities."

"Why, what did he do?"

"Nothing really. You remember him. He had a big mouth. He wasn't against the regime, but every now and then they did something that irritated him. He would say what he thought, but mainly in our own house. He wasn't stupid. We knew what was going on."

I thought about what to say, but no sentence seemed remotely suited to the enormity of her news. When we went back into the front room, her husband said, "Well, send two women into another room and they'll never stop talking. I bet that you covered a lot of ground. Natter, natter, natter. That's all they do, am I right? Er, ... what is your name? I don't think we were properly introduced."

"Osip."

"Well, am I right?"

"I've got no idea. It's far too complicated for me."

"Complicated? Oh I get it, you don't want to upset the little woman, and she is little. Tiny, I would say. Comes from somewhere in the east. Chinese, is she?"

"She's a Surelik like me," Tanya said angrily.

"You two," continued the husband completely ignoring

what Tatyana had said, "should take a leaf out of our book. The whole time you two were going natter, natter, natter, Osip and I were sitting in complete silence. Think of all the energy we've saved ourselves, because it goes without saying that absolutely no good will have come out of all your silly chatter."

After that the conversation became a little more normal. I think that we even talked about the best time to plant cabbages on the Surelik plain. Tanya and I were the experts, but her husband thought he was. And then we left.

"So," said Osip once we were driving off in the car, with the sigh of a man who has wasted a great deal of his time on a lost cause, "there are adult children like us and there are violent adult children like them."

"I disagree."

"You're counting yourself out, I imagine," he laughed.

"Not at all. I'm counting Tatyana out. First of all she is not violent; her husband is. This is no fault of her own but where she has landed up. We cannot know the whole story, but it is sadly a common one."

"And your second point."

"Of course, but you already know. She was never a child even when she was child, so I doubt that she's a child now. Now she has to negotiate a violent man on a daily basis, and that leaves little room for childishness. It is also a constant humiliation, so she may well agree with you and feel that she in her helplessness is some kind of child undeserving of the benefits and circumscribed liberties of adulthood. But she's not; she's a hero."

"That's a bit strong," he said in a peeved voice, and perhaps he felt that I had chosen that day to be independent-minded and I was being too rebellious and possibly winning too many arguments.

"Osip, allow me to be the expert when it comes to male violence to women. You're not a violent man yourself. In fact you're a kind man, so it is understandable that you don't know how much is out there. But it's of epidemic proportions in all civilised countries, I fear."

"What do you know about all civilised countries?"

"I was married to a Little Noisy Music, remember?"

"Oh really. Tell me about it."

"I'd rather not, if you don't mind. No good can come of dwelling on it."

We drove on in awkward silence for a while, and I wondered what he was thinking. Eventually he said in a near whisper that betrayed a degree of emotion. "I was a lucky man when I came across you. I should stop lecturing and grabbing the limelight, and I should listen to you. I could learn a lot."

This was perhaps the nicest thing he ever said to me, and he did say many nice things. All I could say was, "That's the first sensible thing you've said all day." After that day, we were even closer.

To the north-west of the Surelik lands, there was an area where the language was very strong, even though it had been under the rule of the Great Caesar for many centuries. It is known for its gentle and easily defendable hills, as well as good agricultural land. I had never been there before and thought that Osip would also be interested. It is part of another oblast, and when we entered it the topography and the architecture changed. Osip, for whom every day had to be an adventure, gave an ongoing commentary on every aspect – the crops, the houses, the instruments, the settlements, the people themselves, but I was interested in the one thing he wasn't: the language. In the main town we met up with some writers and intellectuals who were keen to meet the great man. They spoke Surelik perfectly – perhaps a few more loan words, given their long familiarity with the Triers – but also and quite oddly their language seemed a little archaic, closer to the oral epics about Vōitleja.

Their approach to politics and the Triers was certainly different. They had no problems with the presence of the Triers' laws and institutions, and they accepted the new regime with a shrug, as though accustomed to following the Triers' lead. "Things had to change," they often repeated, but went little further. Osip soon got tired of them – more writers and intellectuals, and all of them supplicants of some kind and clutching some important project. All the hungrier for being so far from Moscow. He persuaded one of them to take us out of the town to meet the people in the country. These folk turned out to be self-confident, but also uninterested in the writer with an international reputation. This didn't matter to Osip; it was a relief, but their taciturnity was a problem – especially as he relied on me and the local writer for interpretation and his natural affability counted for little. However laconic a society may be, you will always find a talkative person, and we did. A giant of a man with an angular face and regal expression butted into our conversation just as the tiger walks the nocturnal forest with a sense of its own presence and the malleability of others.

"It's a rare thing that the Surelikud visit these parts of the country. Now why would they be sniffing around here? There must be something they need, because as we say here, 'If you see a Surelik, keep your hand on your purse.' No disrespect, but normally when we have people down here sniffing around and counting the livestock, it's in the language of the Triers that they speak."

We translated it for Osip and he immediately picked up what we hadn't – probably because he came from afar. "Isn't he a Surelik? He's speaking Surelik, isn't he?"

To Osip's questions, the man was categorical in his response: "I'm not a Surelik. Never have been. I'm a Trier." He said this with pride and incongruously he continued to say it in Surelik. After the back-and-forwards of translation, Osip was fascinated and immediately engaged with the peasant in his own language, but it turned out that the peasant's knowledge of it was no better than passable. I'll try to reproduce that conversation as best I can.

"Why do you not consider yourself a Surelik if Surelik is your native tongue?"

The man looked surprised at the question, as though it had no basis in logic. "What has language got to do with it?

We have nothing to do with the Surelikud, who all live over the border in the other oblast. Even the ones who live on the plain are only a few generations out of the forest. They're still forest Surelikud for us. Nothing like us. Nothing. They're little more than savages."

Osip smiled. I was outraged, but he was enjoying the intellectual perversity that humans are capable of. In some way, it reassured him of the complexity of human society – its unknowability. "But why do you call yourself a Trier?"

"Why wouldn't I? For three hundred years, we have been part of the Great Caesar's lands and we have defended the frontier."

"And why did you do that? What did the Great Caesar do for you?"

"Well, quite a bit. He didn't take our lands; we were never landless peasants as on the Surelik plain. And we also fought to defend our own property."

"Do you not think that this was why he allowed you to keep your lands once he became your ruler?"

"What difference does that make to me? We kept our land, and we continued to keep it once the frontier moved further and further east. Perhaps he forgot about us, a tiny speck in his empire. Another reason for not kicking up a fuss about this and that, as people tend to do nowadays."

"So why don't you give up your language and use theirs instead?"

"I'm using it now, am I not?"

"Yes, but ..."

"Listen, we're proud of our language and our songs of Võitleja. The Triers allowed us to be who we wanted to be, and being a strong nation they provided us with stability. You're a Trier, why the grilling?"

"No, not a grilling. I'm just curious to know. So how does it end for Võitleja? Did he lose his wisdom, and then did the swan give it to the Surelikud?"

The man laughed. "What nonsense is this? Not even the

Surelikud say this. They say that he died and that was that. End of the epic. But we have a different ending: Võitleja remembered that he was a warrior and in his rage he rose up out of the lake and smote the Muurahvas, all the Muurahvas. He removed them from the face of the earth and their seed was ended, because that was what the gods wanted. And that was that. He took their cattle and he took their lands. He had many more adventures, and he always demonstrated his prowess as a warrior and as a man."

"Do you think that there's any historical truth in these stories."

He thought about this much more than about whether he was a Trier or a Surelik, and eventually and in a guarded manner he granted, "There will be some exaggeration of course, but I'm sure that it is based on some real events. Otherwise why would we sit down around the fire on the long winter evenings and recite these stories?"

"You have a point," said Osip with a grin of comprehension and humanity. I'm sure that he would have agreed with me that mythology says more about current beliefs than it does the past. And to a lesser extent this is also true of modern historiography, however much they insist that it's now scientific. Everything is scientific, we've been led to believe for a long time now, and it is rarely true. In that time in particular, pseudo-science was rife and these things are not harmless. That poor man was drifting towards compulsory collectivisation, and his invincible Võitleja would have been unable to help.

The Parable in which the Stupidity of Human Beings Is Discussed

It is a long time since Saint Francis of Assisi learnt the language of the animals, and given the infallibility of religion, we cannot argue with this and why shouldn't we also assume that the animals could learn the language of humans. Alright, not all human languages, there must be too many of them even for the cleverest animal, but at least the one they can hear in their vicinity (the scribe is pulling a face, but I will ignore her).

So, some time not very long ago in one of the more remote and backward areas of the Triers' lands which could have been the Surelik plain, a donkey, a pig, a dog and an irritating little sparrow were drawn to a bonfire the humans had built. It was warm and comforting on that cold winter afternoon, and the pig and the dog stretched out in front of it, while the donkey just stood and dozed standing up. And the irritating little sparrow sat on a branch and looked on with curiosity.

The donkey, well-known for its stubbornness, is less well-known for its sociability, mainly because we never knew that it could speak. So it started the conversation quite innocently by asking, "Why do humans do such illogical things? They put in a lot of effort cutting the wood and now they're burning it. They're not even enjoying the warmth."

The pig, who was very knowledgeable and respected for its worldliness, was able to provide the answer: "They're burning their rubbish, which they produce in huge quantities. They are the only animal that does this, and they have to think hard about how to get rid of it."

Apart from the irritating little sparrow of course, they all seemed quite happy with that for some time, but then the dog, who must have been giving it some thought, said, "Why don't they bury it? That would be a lot less work than going into the wood, cutting down a tree, and then cutting it up into smaller parts that have to be carried back to the rubbish."

The pig wriggled uncomfortably, having thought that the matter had been satisfactorily resolved and longed to lie placidly in the warmth without another thought in his head. He could have done without the dog's curiosity.

"Come to think of it," said the donkey, "why is it that so many animals are convinced that humans are the most intelligent animals of all?"

"Because they produce so much," said the pig, "cars, aeroplanes, buildings, cities, roads, machinery, packaged food, clocks and container ships. And quite a few other things, I think."

"That's what I always thought," said the donkey, "but it has now occurred to me that all they're producing is rubbish. That is to say that everything that is produced sooner or later turns into rubbish, which they then have to bury or burn. It doesn't sound very clever to me."

"A fine lot of philosophers you are," said the irritating little sparrow, "have you never heard of GDP?"

The pig wanted to say, "What's that?", but he didn't want to show himself up.

"What's that?" said the dog.

"Gross Domestic Product," said the irritating little sparrow.

"What's that?" said the donkey.

"Can't we just enjoy the warmth of the fire," said the pig.

"No, pig, you can't," said the irritating little sparrow, "an animal isn't in this world to loll about, but rather to test its existence by going beyond itself in its search of the truth about our world."

"You still haven't told us, sparrow," said the dog, "what Gross ... you know, this GDP thing is."

"Well, the first thing to know is that it doesn't really exist," said the irritating little sparrow.

"Right, that's enough of that, sparrow," said the pig who jumped up and ran over, but he couldn't get at the sparrow; all he could do was run around that tree emitting threatening grunts, while the irritating little sparrow took its time.

"Please, sparrow, enlighten us to the importance of a thing that doesn't exist. You seem remarkably well informed," said the dog.

"Dear dog," said the irritating little sparrow, "all you need to do is learn one of the six thousand human languages, and you will understand all these things, because humans speak incessantly of little else but the Gross Domestic Product."

"... which doesn't exist," the dog continued.

"That's correct. It doesn't exist because it is a meaningless statistic that can deceive in many, many ways."

"Then why do they put so much store by it?"

"Because they believe that it can tell them how happy they are."

"Then they really must be very stupid," the donkey interrupted.

"The lot of you are quite mad," said the pig, "it is a well-known fact that humans are the most intelligent animal on the planet. You only have to look at all the things they make ..."

"... which turn into rubbish," said the dog, who was really getting the hang of the whole thing.

"Quiet," said the pig, "it is a well-known fact that humans are the most intelligent animal on the planet, and that pigs are the second most intelligent. I'll have you know that our brains are not much smaller than a human's."

"But what does this GDP thing make them do?" asked the dog, ignoring the pig completely.

"It makes them produce more and more things, so that they feel happier or rather appear to be happier, but actually this just makes them madder and sadder," said the irritating little sparrow.

"You irritating little sparrow," shouted the pig whose face was now pinker that it usually was, "you just go around irritating animals who are quite happy with things as they are. You're never going to change the humans anyway. They're the ones in charge and no little know-all sparrow is going to make a difference."

"Quite right," said the sparrow (I think that if sparrows can laugh, then it must have laughed too), "and who would have thought that you could say something sensible? I cannot change anything, but I can find out the truth. You go ahead and have a good snore in front of the fire and enjoy your thoughtlessness, I have other things to do. But before I go, I'd like you to answer one question: what are these?" and it flapped its wings.

"Your wings, of course," said the pig, "what a stupid question."

"But they're also something else."

The pig looked blankly at the sparrow.

"They're my free spirit. They can lift me up, and allow me to observe and to think, and no censor can touch me – not a pig, not a dog, not a donkey. I can go on irritating animals for as long as I live."

"What about humans?" said the dog.

"You're the smart one," said the sparrow, a little peeved but also impressed. "Of all the rubbish they've been producing, the worst rubbish is weapons – and a rifle could be used to kill me, but I'm small and insignificant and they'd hardly bother. So me and my free spirit will be off and I leave you to your idle conversation." And off he went into the sky with effortless grace, while the pig sat down glumly and said, "That was a rum one. I've never come across such an irritating little sparrow in my life."

*

The scribe is objecting again, and saying that it's not relevant to my story, but it will be later in the book, so that was a taster as it were. I won't comment on her other objections, because I believe that the reader – being undoubtedly more intelligent than my scribe – has understood that dialogue well enough. Instead I shall finish the sad tale of the Surelik Triers of the north-west. At the time Osip and I visited them, they were unaffected by forced collectivisation which was almost complete in the country as a whole and only about five per cent of the land was untouched. How had they resisted so long? Certainly there must have been support from somewhere in the hierarchy – either regional or central – but sooner or later they would have to bend. A year later, there was talk of unrest in the area, and later still there were rumours of expulsions leading to forced resettlement in the east. We know today that those rumours were true, and somewhere over in the east there's a town where some of the old people still speak Surelik; there's not a trace of them in their ancestral lands to the north-west of ours.

Was that Surelik-Trier peasant aware of this danger when we spoke to him? He didn't appear to be. Though my experience of being a Surelik-speaker was very different from his, I was pleased that he and his sort existed, and went about their lives as patriotic Triers while not quite being Triers. This shows that there are many ways of being something and many ways of interpreting the world, and this often has to do with history, geography or sometimes just the whims of powerful men. Or perhaps not even that: an order would come down from above, and being a proud, independent-minded people, the Surelik Triers might have resisted and therefore faced the full weight of repression, transportation and, in some cases, death. But would the men in power who made those decisions have known anything about these people and any of their methods and practices which could be useful to know? What possible advantage could derive from throwing them off their land?

This is progress. A simple calculation wipes out the complex differences that are at work, often usefully – so complex that the elites, not only in this land of the Triers but across the world, do not even inquire about what is going on down below where the directive becomes action. Everybody believes in progress, which is odd because every few years the concept of progress changes radically. Progress is simply the current direction of history, which could be in the opposite direction of twenty years earlier; it is always going forwards even when it is going backwards – but always, always, everyone has to move in the same direction and the means of coercion multiply, increasing the efficiency of these waves of change which uproot families and entire societies, causing distress and disorientation for no great benefit, even though the statistics will scream that great strides are being made. Even as we citizens reel under the force of the storm, we hear on the radio that a life free from want and wanton violence is just around the corner.

This is progress, which everyone believes in without really having thought about what it may be.

Still, I had my own ambitions. I was seeking a modest progress, and having been rebuked, Osip was keen to make up for his ill-mannered ways by using all his remaining contacts to arrange a meeting for me with an important figure in the Ministry of Minority Peoples. Eventually he did, and there was some excitement. We discussed tactics and strategies endlessly. Sometimes we argued because I felt that Osip had little hope of a successful result, but that was hardly his fault and the man was doing all he could. In any case, it was all waste of time, because none of it had the least effect on the outcome.

On the appointed day I went to the imposing building, which was not overly imposing as this was only the Ministry of Minority Peoples. The room which I was ushered into with almost religious reverence was large and contained little furniture. There were five telephones on the desk along with a single blank sheet of paper. The smart fountain pen, clearly of foreign manufacture, had been lined up in exact parallel with the edge of the paper, as though looking forward the next opportunity to display its luxurious graphic potential. The man too appeared to be expectant, but possibly even he was unclear of what. Perhaps his life had been a tedious succession of disappointed expectations.

He sat with bovine rectitude, overly comfortable in the comfort of his convictions, surrounded by what he took to be the symbols of his power, and yet his power was limited: real power sat elsewhere in chaos and a bottle of vodka stood totem-like before it. And the glass that would raise the alcohol would be tickled by a grey moustache of banality, while the other men in the centre of power were more spectators than participants and they were drinking too – out of apprehension and foreboding. The real power was new power improvised by paranoia, and what sat before me was at least as old as the first written word. The new power was a creation of the radio and the tank – and humanity's inability to apply new technology to the betterment of the human condition rather than the efficiency of power.

"What can I do for you?" he eventually said, as though coming out of a daydream.

I explained our need to have our own autonomous republic because of our cultural distinctiveness.

"I don't think that I've ever heard of the Surelikud. In southern Siberia, you say ... Were you all Christians before the Revolution?"

I explained that we hadn't been, and he was clearly disappointed – perhaps "put out" would be the better term.

"Not Christians?" said the high official in an overtly atheistic regime. "Do you believe that you're socially advanced enough to take on the complex and onerous responsibilities of running an autonomous republic?"

I answered that I was convinced we were. We had many young people who had benefited the new regime's educational policy, and the Cyrillic alphabet had been adapted to our Surelik language so that our people were often literate in more than one language.

He seemed pleased with these sentiments, but less convinced of the reality. It was good that the enlightened nature of the regime was readily acknowledged, and he nodded his approval along with a weak, uncertain smile, as though he were wondering whether he had permission to dispense that lukewarm, bureaucratic facial expression. He asked a couple of slightly naive questions and then incredibly announced his judgement: "Then you shall have your autonomous republic. Go back to your people and announce the good news." Having concluded the process, he appeared keen to have me out of his sterile office and be free to return to his sheet of paper so overwhelmed by its neighbour, the foreign pen.

I left elated after many expressions of stunned gratitude. And yet I felt cheated. It had been all too easy. Without a proper debate or even an argument, it didn't seem possible that a decision of that kind could have been reached. Of course we celebrated when I returned home, and Osip felt quite proud of himself. "You see. And what little faith you had in me," he laughed as he drank Georgian wine. But the weeks became months, and I had heard nothing more. Osip made a few tentative enquiries which came to nothing. The longer the silence, the bolder he became, but one day he returned quite depressed. He told me to sit down, but only after I had poured him a drink. He finished the glass before he spoke: "We have to let go on this autonomous republic business. It's not going to happen. Before they just brushed me off, but now they're getting hostile and irritable. In the current climate, I can do no more."

"You tried!"

"We were idiots to trust the bureaucracy. They never had any intention."

"Perhaps."

"I'm telling you. That's how they think. And that way you'll never try again."

"Maybe. Or perhaps that man wanted to look as though he had power he didn't have. To convince himself briefly that he could make a decision."

"Oh, he'll have given up on that long ago. This land is run by personal diktat, and those who do have some real power are probably no more than four or five men. They play games. They have their methods." He spat out those last few words.

The civilised world was indeed a well-oiled machine based on reason and intellectual enlightenment. And we Surelikud? We were just savages who could not possibly attain the sophistication of the large powers who look after us so generously.

I must have said something of the kind at the time, because Osip and I started to discuss the concept of civilisation, which with many provisos he attempted to defend.

"I'm not saying that we haven't lost a few good things more primitive people have, but you cannot argue that all the great scientific and artistic achievements of the last few centuries aren't a spectacular monument to civilisation," he said with just a little too much passion, as though I had touched something that affected him like a religion. I sensed that this was not an argument he wanted to have, and he was usually a man who enjoyed one. This was a sacred matter.

"And I'm not denying that spectacular things have been achieved, but I question whether it is worth the price. How many people really care about your monument? Not the majority who drudge too much and eat too little – who are the great majority whichever economic system you look at. Are we here to create monuments? Or are we here to create the intangible and the ephemeral, which leave only a slight trace in human memories and then only for a few decades? And what I'm talking of here are the relationships we all have with others, which we ourselves often forget but which for a short time were important to us and gave us great satisfaction. Our conversations. The things we learn from others, not necessarily as they intended. Our relationship with the land, with the forest, with the sky, with those landscapes of perfect beauty that enter into our mortal souls. Think of this magnificence, and you will no longer need monuments, because they are life itself. And how many people, do you think, never live because they're too busy chasing monuments, either those of others or, far worse, ones that they would want for themselves – not just large physical monuments but also medals and titles like 'doctor', 'professor', 'admiral', 'general', 'king', 'emperor', 'general secretary of the politburo', on and on, endless lists of titles, honours, honorifics and other flattery that can swell the hearts of those who have stopped living. We uncivilised types have none of that. Unless we leave the forest, we're unable to imagine such things."

"Oh please, you know that I wasn't speaking of crap like that," he cried, unable to conceal his irritation. "Art, real art, is the opposite: it is this desire to regain life by looking at the world – and even the drabbest everyday things – in entirely new ways. It is an exciting revitalisation of our lives – not this not-living you think that civilisation is. I'm not standing up for the generals and the bemedalled. They can go to hell, as far as

I'm concerned. But art, architecture, music, literature, these are the things that save us from the dullness of our existences."

"But why is life drab? Why is it so dull, as you keep saying? Only because you've exalted yourself and your civilisation. This is where we misunderstand each other. You're a writer. You believe that writing a book, putting your name on it and getting it read by lots of people is a significant thing. But haven't you ever thought that all that is just distracting you from more important things?"

"Now you're just being offensive. And yes, I'm not that interested in looking at beautiful sunsets every evening or climbing up some bloody mountain. That is fine for people who like that kind of thing. Things, things, things. We keep using that word, but that's not what it's about. It's about the whole panoply. The whole complex mess, if you like. I'm as critical of it as you are, but I want to observe it all, live it all, live it second-hand through my work, understand it, fail to understand it." And here he stood up and smiled. Happy again. "That's living! And it's better than snaring a rabbit in a fucking forest."

Now I was irritated. He had been justifiably irritated by my misrepresentation of his arguments, and now I felt the same about his misrepresentation of mine, though I wasn't sure that either of us had a very clear idea of what we were talking about. Emotion was as important here as reason. Those who prize their ability to reason are often the first to embrace the irrational when their fondest beliefs are under threat, even from weak arguments. Those are the beliefs we take so much for granted that we fail to revisit them in our own minds and possibly forget why we originally gave them so much importance. I wanted to make him understand what I meant by relationships, and he believed that I didn't quite understand the significance of art for civilised people. "You have to agree that man is a social animal, which is what your philosophers have always said, so you must understand then that we are an animal that creates relationships and those relationships can make us better people or worse, they can

164

be shallow and they can be profound and, above all, they can bind us together in a dialogic manner that frees our souls or they can bind us together through power and therefore become oppressive. In both cases these bonds are strong, but these relationships are at the opposite ends of a spectrum when it comes to quality."

"Enough of this sophistry. What you don't understand ..."

"No, don't tell me that again. Art and literature have replaced religion in a godless age. I've heard it so many times, and it may have been original in the nineteenth century but it was always a very individualistic approach. Art and literature are social acts that involve always more than one person; not just the artist but also the person who beholds the artwork or reads the book. Art in our forest society was always public, always an involvement and we had no word for it. Which will only convince you of our backwardness, but while these categories can increase understanding, they also diminish public involvement and public ownership of their culture."

"Have you ever thought of joining the one party allowed by the Triers' regime? You would get on very well, and they talk more or less the same shit."

"No, I never have. Not for a moment, but you are a member..."

"But a critical one."

"Wouldn't it be more critical to leave? Just resign. Say you've had enough. Why not?"

"Because..."

"Because you're afraid to leave and you rely on your contacts there to get work."

"Can't we disagree without insulting each other?"

"That's called losing the argument. The moment when you bring in the sanctity of your remarkable sensitivity."

"Are you being such a bastard because you're angry about losing the chance of your damn autonomous republic which would only be another layer of bureaucracy?"

"No, I'm being a bastard because ultimately you too see the Surelikud as inferior beings."

"Oh that prickliness of small nations. I can put up with it only so far ... No, no, I don't mean that. Okay we're pushing each other into a corner," he said with untypical solemnity because he desperately wanted to convince me. He pulled on his cigarette, as if it could release the tension he felt and perhaps it did. "Look, I'm quite happy to argue my side using your yardstick: the quality of human relationships. In my opinion there is no small act of kindness that doesn't derive from centuries of thoughts interwoven across societies and languages."

I looked at his European face, his pleasant European face, so unlike the Little Noisy Music's, and I realised that it is our relationships that attribute the way we perceive a face. We Surelikud are a mixed bunch at a crossroads of peoples: Central Asians, East Asians, Triers and small indigenous peoples. Our lands were both cosmopolitan and remote, but no one looked entirely European, just as I don't look entirely East Asian. Still we can have our prejudices, particularly against the Triers, perhaps because they're the ones that have changed us all to a greater or lesser extent. I loved that face, just as I loved arguing with him even about something so close to my heart and his. And later I would reflect on the irony that European Jews who were the great propagandists of European culture would also become the victims of the most obscene prejudice meted out by other Europeans whose civilisation they so loved. None of this I mentioned to him, although it seemed relevant to my argument: everything starts from the human relationship; take that away and our psychological health starts to dissolve irrevocably, as does society itself. My thesis is this: wasn't this process initiated by repetitive work without agency and accelerated by technology that cuts across those lines of communication. Something he would never admit. He may have been right that art lessens the pain, but it is the palliative and not the cure.

"I could not disagree more," I said but this time with a smile to signal my respect in spite of our difference. "You're suggesting that civilisation brings what you call civility, because you believe that it didn't exist beforehand. You're suggesting that we had to go through this pain to gain something we never had, but in fact all this pain has made us want to regain something we've lost. And it's not easy."

"I don't believe in the noble savage. Nobody does today. It is a fantasy."

"Well, I don't believe in it either, but for a different reason. The word 'noble' for me is suspect. It originally meant 'well-known' or 'notable', but this implied a society that was so large that some people were unknown. Nobility thus came to mean wealth and power which make a person more visible. In turn this means a society based on class, and a society of haves and have-nots. 'Primitive' society did not have that, and therefore it didn't have the concept of nobility which was retrospectively applied by well-intentioned members of your civilisation. You shouldn't dismiss them for their idealisation, which had a generosity so many other Europeans lacked."

"*You mean* people like me?"

"No, don't personalise it. That's not what I mean. I speak of the European colonisers who despised the peoples they colonised. And thought that they were bettering those peoples even as they stole from them and enslaved through various methods. And even intellectuals like yourself struggle to understand this at times. In a decade or two, you'll understand. Take your time, and remember that even Tolstoy did it in stages. His first break with his early career was to write positively about the Cossacks in relation to the urban Triers and their upper classes while treating the indigenous Muslims as caricatures, and then at the end of this life he did the same for the Muslims whose lands were being taken and criticised condescending attitudes towards them. Some of the characters did in fact look on them as noble savages unable to keep up with progress. An unavoidable tragedy. Perhaps that is how you look on the Surelikud."

"Rahväema, you're an arrogant woman – you know that,"

now he was angry again. "You can't just sweep away Western culture like that."

"I'm not. I admire it too, and have probably spent too much time studying it. It turns out that it's not as useful as I thought it would be."

"Oh my God, you're insufferable..." And it would have gone on, but at that moment his son came into the room and looked at us both. He thought that our relationship was at risk – that is the relationship between his father and the woman who was always pontificating about relationships but clearly wasn't good at them (though I wasn't just talking about relationships between women and men, but all relationships: with relations, with friends, with the person you buy your newspaper from, with someone who stops you to ask for directions, and with plants, trees, forests, the earth – that maternal substance from which all life is born directly or indirectly – and of course our relationships with children who are our future). I don't think that our heated argument would have upset the child, because he probably sensed my disinterest in children and thus in him. Why could I no longer relate to children? Was it something in me or had this civilisation I had to learn about pushed that essential part of my humanity out of my mind? Osip left the room with him, and after that we found more interesting and less incendiary subjects to argue over.

For once the scribe has come up with a good question: why haven't I mentioned the names of Osip's two children? The answer is sadly very simple: I cannot remember them.

Some months later, Halvatud sent a message that I was to meet at a café near Osip's home. I was sitting at a table writing notes, when I saw him working his way towards me with his usual mix of determination and vitality. He sat down and said nothing. He simply threw his newspaper on top of my papers, and looked at me piercingly.

"What's the lecture this time?" I asked. To which he merely smiled with gentleness.

"I hope that this won't take long," I said curtly. That was who I'd become at the time.

"It could do," he replied with an expressionless face which made me turn towards him. I took it as a sign that he had something serious to say.

"Alright!" I muttered reluctantly.

"You do realise that Osip is not going to live for long?" he asked with almost fatherly solicitude.

"Why do you say that?"

"You must realise that not all people with fine rational minds behave in a rational manner. Moreover, just as some people gamble with wealth they may not even have, so others gamble with their lives in different, perhaps more heroic ways. It seems that they cannot feel fully alive unless they put the thing they hold most dear at risk. For me who was born with risk that was innate and held at bay by a constant balancing act, this folly seems very strange – but perhaps it shouldn't be, because it may be the reason why I enjoy life so much. Your friend Osip has flown too close to the sun. On top of that he has a relationship with a woman coveted by one of Yezhov's men – you realise that too, I hope?"

"Of course I do. We're adults and individuals. I've been married twice and neither husband brought me much happiness. It was not the fault of the first, but the second could not have been guiltier, so Osip is the only one who has, and if he sleeps with another woman, I care not a damn. Let him! In these times, we catch our moments of happiness as soon as they come within our grasp."

"That's all very well, but fidelity is not the problem. Osip is a loyal communist, but that too counts for nothing. They can't forgive him his independent spirit and above all his sense of humour. These men don't understand it, and when they hear laughter, they think that it's directed at them. They put up with him, however, as he delivers the goods: novels, short stories and, most importantly for them, film scripts. If Yezhov's man adds him to the list of people to be executed, no one is going to rush forward and defend him. They give all such officials some discretion as long as they don't overdo it – in that case they join the list as well. It's a constant game of nuanced and not so nuance self-abasement. It is a world in which evil is done by people who think that they're morally good, because they're on the side of the working class or history or a Marxism Marx would have disowned. For every great evil they commit, some of them also do a small good, as this convinces them that they are good people with good hearts. They can smile in the mirror where they see their warmth and magnanimity smile back. Greatness of soul, indeed, and it costs so little! Such people also enjoy a good bargain."

"So what do you want me to do?"

"Nothing. Nothing can help Osip now, because he has already thrown the dice and lost the bet. It is a matter of time. Use what's left to keep him content and enjoy your last moments. There is the matter of the children."

"His children! What have I to do with them?"

"Do you want them brought up in a state institution as the children of a spy and subversive?"

"Spy and subversive. Yes, that's what they'll call him. How odd, because he has subverted many things, but never this regime, even when he's been acting the clown. My first husband most definitely rebelled against them, and yet they weren't nearly as bad in those days as they are now. And they weren't good either. Where's the progress? The famous progress they always promised and still do?"

"So you'll bring them up?"

"Not on your life! Neither mine nor Osip's. I gave my son away, remember. How could I take on another's? I have things to do, Halvatud. You said so yourself. Not children. Not in this world. You have no right to even to suggest it, you sanctimonious bastard!"

"That's okay," he responded in his terrifyingly calm voice, "then you'd better work harder at doing what you're supposed to be doing than you are doing at the moment."

I stood up and walked away carrying the burden of my anger and self-pity, and I knew that on his crippled legs he would never be able to catch up with me, but when I inevitably glanced back at him I could see that he had made no effort. He knew that he'd won the argument and he knew what I'd decided to do. His newspaper lay open in front of him and he was reading it while he happily sipped his coffee.

One evening when we went to bed, I knew that Osip was very upset and I knew what it was about: his estranged wife had been picked up by the NKVD and it should have come as no surprise as she was a fairly vocal member of the Left Opposition. I didn't want to speak about it until he brought her up, which he seemed unable to do. I woke early and noticed that he was already up. I eventually found him outside the flat at the stairhead, where he had taken a chair and was seated with his face in hands. When he looked up, I could see that he was crying. "But what about her?" His face was distorted and childlike. Unlovely but also demanding of my sympathy. I'd already known the outcome, but had not fully comprehended it. The company of the civilised is not easy to keep. Even in their better forms, they are unnecessarily complicated.

I said nothing, not to torture him but because I simply did not know what to say.

The man in him, the Trier, resurrected itself. He sat up straight, removed his glasses and extracted a slightly grubby handkerchief to wipe them and tidy up his face. It's unlikely that he knew what he was doing, as his mind was clearly elsewhere. He then looked at me with what? Anger, shame, embarrassment or even pity for me? The human is not a machine; its logic is not binary and its decisions never fully calculated.

"It's not your fault," were the first unfortunate words he chose. Of course it wasn't, but I knew what he meant. "It's me. How can I live in happiness while she is in a labour camp?

Supposing she's still alive. How can I face her children every day, look after them, love them, while she is suffering? How will I feel?"

I said nothing. Still unable to speak.

"How can I do this to you? I should have thought it through. I am not an insincere man."

My silence continued, but I allowed myself to stroke his hair. That was my reply, and I felt him relax.

"Rahväema, I also have another ..."

"Don't say it. I've known about her for a long time, and I don't care a damn"

"These are unforgiving years," he was emboldened and wished to justify himself further, but I had already forgiven him always supposing there was any forgiving to be done. I never doubted his sincerity. "We were made for each other, but ... We are a generation that has been called upon to make great sacrifices. Even though we know that terrible injustices are being committed, we cannot lose our faith in the system, because it has the potential to save the world. The men in power will not be in power forever, but the system must survive. Things will get worse before they get better, and we cannot endanger that for our own happiness."

Here he was confusing different matters: his duty to his ex-wife in the labour camp, to his other lover soon to join her, to me who was somewhere in the same queue and to a flawed regime he could not abandon like a wife who cannot abandon an abusive husband. That was love, unquestioning love, a word he never linked to my name, even though he had clearly won mine.

"In another time ..."

I lifted my left index finger to my lips to silence him. I wanted no more of his excuses, which would only have marred my memory of him. I stroked his head once more and kissed him on the forehead as a parent might kiss a fractious child. And then I turned and walked past the open door to his rooms, down the stairs, and out of the building. I abandoned my few belongings and the work we had done on Surelik history. More wasted energies, more time lost in what was already a very uneven battle. This last thread holding me to the specific, of which all real human feeling is made, had now been cut. I was cured of emotion and free to do what I had come into the world to do.

But it wasn't a happy freedom. Not at all. Freedom in the West is always associated with happiness, but freedom is earned at great cost and often involves acts of cowardice – or acts that appear to be cowardly. He was finished. They'd taken her and would take him. If I stayed with him and the children, then at best I would be stuck with the children. More likely they would take me too. Halvatud was right: I had to survive and I had to do what was most necessary. Once again I was abandoning someone who needed me. I was the one who should have felt guilty, and I did to some extent but this just redoubled my conviction, though I still had little idea of how I was to go about it.

Scribe, don't look at me like that. Did you know nothing of this story? You thought there was only Ilusadev. Don't bother me with your sentimental ravings. But you're right though. Quite uncannily. None of this bit about him crying on the stairs, not a word of it in my book. You will follow my instructions! You're here to work, not to be clever. I dictate and you type. As long as the result is my words – exactly as they come from my mouth, unless I tell you to remove them. And as you wish on this occasion, that episode comes out. The focus will be on Ilusadev in this book. Ilusadev and Perkins. The generous heart and the cruel mind. The handsome and the foul. The courageous and the vicious. This symmetry works perfectly, but that emotional scene with Osip would complicate matters beyond measure, and what would it mean? It shows me faltering, and I think that I had already done enough of that. It is well known that the Triers' regime was brutal at the time; it needs no repetition. And yet Osip is the one I think of most. With guilt, regret and joy at the moments we had together. All that is true and desolating to this day. I didn't weep at the time, but I have often done so since. They shot him, you know. He would have gone before the firing squad still believing in that ism, and not regretting his decision to return from the safety of Paris. They would call this tragedy - and almost delight in it - but I would call it folly.

There's nothing more irritating than my scribe's attachment to the idea of my undying love for Pyotr Sergeyevich, and I've told her time and again to leave such romantic thoughts alone. They're of no interest to the reader - or to me. I left that behind me long ago, and why should I care for a fickle man who couldn't look after himself. My husband indeed. What he taught me was how not to behave. His instruction often derived from bad example. I loved him once with a love too distant now for me to see clearly, and he had, I know, a certain tragic nobility, which is what is leading the scribe astray. And yet she persists in her tiresome questions, which I largely ignore. I only reply when they're pertinent to this book. Of course she respects me and is fascinated by my life or what she would like my life to be. She charges me nothing for her labour and feels that she's sacrificing herself for Surelik culture and humanity as a whole. Humanity as a whole! And she's so young - well, young compared with me. She can tie her shoe laces without difficulty. I tell her that youth should live and love with joy. Yes, even in your fifties. To be serious in youth is to be dangerous, particularly to others. There's time enough for seriousness, and once you've discovered the gravity of life there can be no more pursuit of joy. Not that joy won't occasionally visit like a welcome but uninvited guest. Joy that comes precisely because you have no more needs - no daft desires and impatient yearnings, just the daily rediscovery that life's great gift is life itself and it comes wrapped in luscious nature, as our great forests bear witness. But I believe that even those who live in the torrid desert will feel the same as I, when they look on their granular, apparently lifeless universe, because they will know how to read it, as I obviously don't.

That's why I laugh at travellers; they think that they'll discover the world, but all they discover, if they have any intelligence, is their inability to understand. We don't understand that familiarity is required before we can even start to read our environment, and yet when it becomes too familiar we fail to see it again. We travel in order to understand where we come from – that is the purpose of travel. And if we travel, we should travel slowly, and pause at length in order to understand at least something before moving on. Knowledge is like those abominable oil wells the Triers and Noisy Musics crave so much; it has to drill down on the same spot – but more benignly – and this takes time, unhurried time.

Don't pout! I know that you love the idea of my loving Ilusadev chastely to my dying day, but life is much more perplexing than a romantic novel. Ah! The scribe objects and asks me why I'm turning my life into one. But I'm not; I'm writing a political memoir, and I have a duty to my followers. That's why this passage has to come out.[8]

I didn't want to abandon the Tryer's capital solely because of the killings. The city folk and the country folk romanticise and envy each other, and their ignorance of each other makes them who they are. Those who cross the boundary and familiarise themselves with the other are rejected by both and inhabit a pleasantly unhappy understanding of the world. I sensed this, and knew that I could only protect myself from it by returning to the forest. It turned out that leaving the city was not going to be easy. I was on a list, probably just behind Osip. They found me about twenty-hours later, and must have been following me for a bit in the hope that I would lead them

---

8 As far as we know, nothing was in fact deleted from the first published text. It is possible that Kiryutaya restored it just before it went to the printer's. If that is the case, she made the right decision, especially in light of Osip Osipovich Steinberg's fame as a novelist and scriptwriter.

to others, but once they realised that I was homeless in the city, they decided to act. This meant that Osip had already been arrested.

I was taken to their building and put in a cell, where I was forgotten for several days, which meant that I was not one of their more important prisoners. And why would I be? Eventually some soldiers came and took me to the interrogator. The room was typically spartan and there were a lot of papers. Piles of them. The soldiers left and not a word had been said. The man was sitting with his back to me and puffing on a cigarette. This was clearly a break in his busy day and he was not going to cut it short. Eventually he turned and, still not looking at me, vigorously stubbed out what was left of his cigarette in the ashtray on his cluttered desk. He was a man of about forty, but clearly full of authority. He had a pleasant face, but his eyes were weak and sleepy as though something sometime had broken. Then he looked at his notes and said, "Rahväema Ranavutavskaya Ilusadeva. That's your name?" He looked at me with a bored expression.

"That's correct."

"A Surelik, I see. I was once in that part of the country."

"Really, and when was that?"

"The end of the Civil War."

"Of course you were, Andrei Alexeyevich! Haven't you recognised me? Or my name."

He stiffened suddenly and very slowly he began to understand who I was. His face changed as his emotions changed. Initially there was a spark of pleasure which was quickly replaced once he worked through the implications of this encounter.

"Rahväema, yes of course," he said very slowly as though he wanted to slow time down or even halt it.

I waited. He was of course my interrogator, and his silence gave me a chance to calculate how I could use this to my own advantage without overplaying my hand. I decided immediately never to mention the side on which he fought in the

Civil War or ask him about how he ended up in his current position. That would have been tempting a firing squad. If he brought up any of these things, it meant that he wanted to justify himself, and in such a case I would let him speak. Suddenly I knew that I had a chance of getting out of there alive, a chance to be free to leave for the forest.

He walked backwards and forwards in front of me. Nervous, irritated and uncertain of what to do. Finally he stopped and I waited calmly and patiently until he eventually stopped and spoke, "So you have been mixing with anti-party elements. You are aware of that, aren't you? You are in very serious trouble."

"I don't know any anti-party elements. The man I was living with is a very loyal member of the party and always has been. From before the Civil War. I personally have never been a member, but I am not against the party either. I'm not a political person, as you know."

This answer only made him more agitated. He went behind his desk and sat down in a defensive position, while he tapped its edge with his pen absent-mindedly. "Rahväema," he said as though my name could provide some clue to how he was going to get himself out of this predicament. "I know what you're thinking, but they know all about my background. I never made a secret of it. Don't think that our previous acquaintance is going to get you out of this, because I have to do my duty. I always do my duty and my duty is to the party, its beliefs and the fatherland. I now know that I fought on the wrong side. I am ashamed of it, but after I met you I fought on the right side, the truly patriotic side against the Japanese and we drove them out of Siberia."

I said nothing.

"Don't stare at me. This is an interrogation and you are accused of serious crimes against the state."

I continued to say nothing.

"Do you know that my men rebelled against me ..."

"I thought at the time that it might happen."

"Really! Well they did, and they beat me up badly and left

me half-dead. That's what they did. I was unconscious. The next thing I remembered was that I awoke in a hospital bed. I said to the doctor, 'Why have you done this for me? I fought with the Whites.' And he said, 'The war's over now, and we're all Triers again.' That was such a moment for me. Such a moment, that at long last I could rejoin society. But of course the war wasn't over, because there was still the war in the East. So I volunteered to fight and do my patriotic duty. Remember that I told you of my disbelief that such a shambolic army could have defeated us, and of course you didn't know. But I found out fighting with my new comrades. And I became one of them."

"And no regrets about the confiscated family estates?"

"Of course not," he sensed the implication of my words, and I felt that I'd gone too far. "I've told you: they were right. My family are abroad with whatever wealth they could take with them, and they have completely disowned me. And nothing could give me greater pleasure. I am a new man in a new society which could bring great benefits to the rest of the world." Here he started to be swept along by his own rhetoric, as though I hadn't heard it all before. "What you saw, Rahväema, was a broken man. That's what I was. A broken man amongst broken men."

"Yes, I know. But I thought no less of you for that." That pulled him up short. He hadn't expected this, and it was the truth. But it was also extremely well-chosen, and if there was a chance of avoiding the labour camps, it would come from this. I couldn't know, but I felt that it was. "My husband fought against the Whites for three years and lost his life in doing so." I had decided to gloss over the fact that it was the Reds that killed him. That was probably on my file, but I sensed that I had found a way to his heart and would tell no more lies or even distortions of the truth.

"Yes, I seem to remember you telling me something about that," he said thoughtfully. "I understand your suffering."

That was a line that lifted my heart; the conversation had

moved from him to me, and he had to think about that. Every word in this conversation had to be analysed, and I couldn't afford the slightest error.

"I remember you very well – and the assistance you gave us," he continued. "I never thought that I would see you again, and certainly not in these circumstances." He sat down in his chair and appeared to be doing nothing – to be exhausted and dreamlike, but it is more likely that he was going through all the possible repercussions of his predicament. This meant that part of him was saying that he had to help me, and yet another part was unconvinced.

He looked at me with a mix of perplexity and embarrass-ment, said nothing, fidgeted a bit and then gave me that same look. Someone knocked at the door, and a brisk young woman came in a placed some papers on his desk. He hardly looked at her, and muttered a thank-you. She sensed an unusual ten-sion in the room, and also held her silence. The latch bolt seemed to click very loudly when she closed the door behind her. An empty quietude filled the room and an air of unreality enveloped the two of us, while our thoughts set off on the very different trajectories – each of us with our own fears, feelings and solitude. Of the two, I was probably the more hopeful because behind me I had three days of terror and besides I had to take advantage of this unexpected opportunity. He on the other hand had security behind him, a new faith and a position in society. Why would he risk those for someone who could no longer be of use? Only if he had a conscience and a belief in something beyond his own survival.

When he spoke, his voice was slightly cracked, as though some mechanism in his throat had jammed, and it betrayed his emotion. The last thing a man like him would have wanted. "You understand that there is a legal process here, and I have to follow it rigorously. This is a different society from the one we had before; personal relationships have nothing to do with it."

Of course this was double blow, because not only did this

not bode well for me, but it wasn't true as he must have known. Yet this was not Osip and me having one of our debates. The truth was in second or third place. Or perhaps not there at all. It was a game of chess, and I had to think a few moves ahead. "I fully understand, comrade. I wouldn't dream of putting you in a compromising situation. You must examine the facts of the case and come to your decision. I am here to be interrogated."

This didn't help him at all. His discomfort increased, and there was another long silence.

"Rahväema, I will be frank with you, because we have suffered together. The past cannot be entirely scrubbed out, as though there was only the present, but on the other hand our generation has a particular debt that it has to pay to the future."

This gave me hope, and of course I held my tongue.

"I have to admit," he continued with some difficulty, "that some things have happened that shouldn't have, but it was never going to be easy and everyone and every society has to make mistakes – often mistakes with the best of intentions, namely the defence of the fatherland against foreign provocateurs. You understand that?"

I nodded of course.

"The task we have is to weather the storm – to save this bold society from the dangers of evil forces – and in our zeal we occasionally go too far. It may be that we have to, because if in our fear of acting unjustly we could allow some evildoer to get past us, untold misery would result."

I nodded in the pause.

"Ours is not an easy profession and it is one of great responsibility."

At this stage I thought that some little platitude might persuade him that I was fully aware of his difficulties. "Public morality must always take precedence over private morality, of course."

"Well said, Comrade Rahväema," and the tension his

physiognomy described so clearly was slightly relieved. "I couldn't have put it better myself. I have decided to terminate this ... conv... this interrogation as you have so correctly defined it, and I will go through your papers very carefully and come to my impartial decision. And we will resume this interrogation tomorrow morning." Now that he had decided not to decide, he appeared greatly reassured. We had more or less resumed our proper positions in the relationship, and he was once more in full control. At least for the moment.

The guards were summoned, and having received no counter orders from him, they were just as rough with me as they usually were in taking me from and back to my cell. And yet I was happy.

During that night, I had a very powerful dream about civilisation and its discontents. Like all dreams, it didn't survive the passage from sleep to wakefulness in its entirety. As can so often happen, all that survived was the sense of what happened, and the various bits didn't fit together. But I was so affected by it, that I wrote it down and, as I wrote it down, I made a few changes, additions and subtractions:

The Parable of the Socialist Realist Woman

In 1905, a mutinous sailor was shot on a street in Petrograd by a sniper as he and his comrades marched through the city, and at the moment of his death, his daughter was born and cried in a poor suburb of the capital. They tried to calm her, but she wouldn't stop. They checked her for all the conditions that upset a baby but couldn't find one of them. She cried for days and then for weeks. She stared at her mother as though furious that she had been brought into such a world, and she only stopped crying when she started to dream of a perfect world in which there was no violence, everyone worked hard and there was no strife. All they wanted to do was work and march, and they all marched in the same direction even though no one seemed to know exactly what that direction was. And they sang continuously in their joy, though they weren't absolutely sure what their joyfulness was all about.

Nevertheless she grew up strong, her features chiselled by some divine hand, her chest exhaled the health and healthy thoughts of her organism, and inhaled the force and right-eousness of the new regime that came in her childhood. She could lift a sledgehammer as though it were a twig and work endless back-to-back shifts at the coalface, or make hay from dawn to dusk without putting down her pitchfork. But she never did.

Her trade was much more important than such humble tasks and involved standing absolutely still with either a hammer or a sickle in her hand. She was a model for sculptors and artists who were representing the workers to themselves and to anyone else who believed in the new order.

For some reason, she always had to stand next to a man who was also strong and handsome, and would have been working from dawn to dusk if it weren't for this important task of representing the power and confidence of the working class. She resented his presence, and he may very well have thought the same of her. He may very well have thought that though she was strong, he was stronger still, and though she was steadfast, he was still more steadfast.

The Socialist Realist Woman said to herself, "Sometimes I feel like I'm made of stone – I feel that I cannot feel – that I'm so concentrated on conforming to an idea that I cannot enjoy my divergence – that my heart is as flabby as my muscles are taught. In fact my muscles are always flexed, unaware that being is not an idea but a collection of conflicting ideas that obtain meaning from that conflict. An idea that exists in solitude is necessarily static. I am oppressed by stasis even as I wield my sledgehammer or cast my seeds and my body glows with sweat. I am chilled by my own perfection."

She asked the Socialist Realist Man if he occasionally felt the same way. He laughed histrionically and a little diabolically, not without a tinge of self-irony but very subdued. "Of course not, not when I'm doing the hardest and most taxing job of all: symbolising the immense efforts we are all committed to in the construction of a socialist fatherland. Sometimes I come home and my wife asks me if I've worked, and I reply, 'Yes, I have been symbolising myself into an allegory all day long until the sweat dripped from my forehead and my powerful limbs started to flag. But I was steadfast.' It is not an easy job being perfect, but when I feel my strength flagging, I think of the fatherland and my strength revives."

The Socialist Realist Woman was very depressed to hear this. She never flagged and rarely thought about the fatherland. What is there to think? Her problem was stasis – her inability to feel. She had her suspicions that the Socialist Realist Man was telling lies. It was very difficult to find a spouse in this line of work. Who would want to marry a statue for a start? Who would marry someone who had so little conversation? Who would marry someone was so unspeakably perfect?

Her anger at the Socialist Realist Man was the only real emotion she'd ever felt, and so it was unsurprising that one of the days in which she was holding the hammer and he the sickle, she made an enormous effort to move her powerful muscles and swing the hammer as hard as she could into his muscly abdomen. The Socialist Realist Man shattered into a thousand pieces which radiated outwards like an exploding star. Some fragments even struck the Socialist Realist Woman and she steadfastly brushed them aside.

The nation was now in a state of great agitation. The politburo had been notified, and they of course instructed the NKVD, who promptly appeared at the Socialist Realist Woman's pedestal and arrested her forthwith. Arresting a statue proved to be serious business and they had to request a large van, after two agents had spent no less than an hour trying to handcuff her.

All legal experts agreed that this was a serious case of

mutiny and that she should have a military trial, partly on the sound basis that military men are less likely to feel ridiculous when judging the behaviour of a statue. A court martial is always going to find the accused guilty unless the accused were accused of something exceptionally bloodthirsty such as torturing prisoners-of-war or machine-gunning the entire population of a village, including women and children. In which case the accused will be acquitted and given a medal one year later. So she was condemned to twenty-five years of hard labour.

Off she went to the labour camp where she could finally work from dawn to dust in a manner that would have put Stakhanov to shame. She got so much work done that her fellow-prisoners could put their feet up, which made her tremendously popular. She really did feel the sweat on her brow, and she really did feel that she was making a difference and contributing to society. And most exhilaratingly she really did feel alive as she paid her debt to society. And strangely enough, it was all a storm in a teacup, because society quickly moved on and forgot all about the Socialist Realist Couple.

*

As the readers will now also be expecting, the scribe is not happy with this one either. There never was any doubt about that. I want to get back the interrogation, but I will add a few lines that put this little story in the context of more recent history: like the Noisy Musics would later argue, the Triers in this period believed that happiness could be manufactured. The real difference is that the Noisy Musics would think that it could be summoned up by the self, and the Triers thought that this could be done by the collectivity. Even though the Triers barely uttered a sentence without the word "dialectic", they struggled to understand the concept, and the Noisy Musics – more simplistic still – thought that happiness was a hare to be hunted. Only because I am a Surelik and an outsider could I find myself unable to believe in the supposed bright future of the Triers' wonderful new state. For me, the tumult of ideas was incessant and irresolvable, whilst my friends and colleagues in the majority community placed their confidence in the "scientific" necessity of progress.

The following morning I was taken back to see my interrogator. Nothing in his face gave a hint of what he intended to do, which I took to be a bad sign.

"Rahväema Ranavutavskaya Ilusadeva, I have read the papers in your file and I have found that you most definitely have a case to answer."

He said this with complete bureaucratic confidence – a speaking-clock of a man who takes no responsibility for his actions because they are governed by higher authorities – and then he looked at me as though I should clap, such was his belief in what he would surely have called "his integrity".

I responded with an asymmetric smile carefully engineered to express my disdain for his inability to rise above his "professional" station.

He got the message and stood up. He walked backwards and forwards behind his desk as though he were on stage and I were his audience. Occasionally he would turn his head to scrutinise my expression, and I attempted to maintain my ironic smile as best I could, though it would not have been easy at the best of times, which these weren't.

He stopped and looked at me angrily. "Do you think that you're a special case?"

I remained silent and smiled.

"Do you realise how many prisoners come through here in a week?"

I said nothing, and sustained his glare.

He came towards me threateningly. "Many, many people from all backgrounds come here for interrogation. The dangerous, the very dangerous and occasionally, yes I'll admit it, the innocent. I've admitted that already. We don't allow them to sleep. We don't give them any food. We interrogate them for hours." And then in a lower voice, "We have them beaten. In order to get at the truth, you understand. Why should you escape that trail of misery? Maybe you're innocent, but I can't be sure."

"Guilty of what? Guilty of sleeping with a man who was sleeping with a woman one of Yezhov's men fancied? Are these the priorities of the regime that wants to save humanity?"

He came closer and raised his hand to strike me. I tried not to, but I winced – and he dropped his arm. He circled round the room and then rushed back to grab me by the shoulders. He shook me violently and shouted, "Do you think that I'm going to put at risk everything I've been fighting for? Just because you gave us a hand long ago. How to snare rabbit!" He was still shaking me, but not so hard. "We're not talking about rabbits here. We're talking about the grand issues of history. The fate of nations. The liberation of millions from drudgery and bestialisation. It will be a long road, and I probably won't see the day, but I shall fulfil my duties with exemplary rigour."

"By torturing the innocent? In Surelik, we say, 'If you beat a dog, don't expect it to bark.' It won't get very far."

Here he almost lost all self-control. I say "almost" because he refused to strike me. Something held him back, and I cannot say what it was. Some things never become clear, but what I definitely saw in his eyes was fear. Whether it was fear for his own safety or fear for his own sincerely held beliefs I have never been able to fathom.

"Your afraid, aren't you?" I asked, "Admit that you're afraid."

This was the last straw. He released his grip and walked away. He rang a bell, and two guards appeared. Probably different ones. I barely noticed, as I was terrified myself. I was alone. Just as Osip would have been in that moment. I would possibly not see a friendly face for years. In the camps they would look on me as a foreigner, and some of the convicted criminals would vent their racist ferocity on me whilst camp guards would look on with indifference. I had gone too far.

I had said too much. I had lost my chance. Or perhaps there never had been a chance.

Having noticed my interrogator's anger, the guards gave me a beating in the cell and left me in a pool of blood, which almost definitely worked in my favour. For when they dragged me for the third interrogation after a night with very little sleep, I must have looked a pitiful sight when they placed me on the chair. "Oh my god, what have you done?" was all he said to them.

And they replied surlily, "Nothing to do with us. Ask yesterday afternoon's shift. Is this work getting too much for you?" They left to get on with their day's labour.

"Rahväema, I'm so sorry," he said in a soft voice - as though to a hurt child.

I could barely speak and had lost a tooth. Several replies offered themselves to me, but I settled for: "A fine utopia you have here!"

He ignored the remark in a way he would not have the day before. Tiredness crossed his face like the drawing of a curtain. What had originally been his intentions that morning, I cannot tell you. But the man before me was now one put to shame. Everyone has their limit, where humanity finally rebels. That is what I believe, and the more cynical of you can continue to think differently. There are psychopaths, I suppose, but I'm no expert. The powerful are all at least slightly psychotic, I expect, but nearly all the people I've met during my life have not been. Perhaps it was luck. It certainly was luck in the case of Andrei Alexeyevich. There would be no more discussion of duty and history and the liberation of the masses. He crouched so that he was at my level and said very simply, "I'll get you out of here."

I know nothing of his life at the time. Whether or not he was married or had children. Whether he had friends or was a loner. Whether he had other pursuits beyond his work and his passion for order. And he knew very little about me except, I suppose, what he had read in the reports. It took a few days in the cells before I was released. How he managed it is another mystery, and the more important unanswered question is whether he managed to do it without consequences for himself. What I can say is that he must have followed me after my release, because shortly afterwards he appeared and took me to the station. He gave me papers for going to Väikelinn, a train ticket and more than enough money for the final leg overland. I tried to hug him, but he resisted. The civilised are sometimes quite incomprehensible.

So I left the city with a battered face, a battered heart and a battered ambition. I had studied the culture of the triers and the wider European context to which it belongs. I did this not to obtain an education that they could endorse, but to understand my enemy and how to minimise the hurt they could inflict on us, or this is what I told myself. At the time, I didn't understand many things; for one, I believed that all the Triers were well-versed in their own cultures and had read all the classic writers, such as Tolstoy, Dostoyevsky, Turgenev and Gogol. People may laugh at my naivety, and I see my dutiful scribe smiling benignly in my direction. No need for condescension as I see no shame in this. Far from it. What concerns me here is what I'd lost: by engaging with the Triers' culture, I had become deeply rooted in the enemy camp. It wasn't so much of a problem when I was isolated and defeated, but it would be when I became more powerful and the fine line between representing the Surelikud to the Triers and the Triers to the Surelikud would become blurred.

I don't deny that I also gained a great deal. I learnt to reason more deeply – for this is not an innate ability – and this did help me in my struggle. But the time had come to get back to my roots and relearn what I should never have forgotten. I knew that the Triers' civilisation, like all the other ones, was rotten to the core.

On arriving at Väikelinn, I decided to stay for a few days and meet some of my old friends. When I turned up at Tatyana's house, she was sitting on one of the wooden steps that went up to the front door – relaxed and relaxing in the autumn sunlight. She greeted me lovingly, and immediately invited me in.

"When I heard that you were back here, I prepared some food." She waved her hand at the spread. As she didn't know when I would come, she had bought sausages and cold meats as well as Moldavan wine.

"You shouldn't have."

"Why not? I'm in charge here now, and I know what a terrible greeting you got last time. I'm going to make it up to you."

"You're mad."

"I know. Even my son says that. But sometimes ... well, it just seems the right thing to do."

"How do you mean ... in charge now? Has your husband left you?"

"I'm afraid he has. But not voluntarily. The NKVD, no less, came and took him away. I've no idea what it was about. But a week or so beforehand, he spoke to me at the breakfast table very solemnly, 'Tanya, there are terrible things happening in this country. They are coming in the night and taking people away.'

"I had gone to the sink to get a glass of water, and I then did terrible thing: I picked up a knife and threw it at him. 'How dare you insult the fatherland!' I shouted, and I had never returned his violence with violence of my own, but something snapped. 'And you're a fine one, you snitched on my father, and who knows where he went.' He didn't deny it: 'Yes, because he was a counter-revolutionary, but this is different. They're picking up all the communists. Not the dissidents, but anyone they feel like. It's crazy. I'm very frightened because they took away Vladimir Nikolayevich who, as you know, has been my patron. I owe everything to him. I'm a loyal communist. Why should I be afraid?' Then I felt sorry for him and ashamed of my behaviour." She laughed, "Just as well he ducked, because otherwise I'd be the one in the camps as a common criminal. I knew that it was serious because he didn't react to my vicious attack. He wasn't a good man, but he was my husband and the father of my son. I can't say that I miss him much, which troubles me. He wasn't easy on the boy either. Anyway let's talk of other things."

I listened and said nothing. She was right. At the time of the Kirov's assassination, we had believed many of the regime's lies, but later we all became more sceptical. There is a moment in all regimes when their lies lose credibility, and regimes can never understand why. They just keep going.

I offered her some money, which she refused. Later I would hear that she too was sent to the camps with a twenty-five-year sentence, but she only served eight. But that was much later.

I left for the safety of the forest – for my home and the creator of all I was or had been. I would pass most of the war there. I had a few books in Surelik and the language of the Triers, which I had stocked up on whilst I was in Väikelinn, and I was able to get more on my rare visits to the town which always came with the risk of arrest for vagrancy. I have never understood why that should be considered a crime, and yet civilisations never stop boasting about the freedoms they have brought to humanity. So my studies were not entirely interrupted, but there were considerable obstructions. My experience of learning is that a few (but not too many) obstructions galvanise the student to greater efforts.

The land of the Triers was increasingly in turmoil. War had been in the air for a long time, and then it happened in the West. Then a year or two later, the Beer Cellars opened up an eastern front: their invasion came like a massive rupture in a dyke. Not only did the flood kill humans and animals alike, it changed the landscape. Cities and towns disappeared; the land was pockmarked with craters and where there had been green, brown mud oozed and resembled a lifeless, toxic substance – or perhaps more correctly a pustulation caused not by the methods of modern warfare, as was the case, but rather by some strange disease that had infected the earth itself. The disaster derived from a mix of political ideas, the power of modern bureaucracy and the human machinery of death, but it felt like a biblical plague. A force that came from the heavens and could not be stopped. But it would be, after more suffering for the Triers on a colossal scale which the world would intentionally and quite shamefully forget.

For a bit it seemed all over and that defeat was irreversible and the enemy's advance unremitting in its apparent efficiency. We knew that the wave was coming closer bearing its well-equipped army of hate, which was pitiless in the business of killing men, women and children. In every city, town or village they conquered, they requisitioned the food and homes, and left the people to starve and freeze in the open. And later when they retreated, they took everything and burnt the house down. Surely the consciences of one or two must have been moved to the odd act of clemency, but memoirs appear to suggest not. The population was to be more than halved and the survivors enslaved by the colonists who were supposed to follow. That was their plan. They believed that the Triers were subhuman. God knows what they would have thought of the Surelikud if they had ever got as far east as where we lived, and then it really did seem only a matter of time. But that was their mistake and eventually the waters of vile hatred were spread too thin and they sank into the mud of their own making.

When winter came, the mud turned to a hard brown rock that seemed to prophesy a dead unchanging planet. This could have been a prophesy of what still awaits us. The Beer Cellars were defeated by the courage and sacrifice of the Triers, and also by the vastness of the Triers' lands and the vastness of the Beer Cellar's rapacious greed. So many people to kill and replace, and so many resources to capture – and it looked so doable. But no map could explain the vastness of their project and their desires and ambitions. All in the name of progress of course, because humanity had to be bred like the best horses. But would horses know how to choose the best horses? Humans breed horses not in the interests of horses, but for their own very specific purposes. Only nature knows to breed properly through its law of diversity.

No general who flew to the frontline could conceive the vastness of the land, because to understand that, you have to drive, ride or even walk across it, carrying equipment and limited supplies. The rules of war - always an atrocious game - appeared to be overturned in the name of progress and racial superiority. Mules and men of inferior races struggled stubbornly to supply the conquerors, and left their bones along the roadsides, when the road could be found. Finite resources spread across a vastness that appeared to be infinite, whatever the map said when unfolded on a table. In that neat representation, a general could observe and dream - unconscious of who and what he had become. Something even his countrymen would in later decades despise and feel ashamed of. But he didn't know that then. He couldn't think that. He couldn't imagine that, because a different future had been written in his head.

If vastness was the necessary element for defeating evil, then how can God exist? The Triers' God, the Beer Cellar's God, the Beautiful Ceilings' God, the Little Noisy Musics' God. The same God, but apparently supporting all the sides, if the Churches were to be believed. My beliefs were lost in the vastness of history and of the Triers' lands, and all I wanted was the comfort of the forest again. The chance to escape the vicious cruelty of civilisation and return to the innocence of a small domestic world whose greatest ambition is the next meal offered up generously by the wooded land. What hope is there if, once lost, such things can never be regained. I am not a good witness as I was mainly absent and, besides, others have done such an excellent job. Mine was a different story - the story of the periphery that apparently never matters but was always in credit, giving much more than it could take or want to take in terms of both goods and men. The Triers were using us again, as well as all their other minorities. For many decades, their men would be ageing in the absence of a limb or two. Did the "mother country" really appreciate their sacrifice, which very probably they gave willingly to prevent the unthinkably immense barbarities of the Beer Cellars, one of the most civilised countries in the world? For that matter did the rest of the world value the sacrifices of all the Triers in that most cruel of wars – particularly for non-combatants? History is written by propaganda and not real events in the cold mud that is the substance of the obscenity we call war.

The elk shall travel the forests until finds its fellow kind. And so it was. I wandered and first found almost no one, and none of them Surelikud but only Triers keeping out of sight. Mainly criminals and young men who wanted to avoid war at all costs either out of fear or principle. I kept going and then I found the first Surelik encampment with their traditional huts. When I saw them again, they looked like palaces. Once you have lived inside an NKVD cell, everything is luxurious, even a Surelik "shack" as my scribe likes to call them. Of course it was more than that: it was memories of childhood and friendship, where everyone was part of everyone else and no one was a stranger. I remember those crowds in the capital, and how they rushed along and did not see each other – did not want to know each other. At first, it had been a shock, but eventually I became more like them. Now I was back home.

The Tank

The invention of the tank could not be more different from that of the radio, however self-important that voice through the ether may have been (today it is a modest, diminutive, transistorised object to match its educative, self-effacing role now that populism and pomposity have gone elsewhere to have their voices heard). The tank has no saving graces and never will have; in fact it is a graceless monster, a blasphemous curse and a reminder of all the energy that goes into destruction. As an object, it is ugly beyond measure, and whilst it started with a degree of quirky cloddishness, its continuous enlargement and streamlining have only made it uglier. Nations display their tanks with pride and their politicians like to be photographed pretending to drive one, when they should have been ashamed of them and talking to their confessors.

The tank was invented by the Little Noise Musics during the war that led to our revolution. They supplied six of them to the Whites who besieged Petrograd. They came out of Estonia with regular troops and a white army, and the long-suffering city experienced the first of its two sieges and resulting famines during the last century. The Leather Glove appeared on his train and pushed them back, but only because the clumsy creatures kept falling into craters and rivers from which they couldn't extricate themselves. Half-blind, their biggest danger was themselves, but in a cavalry war they could kill untold numbers of people.

This Great Patriotic War was the first and perhaps the last war in which the tank would play a primary role. It was technology that could go almost everywhere but, like heavily armed cavalry, it was best suited to the open plain, and then the numbers counted as did the cleverness of their design.

The tank was a carapaced Titan that escaped from Tartarus or a metallic monster worthy of H.G. Wells's *War of the Worlds*. It was the weapon for the machine age, and the people operating it, hidden inside, could have been beings from another planet, but were in fact soft-fleshed, frightened men and pawns in a gruesome game of chess. Yet it was a monster that had its articulated steel belts firmly on the ground. Whilst planes had views and space, this wretched steel box was claustrophobic and still had limited vision. Great waves of these ridiculous clockwork warhorses charged awkwardly into battle against each other, with their lances lowered and firing balls of fire, as though the helmet and the visor and had replaced the man and the horse, and the knight was rarely to be seen in the aftermath. Here the battlefield was not full of dead bodies, but merely torn metal, while the human bodies were forgotten in the cruel plenitude of industrially produced military hardware and high explosives.

*

Kurat suddenly appeared after the war, and walked confidently up to my shack. "Still wasting your time, Rahväema? You don't seem to be getting very far. You won't find anything in your studies that will help with your struggle."

"Don't you ever get a little bored with your line in wheedling cynicism. Don't you ever feel like a change?"

"Change?" he screamed in outrage. "Why would I want change? Of course there are fat times and lean times for me, but they are all my times. These last one hundred and fifty years have been wonderfully fat times. Never fatter, I would say." And then he warmed to his subject, raising his voice almost excitedly and reducing to it to whisper accompanied by a sneering smile when it came to his glosses, which should be put in brackets: "And never so linguistically inventive – such expressions as *laissez-faire* (how many starved for that one?), *menefreghismo* (that's I-couldn't-give-a-fuck-ism, such brilliance from the land of the Beautiful Ceilings, so free of nuance and moralism) and *Arbeit makt frei* (never was a promise more cruel or such cruelty dressed up with such delightfully faux moralism).

"And the cleverest are yet to come, and you'll love them when they do: 'extraordinary rendition', 'humanitarian warfare'. 'shock treatment,' all delivered with the pained expressions of the high priests of the market. You see, Rahväema, there is progress."

"On that we can agree. And only that. There's a thing called progress, and it brings only death, misery and destruction. It is the evil you delight in, and the essence of what I struggle against. I thank you for making it so clear to me."

Thankfully Halvatud also came to see me, because I will be honest once more: life in the forest lacked intellectual discussion. No, that's not right, but it lacked the kind of intellectual discussion I'd become accustomed to. And there he was in the depths of the forest. He walked into the clearing with that wry smile of his, and I could feel his contained pleasure rising within him as he came closer. He hugged me without uttering a word before reciting, "The Trees Gave Us Our Language"[9]:

> They drew. The roots they drew
> the juices of the earth –
> and how did they find them?
> But find them they did.
> All this rich bounty brought
> from the black earth we hardly see.
> Such is the maternal magnanimity
> of crumbling dark brown soil,
> the forest floor, shaded, housed indeed
> by the canopy who stole the light,
> is green with lush, lush opulence,
> a solum that blooms with jostling weeds
> who strongly know,
> "This is the last free land
> for plants and Surelik alike."

"Ah yes," I said, "without the forest there is no Surelik language. According to Suurluultaya's words, the language grew up within the humours of the trees, sprouted on the

---

9 The poem was composed by the great Surelik nineteenth-century oral poet, Suurluuletaya, who was both traditional and influenced by European Romanticism. We have attempted to render this popular anthem of the forest in passable English [*translators' note*].

forest floor and drank in the sun's warmth on the canopy, and so did I. It is everywhere within the forest, and could not survive outwith."

"But it can. It must," he said in a serious schoolmasterly voice and then smiled and hugged me once more. His feeble arms could not squeeze tight, but I still felt the warm emotion of his embrace. "So you're glad to be back in the forest?"

"I think that I am. Like you, I'm now caught between two cultures. You know, when I first walked in the city, it was like a civilised man who walks in a forest with no previous experience. He hears the wind play with the foliage, and it feels like the stirrings of some animate being, a warning perhaps, an awareness of being in an alien environment, like a whale on a beach. Occasionally the man feels that a walk in the forest is no longer as adventurous as it seemed in his warm office whose white walls shone like a cemetery, a rest home for the dead. For me the city was no less uncomfortable, and the excitement of its grandeur is diminished by the demons who watch over you and question your right to be there. The endless sequence of offices filled with seated men and some women, whose purpose is unclear but surely directed against me who in the forest never feared the wood whether it was sunlit or dark. And yet beyond the murk of diffidence and deceit, the signals of the city are so horribly transparent and crass. Stop! Go!"

He asked about my studies, and nodded in approval. We chatted about acquaintances, Väikelinn and the war. In spite of Moustache's refusal to prepare for it and perhaps because of it (since it encouraged the enemy to overstretch itself), the invaders were now in flight. One terror had thus been removed, and what's more, the Moustache had relaxed the oppression of the pre-war years and promised changes once victory had been secured, not that his promises had much currency.

"What does this mean for us?" I asked.

"Impossible to say," he replied. "A little hope perhaps. Not much, I fear. Now *there's* that word again: 'fear'. There has been so much of it in recent years. It wasn't something we really experienced in the forest, was it? Of course, when a Surelik climbs a tree, he has a proper respect for the dangers his work entails, but it is never this anxious fear not just of real dangers but those imagined in a climate of fear."

"It has been used as a political weapon."

"Of course, but you are widely read and must know that it was always thus with civilisation: they call it terror and it was always used in war. The besiegers would threaten the besieged, 'Open your city gates now, or when we finally enter we'll run amok and kill and steal and burn and rape.' And so they would if they were kept waiting, for many reasons: as a warning to other cities and as a reward to rapacious soldiers who had suffered months in death's companionship and the harsh business of overcoming city walls. Angry armies could turn on the leaders. Terror is not new, even terror inflicted on one's own citizens or subjects, if they didn't do or think as they should have. What is new is the extent of it, made possible by the efficiencies of progress, which sooner or later will arrive as mercilessly in the Surelik lands as they currently are in the Triers' ones. That is the problem we have to solve, Rahväema."

"This diffused fear, what does it do?"

"It fragments. Individuals cannot really communicate their fears to others, partly because they can't really define them or assess what most concerns them, and partly because they can't trust anyone anymore. This is recipe for national psychosis."

"And of course fear comes out of uncertainty."

"Well, this is often said, but I don't agree. It arises from a mistaken attitude to uncertainty, which will always be with us. It is not the case that people in insecure situations are the most fearful. Fearfulness is more common amongst the median classes, and reaches a frenzy amongst the powerful and the rich. Whereas those around us now, the Surelikud of the forest, live with uncertainty as a fact of life. Their death rate is undoubtedly higher, but they enjoy more time with each other and develop as an organic whole and, paradoxically enjoy greater individualism, in the sense of being their own person, than do people in civilised countries. The desire to understand – the compulsion you've now acquired and will never shake off – does not lead to greater certainty, because with every new understanding, many more unknowns and uncertainties are opened up. The trick then is to make peace with uncertainty, but continue to follow the curiosity of your intellect in the certainty that truth does exist, but the path to it will and should only lead to greater uncertainty. In short, uncertainty is an inescapable human condition and any denial of this leads to fanaticism. If you embrace it, you will no longer fear it; it becomes part of the bewildering experience of this small but uniquely fecund planet – fecund not only in flora and fauna, but also in the ideas produced by the human being, that most extraordinary product of the fertile and now much mutilated earth. We should perceive uncertainty as an invitation to an adventure that leads to the knowledge of things and the knowledge that there are still more things we do not know and which will remain unknown for long time or perhaps forever."

"You talk of practicalities, and then end up speaking of abstractions. Where does this leave us in our struggle?"

"Rahväema, you disappoint me. These 'abstractions' are fundamental to our struggle, which in any case has no chance of moving forward whilst the Moustache is around. This would in any case be the moment for 'abstractions', because I don't want you to be simply the campaigner for one of the many little peoples of this world who will face the danger of extinction in the next half century; I want you to arrive at a wider understanding of your role and that of the Surelikud. I want you to understand the global picture, whilst never losing your intellectual attachment to this, our Surelik land. It is not perfection, or if it is then only in the limited sense that it lives harmoniously within the community of the earth and the forest."

"So what are you telling me to do?"

199

"I'm telling to carry on doing what you're doing at the moment. Observe and understand your fellow Surelikud, love them and don't put yourself above them, consider the language and think about how it works in relation to the other languages you know, particularly that of the Triers. Continue to read the works of the Triers, as they have powerful things to say, but don't become a Trier – don't become anything but yourself. Humanity will win this war against the Beer Cellars, but it may not survive the peace in the long run. As the years go by you will start to understand how important the example of the Surelikud is.

"Rahväema, you have often said that the only things you liked about the priest's lesson on Christianity were the parables. We are a people who tell each other stories, after all, so of course it makes more sense to us. So I have been thinking about all the refugees and displaced peoples in the lands of the Triers and in Europe. So many peoples, great and small, fleeing in haste to other countries which have their own problems and are not always welcoming, and I have thought up this parable which I want to tell you. It is:

The Parable of the Two Kindly Men

A refugee escaped a war zone and arrived in a peaceful land. A kindly middle-aged man goes through an endless sequence of extravagant kindnesses in his treatment of her. They end up at his well-furnished home.

Eventually the woman was so overwhelmed that she said, "Your kindness has been extreme, much more than I could have dreamt of as I left my homeland in tears. I feel that I know you and trust you, so I will sleep in your bed tonight and for as long as you may want me."

"You may sleep in my bed, but I will sleep on the sofa."

"Why? Do you not find me attractive?"

"It is not that at all," he replied grandly, "but if I sleep with you, then all my kindness will turn to dust – to mere wiles and enticements. It'll become meaningless and self-interested – it will have been instrumental in seducing a young and beautiful woman who is alone and defenceless. And I would concentrate on my love of you, when actually I want to love all humanity selflessly."

"But this," the young woman said tearfully, "only makes me love you more."

"That is as may be," still adopting his detached and philosophical tone, as though engaged in an important experiment. "Moreover, I have to tell you that tomorrow, you must be on your way as I will go out into the world to find someone else in distress – whom I must give succour to for twenty-four hours."

So the next day the woman thanked him warmly and said, "I'll go as this is your wish, but however long I live, I shall never find such a good and upright man. I have thought about this in the night and I will never make love to any man but you, and if I can't have you, I will have no one. I'll live a life of celibacy, that is what I swear."

He smiled at her, clearly gratified by her love and passion, but his voice was unchanged. "Go, my dear woman and live that good life, and I shall know that we are both doing our duty." He allowed her to peck him on the cheek.

She hadn't walked for half an hour when she encountered a young man with an unhappy face who stopped in front of her and sullenly offered to carry her bags. She refused and he insisted. "I am only a defenceless woman, a refugee who has no friend in the world. I can offer you nothing in return – no food, no money, no companionship and in particular no love, for I have none left."

"That is quite adequate for me, because all I want of you is the right to serve you." And so it was that he served her unstintingly and with equally generosity of the other man, or more, because he had very little money. Time passed, and the months turned into years.

One day she said, "Why do you serve me so loyally and with

such servility? Never asking for anything except my uncompanionable company. What are you trying to prove?"

"To prove? I'm not trying anything of the kind."

"But you must be! Are you not trying to prove your goodness, if not to me at least to yourself? What is your religion? What is your philosophy?"

"I know nothing about religion and philosophy. These are for cleverer people than I am. I saw a woman and I saw that she had a good heart. I don't know exactly what that means, but I know that it's important. And I said to myself, I shall serve her if she so wishes, and demand nothing of her, because we're all free spirits. And here we are. In my ignorance, I cannot tell you where philosophy and religion come into all this."

She thought about this and came to the conclusion that she had made sacred vow to one good man but another one came along and seemed to be even better.

"Yes, dear youth, you have been kind to me and loyal to me, but asked nothing in return, so you may sleep in my bed tonight."

"Are you sure? Because I am happy as we are and would not want to push you into doing something you do not want as much as I do. I dream of you every night, but in the morning I see that you can only just tolerate me."

"This is terrible," she said and took him by the hand and led him to the bedroom.

The next day he got up early and started to prepare breakfast, and when she came into the room, she sat down under the weight of some personal misery.

"I haven't slept last night because I have broken a sacred vow." And she told him the whole story of the older man's kindness and how he had refused her love. She thought that he would understand and commiserate with her, but her story had an entirely different reaction. She was so used to his submissiveness that she thought that this was all he was.

"Let me understand," he asked coldly, "this other man was kind to you for a day, and I have been kind for many years which are made of many months, weeks and days, but until last night you couldn't show me any kindness in return. And now, not twelve hours later you recant, and feel guilty to someone more interested in his halo than where humans meet humans on an equal footing, and see only who each other are and try to get along. A necessary but difficult task.

"I cannot forgive such treachery, in spite of the years I've spent with you. I'll leave you as I met you with the clothes on my body and a little money in my pouch. I leave you to your vow and I leave you to your memories of a single day."

With that, he left.

And what did she feel about that? You think that she ran after him and fell on her knees and begged, and he eventually gave in and returned to the house where they lived happily ever after, as befits a romantic tale.

Not at all!

No, she was quite uncertain about how she felt. He had a point, she could not deny that, but did she impose that other vow he made to himself – that he would gift to her his life of sacrifice? No, she had never asked for it. She took some tea from the samovar and went to the sofa, where she kicked off her shoes, so that she could meditate in peace. After a few minutes, she smiled to herself and said, "These men, what do they want? The people in this land are far too complicated, and wish too much to be good." But of the two the best one has just left the house. Did she love him? Perhaps, or was it more that she was in the habit of him – always there, always willing, a presence who was genuinely kindly without trying and who impinged but little on her life – or so it appeared.

Meanwhile the angry man, the hurting man was counting up the days, months and years of his sacrifice that had been valued so little by her. The blinkers of love had been removed from his eyes, and he knew that he could never feel the same about her again. On he went and his anger subsided a bit, and he thought to himself, "No, I could never love her again in the same way." But he would miss her. She gave him a purpose in life. She had a good heart, that was true even though he never really understood what that meant. Even a philosopher probably couldn't define what it was. In fact he could bet on it, though he never knew what a philosopher was either. As for a theologian, he wouldn't even know where to start on such a question. A good heart meant little, when there were all those sophistries to have fun with. Rituals and hidden meanings. Philosophers and theologians love such things.

Back at the house, she drank her tea and smiled at her freedom. Men, who needs them, she thought. But then lunch came, and she had to make her own lunch. This was not much of a problem. Slightly diverting, in fact. But the idea of the evening meal was looming behind that lunch, and she realised that her routines were about to change. By mid afternoon she was even considering whether she should run after him, as you most probably thought she should have, no sooner had he departed from their door. She didn't know which direction to run in, and besides she soon realised that even if she did beg him to return, he would never feel the same way about her.

Supper came.

She could hardly be bothered. Now she was feeling angry with him. Would she run after him? Only to slap him on the face! And yet she was slightly bemused by her own feelings. Was this perhaps how marriage worked? The imperiousness of habit. But it would wear off. In two months she would have forgotten him.

And in her ravings not once did she think of the middle-aged saint to whom she'd promised eternal chastity.

Late in the evening she heard the latch on the door and a blast of cold air. There was no sound now, but she knew the young man was in the house. Even now her joy was not unalloyed.

He entered sheepishly, but she recognised that he was as conflicted as she was. Older than him and a woman, she knew instinctively that talking it through would lead to an argument. He started to speak, but she pushed her index finger across his lips even as he articulated some lost word: "This is not the time for talking or even apologising. This is the time for ... action ... physicality ... the comfort of togetherness ... call it what you will."

"Then why are you talking," he complained.

"Shhhh!" she smiled, and they lived together ever after. I cannot say that they did it happily, but I can confirm that they didn't do it unhappily either. It was a bit of both, mixed in endlessly differing proportions, just like most people. The spell of the pious man's evil was broken, and they never mentioned him again.

*

Well, reader, that was all very clear. Halvatud is good at anything he turns his shaky hands to. Surely the scribe won't have anything to complain about this time. ... But I'm mistaken, and this argument we'll record in full. It will be extremely worthwhile.

Scribe: Now I understand where all these parables came from. That Halvatud was behind it all along. To my mind he turned your head, and not in the right direction. And there's something else that's becoming all too clear, you have been reading far too many books.

Rahväema: You sound like the old man in Väikelinn who spooked Osip Steinberg ...

Scribe: ... and prophesised correctly.

Rahväema: Sadly yes, he prophesised correctly. And he also told me that it was wrong to put our language onto paper – that we learn from life and not from books.

Scribe: And he was more right than wrong!

Rahväema: He was right to say that we learn from life, but it takes a lifetime to learn from life, so why not read a few books and learn what other people learnt from life – and get ahead. Many books, if they've been read by different societies and over many centuries, must have been written by insightful authors. Some degree of wisdom must have been accrued.

Scribe: Yes, but you can exaggerate.

Rahväema: You can exaggerate in anything, it's true. As an addiction it's fairly benign, besides I have always told myself that I did it for a purpose. Halvatud thought so, as you can tell from the conversation I just dictated to you.

Scribe: Halvatud again. Do you really think that this memoir – or whatever you want to call it – will be edifying for young Surelik minds?

Rahväema: I do.

Scribe: His parable is utterly improbable. The plot's insane. It's stylised like some nutty religious text. It has no psychological depth. And who are these people and where are they from?

Rahväema (sighs): The plot is intentionally improbable. Those are very improbable characters, but in less extreme but more complex forms they can be found. It's an apologue or moral fable.

Scribe: Moral? Doesn't sound very moral to me.

Rahväema: I think that our Surelik morality is more a morality of the self. It is about self-criticism and not being judgemental of others. Particularly in their sexual behaviour.

Scribe (spluttering): What nonsense! You're giving them a blank sheet of paper.

Rahväema: It's not my business to give anyone instructions at all – no sheet of paper was requested and none will be given – either blank or covered with new commandments. Haven't we had enough of that in the last century? All Halvatud is saying is that sexual fidelity is not the most important thing. In fact it's not important at all. What's important is to have authentic relationships – honest relations – true dialogues in which both interlocutors engage, listen, consider and either agree or decide respectfully to disagree. That can't be legislated by state or church, because only the individuals involved know what's going on in their own heads, and even then their knowledge is not complete because much is hidden from the conscious mind.

Scribe: Well, if that's all it is, why go to the trouble of inventing all that rubbish. It's not entertaining, you know. It's quite embarrassing really.

Rahväema: Scribe, you can be a very tiresome person. I've probably told you that many times, and I should thank you for continuing to assist me with my work, sometimes by raising these objections of yours which will be shared by others, no doubt. I am not attempting merely to entertain you or anyone else, because this would produce a book that I would consider very dull. I am attempting to engage with people, but more than that I'm trying to go beyond those who may find me entertaining and persuasive. This leads to the primary purpose of my memoir, which is not so much to persuade people of my opinions as to provoke new thoughts, which hopefully will go in directions I have never thought of.

As for Halvatud's parable, it is much more than rejecting judgementalism; it warns against those saints who despise people and only perceive them as a means to demonstrate their own virtue, and it advises against making promises to govern an unknowable future. This is not a great deal, and may also be obvious to subtle minds, but he did no harm by turning these thoughts into a story. He was also saying that when we help others, we should not humiliate them, and by helping them we take on a long-term commitment to help them in the future. Equitable and reliable assistance is a task of the state, and the task of the individual is to help those closest to them in any way they can without thoughts of getting anything in return.

Scribe (sighs): What a lot of fantasies! Rahväema, sooner or later you're going to listen to me and thank me for talking common sense.

Rahväema: Ah, how many terrible crimes have been committed in the name of common sense.

Scribe: And how many more by the dictatorship of unrealistic fantasies.

Rahväema: And that too, which is why uncertainty should be embraced.

Scribe: I don't see much of that in you.

Rahväema: That's because, dear scribe, you're half blind. Anyway, thank God that we're Surelikud who will never rule the world or want to. Can we agree on that, dear Kiryutaya?

Scribe: Don't talk down to me, Rahväema. You started this conversation by reminding me of what a tiresome person I am, and I will finish it by reminding you of what an arrogant and manipulative person you are.

Rahväema: I am arrogant. Sometimes, I'll admit. I have to be, as I'm on my own.

Scribe: What about your Halvatud?

Rahväema: Halvatud is no longer with us, but you're making me run ahead of my story. I'm not looking for pity. I chose my path and I have to stick to it. Frankly it hasn't worked out as well as I'd hoped. Not at all, in fact.

Scribe: Were you hoping that the Surelikud would rule the Triers, or that they would be more reasonable, every other month perhaps?

Rahväema: Now the conversation has become foolish. Let's drop it. It's undignified. I apologise for my rudeness on occasions, but the truth is that you irritate me very much, as I do you. We're opposites and to some extent our conversations help guide the reader through this book. That's why I chose you, and you accepted, remember, because I promised to ensure that you become my replacement when I retire or die. No, no, don't take to the moral high ground. Let's be honest with ourselves, because we have at last started to do that. You know this is the case, so don't object. We're both getting something out of this, but I have to say that you genuinely were my first choice, not because I think that you'll make a great job of it. You're simply the best pup in a bad litter. You can bark, but you couldn't even follow the scent of a skunk on heat.

While I wait, I'll type in for the reader's information that the scribe has left the room to cool off for a bit. We will resume the dictation in ten minutes. That's the way we work!
    I should have mentioned that when Halvatud came to the forest after the war, he was wearing a leather bomber jacket.
    "I've heard about these," I said, "how did you get hold of it? They're very expensive."
    "It's second hand," he said, "and it keeps me very warm. I owe my life to this jacket."
    "Even second hand, they're expensive."
    "You're right. And when I say second hand, I mean somebody handed it to me with a ten-rouble note."

"Lucky man. Who was it who gave it to you?"

"All he said was, 'This is supposed to be socialism'."

"And then?"

"He walked off. He was an army officer, I believe."

"Osip would have loved it, with all those zips - and all those pockets. It's a pity we don't have anything to put in them. One day, perhaps."

"I couldn't see Osip in one."

"Oh no, he wouldn't have worn one, not even if he met your generous officer. He would have seen it as an object typical of modernity, a metaphor for the next modernity, a garment that suggests not only practicality in design but also a promise of better things to come, because it is a highly masculine statement of confidence. Don't take this badly, but it doesn't suit you."

"I know it doesn't! That's why I wear it - even more important than its warmth. I don't know the motives of the kind officer. Humanity certainly, but perhaps also a sense of humour."

If I had known the term at the time, I would have called Halvatud an ambulating work of conceptual art - a living paradox: the coat of machismo inhabited by the courageous man almost free - or should I say totally free - of the defects of human masculinity. We didn't only talk of our struggle for Surelik autonomy, but also of other things, many other things and often of Osip. We talked and we laughed, another element that no life should lack, though in those unforgiving years it was as sparse as dried leaves in the spring.

I'm going to leap over a very long period of my life - two periods really. Firstly I continued to live in the safety of the forest even after the war had ended, and Halvatud stayed with me. I read, I wrote and I discussed things at length with him. It was the period in which we became intimate friends. It was a lifestyle that was both relaxed and busy. The business of survival claimed a part of the day, but not too much - perhaps a quarter of my waking hours - and my studies took perhaps another half, which left a substantial remainder to chat and enjoy the company of my fellow Surelikud. Then in the late forties, Halvatud announced that he was going back to Väikelinn and possibly on to the capital. He suggested that I follow him in six months to a year, when the spirit moved me. When I did that, various things happened; I'll not go into them here and I don't think that they're very relevant to my story. The Thaw would come in the fifties and suddenly I found myself in a very new environment which I could exploit for our cause. History started to speed up, and our story reaches its climax.

The Moustache died, and the Gulag was emptied. In the not quite three-quarters of a century that the regime survived, it never came up with a workable system for succession, so after a fractious interregnum, Khrushchev took the reins of the vast territory of the Triers' lands. The scribe, sensitive to my every inconsistency, has drawn my inattentive attention to the fact that Khrushchev has got his own name, and isn't called the Fat Little Man in the absence of anything particularly remarkable about him. But as the astute reader has probably already guessed he was the man who laid bare all of the Moustache's horrific crimes against so many innocents, my beloved Osip included. He wasn't a saint, and he had Imre Nagy shot. No doubt he felt that, given the brutal and hard-fought suppression of the Greeks by the Noisy Musics and the Little Noisy Musics and the failed invasion of Egypt by the Little Noisy Musics and the Viticulturalists, the Triers could not relinquish their own pawn on the international chess board, and the land of the primitive Surelikud's supposedly civilised descendants would quite possibly have contributed to his being driven from power a few years later. It's also true that an enemy's crimes can never exonerate one's own, but as the reader – whether astute or not – will shortly discover, I have other reasons for being grateful to this little man.

As soon as I could,[10] I set about my life's work with vigour. This initially meant building a network of people who held dear the language and culture of Surelikud. This was a long and complex process, which doesn't lend itself to a narrative like this, but it was the most crucial and fruitful work I ever did. It was principally a corresponding society, though in the capital and Väikelinn meetings were held, often in people's homes. These meeting could be political, but equally they could be cultural events at which traditional songs were sung and readings were given of poetry and prose in Surelik – mostly unpublished. Gradually we engaged in street events, starting in Väikelinn and then more boldly in the capital. After much discussion it was decided in 1956 that one should be held in Red Square, and I travelled with some difficulty to the capital to take part.

It was a cold spring morning and there was still some snow on the ground. Disappointingly there were only about fifty people there or sixty at the most. Many had clearly thought the better of it at the last moment, and as it happened, this wouldn't make much difference. No sooner had we started to hand out a few hurriedly cyclostyled leaflets than a solitary militiaman appeared. He looked bored and at this stage relatively unconcerned.

"If you hang around here, I'll have to arrest you," he said in a world-weary drawl. "Don't make me do it; it's not as easy as it used to be. I'll have to explain myself and that's time and paperwork."

"Arrest us! Arrest me! Do you think I care?" I shouted.

"You see what they've done. They've diminished their own authority; there has to be fear. Or no one will do a damn thing, and they'll be protesting day and night," he spoke disjointedly as though to himself. "It's not as if there aren't things to protest about, even though it's a waste of time – theirs and mine. And what is this one about? Who are the Surelikud

---

10 See Kiryutaya's statement, "The Scribe's Retort", pp. 355–363

anyway? Are you a Surelik then? You don't look like a Trier. There are foreigners everywhere."

"That's because you keep taking over foreign lands. The system may be changing, but the peoples haven't. We're still here, great and small."

He looked slightly insulted, yet unsure as yet about what to do.

"The Surelikud want the status of an autonomous republic. Just like peoples in other parts of the country."

"No one has ever heard of you. Where have you been? You've left it too late," he fired off his questions as though he had to engage with us, but found it humiliating to do so.

"Because we've suffered..."

"Don't talk to a Trier about suffering. We've suffered more than any people in the world. We've suffered. I've suffered. They took a dislike to my father, but because he had once been a powerful figure in the local party where we lived then, they didn't go after him directly, but one move at a time to encircle him, starting with his father-in-law, who they shot, and this drove my mother mad. Then they arrested his assistant and his assistant's wife, so he felt like a leper whose contagion was more virulent amongst those he handed it on to. I think that he was relieved when they finally came for him. That was before the war, and then while I was at the front, the Beer Cellars came and shot my whole family – in fact the whole village – and then burnt everything down. In some villages they killed everyone, and in others only those they hated most, while those left alive were to be kept as slaves for when the new Teutonic lords would come to take lands allocated to them. You don't know what suffering is."

"I understand," I said, "but you have to understand that we too suffered under the man with the moustache just like you Triers, and on top of that we have suffered as Surelikud."

"No! The higher up the command structure you were, the more of a Trier you were, and the more you believed in the system and perhaps even worshipped it, the greater the danger

213

you were in. I'm not saying that this was necessarily wrong: we need to be a disciplined people, we need to be kept in a state of fear – it's probably a stage we need to go through to get to the society we want. I think that the new man in charge is releasing the pressure too fast."

"We live in different worlds: you cannot know the nature of our suffering or gauge how it has affected us. There was danger in the east too. If the Samurai Swords had broken through, we would ..."

"How could I forget. I fought in the west and then we celebrated our victory in Moscow before being sent to the east to fight the Kwantung Army which we defeated in twenty-two days. That's why the Noisy Musics dropped those atom bombs on the Land of the Samurai Swords. It was a message to us Triers and not to that broken people and its emperor – a callous and cruel act. And you're kicking up a fuss about your silly little language."

"It's not silly to me," I shouted. "Every language is a people's store of knowledge. Even in a small one, it is the creation of many, many people over centuries or even millennia. Peoples large and small are scattered across the lands of the Triers, and many of them you may not have heard of and others may not look like you do; they have sometimes been transported and have sometimes fled, wandering arid lands in hope of safety with no particular plan. You live with your personal tragedies, and we with the tragedies of peoples."

"And which were you: forced to leave or left of your own volition?"

"Neither, we just withdrew into our forest, which may be why you've never heard of us. There were no hate campaigns in the newspapers, but of course some of us landed up in the labour camps and some suffered hunger. The enemy soldiers never got near us, so it's true that many have suffered more than us, particularly Triers. I'm not here today for a competition over who suffered the most."

By then five more militiamen had appeared, and their faces

expressed both bemusement and disapproval. Now he was no longer alone, the first militiaman decided that he had to assert himself: "I'm afraid that if you don't disperse, we shall have to arrest you!"

Most of my followers shifted away as though this was exactly what they were always going to do, but after so many years of ineffectual action, I was not going to let this chance go. I started to shout slogans very loudly and when the militiamen moved towards me, I moved away. I cannot remember what I shouted, because I was barely registering it myself. I was provoking them. The lead militiaman finally grabbed my arm in a firm grip, but I managed to pull it free by stamping on his foot at the same time. After this all of them pounced upon me, and my fellow protesters scattered like deer in the forest.

Once again I was in custody. It wasn't as brutal as it had been the previous time, but nor was it kindly. They interrogated me in a particularly futile manner for some hours and then put me in a cell to cool off. The following morning, they reappeared. There was the militiaman who arrested me, some high-ups in the militia and a man in civilian clothes who must have been a political commissar. They started by explaining the gravity of my actions, but the militiaman who complained about his foot was largely ignored. They understood that I was aggrieved about the plight of the Surelikud, and the new regime was well aware of such problems, but Rome was not built in a day. We needed to be patient, and eventually our arguments would be listened to in a civilised manner. They shouldn't have used that word, "civilised", which always rankles. When they told me that they had kindly decided to overlook my misdemeanour and release me from custody if a signed a document promising not to repeat my offence, I told them that I would not even contemplate such an undertaking, but in any case I had decided to go on hunger strike. This silenced them; they looked at each other in dismay, and then without saying hardly a word they left. I commenced the hunger strike, rejecting all food but taking the water they offered.

The days passed, and they made half-hearted attempts to persuade me. It was always the same people but not all of them at the same time. One day it was one group, the next day another, as though they were taking it in turns to test out their different methodologies. The sign of the times was that the political commissar was the kindliest but also the most manipulative. He was the most entertaining to reject. After eighteen days of hunger strike a guard came and said, "You've won!"

Unknown to me, important things were happening in the land of the Triers which were having repercussions around the world. Shortly afterwards the usual people turned up but without the militiaman who arrested me and with the addition of another man in civilian clothes who must have been even higher up the hierarchy, I was ready for the fight of my life. I had suffered: "If you've come to persuade me to desist, you've wasted a journey," I almost spat at them in spite of my weakness.

"Rahväema Ilusadeva," the important-looking stranger said, not without the hint of a benign smile, "we've come to offer you the autonomous republic you so desire."

Victory is not so sweet as they say it is, or at least not immediately. The instant reaction is one of distrust: was this a trick to get me to suspend the hunger strike and extend the whole process? How could what had always been so difficult suddenly become so easy? These were the words I had always wanted to hear, but now it didn't seem possible that I had heard them. I was also quite suddenly aware of my overwhelming weakness and tiredness. I practically fainted, and someone caught me from falling out of bed.

The uniformed men looked on with discomfort and displeasure, but the important man was positively solicitous. "Rahväema Ilusadeva, this is a genuine offer. Things are changing in the country. Not only do we want the new autonomous republic up and running as quickly as possible, but we would also like you to meet the First Secretary himself before you return to Väikelinn. Think of that return, Ilusadeva; it will be a great moment for you to savour, after all your efforts."

I still thought that it was one of their games. So accustomed was I to their contempt, I could not believe them. The important man spoke reassuringly in the normal language of the Triers instead of that bureaucratic language they usually use – not a "comrade" to be heard. It gradually occurred to me that this could really be happening. The First Secretary himself! There had to be a reason for this, and yet no reasonable explanation sprang to mind. But then with the perceptiveness of the oppressed, I sensed a glint of fear in their eyes – mixed and almost obscured by a much larger dose of impatience. "It's true, you fool," said one of the guards, "you don't even know when you've won. You'd better snap out of it. Tomorrow the Secretary-General is coming to visit you. You cannot be stinking like a rat when he does."

Suddenly a feeling of overwhelming tiredness and weakness poured through my body, and my body no longer felt like it was my own. It felt like an unbearably heavy overcoat that I could no longer sustain. They thought that I had fainted, but I saw everything with great clarity as though I were in another part of the room. And I saw the terror that now prevailed amongst their emotions. I gloried in my victory and cared nothing for that crumpled body on the floor and its staring eyes – my eyes. But where was I?

It was an extraordinary moment of pain, exhaustion and exhilaration. To this day, I cannot understand that experience. They moved my body as if it were a thing – but a fragile and important one, on which their own careers depended. They undressed me and washed me carefully but not lovingly – their disdain was unabated. They held me responsible for their predicament. And I observed indifferently – almost with sociological curiosity – the scenes that unfolded before me, because I was always conscious even though they eventually thought that I was having some kind of fit.

I was taken to a hospital and laid in a wonderfully comfortable bed. A nurse came and took my temperature and measured my pulse and, yes, I suddenly felt the presence of an almost maternal kindness. Once she had checked my physical state, she gently caressed my cheek and said – oh how clearly I remember those words – "You've been through a lot, haven't you?"

I had rejoined my body. I don't remember when that happened, but her caress made me aware of the change. And I immediately wanted to cry – whether out of pain, relief, self-pity or joy I cannot say. Perhaps it was all of those things or none, just some meaningless physiological trigger, but I think not. I felt so warm and comfortable – and so protected. But of course for someone of my generation, this emotion could not be experienced without a sense of guilt and embarrassment. Her hand caressed me again, but this time to remove a tear that had somehow escaped and I felt the dampness of the smear across my cheek. She smiled and said, "Don't worry, dear; you will pull through."

This mattered to me now, and again I wanted to cry, but this time definitely with joy. I wept. The tears came out in floods, and I must have been smiling as well, because she started to laugh, "You're a fighter, I can see that."

Eventually they brought me a little food and a lot of water. I noticed that they treated me with deference. This was a completely new experience, and one that I would get used to, but at the time it felt inappropriate and even a little unsettling. But it was also a pleasant and powerful tonic. I had previously attracted a little attention with my solitary voice in favour of the Surelik cause, and now when solicitousness prevailed I was unable to give voice to that voice. It was not a reaction to me as an individual, but to an idea of who I am that had been manufactured elsewhere – something I would only understand later.

The following afternoon Khrushchev really did visit me. He entered the ward in which I was the only patient, along with his entourage which included a photographer and a sullen man who looked as though he had long before decided to go through life looking permanently unimpressed with a world that could never measure up to his expectations. The First

Secretary, on the other hand, was in boisterous mood and gave the impression of having been encouraged by a glass or two of strong liquor. He was in the middle of telling a hilarious anecdote when he turned to look at me. And he stopped. "Why didn't anyone tell me?" he said with irritation, which may well have been caused by the lost opportunity to tell a good story. He shouted and waved everyone out of the ward except that permanently unimpressed gentleman. He then took a chair, approached me, swung the chair into position and sat down next to me with the chair's back in front of him so that he could lean on it – almost in the same brisk movement – while the other man hovered at the end of the bed. "How are you feeling?" the First Secretary asked, but before I could answer he followed it with another question: "Can you understand me, when I speak?" I nodded that I did. "Well, comrade, I am a busy man but I've come to tell you in person that you will have your autonomous republic. This is something we believe in just as much as you. Things are changing."

Few people, I believe, have ever experienced such a sudden improvement in their fortunes. It's true that this is more common in a country in which great power – both untransparent and unchecked – is concentrated in the hands of the few or indeed a single man, and more generally such concentration of power favours the downward swing of fortune's wheel rather than the upward one, but this First Secretary was an unusual one. I was unable to speak while I fumbled around for the appropriate words.

"Wasn't that what you wanted?" he said in a voice not entirely concealing his annoyance. I managed to say that it was. And of course I was extraordinarily grateful. It was just that ... "Yes, yes, of course," he continued in a more relaxed tone, for there is nothing a powerful man fears more than losing face, "you are unwell, and it'll take a little time to get better. We'll monitor the situation, and when you are ready, we'll meet again – quite soon, I hope."

He seemed to have something else to say and sat in that state of indecision for at least two minutes. Then the other man came over and said in a firm yet mildly subservient manner, "I think that we had better be leaving ... and the patient probably wants a good night's sleep."

They left, and the doors to the ward swung gently but noisily for a few seconds, unaware of the sudden vacuum in the room since the end of the fleeting visit of power and its entourage. I felt incredulous and still slightly alienated from all that was going on, as though what I had witnessed had been a play – a fiction or even more terrible some kind of practical joke – but in my soul the seed of elation had been planted, and I fell into a deep restorative sleep.

During the days that followed I started to recover, first slowly and then dramatically. The kind nurse who had stroked my cheek was soon chatting to me about the minutiae of life – hers and other people's – and some of the grand events that were occurring. She was the one who told me that during my hunger strike, the twentieth party congress had revealed the full extent of the Moustache's crimes, and the country was in a state of shock and uproar. News of a hunger strike would have struck a false note in that moment, while the announcement of a new autonomous republic of little importance would have maintained the momentum of a regime under a process of extensive reforms. This revelation explained the events of the previous few days. This was even more surprising than what had happened to me. It seemed that with his slogan of "peaceful coexistence" the new general secretary, who had changed the name to "first secretary", was trying to lead the world in a more enlightened, or at least less belligerent, direction.

And once the doctors considered me to have regained my health sufficiently, the blandishments of power were to follow: my friends informed me that the news had all the party officials in Väikelinn running around in a panic and doing little else but praise me. There was much laughter when they told me this, and it all seemed too good to be true, but in fact it would be even better than I could have imagined. When regimes have to concede something, they very quickly want to prove that this was what they had always wanted to do. But first I had to see Khrushchev, and a woman came to take me shopping for better clothes. When I rejected this idea, she argued quite heatedly and ultimately when I was still stubbornly dismissing all her approaches, she told me that it wasn't a request but an order, and it was required for the photos. Khrushchev himself was charming or in charming mode, and he made a speech about the Triers' "family of nations" and the importance of keeping all these cultures alive. Peaceful coexistence wasn't just for international politics. Then photographs were taken of us in various poses, mainly shaking hands, followed by a quick toast to the new autonomous republic. I was out of his office in ten minutes or fifteen at the most, and that included the time-consuming business of the photographs. The photographs were published in the papers but not prominently as there was so much going on in the country and abroad. How much this incident registered with the great majority of Triers is difficult to know, but I would say not much. In the little world of Väikelinn it was an earthquake.

For some reason they insisted that I be driven back in one of their more comfortable cars with a driver and the more junior of the two men in civilian clothes. He was extremely well-mannered and attempted to get me to join the party. I decided to reject this very politely while paying many compliments to the party and its new policies. How could I not, after all they'd done? I hid behind the supposed naivety of the noble savage, and after considerable efforts, he seemed to accept this. Indeed they did not hold back in their support at this stage in our story. Nothing had prepared me for the reception on reaching our small capital. The streets were lined with people waving the Triers' flag and a Surelik one that had been improvised over the last few days. I did not approve of it and had it changed. No one raised any objections. I quickly understood that I was now in a situation of some power to change things, and yet at the back of my mind was the sense that I was a hero more because of a lucky coincidence in the political firmament than because of any act of acuity or courage. Still it was a reality and it was up to me to use it wisely.

My triumphal arrival in Väikelinn was a mix of official orchestration and popular spontaneity, which were not always easy to distinguish between, in part because rarely is human behaviour governed by a single motivation and in part because I was intoxicated by success which obfuscates our senses just as much as alcohol and other powerful drugs. I wanted to believe that the love they showed me was sincere and not manufactured, that I was on the threshold of leading the Surelik people out of bondage like a Surelik Moses and that I was the mistress of my destiny – and theirs of course. Only I would have the abilities required to change the course of history.

Nevertheless I still believe that the Surelikud of the plain did in fact admire me and hold me in great esteem at the time, and did so for various reasons. Above all, I had momentarily drawn the attention of many more Triers to their existence. Triers, who had their own problems, were not always that aware of the minorities who lived amongst them, especially the smaller ones. Suddenly we were on the radio and the new invention that was spreading gradually across the nation – the television. And it was all my doing, or so it seemed. With the intelligence that comes from looking in the back mirror of life, I can now see that several other factors had to align with my hunger strike to create this happy ending: Khrushchev, the revelation of the Moustache's crimes, the world being momentarily even more interested in the Triers than some Triers were in me, and the relative unimportance of conceding autonomous-republic status to the Surelikud. Tell that to a politician who has just achieved an unbelievable breakthrough in their lacklustre career! It could easily have ended in my death, which after so much suffering I was perhaps seeking out. Besides there are no happy endings in reality, just a monotonous pursuit of some elusive objective along an endless path of strictures imposed by that reality itself. Reality can be surprising but it has a preference for the highly predictable.

In the choreographed procession, much was made of both Surelik and Trier cultures wonderfully blended in the Surelikud of the plain. The enthusiastic Pioneers were out in strength and some soldiers from the local garrison were rounded up, though they could hardly conceal their reluctance as they were all Trier conscripts. They marched up and down between the orations, perorations, homilies and secular sermons. I was garlanded, I was speechified, I was lionised, I was given the citizenship of Väikelinn and I was given some kind of medal which was given to those stubborn people who had refused to join the party but were, at least for the moment, perfumed with the grandeur that can only be bestowed from above. And who would argue with that? Again, when I look in that back mirror, I feel that the whole thing must have been tiresome, but I am afraid to say that I was enjoying every moment of it.

Naturally, I too had to make my own stirring speech and initially I wanted it to be radical. My notes referred to a journey that could only end in independence. But whatever my state of euphoria, that would not be my final draft: I was, at least unconsciously, aware of the restraints upon me. I was obliged to make my first compromise before I even entered the temporary offices of the new republic. What did I say? Well, as far as I can remember I thanked a lot of people including the First Secretary, I spoke of the historic bonds than held the Triers and the Surelikud together ("one of the most successful unions in the world", in spite of one side never having noticed that the other existed), and I ended the speech by asserting that the Surelikud had now achieved all of their political objectives.

Was that a betrayal? If so, only of myself, as the Surelikud certainly didn't want full independence. Meanwhile and in as much as they had a concept of nationhood, the Surelikud of the forest did want it – or rather they wanted to be left alone to live as they always had. At that time, this was the belief of the great majority of them, and the others had no view at all. This is the paradox that I want to investigate along with the reader, but not even at the age of one hundred and fifteen years do I have the answer to that question.

Following the alcohol, the heady rhetoric of the speeches and the barrowloads of self-congratulation that were apportioned to one and all, I left the main hall where it took place to walk in the quiet of the night and reflect on my new situation. Once the noise emanating from the festivities could no longer be heard, my mind started to clear and in the dull light of a streetlamp I saw the unmistakeable figure of Kurat leaning against a post in his customary state of complete relaxation. I felt no concern; I was powerful at last and it was time to make my plans. What could he possible say to upset me? When I was close, he pushed himself away from the lamppost in that gesture of his, which for some reason always contained an element of menace, but this time his face wore the mask of a supplicant.

"Rahväema, we meet again and at such an auspicious moment. You must be planning your next step."

"How intuitive of you! How do you do it, Kurat?"

"Centuries of experience, young woman."

"Not so young anymore."

"Young enough to have so much power over the Surelikud."

"What do you want? Get to the point."

"I feel that you owe me something, and would like a little favour back from you."

"I can't imagine why. The only thing you ever gave me was a sense of nausea."

He sniggered snidely and circled me with his wheedling glare, "Rahväema dear, do you not feel a little something for handsome Kurat. I love your new clothes. Very fetching, but if you come with me, I'll dress you even better than I am dressed myself, and I'm told that most men die of envy when they see me."

"You're mistaken again, Kurat. These clothes mean nothing to me, and they were required for a particular event."

"Yes, I heard. How wonderful, I thought, Rahväema and the party's First Secretary together. What a powerful mix, I said to myself. Those two in tandem could achieve so much. Why don't you take out party membership, dear girl? If you do that and then follow my instructions carefully, I could get you to the very apex of power in this most powerful of countries. What do you say, my lovely one?"

"I say go to hell. I'm happy with my position in the new autonomous republic, and also overawed by it. It's a big responsibility, and will take all my energies, thank you very much."

"Don't thank me. Follow me as so many other have. Tallyrand, for instance, I always look on him as one of my finest students, and all I did was whisper in his ear and he followed me to the letter. Do you want to hear what I whispered?"

"If you must."

"I whispered, 'The trick is not to be opportunistically blown along by every wind of history, but to perceive what is about to happen before it happens, and make it happen and happen in the most brutal and dramatic manner. Be an artist and sculpt the future vigorously with your head and hands, but stop regularly to sniff the direction and scent of the wind, and sense what is coming next.'"

"That's quite a whisper."

"Listen, that position of power you're so pleased with is very vulnerable. This First Secretary won't be around for very long, and who knows what the next one will think about a handful of savages who have no significance in the political game... No, don't look at me like that. No offence was meant. It is just that that will almost certainly be the attitude of the next general secretary."

"You heard me: go to hell." He laughed awkwardly the second time I said this. "I don't know who you are, or what you want, but I know that you're an evil bastard and I'll waste no more time with you. I have things I need to think about."

Kurat became slightly agitated – an almost impossible emotion for such a man. "Rahväema," he said, "I have always liked you, because unlike most others I meet, you stare me in the eye and do not flinch. You argue back and treat me with disdain. All of which is inexcusable insolence, particularly from an insignificant Surelik woman, but I find it captivating – even a little titillating for some strange reason. A whim, you may say. Even a weakness on my part, and it may have been my only one. You are, I thought, a worthy opponent, but this time you have gone too far."

"Not far enough to my mind. I want your poisonous face out of my sight."

"Very well, I will go but I will also punish you by making you live so long that you'll have to witness the terrible degradation of the Surelikud and their culture, and not only that," he smiled spitefully and feigned offence. "Also the relentless destruction of the Siberian Forest that you love so much." With this he turned his back and walked away nonchalantly, starting to whistle a catchy tune. I shuddered, and fortunately I would never see him again. But the curse lingered and I wondered about its efficacy.

Now the scribe is furious with me, and has stood up waving her arms around and looking quite red in the face. She doesn't understand: she's supposed to be typing, and I'm meant to be dictating. She somehow thinks that she has a right to comment on my work, which I don't mind but there are limits. I'll be generous again because I think that this one is also going to be really good:

Scribe: Who's this supposed to be? The devil? And he's cursing you. This is insane. Will anyone take you seriously once they've read this book? Can't you see the risk to your reputation?

Rahväema: What a lot of questions! Far too many in my view! I've no intention of answering them all! Have I mentioned the devil? Of course not.

Scribe: There's much in this book that makes no sense, but this time you've gone too far. In every age you have to live within the parameters it lays down. Otherwise you're just making a noise no one can understand. Your family probably didn't realise it as they scrabbled around in the forest, but even by that time most of the world had left the Middle Ages far behind.

Rahväema: And what do we know about the Middle Ages? We do know, however, that you became a Christian – an Orthodox Christian – and when was it? 1993 or 1994, if I remember correctly. Such excellent timing. Coincidentally of course, because you genuinely believed quite suddenly that there is a God and therefore a Devil too. And so many other things: the divinity of the carpenter's son, the virginity of his wife even after that son's birth. After he has been brutally executed by civilised Romans, Jesus removes the boulder that blocks the entrance to his tomb and after a few conversations flies up to the heavens. But you object to a character in my book who appears not to age and curses me. I do not confirm that there is any causal relationship between his curse and my having so far reached the good age of a hundred and fifteen years. For the benefit of readers not from these parts, longevity is quite common amongst the forest Surelikud. Now tell me, which of us is the insane one?
(At this point, the scribe, who is much taller than I am, came up close and screamed incoherently. Some mention of abandoning her work as my scribe, I think. I am unclear because I was backing out of the room before her threatening behaviour – I have only persuaded her to type these words on the agreement that it is made clear that she does not accept this version of events. Once we had both calmed down, we resumed our conversation.)

Scribe: I am merely trying to protect you from yourself. Christianity was founded a long time ago, but you can't have such things happening in our own time.

Rahväema: Scribe, I'm going to be patient with you, and take you through things logically – step by step. What is the purpose of this memoir?

Scribe: To tell the story of your life.

Rahväema: That's the definition of a memoir. I'm asking you what you think the purpose of this memoir is.

Scribe (after a long pause): You want to show how much you've suffered and how much you've fought for our culture.

Rahväema: Is that what you think? Fair enough, because that's what most memoirs are: self-aggrandisement, self-justification and the settling of old scores. But I have another purpose. I seek the truth. When I started to dictate this book, I had no clear idea of what I would say. As I dictate, things become clearer or sometimes their complexity becomes overwhelming and things that appeared clear are no longer clear, and I must express them in new ways.

Scribe: But did it happen? Did you really meet this Kurat? Did he really curse you?

Rahväema: I did of course, and of course he did curse me.

Scribe: You can't go around telling lies in order to get at the truth.

Rahväema: Scribe, that is exactly what I can do. That is what I have to do.

Scribe: Nobody can believe in the devil and not in God. Everyone knows that. Why are you so perverse?

Rahväema: I can. But you have got it the wrong way round:

I can believe in God but not the devil. The opposite of God is not the devil but nature, which is beautiful and inspiring as well as cruel and necessary to the non-human world. Ultimately humanity is also reliant on it, but parts of humanity can opt out and rely on other people to interact with it. This is why humanity is such a threat to nature, because if the unengaged part of humanity becomes too great, there will be a breaking point that will destroy us and many other things. God, who struggles to exist in things but does, finds it easier to find a place in human beings. He is the spirit who detaches people from themselves. So in the minutiae of everyday life, those who have nurtured a relationship with God don't get angry when someone skips the queue, because they say to themselves, "Leave the person alone; they are unable to fight against their nature and therefore cannot be blamed." Of course those who skip the queue are more likely to obtain whatever the queue promises, but this doesn't worry the nurturers. Some in the queue will make it to success and some will not; their order in the queue is not the result of a greater claim but of mere fortuity – such factors as proximity, prior knowledge, connections, fastness of foot.

In more terrible situations, such as the Nazi death camps, witnesses who have survived spoke of people who cared for others, shared their food and listened to their sufferings. Those people rarely survived, as some memoirs suggest. There is no advantage to accepting God, other than the peacefulness in the soul or the strength of a spiritual existence.

Scribe: And do you have a spiritual existence?

Rahväema: Yes and no. Those who move from political thought to political action are obliged to act in the selfish interest not of themselves but of their social group. God excludes no one, but even those who believe in a universal good – religious or political – will tendentially or even tendentiously exclude those who don't believe in universality or in their universality. Excluding no one is very difficult for human beings to do. It may be oxytocin which creates bonds between human beings, but that hormone is also supposed to seek out pariahs with which to strengthen those bonds. The instinct towards ostracism can only be overcome by something like God, which is outside nature – and yes a construct useful to civilisation.

Scribe: This is meaningless nonsense. And why do you use the word "God"? Yours is clearly some secular surrogate for religion.

Rahväema: Not at all. Progress loves to rename things and concepts that already exist, and they do so because they do not understand the past. I could call God the "Human Soul" or "Morality" or the "Moral Instinct". But why? The concept of God has always evolved, and was never an old man in a long grey beard sitting on a throne; that was just an allegorical depiction suited to a specific society. The other problem is that the new names always sound so restrictive or even ersatz: Human Soul, like the word Humanism, suggests that humanity is not an inherent part of a wider system. We are what we are not only in our relationships to each other, but also in our relationships with the other species, the plants and the inanimate seedbed out of which all life springs – in other words, the entire planet.

God is a necessary concept for civilisation, because civilisation is humanity's attempt to tame nature, and to homogenise and rationalise it. The cruelty of nature works because it punishes overarching success, but man's progress puts this defence mechanism at risk. Nature thrives on diversity, randomness and opportunities provided by its wastefulness. Something is always there to mop up what has been discarded. Homogenisation and rationalisation are toxic to nature, but nature will eventually win, because the higher humanity builds its fortifications against nature, the harder it will fall.

Humanity will destroy itself unless it changes its ways and it is probably incapable of doing so, but the price of humanity's overarching success will be much more disruptive and toxic than anything that has happened in the past.

*

One of the first people I met in the street during the days that followed was Ärrituv. He was bounteous in praising me and the new republic, in spite of the fact that the previous time he met me during my short stay in the Surelik capital while I was a vagrant on the run, he had been snarling about not being included in Osip's film as promised. The new Rahväema was just about to snub him, when she stopped herself and I became myself again. His conformism was irritating, and the fact that he was irritable himself made this worse, but he did not deserve to be mistreated. His complaint was justified; Osip wasn't ordinarily a manipulating liar, but in matters of his art he could throw aside his very last scruple. Poor Ärrituv never had a chance of getting what he wanted, and Osip should not have played him along. Besides he seemed genuine in his amiability, and not in search of any advancement.

"Hey, Rahväema! You remember me? Ärrituv."

"Yes, of course."

"You know ... that friend of yours wanted me to be one of his actors. I've forgotten what happened. I had a lot on."

"Yes, of course."

"Well, Rahväema, you've certainly gone and turned the world upside down. This is more than we could have ever hoped for. An autonomous republic! And it's all down to you."

"I have, haven't I? Thank you for your kind words, Ärrituv."

"It's not just me! The whole place is talking about you." At this stage I started to feel a little embarrassed – uneasy at the idea that everyone was talking about me. Wasn't this what I had always wanted? Perhaps just as much as the autonomous republic, and where did all that ambition come from and when? When I was a lexicographer, any thoughts of that kind

I would have been considered madness. This conversation also told me that people have no memory – myself included. And if a good reputation can be switched on so quickly, surely it can be switched off at the same speed – or equally it could slowly fade. This was someone I hardly knew, and someone Osip and I had laughed at – a little cruelly. But he was no more laughable than I was with my new-found powers ... yet no one would have laughed at me when I was at the height of those very powers.

"Ärrituv, what are you up to these days," I asked awkwardly as I was at a loss about where this conversation was going.

He looked disconcerted and finally found the words, "This and that. Down here things haven't returned to pre-war prosperity. It's difficult, you know ..." Here he seemed just as much at a loss as I was, and with some discomfort he brought to a close the conversation he'd started so buoyantly. He disappeared amongst the passers-by after politely taking his leave.

I realised after that brief conversation that my job required me above all to listen, because such exchanges would help me to understand the society whose fate, I thought, was in my hands – particularly as I had been away for so long.

I was busy, not with planning but with setting up the new organisation, which I was entirely unqualified to do. Naturally there were plenty of advisors, who sprouted out of nowhere with some kind of official stamp of approval. New offices were to be found, but looking ahead we had to plan for an assembly which was part and parcel of the new order. They would be relatively modest, but they brought jobs and status with them. We had to hire people for new jobs, and I was given a list. It seemed overwhelming, and I had barely thought about this while I had been writing pamphlets and giving speeches. It is easy to judge people and know what's best, but now I was responsible for the outcomes rather than criticising those of others. I was still intoxicated, but I was also taking in the enormity of what this longed-for ambition would mean in terms of decision-making and the uncertainty about where those decisions would take us. Several months had passed, and I hadn't given Tatyana a thought. But when I did, I was impatient to see her. I don't know why it suddenly became so important. I possibly hoped that she could assist me in some way.

Her house was exactly as before, but in need of maintenance. She happened to be sitting once again on the steps to the front door, and she was immersed in a book. She looked up when I reached the first step: "I was hoping that you'd come, Rahväema, but I also thought that maybe you would be too busy." She threw her novel on the steps, and smiled the tired smile of someone who had seen too much and aged before her time.

"Well, the First Secretary certainly sent the tiger into the clearing when he revealed all the Moustache's misdeeds," I said for no particular reason, and still today I don't know why I said it, instead of asking after her or her son. Probably because she was silent herself. It's difficult when after many years of suffering you meet an old friend. You're no longer the same person and you know it. They say that if your friendship is deep enough, then you can pick it up where you left off, but it's not that easy if you've been through what I'd been through – and what she had too.

"You call them misdeeds, but I'd call them pointless crimes. Inhuman. We had always believed in him."

"That's how socialism turned out, I'm afraid."

"I still believe in socialism."

"Really."

"I do. Very strongly, but perhaps the Triers weren't ready for it."

"Oh they were, always supposing it's a good thing. They were. Their mistake was to emulate all the other empires. Steel, arms, canals, roads, railways, but not the existing resource of village democracy."

"I didn't know you were a Tolstoyan, Rahväema. Such an

idealist! The trouble was the other industrial powers kept invading the country. The regime had to protect itself. Perhaps the old Marxists were right, and the Triers really weren't ready. The country had to go through other stages first."

"Nonsense, Tanya, but you have a good heart. When you have to become a mirror image of your enemy to defeat them, then it would be better not even to try. They choked off debate and manipulated the assemblies. I'm not saying that you're not a true Surelik, because your parents brought you up to speak the language beautifully, but if you were a Surelik of the forest you wouldn't think in these fancy ways. It really is much simpler than you think."

"I could say the same to you. Precisely because I have a better understanding of the Triers, I know why they had to do the things the way they did. My parents were Surelikud and proud of it. Always."

"And yet they gave their children Trier names."

"Yes, because they thought that it would help us get on in life."

"And did they?"

"Yes and no. We're scattered across the nation, and Sergei went abroad. I'd have left if I hadn't got pregnant."

My first thought was that this kind of the thing was bad for the language, but I suppressed that product of my monomania, and changed the subject. "What happened after they took your husband away?"

"I got married again. To the kindest man. I loved him terribly." She grabbed a handkerchief in fat hands and blew her nose, frustrated by the debilitating emotions that were convulsing her body. "He was a true father to my son. A good communist too. At the very same table my first husband had spoken at, he broached the question of the purges: 'They're taking people away in the night, and they're shooting them or sending them to the labour camps.' I didn't throw a knife at this one, but rushed over to him and grabbed his hands. 'Lev, promise me, promise me you'll never mention this to anyone else. Or you'll be sent to the camps yourself.' I wept, I pleaded, I cried out in pain. And of course he promised. It didn't change his fate. They came in the middle of the night, just like the previous time, and they took him away. He seemed quite calm, as though he had been expecting it. He was never heard of again."

"What happened to you after that?"

"Then they came for me, just before the war. Fifteen years, I was in the labour camp. Fifteen years out of a twenty-five-year sentence. For what?

"Oh, what a life, Tanya, how can I help you?"

"There's nothing you can do, unless you can change the past."

"I mean your son. How is he getting on?"

"Well. Well enough. The university seems to think so, but the disappearance of his stepfather in his childhood has hit him hard, more than his father's. He never really got over the idea that someone could read him the classics in the evening and still be there at the breakfast table. His own father kept strange hours and never really noticed his son."

Tanya only lived for another five years. She never really regained her health after she'd returned from the camps. Did I do anything for her son when I had so much influence in the autonomous republic? No, I didn't. I did perhaps very occasionally think about it, but never got round to it. I could say that I didn't have the time, but I did. I was often caught up in things of lesser importance, when seen from the distance of half a century.

This was the highpoint of my career, though I didn't know it at the time. It justified my suffering and the suffering I'd caused to others, which afflicted me to some degree: the abandonment of my son, my failure to stand by Osip, my ... yes, my arrogance which showed itself at times, particularly when it was important not to lose face. For you cannot survive in this business without a bit of that. You cannot survive in politics through niceness, perhaps especially in small countries where there is more familiarity. I don't say that you should lie, but you have to keep silent about anything that could reveal your weaknesses. And you must never be violent, especially if you are a small country. Large countries can be as violent as they want and at any time, and they can justify it with the flimsiest of arguments. The only thing that holds them back is their conscience, which they almost always lack, and ultimately an awareness that all power does not come out of the barrel of a gun, as it can also come out of a much more complex fermentation of violence, culture, alliances, reputation, narrative, propaganda and, yes, humanity.

We set about changing things in Väikelinn, and the authorities were very helpful. Sometimes we had to compromise, particularly where the Surelikud of the forest were concerned. The authorities of course wanted everyone registered – they always had insisted on that. It could not be avoided, and they wanted the children to go to school. It was pointless arguing that they already had a very thorough education and one suited to their lifestyle, but we did try. On such things they were immovable, but at least their intentions appeared to be good. It was agreed that schools would be set up in settlements to be created across the forest at some distance from each other (we were insistent on this). This meant that areas of the forest had to be cut down for permanent settlements, which were still very small. Roads or rather dirt tracks wide enough for a lorry to pass would also have to be built to connect these settlements and the settlements with the plain. When I asked about how the lifestyle could be protected, and quoted our proverb, "If men were meant to stay in the same place, they would have roots like the trees," they laughed politely but were unconvinced. When however I mentioned the economic activities which could die out, they were suddenly open to persuasion. We suggested a steady flow of game could be established through legal channels which would be very profitable to the state, though we knew that this would be unpopular with hunters who were running lucrative, illicit businesses. One of them asked if there was any fur-trapping. Not really but it could be arranged. This proved to be a solution that made everyone happy. They saw a way to earn foreign currency, and we saw a means to containing the damage to our lifestyle. Like the Tuva whose men worked two-weeks-on and two-weeks-off herding their reindeer, our men could go trapping for two weeks and spend two weeks in the settlements, but we insisted that women could also pursue this career. We were introducing the state, it's true, but the alternative seemed to be the gradual disappearance of the forest Surelikud.

There was of course a huge cultural difference between those who represented the centre and thought as Triers and those who represented the autonomous republic and thought as Surelikud. When I said that the Surelikud liked to absent themselves from the economy, and just wander taking what they require and no more, one of the bureaucrats – and by no means an unpleasant man – said, "But why? Without a reason, even a crow doesn't fly."

And I replied, "I recognise your proverb, but we have one that implies the opposite, 'A breeze whistles through the trees for no reason, but it still caresses your face.' Mankind had lived outside the economy for many more millennia than he has lived inside it. It was there that we were made, and you could say that it was here in the economy – of whatever kind – that we have been corrupted and lost our way." One of them attempted to take my side by asserting that orthodox Marxism agrees with this and here in the land of the Triers we were working our way slowly back to that freedom but on a higher and more civilised level. I kept my counsel, which was that I could see little sign of it, and if that was the case, was all this unpleasant multi-millennial detour really worth it?

Fundamental reforms recognised Surelik as an official language which meant that lessons were taught in it, newspapers were printed in it, government propaganda and applications appeared in it and its use in publishing and radio was expanded.

New offices and cultural centres were opened in Väikelinn, and the status of the language was greatly enhanced. This was not so much a period of ideas as one of practical application of ideas that we hadn't fully thought through and which then had to be negotiated through the ever-present delegates of higher authorities. What was happening appeared so enormous, but given the vastness of the Triers' lands it was in fact a change of infinitesimal proportions. And much was happening beyond. Our Trier friends, as they now seemed, were at the centre of the globe and upstaging their hyperactive competitor.

Where the Things We Leave Behind Go

Even today there are many who don't know that the Triers got to the moon before the Americans. The evidence of this is all around you, as this parable will reveal. And it was none other than the intrepid Yuri Gagarin who was the first man on the moon or at least the first man from earth to be on the moon. On his one trip into space, Yuri's spaceship carried a spacepod, a small, highly manoeuvrable spaceship designed to allow a safe return to earth in an emergency, but it could also return to dock at the spaceship once the latter was in orbit. Some problems did arise, and Yuri had to put the ship into orbit around the moon, but when he had completed the repair work, he couldn't resist a visit to the moon.

On leaving his spacepod on the other side of the moon where no prying eyes could see him, Yuri found that the moon was not entirely barren. There was a single very large building and outside there was a flag fluttering in the wind. He didn't recognise it, but it looked pretty much perfect. "There must be an atmosphere after all," but he still didn't dare take off his spacesuit.

As he walked towards the building, a woman came out – a woman of outstanding beauty: she was brown-skinned with large dark but slightly narrow eyes, and high cheekbones.

Every part of her seemed to have followed a blueprint for perfection.

She had a radiant smile that beguiled as nothing Yuri had ever encountered could have beguiled. And in that moment his life changed forever.

"How can anything be living on the moon?" he muttered to himself.

"There are more things in the heavens and on your earth than are dreamt of in your philosophy, Yuri," she said with perfect command of the Triers' language.

"How do you know my language and how do you know my name?" he stuttered in amazement.

"I can speak perfectly and only perfectly every human language, and of course we know everything," she smiled again, but not that have-a-good-day smile of a tired end-of-shift air hostess; it was an effortless but perfectly calibrated smile that appeared to come from the heart. In fact every time he looked at her or a part of her, the word "perfect" echoed through his mind which could think of nothing else.

"And what are you doing here?" he asked.

"I was about to ask the same thing of you," she said. "You do realise that this is a restricted area?"

"No," he said fearfully, and Yuri was a fearless man.

"Don't be afraid," she reassured him, "no inhabitant of Platonia is ever angry or aggressive."

"Platonia, is that your name for the moon?"

She laughed a suppressed laugh as one might when someone demonstrates their ignorance. "I am from Platonia, a distant planet, and for a month of every year I come here to look after – well, I'll explain that later. I can see that you are very tired and probably hungry, so I'll take you to the guest apartment and prepare some food."

All these extraordinary things were not dreamlike at all, as I expect most readers are thinking. No, for Yuri everything was very real, more real than reality back on earth – nothing was like a shadow on a cave wall. She sat him down at a most perfect table, but only after she had convinced him to remove his spacesuit. He could breathe perfectly but he felt inferior amongst all the perfection.

"Yes," she started to explain, "I come from Platonia where all the inhabitants are what we call forms or ideas – and our essence is most perfect and unchanging. Eternal, if you like."

And the food he ate could not have been more exquisite. It was all meat, vegetables and fruit that he recognised, but he didn't recognise their perfection and balance.

"If you don't come from the moon, why do you measure time in months?" Yuri quite reasonably asked.

"Oh, we don't use months on Platonia. You see, we have just one of everything on Platonia – I mean everything in the universe. We have one of all the creatures on the earth of course, but only in their most perfect form. Do you understand?"

"Yes, I'm not stupid, but I don't see the point."

Now she laughed loudly. "I like you, Yuri, you make me laugh and it is so good to have a laugh."

"The most perfect laugh of course, not like mine," said Yuri.

She laughed even louder. "Yuri, really you are a joy. It's a long month the month I have to stay here. We don't see many people. Astolfo he was called – and he had some crazy story about so many couples, tragic deaths, battles and someone's insanity that even a perfect brain like mine couldn't sort it out. There was never time to discuss Platonia and he showed no interest. Who knows what he wanted? But he left almost as soon as he got here. And he came on a hippogriff, that's the method most people use, but they don't come often. What was that thing you came in?"

"A spacepod, and my rocket is orbiting the moon. I thought that you knew all there is to know."

"What a tiresome thing. I suppose we'll have to have one of each made on Platonia."

"Most perfect ones, I imagine," said Yuri with the grumpiness of the imperfect or rather of a sensible mixture of perfection and imperfection.

And the woman laughed again. Raucously. "I love your jokes. You Triers are very witty."

"Okay, if you find me so funny. Perhaps you could explain why you're a woman. You're supposed to be the man in the moon, not the woman."

Again she laughed uproariously, which offended Yuri, because he didn't think it was that funny, and the repetitive nature of her perfect behaviour was beginning to irritate him. They probably didn't have too many jokes on perfect Platonia. It took her two minutes to calm herself down enough to wipe tears from the sides of her eyes and say, "Actually there is a man on the moon, but he comes at another time of year also for a month. So there is one ideal man and one ideal woman, and we come close to the planet we represent twice a year. We do our research quota for the year and then go home. So they're not entirely wrong on earth: there is a man but there's also a woman. Human imagination is a wonderful thing, but it's not entirely accurate. That's what we want. Perfection is only for Platonia."

"That comes as something of a relief," said Yuri.

This time she only chortled. "Perfection in all things, Yuri. Next you need to rest – to sleep the most perfect sleep, but only after we've made love..."

"That would be to make the most perfect love?" Yuri said and he thought very briefly of his wife and children, but in that moment they felt far away and insubstantial. This was reality – hyperreality, while reality down on earth was no longer reality. All those things that mattered back home no longer did. Things that humans fought over – insanely. It occurred to him that perhaps everything significant about humanity was contained in this building. He didn't know why he thought that, but he did. Perhaps it was just that he was looking through a telescope from the right end.

So they went off to the guest bedroom and had sex. It was remarkable in its athleticism, but lovemaking with a perfectionist is never going to be very loving. In spite of being an extremely fit cosmonaut, Yuri found it tiring and afterwards he slept the most perfect sleep.

When he woke, the woman was there fully dressed with a cup of tea. "Triers like tea," she said as though to display her encyclopaedic knowledge.

"They certainly do," said Yuri, and he drank it. It will come as no surprise to the reader that it was the most perfect tea. And it was the tea that made him think about it. Later he would tell Nikita Khrushchev that after this experience nothing could satisfy him back in the harsh realities of Earth. Living like a god for half a day had taken away all his pleasures for the rest of his earthly life.

The woman wanted to show him the building which contained her research samples, and he was only vaguely interested, as a certain nostalgia for the less than perfect was growing stronger, but she insisted. And a man like Yuri could never disappoint a perfect woman with a perfectly beguiling smile. He was taken from one room to another, and they were all the same. There was floor-to-ceiling shelving everywhere and along each shelf there were jars of various sizes with strange objects floating in a liquid. It was all slightly repulsive and as far from perfection as you could possibly think.

Seeing that Yuri wanted to run, the woman smiled her perfectly beguiling smile and explained in a school-teacherly manner, "When children are born, they have all the virtues, but gradually as they go through childhood they cast some of them off and we catch them and bring them up here for preservation in a special liquid. That way we can study them and fine-tune our concept of perfection."

"You mean you learn human perfection from us?"

The woman pinched her perfect lips and, revealing a little too much unease for a perfect person, said with matter-of-fact simplicity, "Well, you people are getting a lot of practice, however lousy you are at it."

Yuri went over to the shelves and looked along them: "Great Caesar Nicholas II's Common Sense", "Jean Calvin's tolerance of other people's views", "Winston Churchill's kindness to peoples who don't speak English", "Mao Tse Tung's Judgement", "Louis XIV's Common Touch", "Napoleon's Contentment with Peace", "Cesare Borgia's Moral Purpose", "Henry VIII's Marital Skills", and Hitler, Mussolini, Stalin and Franco had too many jars to list in full each containing many of the same things: "Tolerance", "Humanity", "Compromise", "Trust", the list was very long. And he asked, "Tell me, how is it that I know most of the names."

"Ah well, not many common people provide samples. It's mostly the rich and powerful. We're having to build an annex because of the Noisy Musics and the Little Noisy Musics."

"Why's that?"

"All the future Noisy Music presidents after Carter and the Little Noisy Music prime ministers after Callaghan are going to inundate us with jars. We've got a jar with intelligence from every one of them."

"Well, this is good news from us. The West will decline, and the Triers will be safe for once."

"Not necessarily. The only thing more dangerous than a ruthless man with a powerful weapon is a stupid man with one. Some of them will be both ruthless and stupid."

"So you can look into the future. How can you do that?"

"I think that you'll find that the future, the past and the present all exist in the same moment."

Yuri had had enough of stolen virtues. But as he started on his way, he noticed an empty jar with an ancient label with "Orlando's Sanity" on it. He pointed this out to the woman, and she frowned. Is it possible to frown in the most perfect manner? If so, that is what happened, but a frown it was – an admittance of something less than omnipotence. "That should never have happened. The sample has been stolen."

Yuri had had enough of the outreach unit of an intergalactic archive. He wanted to be back home on earth, and to touch a tree and not think of it as a mix of molecules which are no more than a store of energy. He wanted to think of a tree quite simply as a tree – something with deep roots and branches branching out and up towards the sky, holding all kinds of creatures and calmly embracing their endless struggle for survival. He said, "I believe that you don't catch these virtues as children discard them, but rather you steal them. Am I right?"

The woman frowned, "You're too clever for your own good, Yuri."

"Yes, you steal them, and that why there's so much conflict and misery down there. You have a lot to answer for."

Yuri had had enough of perfection and all its subtle ways and uncertain motives. He wanted to go immediately, and the most perfect woman wanted him to stay a little longer. She smiled her perfectly beguiling smile, but he was having none of it. Perfection was exhilarating like a fine painting or sculpture, but it was flat and strangely lifeless because it was unchanging. Sterile. Fragile perhaps, but apparently not on the moon. He had to go, he had to flee, but life would never be the same. Less enjoyable, he already feared. She followed him all the way to the spacepod, beseeching him to stay but only very gently as befits a most perfect woman.

"You must never tell anyone about this experience, and besides they will never believe you," she told him.

"I'll have to tell someone," he said.

"Then I'll give you this," and she handed over a small plastic card which was identical to the credit card we're all familiar with, but Yuri couldn't recognise it because it hadn't been invented then. It had an intricate and hypnotic design on it which meant that it was very difficult not to take it out of your pocket every now and then.

Yuri looked at it and said unenthusiastically, "I don't know. To me it looks harmful. What is it supposed to do?"

"If only one person hears your story and neither of you tell anyone else, then it will convince your chosen person that you're telling the truth. But if one of you does pass on your story, this plastic card shall take its revenge and multiply over the whole planet reducing millions of people to a state of miserable indebtedness. There shall be a plague of acquisitiveness because of cards like this one. It shall scatter your small planet with object of all sizes that are useless and unwanted and unnecessary. To produce these pointless objects, humans shall cut down the forests, empty the bowels of the earth of all their most toxic secrets, and clog up the rivers and the seas."

"I don't know," said Yuri, "that's a big responsibility. What if my chosen person doesn't keep his promise? And if all these plagues you threaten came true, all the children wouldn't be playing with each other but with extravagant toys as if there were no tomorrow, and then they would become unhappy adults. It doesn't bear thinking about, but of course you'd be happy..."

"Why?"

"Because you'd be getting more and more samples."

"Yuri, you surprise me again. I suppose they do send up their cleverest, just as some primitive peoples offer up only the best in sacrifice."

"Not only primitive peoples."

"Yuri, you cannot be perfect because you do not hail from Platonia, but I think that you must be the closest to it on that fair planet we see below us. It saddens me that you must rush off – a little rudely, given my hospitality – but you must decide: do you want this plastic card or not? All you have to do is choose someone you can really trust."

"Very well, I'll take the card. I do have someone in mind."

The woman looked relieved and made no further attempts to keep Yuri back. He clambered into the cramped cockpit of the spacepod and looked out of the window. The woman was waving brightly but only in the most perfect manner. He shot off on his trip to meet up and dock with the main ship. His journey home went smoothly and he landed in the Kazakh desert.

There were the usual ceremonials and when Yuri met Nikita Khrushchev, he leaned forward and muttered into the First

245

Secretary's ear, "We must talk." Khrushchev was intrigued and very soon they were in a private room. Yuri told him the whole story, and Khrushchev just laughed. He asked if it was April the First, and then laughing he poured Yuri a vodka and said, "I think that you need this."

But Yuri was not amused and didn't touch the spirits. Instead he took the plastic card from his pocket and handed it over while he looked Khrushchev in the eye desperate to see his reaction. The other man was still chortling and taking the card, nonchalantly said, "And what is this supposed to be?"

Then he looked down at it and his expression changed. For a minute it was subdued and concentrated, as though he were reading something. Then he looked up with a huge grin, "The Noisy Musics are really going to hate this." And he hugged Yuri, but Yuri was too agitated for hugging.

"No, no, you must tell no one." And he proceeded to explain the magic properties of the piece of plastic.

Khrushchev looked at the plastic card again, and mused, "I'm not surprised. As soon as I looked at the card, it seemed to speak to me. Not only did it confirm your story, but it also spoke of all its own possibilities. I don't know exactly how, but I believe that this is an important invention that will lead to enormous social changes. Whether they will be good or bad is another matter."

"Bad, bad, definitely bad," said Yuri, "that's what the women said. But only if you tell someone else. This must ..."

"It's not your job to tell me what to do and not do, Yuri Alekseyevich Gagarin, but I will keep it secret for you. You are after all a Hero of ... etc, and we have been warned. Definitely bad, you say?"

Of course Khrushchev didn't keep his word. Being gregarious by nature, he had to tell some people, but he didn't show it to them as he was aware of the curse. Then he had a great idea which came to him when he was speaking on their special hotline: he would send it to JF Kennedy, and who knows who he told? It was foolish of Yuri to think that a man like

Khrushchev could have kept such a story secret. And the rest, as some people keep stupidly saying, is history, as though it were a constant like Platonian perfection and didn't constantly change geographically and through time. The Triers' history is not the same as the Noisy Musics' history, and neither of them have much truth.

There is one last thing worth mentioning. Just before Khrushchev and Yuri separated, Yuri was telling the First Secretary about another member of the politburo. It appears that there was one quite unique exhibit: an enormous jar of formaldehyde containing a physical item rather than an abstract trait to be preserved in its special liquid. No one knew how it got there and on the side was written in large letters: THE BRAIN OF LEONID BREZHNEV [known here as the Moron]. They didn't know what to do with it and someone had left it at a window where the label had yellowed in the moon's sunlight.

Yuri had thought that this story would be well received by Khrushchev and it was. He looked at Yuri and said with his pleasant smile, "After we'd gone to all the trouble of sending you all that way, could you not have brought it back with you?"

*

The scribe is beginning to understand the point of these parables, and she has made a joke of it. She told me with a wicked smile, "There must be quite a few jars with your name on it, Rahväema." Of course she's right; there must be more than a few.

This unexpected reaction of hers is unfortunate because I wanted to explain to her – and therefore to the less insightful readers – that not only is perfection impossible without imperfection, but also that imperfection is often better than perfection, which in itself is almost worthless and ephemeral in spite of whatever the man and the woman on the moon may think; the struggle for perfection is the only benefit of perfection. Still, if the scribe has got the message, I can be sure that every reader has.

Was our autonomous republic a success? I like to think that it was. Mainly for the Surelikud of the plain, I have to admit. The schools were improved and most of the time the children were taught in their own language. As a republic we got more funding from central government, so roads, hospitals, libraries and the like started to catch up with the rest of the country, although money continued to be tight. It was a different matter when it came to the Surelikud of the forest. This became clear a year after my return to Väikelinn: I was visited by Vladimir Paulusev, a pleasant young man and an ambitious one who had been co-opted to us from who knows what part of the labyrinthine state – presumably to keep an eye on us and guide us. Every kind of person must exist in every kind of civilised society, I think, but in different proportions according to the kind of civilised society. However he was a type that most definitely exists in copious numbers under all regimes: he was affable and would listen to everyone, demonstrating at every stage his tolerance of others, but in the end he would always come down of the side of the status quo, whatever that status quo was at the time. He was also a man who had happened on ideal times for someone of his nature; Khrushchev's slogan for international relations was "peaceful coexistence", but this was also the atmosphere of domestic politics.

"Rahväema, we have a problem in the forest," he was also a man who liked to come straight to the point but never in an aggressive way. "The settlements aren't working exactly as we had hoped."

"Meaning?"

"Well, there is a degree of resistance from the forest communities."

"All of them?"

"I'm afraid that's correct."

Perhaps I should describe Vladimir Paulusev, but I find it difficult because he had no distinguishing features other than a fairly pleasant voice. Not one that makes you weak at the knees, but pleasant. I cannot think of another word. You couldn't dislike him because he seemed to be so accommodating, so amenable, so damn nice, but you wouldn't seek out his company either. I wouldn't say that he was duplicitous or inauthentic, because he was always honest to himself: a man who wanted to keep everyone happy, but most of all he wanted to keep the powerful happy, because he sincerely admired them – not for what they were but for who they were in the hierarchy: I'm sure that he would have admired the First Secretary's successors once they had removed the First Secretary. This was not deviousness or even pragmatism; it was an instinctive desire, just as a dog will follow its current master.

"What shall we do about it," I asked. I didn't even ask for further explanations, possibly because my first reaction was one of irritation. "The Surelikud of the forest again! When we will they stop being the problem?" That was what I thought, I am ashamed to say.

"I think that we'll have to go down there and talk to them."

I thought of how Halvatud had showed me up, or rather how they disliked me and my behaviour for reasons I still wasn't clear about. I had no desire to go there: "I give you full powers to deal with the situation," I said grandly, ignoring the fact that I didn't have full powers to grant to anyone. Even the full-blown republics in practice didn't have full powers.

"I don't think that they would listen to me," he argued, "we need someone with authority. And then I'm from the plain and you're from the forest – originally of course, because you've lived outside it for so long and learnt so many other things. Who better to carry out what will be quite a complex and delicate task?"

It took quite a bit more flattery before I was persuaded, and we departed with a sizeable entourage which he put together very carefully. On our arrival, I soon realised the depth of the crisis. Initially the Surelikud had liked their new homes, but when they were told that they had to stay there all the time and their children had to go to school, attitudes changed. Women in particular didn't understand why they had to stay behind. Some of the men didn't want to hunt for furs. There were even some who didn't want to hunt anything that wasn't for their own consumption. Some of the children liked the schools, but most of them did not. All the teachers were from the plain, which immediately created a cultural rift which was perhaps heightened by the fact that they spoke the same language.

And then... And then I knew I was in trouble when I saw a large group of angry parents coming towards us – very slowly because they were being led by Halvatud himself. He was already shouting and waving his stick, though he was too far away for me to understand his words. Vladimir's first words were, "Who is that idiot?"

"Not a useful one at this stage," I replied.

"He doesn't look like too much trouble to me." How wrong he was. But then his belief in progress was a faith so strong that it would have put Ignatius Loyala to shame, though Vladimir was a more sensible and practical man than the founder of the Jesuits, and therefore he would have little influence on our history.

Eventually the agitated crowd came up close, shouting incoherently as it did. It was Halvatud who fired the first shots in the hostilities: "Rahväema, what in the name of the vengeful God of the Triers are you doing?"

"I'm doing my duty as an elected official...," I said grandly.

"But you haven't been elected; you were appointed from the top."

"Alright, I'm doing my duty as an appointed official..."

"Then why are you forcing people to settle when they don't want to, and sending children to a dull school when they would like to be travelling through the forest? This is not what we were fighting for."

"I was fighting for an autonomous republic..."

"...which you would become the president of. If it's autonomous, that must mean that you can make the final decision."

"You know that's not true, Halvatud," I hated having to admit this in public. "We live in a state in which an autonomous republic is even less autonomous than a republic that isn't an autonomous one. There's a limit to what I can do."

Vladimir was feeling very uncomfortable about this conversation because it failed to comply with the existing template for political discussion, and besides he couldn't understand what it was about. The people upstairs wouldn't like it; that was a certainty. "Comrade Halvatud," he cut in, "I think that in your condition, you would much rather ..."

"Comrade tiresome comrade, you have no idea who I am, what I would prefer or what my condition is, so kindly don't interrupt. Rahväema, who is this person anyway? Are you partially in charge or is he? He can't be the person who's really in charge."

Young Vladimir was beside himself and managed to get in before me: "I was merely trying to offer you the comfort of the settlement's administrative office, where we could discuss this whole matter – in a civilised matter."

"Civilised? That means that you get everything you want, and then turn the screw even tighter in six months. That's not going to happen."

"Comrade Halva... Citizen... Well, whoever you are, stop twisting my words. The fact is, and you'll have to face up to it sooner or later, that we have to remain within the parameters laid down by the politburo. That's the legal position, you understand?"

"No, I don't understand and I don't agree. What we can do is go to your offices – just five on your side and five on mine – where we'll come to an agreement and it will all be like Valmistaya and Kõblus were back together again, or we'll go our separate ways and the fight will continue."

Vladimir said no, but I said yes, and what I said was adhered to, which slightly surprised me.

More offices. The autonomous republic may not have been

doing much for the Surelikud of the forest, but it was certainly doing a great deal for offices and those who work in them. We sat down, five on one side and five on the other. I cut across Vladimir when he started to speak, as I had decided that I had to be at least the one who appeared to be in charge: "First of all I want to explain why we want to establish these schools across the forest." I said "we" because over the previous year I had unconsciously started to identify with the whole edifice of the Trier state. Comfort, respect, civilised manners and esprit de corps are much more effective ways of changing someone's thinking than torture and the threat of a firing squad, because the latter are only effective in the short term. The former digs deep into your soul. That word again. Funny how it recurs in this memoir written in a language that had to borrow the concept. However I was also proving the truth of the proverb, "If you beat a dog, don't expect it to bark." And I was now barking as loud as I could on the Triers' side. When I said "we", I noticed that Halvatud winced.

So off I went talking a lot of well-meaning garbage, and then Halvatud came back with a speech almost exactly of equal length in which he said many wise things, but principally that the Surelikud of the forest were used to doing what they wanted – going as it were where the spirit took them. Even if it were a good idea to change their lives, it would make more sense to do it gradually.

Vladimir, who had clearly been carefully instructed before we left Väikelinn, then told us that he sympathised deeply with our arguments, which were good ones and worthy of consideration. There was however an overriding problem: namely that the nation, after a proper examination of various pedagogic models, had decided that education was the absolute priority and all children in the Triers' lands would have to go to school at the same age and follow their education as far as they could take it. This was in their interests and in the interests of the nation and human progress. That ultimately was a firm obstacle in the way of relenting on a single clause in the legislation recently passed through the Assembly of the Surelik Autonomous Republic.

Halvatud obviously disagreed and suggested that I ring the First Secretary, which was greeted with alarm by all five of us on my side of the table. Halvatud giggled, and Vladimir adopted the grand air of the civilised man who has been unjustly offended but has decided that he is going to forgive in a divinely civilised manner, "I think that just about tells us where we are. As they say in the language of the Triers, 'Laughing without reason is the sign of a foolish man.' I believe that we can bring this meeting to a close."

And despicably I backed him up by saying, "Yes, I think that is quite clear. As the Surelik proverb says, 'Laughter that's empty is the sign of an empty head.' This meeting is now over."

At this point Halvatud started to howl with laughter. And he laughed and laughed and laughed. Even his stalwarts looked a little embarrassed. It seemed that he wouldn't stop, and every time that he did stop, he started again just as soon as he tried to speak. He wiped his eyes even as he laughed. And then he did stop. With great aplomb as though he hadn't been acting very strangely for the last ten minutes, he said very firmly, "Rahväema, go into the office next door and ring the First Secretary. It won't be easy, but everyone thinks that you're closer to him than you really are. Put your argument across as strongly as you can, and get the best deal you can for your people."

Without making any objection, I stood up, went next door, worked my way up the various echelons until I finally got to him. He didn't sound too happy to be bothered, and I put Halvatud's arguments to him very strongly and threatened to resign. He told me what was the most that he could concede, and then asked for the flunky to come on the phone so that he could be reassured.

Once Vladimir had spoken to the First Secretary and returned sheepishly to the committee room, I read out the new agreement. No one would be obliged to live in the settlements for the next five years, and the obligation to go to school would only apply when the families were resident in the settlements. The obligation for at least twenty Surelikud trappers in each settlement would not be enacted for the next two years, and then the numbers would increase in line with the autonomous republic's production plans. The registration of all citizens, the failure of which had been a quite unforgivable oversight on the part of previous administrations both locally and nationally, had to be completed in a matter of months.

This felt like a victory and it was. Vladimir went off on one of his speeches about the greatness and magnanimity of our First Secretary. After a bit everyone stopped listening to him, and I suddenly thought that this was not a successful young man to be envied, but one of a huge tribe – not just across the extensive lands of the Triers but across most of the modern progressive world – which is obliged to carry out the most pointless tasks merely to give the impression that there was some kind of civic decision-making process where in fact there is a command structure more typical of an army. This was true of that Trier regime and it is true of the corporate economies we have today.

When Vladimir finally ran out of self-justificatory things to say, I sniffily asked Halvatud what he had found so funny, and he answered without any hesitation, "I just looked at you two pompous halfwits and thought just how funny and pointless you are. Toothless tigers, I would say." On his side everyone was laughing and on my side the other three couldn't suppress the odd chortle. Vladimir and I sat in pained silence, but I now realised just how much I needed Halvatud and his extraordinary behaviour.

At the end of my phone conversation with Khrushchev, he told me never to try ringing him again. He was giving in because frankly the Surelikud were of no great importance, and it would be bad public relations to fall out so soon after my story had demonstrated his magnanimity. He didn't say so in those words, and it was in his character to be magnanimous in a fairly erratic manner. It didn't matter, because I never reported that part of the conversation, and this meant that everyone continued to think that I had a permanent backchannel to the First Secretary. This was going to give me a great deal of power for quite a few years.

Did I use it wisely? Well, that is a good question, and with the aid of that rear-view mirror, I can tell you that there were successes but also failures. The fact is that on the 14th of October 1964, the First Secretary – the nearest thing I've ever had to a patron – was deposed. By that time, I knew that the best thing was to keep my head down and keep going in the hope that no one noticed us, which is what had been happening for quite some time. One of the first things I did after that trip to the forest was to appoint Halvatud to Vladimir's job and promote Vladimir to a more senior but entirely sinecural position where he spent many happy years.

When the five years were up, no one remembered that all the men were meant to be in the settlements and all the children in the schools. I kept that going until October 1964 when I considered it diplomatic to comply with the law in a changed political environment, even if it did mean a stand-up fight with Halvatud. On the whole I think that we worked hard, and the Surelikud of both the plain and the forest seemed to be as happy as you can expect any people to be. I'm not going to list our achievements as you would expect in a memoir of this kind. It was humdrum, that's what it was. Gradually the Moron took over more control, and you could have fallen asleep until the Birthmark came along and not missed very much.

In 1961 I was visited by a Noisy-Music woman who worked with us for six months. She was a thin woman who had a quick smile and smiling eyes. She was a furnace of enthusiasm and excessive energy. She was like no one I'd ever met, and I thought to myself that if they were all like her in the lands of the Noisy Musics then it must be an exhausting place to live.

But I admired her and of course I was grateful for her interest in us and our culture – an interest that was unlimited and sometimes as exhausting as her enthusiasm. On the other hand I was, as previously mentioned, at the height of my career (if we can call it that) and I had an irrational diffidence to all her effervescence – an inability to admit quite what a wonderful and extraordinarily generous person she was, and an asset I could have made more use of. The few Noisy-Musics I've met – mostly officials on short visits – have always displayed a nonchalant arrogance – one that was so secure that it had no interest in persuading others of it, but this Noisy-Music was apologetic for her country's behaviour and seemed to feel responsible for events over which she could not have had any influence. She demonstrated the folly of national stereotypes, particularly ones based on very little knowledge – a few brief encounters and the rumblings of a distant power. Such prejudices personalise barely understood and complex societies, whilst confusing elites with the people.

Her name was Meg Murphy-Ifurmov, which implies a Trier heritage and, I'm told, an Irish one. For five years she had been learning Surelik which was not easy because of the lack of teaching materials. She had found a Surelik willing to give her lessons for an astronomical fee. There must be at least one of everything in that country, but it turned out that finding him wasn't entirely coincidental. Before she attended it, her university had run a course on our culture and this old man had been hired to teach the language. When the professor who ran the course died, the course was dropped and the man had difficulty in finding work, and when he did, it was because of his knowledge of the Triers' language. Meg told me that he was a mournful man, caught between three cultures he knew well. Some people are enlivened by such situations and others find it a heavy burden. Some have to work hard to achieve this and some are provided with it by circumstance. It seems that he was nostalgic for the Great Caesars and for a time when he knew who he was. He was slightly ashamed of his

Surelik background and also thought that his was a "primitive language", an attitude Meg obviously didn't share. Whether it was his teaching or her studying or both, Meg arrived with an excellent command of the language which is unusual for someone who has not lived amongst a language community. Her intellect was quite remarkable, and I now wish that I had spoken more often to her about the motivations that brought her to our lands.

When we found that some schools in the plain didn't have enough Surelik speakers to form a Surelik choir, Meg came up with an idea which incensed the elders, as we called the old men who had appointed themselves to be the guardians of Surelik purity. Always aware of her outsider status, which she enjoyed, she selected her words very carefully: "I do not want to speak out of turn, but I think that the easiest thing to do is to invite the Trier children to join the choir and learn the Surelik songs. This would give them some familiarity with the language and change their attitudes to it; it might even encourage some to learn the language."

I knew immediately that this was a good idea, but for some reason ... no, I think that I know the reason: somewhere down in my thick skull, I objected to this foreigner telling us what to do, forgetting of course that it was highly unusual that she even cared. Mutterings from the old men immediately moved clumsily through the air like a flight of venomous vultures: "There will never be the like of us again!" – because no one would ever know their culture like they did. Their faces expressed their shared conviction that things, which until that moment could never have worsened, had suddenly achieved that impossible thing. One of them rose unsteadily and in his slow, lugubrious and baritonal voice communicated the gravity of the situation, as though nothing amongst the horrors of the last century could match it. "And will they use the locative case correctly?" Realising her blunder Meg withdrew her suggestion immediately, but this only encouraged the elders who with unexpected sprightliness pursued her like hounds that have seen a deer in flight. They were personal; they were xenophobic. I don't know why it took so long, but eventually I intervened.

"Thank you, Meg, I think that's an excellent idea."

Then they argued with me but in a more subdued manner because they knew what I was capable of. They pleaded with me but lost their momentum, like hounds that have been called off and have to overcome their natural temperament. Her plan was implemented and was very successful; it drew in children and parents alike.

The next crisis was that her six-month visa was going to expire, and I did all I could to get it renewed, but the system would not give. When the day for her departure neared and she knew that she would have to go, she was increasingly upset. It became clear that her decision to live amongst the Surelikud had been carefully planned and she had hoped that it would become permanent. We spoke about it a great deal and I tried to support her as much as I could, but when she wrote a long letter to me after she'd returned to the homeland about which she was at the very least ambiguous, I never replied. I meant to, I think, but like so many other things I should have done in my life, I didn't find the time. I only really thought of her again, when the Drunkard's Noisy-Music advisors took control of the country and discovered to their horror that it didn't have a stock exchange, which not only revealed their ignorance of the country they proposed to govern but also the bizarre idea that a casino at the centre of society was an inherent part of human society – presumably all the way back to Adam. I was dismayed at what happened and vaguely recalled many things she'd talked of, which I'd only half understood at the time. I thought of all the effort she had put into getting to the Surelikud – the investment in time and intellectual effort – how we had all failed her, primarily because we'd never tried to understand her. Truly every human being should enjoy Kant's cosmopolitan right to go anywhere on the face of our planet, particularly if they respect the culture and practices of the societies they visit, and that she most certainly did.

In 1972 when the Moron was securely ensconced as the hardline General Secretary, some zealous administrator discovered a particular anomaly – indeed an illegality – down in that forgettable part of the nation where Surelikud live. I was summoned to an office in Biysk, where I faced a middle-aged man who'd also lost his way in the labyrinth. The reader may be getting bored with the number of offices in this memoir, but offices played a large part in our lives during those times, so the reader will just have to put up with it, as we'll soon be in the go-getting part of the story: modern capitalism with all the progress you could possibly want.

He had a whole lot of papers on the Surelik Autonomous Republic, and on my arrival he started shuffling them around with an air of frustrated perplexity. "I cannot understand," he spoke slowly after quite some time, "how this status has been overlooked for so long, comrade. And who are you? You're not even a member of the party."

"Is that your final word, comrade," I managed to say, although my head was a storm of conflicting forces. I had to be polite to this idiot who was more powerful than I was. Or did I? It was clear that a decision had been made far above his head, and having assessed the risk, I added boldly, "Isn't there something a little uncomradely about the word 'comrade', comrade?"

He looked at me with a vexed and uncomprehending glance before switching to a more headmasterly approach. "We have very clear parameters when it comes to this particular status, and they have to be implemented with neither fear nor favour, as I'm sure you will understand."

"Not really, unless the parameters have been changed since we were awarded it."

"No, they haven't changed at all. Under Khrushchev, changes were made that were neither legal nor in the interest of the international working class."

"So the people who gave us the status of an autonomous republic got it wrong. Did the international working class even notice our little republic?"

"That would appear to be the case," by then he was on autopilot. "It was a period in our history when many mistakes were made."

"Really? And I suppose that during the last eight years there has been a period of gentleness and brotherly love."

"I should warn you, comrade, that it is still an offence to speak ill of the socialist fatherland and even worse to ridicule it. I will disregard it on this occasion, because I can understand that all this has come as a great shock to you - personally. I understand. I am an understanding man, but having looked at this case in great depth - from a legal point of view, of course - I have no choice but to discontinue the status under discussion from the end of next month. There is nothing more to say. You could of course appeal my decision, but I can tell you now that you have no chance of winning it, and you may alienate those whose onerous duty it is to defend the fatherland from external and internal dangers. I suggest then that we bring this meeting to a close, as I am busy man and I'm sure that you have some things to do as well," he injected doubt into his voice when he articulated the last part of that sentence.

Why have I told you this? Well, this was the dismal end of our autonomous republic, which I had won by threatening my own life. That had been dramatic; that had been news. I had briefly become a well-known figure, but its demise came as a whimper on a grey day in Biysk of all places. A backwater passing judgement on a community that was even more of a backwater. The man had no memory of my struggle, and would the Surelikud notice this change in their status? The end of the Surelik Autonomous Republic was not tragedy but farce. And I certainly wasn't going to go on hunger strike again. I liked my life. I liked my own personal status. But we were going to fight on. Surely?

It was not quite true that nothing happened in the lands of

the Triers between the overthrow of the First Secretary and the appearance of the Birthmark: millimetric changes had been taking place and by the end of that long period, they'd become hundreds of miles. There was a great deal more corruption, and with that there inevitably came a loss in the regime's credibility. Even the *apparatchiki* no longer believed in the ruling ideology, as could be seen later by the way they rushed for shares in the assets newly privatised by the Drunkard – often buying them for some trifling sums which had them on a Mediterranean cruise before you could whistle the Internationale.

It is time to take pity on my readers who are mightily sick of offices and bureaucrats, stamps and pens, and papers to be shuffled by plump hands with too many rings and all the other monstrous things that make up the few precious days that the God of the Triers has given us. Fate has counted their number and we have to use them sensibly. So why would a reader pick up a book that's full of offices and bureaucrats who speak in dull, empty little sentences? Let's get away from all that, because man was born to dream and not go from one office to another to get a piece of paper stamped and dated. Surely not!

But first, because I have no intention of spoiling you, I'm going to take you back to the prehistory of the Surelikud. We know from the Triers' records that the first encounter between their explorers and the Surelikud occurred on the 16th of August in the year of our Lord 1537. And we have an oral tradition which merely says "long ago". The Surelikud who were out on a hunting trip were surprised to see such strangely overdressed people, given the heat of the summer months. The strangers were in uniforms that had stripes and badges to denote their rank and bravery, but the Surelikud knew nothing of that. In those days we had no cloth, so our clothing – such as it was – was made of leather and furs in the winter. The Surelikud thought that the Triers must have been hiding something under so many clothes in summer. And eventually we realised that they did.

"Their leader had a funny hat," the Shennakhud related, "which he took off and placed on the head of the most vociferous of our company. We didn't have leaders then and nor do we now in the forest, but the Triers were equally ignorant of us, so they thought that he was our leader. They invited our hunting party to their camp just outside the forest and made us a meal. We found their behaviour amusing and were very impressed by the cartloads of supplies and so many horses that we couldn't count them.

"We fell asleep because of the heavy food and we had never drunk wine before. When we awoke, we found that they had taken away one of our number. It was the vociferous one, and we looked around for our bows and spears, but they had also gone. We didn't know each others' languages, but still we persevered and eventually they took us to him. They had given him more presents and somehow explained to him that they wanted to show him to their king, who must have been the Great Caesar. Once he had expressed his desire to go, we left him with some misgivings."

I found the Triers' version in their archives, and the stories are strikingly similar. Our near nakedness was remarked on repeatedly, but they were complimentary in their description of our physical presence and our posture. They claimed that the vociferous one was our king, an inaccuracy which confirmed our own version. What surprised them most was our "innocence" or "simplicity", a judgement that they arrived at without any knowledge of our language or culture. I won't say that they were wrong, because it seems that they were arguing that we were honest and didn't indulge in lies. No wonder that they have to have an order from heaven, "Thou shalt not lie", to keep them from not lying too much. They also noticed that we had no concept of property. Of course, that too was right: everything belonged to Kōblus and Valmistaya, who jointly held the world together so that we, the animals and all the forest could benefit from it.

Much later the Shennakhud added a coda to this story: the

thing that they hid under their clothing was their deceitfulness, typical not just of the Triers but of all Europeans.

And what of the vociferous one or Haalekas, as he is remembered in our oral tradition, who left with the Triers? He did not return for many years and when he came, he came with many incredible stories of great achievements and great adversities which the Shennakhud refused to believe, but nevertheless recorded in their memories because they were so remarkable – more remarkable than the epics of Võitleya. But Haalekas could not stay long amongst the Surelikud, as the Shennakhud will always tell you, because he had to leave for other destinations. He went south-east into the lands of the Wall-Builders, east to the Tuva and far beyond and west to the many-languaged mountains, where he adopted their religion and their way of dress, which he never relinquished. The Triers had unsettled him, and he could never again feel at home in the company of the Surelikud.

The Parable of Malice and the Impossibility of Unlearning Things

Andrei felt indebted to Masha. She was the one who revealed the fundamental misunderstanding in his marriage. She appeared out of nowhere when he was walking to work. He was taking his usual route, or more precisely his only route, because he was a creature of habit. He enjoyed its familiarity. The library, built before the Revolution, is considered a masterpiece, but what he liked about it was that it was always there – part of his landscape and part of his tedious existence. He had even been to a lecture there on the library itself. It was by a celebrated academic, or at least that is what the man who introduced him said, adding too that the illustrious academic had been his mentor and role model, and without this the mentee would never have made such a success of his life, though Andrei couldn't remember what he was successful at. So the academic said that our library was one of the three finest libraries in Europe. Andrei forgot why this was but the factoid remained embedded. This was Andrei's landscape, and it was a joy to have a good reason for being proud of it. I'm not sure that he understood much at the time, as the academic spoke for an hour and a half, and occasionally Andrei's mind must have wandered. There was no time for questions at the end, which the presenter regretted, but they had to go partly because the janitor wanted to go home and kept ringing the fire alarm. They had overrun and there was a match on that evening between Spartak and Dynamo. You could see the janitor's point and, besides, Andrei hadn't been able to formulate a proper question and probably hadn't wanted to. He would have been nervous about asking it, had he been able to manage that formulation. He probably felt that he'd learnt all he needed to know about the library that evening, and would in any case have failed to retain that knowledge, which is what did happen, demonstrating, if nothing else, that he knew himself well and could predict his future behaviour. And even though he didn't take any books out of the library and only visited it on that occasion, he felt very good about having such a fine exemplar just round the corner.

He also liked the mini-supermarket on the corner. It seemed reliable and had all the essentials. This of course is no longer the case, and now it is constantly in search of the untried and the unknown.

Remarkably he even liked the empty plot. The building had burnt down when he was five or six, and they never did anything with it except bring out plans that never went beyond a newspaper article. Why did he like it? Not because nature was taking over, and trees appeared to signify the passing years. He liked it because it was there and had become part of his landscape. Maybe he would have felt differently if it had been burnt down when he was ten or eleven and the original building had wormed itself into his psyche so attached to constancy.

He actually liked the two apartment blocks everyone said were an eyesore. They have demolished them now and replaced them with a meandering, shiny plastic-yellow construction.

Chorus: *See how the hero walks, his gallant acts to perform. Like Greek heroes of old he travels through the canyons of his wide and wild world, venturing into unknown buildings and learning of great exploits he can surpass. His Penelope has begun to weave. But a Circe hides in the labyrinth of the provincial city, ready to drive him mad by weaving a duplicity of words.*

So one day Masha popped out from behind the famous library and waved to him. She was going his way, she said, so she must have known his way to work. And she added that she was really pleased to see him because she wanted him to know that she cared deeply about him and his wife. This surprised him a bit as he hardly knew her, and though his wife was the same age as her and went to the same school, she hardly ever spoke about Masha and never with any great warmth – though if they did meet, his wife was very polite and asked her all the right questions.

She cared about them, she kept saying, and Masha did seem a very kind, sensitive and reliable person. She spoke as if she knew a lot of things. Most importantly those things – those arcane things that govern how we behave, which he and his wife never really thought about, because they were happy with where those things were leading them. He loved her, and was happy enough with his job. The salary wasn't bad, but could have been better. He loved his wife and she appeared to love him. They both liked skating and walking in the hills nearby, but never thought of travelling. Why would you want to do that? So expensive, when they had everything they wanted in their own city.

But Masha put him right. She cared about them because she and his wife had been very close and always would be. Of course they'd been close, they had so much in common. But now they were less close because Masha was doing so well. Luck may have had something to do with it, but whatever the cause, his wife felt a little bit threatened and frustrated, so she, that is Masha, decided to seek her out and they had a get-together, a heart-to-heart, and his wife had confessed her frustrations. His wife, according to Masha, did care about him deeply – and of course by this stage he knew that he wasn't going to like what Masha was about to say, but he knew that she was saying it for the right reasons. He had to listen, he had to take his medicine and then do whatever he had to do to put things right, for he didn't just care deeply about his wife, he loved her as the moon loves the sun whose beams bring it to life.

Chorus: *How can bold Andrei listen to the malevolent enchantress as she sets out her potions of thoughts and fabrications to trap our hero and turn him into another animal? What does it mean that she would upset the universe for a whim? And can wise Penelope save him from his fate?*

Masha explained that he was too conventional and predictable for his wife. She needed a little excitement in her life, she needed change, but she didn't know how to broach the subject – the difficult subject of change. Afterwards he remembered that she used precisely this awkward word "broach" which carried the devastating news that his wife couldn't open her heart to him. Apparently they were in a rut, and Masha had kindly taken it upon herself to intervene before it was too late. At first he couldn't believe Masha. She was exaggerating. His wife could not have said any such things. She was happy. She often said so. If he got home from work after her, as he usually did, she would walk towards him in a very relaxed manner and hug him. Sometimes she would say, "Welcome home, darling," and sometimes, "Love you, pet." He never wondered whether the alternation had any significance or why the frequency of the endlessly repeated formulas rarely varied. That was his life and he was secure within it. She appeared to be the same.

Chorus: *Thank the gods of all the Triers' lands, he falters before rash acts. He hears the music of Penelope's welcome words, and cries out for stasis, steadiness and the unchanging nature of rose-fingered dawns. Andrei, hold firm! Andrei the hero of the quiet lives of progress which never change but slip through the valley of tears without shedding a single one; oh soft-cushioned lives with no feral force, hold firm! we sing in choral fortitude.*

But gradually the seed of doubt that Masha had sown began to do its work. Perhaps his wife's laconic approach to the marriage was not as relaxed as it seemed. Perhaps the way she sauntered up to him was a sign of resignation. She had given up all hope of changing her life. She looked at him in a certain manner, and he had always thought that it expressed love, but it could have been the realisation that this was all she could expect of him. She was nobly holding the marriage together with almost motherly care for an awkward son whose egocentricity would be acceptable in a child but not in a companion for life.

The thought of it made him shudder and he knew what he had to do, but first he had to do his research. Of all the cities he examined, Kathmandu seemed the most exotic. He bought the tickets and took them to her. She looked at them in unexpected astonishment. Was it joy or discomfort? That wasn't clear. "Kathmandu? I've never been to the capital. Not to Novosibirsk or even Omsk. I once went to Tyumen for a week when my grandfather took the waters there. I was glad to get home. We weren't poor; we just didn't go in for that kind of thing."

Chorus: *They will descend into history. Dangerous but compelling shall be the helical flightpath by which the plane shall make its way down to the valley floor surrounded by magisterial mountains. It shall be a descent into hell for her and for him it shall be into an earthly paradise. A few words can be stronger than the strongest human bonds of love and friendship. The malice of the few governs the goodness of the great majority.*

She went but was not impressed. It was hot and sticky. The

food was strange. The language incomprehensible. She would have preferred to go to Tyumen if she had to go anywhere. He on the other hand could not stay still. The weather was not excessively hot because of the altitude, the food had a flavour that sent you half way to heaven, and the language sounded wonderful. He had to learn it.

Chorus: *But no! He does not turn, but carries on along the road Circe had directed him. He does not turn, but on he goes and see how he transmutes. He is lost to the* civitas, *he is lost to civilised manners and he is lost to the covetousness of the civilised who only move to take or destroy. How Penelope shall weep as she weaves, for he shall never return.*

He thought that he knew his wife, and in a way he did, because she had been happy and loved him. But he couldn't be sure, because we never know anything – even and perhaps especially the things we're most certain about, because certainty is not something we can attain, and yet we lose so much in our striving for it. We cannot be happy with a strong impression, a belief in its fixed place, just as we destroy our security by striving too much for it. Complete security is also unattainable. He fell for Masha's meddling because he wasn't certain and that is a sensible place to be, but it should be comfortable too. Uncertainty is what keeps us alive. Uncertainty does not exclude the possibility of being fairly sure.

And the lesson he learnt was to distrust those who speak as though they know – who have learnt to speak convincingly. He learnt that lesson too late for himself as now he was another person, just as happy and miserable but in a different way: he was hooked on uncertainty. He enjoyed not having a permanent home and not knowing where he would be next month. He missed his wife occasionally, but not the certainty and security of their happy life together. They grew apart and all because of Masha's malicious meddling.

Chorus: *Move your dwelling often and you'll always know your place in the world.*

*

The scribe is puffing her cheeks, but she is beyond attempting to put me on the right road. Not a word does she say, which for some strange reason displeases me. I had prepared my script once more. Still, I'll not complain, for she has done me proud. We'll get back to our story.

And then everyone woke up with the Birthmark in charge, and many people thought that they were having a nightmare. Halvatud disliked him, but I was of the opposite opinion. There was something of Khrushchev in him, but this one didn't have a plan. And it ended badly. Ah, progress and my war against it. Well, things had not been going well during the period between the demise of our autonomous republic and the arrival of the Birthmark.

Halvatud had been right to argue against my prudent decision to respect the law when my only mentor could no longer mentor. Once I made that decision, I had to enforce it, and the consequences were disastrous. The resistance continued for three or four years, and I was getting angrier and angrier, but then something broke in the Surelikud of the forest, and they gave in completely. They filled the settlements and the schools were overflowing. Alcoholism reached unheard-of levels, few people wanted to go out trapping and everyone wanted to have a job at the settlements. Worse was to come: it soon came apparent that, given the lack of jobs, people were moving to the Väikelinn and even people who lived in the settlements were switching to the language of the Triers. I couldn't understand why, but then it suddenly occurred to me: they were inseparable from their television sets. How can you expect someone who has just spent a cosy evening alone or in company of a half-bottle of vodka with that magic box in front of them – entertaining them, mesmerising them, entrancing them and anaesthetising the pain that progress had brought them – to then get up at five in the morning and trudge out into the snow and deep into the forest to set traps, when nothing in that humdrum can match the vicarious excitements that are repeated throughout the evening with the aid of a cathode tube!

If it was humdrum then, it must have been humdrum beforehand, says the scribe. Oh no, not at all. Not at all, dear scribe! For a normal person, by which I mean a person who hasn't been anaesthetised by television the previous evening, the trip out into the winter landscape is an adventure of odyssean proportions in which the freeze has dried the air to a crispness that makes it headier than vodka but doesn't blur the mind; it sharpens it. And then the forest reveals itself in all its variety and busyness: the trees stand static in their solid wisdom, plants clamber up them thirsty for their juices but take care not to take too much, the birds call out but cannot be seen, a squirrel runs nervously, and somewhere out there a bear lumbers along deceivingly alert and in search of its next meal. Rare, it's true, but a few tigers are still in our forest. But most of all the adventurer is interested in the small animals whose fur Western women want on their backs.

Unanaesthetised man didn't go out for the money, as he would get very little for his labours compared with the end-value of the furs; he went because he was addicted to the journey which sometimes took him a couple of weeks. Some of the trappers were proud of their contribution to the nation's wealth, which came from a practice they'd grown to like.

When did anaesthetised man last touch the earth? He only touches the smooth, cleansed surfaces of manufactured objects, mostly made of plastic. He lives in a virtual world. Maybe matter really is only a mutation of energy, but when I touch a tree, it is solid enough, and when I run my fingers across a leaf and feel its fragility and the perfect architecture of its veins, I know that this tireless luxuriance planted in the moist earthiness of much of planet's epidermis is a gift, and

I understand that this beauty and constant transformation through long cycles and short constitutes a remarkable destiny we must stop progress from destroying. As a child it was my homely universe, as solid and constant as the many-languaged mountains, but now I know it to be a speck of green and blue in the grey infinity of an arid universe.

The Television

Television revealed itself to have some of the strengths of the radio, which I previously ignored, while exaggerating its defects. The problem with television is not just the rubbish they pour into your sitting room, but also and most particularly what it stops you from doing. At the risk of overdramatising it, I would argue that the television stops you from having a life. It has its uses, but generally what good things it can do can be done better by books, newspapers and, I now admit, the radio. The TV is toxic, and all the more so for minority languages. It has been the main driver in pushing Surelik towards language death, and the remedy is for the language to be on TV with material that can compete with the Triers'. We've never had this.

For many the reality of the cathode is more real than of the physical world we think we know, but never will. For some in our fragmented society, soap-opera characters are real people they care more about than their neighbours. The viewer is a lonely spectator of people with whom there can be no dialogue, no interaction. These characters entertain but also underscore the chasm that divides their exciting fictional lives from the tedium of the viewers'.

Television is to human beings what a light bulb is to moths. A human being in front of a television enters a catatonic state in which it cannot switch the TV off or even switch it to another channel, even when the programme is clearly an idiocy. When confronted with a TV, a human being is like any other animal whose normal behaviour patterns have been interrupted by some unnatural phenomenon for which nature had not prepared it. And yet TV is a most useful propaganda tool, and determines every debate that occurs across a nation, marginalising movements that had been powerful in the past.

Like the radio, television unites and fragments at the same time: vast numbers of people are watching the same thing, but they're mainly doing this on their own or, at most, in the company of their family or a few friends. The process of taking the source of culture further and further away from the people who can rightly be said now to consume it – a key element of progress – was enhanced by the arrival of the box in the sitting room, and then in the West in practically every room in the house. We had no escape. And we went out of our way to obtain and pay for the tool which would mould us into clones of each other.

*

Ah the scribe has woken up and asked me about the last parable. "What time was it set in?" she asks me. And it is a very good question, and my answer will not convince her. She has certainly detected an inconsistency. But the reader knows by now that I rarely listen to her advice. She's not here to give me advice, but to type and have the occasional argument. My answer is simply this: the bit in Kathmandu must have been in the late sixties and the bit in the land of the Triers in the present day. When she protested, I asserted in my plain-speaking manner: "If I can put Yuri Gagarin on the moon, I can do anything." A parable is a fiction; now let me get back to the facts.

Halvatud never reproached me for not having taken his advice on not enforcing school attendance. Small nations cannot afford a single mistake, while empires can be ruled by idiots and still prosper, even when they descend into civil war and other horrors that civilisation inflicts upon us. Of course that is also their weakness, because when circumstances change dramatically and a moment of wisdom is required, they are incapable of finding any but only want to carry on in their usual chaotic manner as though the world will always tolerate their arrogant behaviour. What can I say? I was responsible for that mistaken policy and the consequences that followed. I didn't mean to admit these things when I first decided to write this memoir, but the process of writing it has forced me re-examine these events I prefer to forget. And I don't have to think that hard before realising that my culpability is undeniable.

It was during the rule of the Birthmark that I started not only to doubt my own decisions but to question the concept of leadership – particularly the sole leader, the leader as an exceptional person produced by history, destiny or the God of the Triers. Napoleon, Bismark, Lenin. Rarely women, of course. Surely if peoples are to be emancipated, then they should rule themselves and not subjugate themselves to a single human will. Ah, the scribe objects and wonders why I am the leader, if I feel so strongly about it and have done for so long. She has a point, but my response is immediate: "You know very well why, because you were amongst the petitioners who came to me and wanted to give me my job back. Don't you remember? Every decision involves a choice between at least two outcomes, and so our actions are constrained by the lack of possibilities in any moment of our lives. What would have happened if I'd refused the post? You would have chosen someone from your own little group, and I can tell you, they were all more incompetent than me. Every one of them. I can see them now, including you at the back. The idea of not having a leader, but some kind of democratic body re-elected very regularly, for instance, was not on the agenda. So if there had to be a leader, it was only logical that I should be the one."

That's what I told her and it put her in her place, but we've jumped ahead of ourselves. The Birthmark, that's right. And my rethinking of my fundamental beliefs. I was in my eighties, as even a not very astute reader will have realised. This is not the moment for radical thinking. Apparently it is the time for staying at home with the television and a cat, but that was not for me. By the late eighties, the number of Surelik-speakers had fallen from the level of three hundred thousand when we won the autonomous-republic status and was approaching two hundred thousand, so when the committee approached me and asked me to resign, I wasn't altogether surprised. If I was caught mildly off-guard, it was that they had the courage to do this. Certainly they were sheepish, so sheepish. Laughably so. But beneath their shamefaced expressions, I could detect a glint of intense joy. Of course there was, and who could blame them? They were frightened of me. I can't imagine why. Surely not because I am straight-talking, unlike the Surelikud of the plain who have to exchange five or six compliments before they can get down to business? Quite possibly that glimmer of exultation in their eyes was the product of my hubris. I admit that at times I am a little arrogant – with the arrogance of someone who has looked death in the face and even yearned for it, and then has suddenly seen it off and achieved what had for so long seemed an impossible dream. After an experience like that, you expect a lot from life.

Now who do you suppose took over my post and became the chairman of the West Siberian Surelik Cultural Committee? I'm sure that the reader can guess, although I have to admit that I didn't see it coming. It was, of course, none other than my old friend Vladimir Paulusev. They must have already chosen him on the basis of his unassailable self-belief: I was shocked, as he had been doing nothing for thirty years – enough years to give him an expression of grey-haired experience, but I knew that he'd learnt nothing because I had designed his job to be utterly pointless. The great advantage of doing nothing is that you can never get anything wrong. When I gave him a sinecure, I unwittingly gave him an unblemished track record. The Paulusevs of this world will end up running everything – that was the thought that struck me then, but in fact the Paulusevs are never in power for long because of their incompetence.

This dichotomy between the plain and the forest is perhaps best described by our prejudices against each other: the Surelikud of the plain like to say, "What the Surelikud of the forest know about a tree would surprise a monkey," and the Surelikud of the forest like warn their children, "Don't believe that a Surelik of the plain is not a Surnudhing [foreigner] just because you can understand his speech." I am, I suppose, still very much a Surelik of the forest in spite of my learning – my obsessive desire to understand the Europeans and their cultures. I'm in the midst of them, and yet I always feel – even now – that I'm on the outside looking in. I am alone. And yet I'm in amongst them, caught up in their diatribes and bitter disputes, championing one side, championing another, staring them in the eye, holding my counsel, but always keeping a lookout for any signs of danger. Those were the lessons I learnt in the thirties and forties, but how can I unlearn them. They are not needed now, and nor am I what I was before those years – those unforgiving years.

So there I was in my late eighties freed of my responsibilities to the Surelikud, their language and all their other problems. At the same time, many things were happening in the lands of the Triers: the Birthmark had opened up the society, which was a good thing, but he was also hellbent on shifting the economy towards the free market, as he had convinced himself that the Noisy Music propaganda was correct, which means that it wasn't propaganda but a golden thread of truth. Perhaps I do him a disservice, because I cannot know his thoughts, but only his actions. Readers will know about these things, and I mention them because they attracted me. History was being made, and it wasn't happening in Väikelinn. I made plans to move to the Triers' capital again, but before I left I want to tell you an amusing incident that occurred shortly before my train journey.

I was in one of Väikelinn's cafés reading the paper and was trying out for the first time a coffee drink called a cappuccino when a fat man with an air of importance temporarily mitigated by his desire to solicit my assistance appeared in the room.

"I've written a great book," he said grandly.

"Really?" was all I could say.

"You'll love it, Rahväema."

"Do I know you?"

"No, but you soon will"

"Really?"

"Oh you will when you've read it."

"What is your book about?"

"Great Surelikud in history."

"Then there are some? I thought that the Surelikud were more sensible than that."

His flabby, expressionless face was unable to move as he stared at me with incomprehension which he struggled with for a bit and then gave up on. "Do you know who Eisenstein's assistant cameraman was?"

"No idea!"

"A Surelik! Yes, his name was Kaameramees and he came from Väikelinn."

"Ah, now I understand your game. You must have been working on this for years."

For some reason, he was now exultant. "Do you know, for instance, who Ronald Reagan's cook was?"

"Again, you have me speechless. Do we have to go on?"

"A Surelik again! His name was Kokkama and he came from Väikelinn"

"Väikelinn. What a place! We should name it after the cook."

"And do you know ..."

"Stop!" I interrupted him and quite absurdly my anger was genuine. I forgot that members of small cultures deal with their marginalisation in different ways, particularly those who live their culture in the shadow of another overbearing one, as in the case of the good people of Väikelinn. "Mr Surelik, you are an incredibly stupid man. We've lost our status as an autonomous republic, and you would have us scrabbling around in the trivia for some paltry association with what the West calls greatness. We have other definitions: we never won battles like Waterloo or Stalingrad. We never had orchestras, and high buildings, but we did have great poets, sagas, songs, belief systems and a beautiful, beautiful language. Have a bit of pride instead of nationalistic bombast which is cruel in large countries and merely ridiculous in small ones.

"For your information, Eisenstein would have agreed with me. He was a Russian Jew born in Latvia, and he cared nothing for nations. He was interested in other things. More important things!"

And the man paused for half a minute, possibly to digest what I'd said, and then he spoke: "Rahväema, if you give me your address, I'll send you a copy of my book."

Dismayed by his obtuseness, I gave him my work address, shook his hand and left. No doubt he sent the manuscript and it ended up on desk of Vladimir Paulusev who probably liked it, because I took the train to the capital and left all that behind.

Ah the city again! How different was my reaction in 1989 from what I had felt when I first went there! Now it held no surprises, only memories – not all of them good. But it felt as though the city carried the world inside it – certainly all of the varied lands of the Triers. There would be the Tuvans, the Mari, the North Ossetians, the Chechens, the Dagestanis, the Baltic peoples, the Tartars, the Kalmyks and there amongst them a small group of Surelikud. I, who had fought so hard to maintain one of the most "primitive" lifestyles – that of the semi-nomads of the Surelik forest – welcomed the city and its anonymity and felt that I was welcomed by it, simply because it did not rebuke me. The innate self-importance of the city is mitigated by its failure to notice you. I was away from the endless dissatisfaction of the forest Surelikud and the increasing impatience of those of the plain. I was alone, and I was nobody again. It was easier now to think in the city than it was in Väikelinn and still more so than in the forest, which should have cradled me as one of its own and opened its expanses to my wandering thoughts. But no, the bustle of the city was now more conducive to a productive solitude than was the small town or the forest. And that bustle spoke of many things, but most of all and most loudly it spoke of the enormous energy of human beings and the many exciting and wonderful things we could achieve if only we could invent the one thing that eludes us: a political system that involves us all and looks after us all and above all after the beautiful planet and the future generations who will have to populate it.

The city no longer contained those I'd known held in its stony chambers and behind its grand facades – except perhaps some acquaintance I had no interest in seeking out. There were just those ghosts we call memories. Osip mainly, and he revived feelings I'd buried long ago along with my guilt. I thought of my disloyalty and lack of courage, both misplaced because my survival was entirely due to a happy coincidence and my arrest could not have been avoided. I thought of his mannerisms, his intellect and above all his love of life. The pointless cruelty of those times was the product of fear, and he was fearless, a figure of strength that had to be cut down by the fearful progenitors of fear. And yet he believed in the regime more than they did.

I saw a hotel where I and that bastard bigamous husband of mine had stayed, and that was a ghost whose haunting I could have done without. But I had to admit that he too was a part of that messy thing that is my life – a man for whom I must have felt something at some stage, and the reason why I did I did not want to examine too closely. Everybody we live with or even just frequent, like every place we live in, becomes irredeemably part of who we are. We are indivisible from

278

each other – for good or for bad, enhancing our creativity or dampening it down, communicating some indefinable spirituality or drawing us into a culture of grasping desires. If Osip had met me when I was with Edwin, he would never have had anything to do with a woman of such bad taste. The two men couldn't have been more different: one worshipped power and the other did not hate it, but rather liked to observe it while holding it in contempt and finding it ridiculous – that was his fundamental mistake. At some level they had understood this.

These were indeed interesting and upsetting times, but I'm not going to give you a history lesson because this is our recent history, and the readers know it as well as I do. A lot happened before and after the coup, but it was really only of interest to me and not the readers. The morning after the failure of the coup d'état was in effect another coup – supposedly when a coup fails, a country returns to the *status quo ante*. Instead we awoke to a new dawn and a new narrative: suddenly we were escaping from nearly three-quarters of a century of unremitting misery, whilst the rest of the world had enjoyed milk and honey flowing from an endless fountain, because democracy ruled and no one was surveilled! The enlightened leaders of the West had no desire to pry into their citizens' thoughts or even discontents, though – heaven knows – why would they have had any? That is a historical truth and anyone who denies this is either a fool or a villain. And I am both fool and villain.

It could be said that some of the leaders the old new regime that came to power when I was seventeen and accompanied me at a distance throughout my adult life until then had also persuaded themselves of the above fairy tale. The regime fell with a whimper, so different from its birth, and in that it resembled a human life, which starts with a scream – so I'm told, though I don't remember my son's – and the vigour of a new life, and after a lifespan of an average length in the West and the land of the Triers it came to a sudden end, although its supporters had been at its bedside for some months – some might say for years. To be fair, many supporters remained for quite a while, and the country felt that it had never been consulted about the bulldozer of shock treatment before it went storming across the land like a natural disaster.

Then in the afternoon, the weather changed and a thunder storm had everyone heading for home. I reached my flat in a state of mild euphoria. The running for cover had quickened my mind and I felt that the coming change might after all be good for the Surelikud. But when I closed the door behind me and heard the heavy drops rain drops clatter against the windows, suggesting their fragility and perhaps that of the building, my first opposing thoughts emerged through a fog of uncertainties and a sense of impotence. And I saw the water pouring down the panes, expressing perhaps nature's dominance of all things living and inanimate, in spite of man's heavy-handed attempts to tame its forces. It felt like a siege of the building and all the buildings in the city: perhaps both nature and man had conspired together to have us alone, fragmented and insecure.

The scribe has looked at me in disbelief. "Were you in the capital that day?" I ask, and she shakes her head and continues to type even these very words, but her expression is sceptical.

Well, what I do remember is that we were left in the dark. We didn't know what was going to happen, and we could never have guessed what did. Nor were we ever consulted.

How they fell for it, the Triers. Just as they'd taken to no property, so they switched to a mania for stuff like children at a circus that has just turned up in town. Long before that, they had queued outside a well-known chain of hamburger joints in search of this wonderful culinary experience, not knowing that they were the ones to be eaten. Their souls were consumed as they munched on tasteless food you had to smother with a sweet, red, viscous liquid, without which it was like chewing on cardboard. Still, the restaurants were colourful and reliably identical wherever they appeared. The staff spoke like robots, which made them suitable representatives of progress and the hybridisation of the mechanical and the humanoid which surely is to come and has long been trailed. The crude over-taste of the liquid was even worse than the under-taste of the food. But they didn't care because their brains were being blasted by noisy music which announced the invasion, not of soldiers in this case, but of mad ideas and stuff they'd have happily gone without up until that moment. Invasions of this kind can be more devastating than a military attack with tanks and bombers.

After nine months, there were child prostitutes on the streets of the once Great Caesar's Baltic capital. Did anyone care in the west? Of course not. The shock doctrine was a real shock. Secret policemen became billionaires and their bodyguards became quasi-policemen responsible not to the state but to billionaires who quarrelled like feudal lords. And people lost their jobs, towns lost their townspeople, and after four or five years, I had finally understood the meaning of a word I'd often encountered on the page but not in life: *bourgeois*.

Oh, the civilised! How they live with their death throughout their tortured existences, both the slack ones who live off other people's work and the ones who work so hard that they never have a moment in their lives that they can actually live. No wonder the Triers had their revolution shortly after my arrival in Väikelinn – at least with the old new regime, the pain was shared out a bit.

The civilised, yes they love their death. "I can't believe I'm thirty," they say. And then forty, fifty, sixty, seventy. Always with their eyes on the clock and never on the moment.

Ah the civilised! They want so much from life, but get nothing from it. Instead of being grateful for the life Nature gave them, they complain of not being able to live several lives and finding out which is best before finally deciding – and they call this the lightness of being. Unbearable insatiability! They want so much, and all they get is a sense of having been robbed by fate. They cannot live with the curve of life which changes us – like a tree which while it ages digs its roots further into the fertile, generous earth that feeds us all."

When I think back to those times, I find that the episode that most typified them was the evening Troyanskikonyev invited me to a soirée. He was a very rich man and donated sums of money that were small change in his pocket but substantial enough for the charity I worked with to feed a considerable number of mouths. I never knew where he made his money and I never asked. He was useful to me, and I was a route to salving his conscience – if it needed salving. I can't remember who was talking the usual drivel when we came in, but I remember his words: "... Our president may be a drunk and a bit of a fool, but he's doing a good job of modernising the economy – with the help of the Noisy Musics, our new-found friends. It's results that we're concerned with, not ideology. We've had enough of that in the twentieth century."

I immediately wanted to shout at them – them being ex-high-up officials and the ex-spooks of the old new regime – but all I could manage in that exalted company was to jerk forward a little and mutter a little clumsily, "You say this in jest, I imagine?"

Having seen this, my companion Troyanskikonyev spoke up, "Perhaps Rahväema could provide another view of what's happening in the Triers' lands – or what's left of them. But first I'll introduce her, because not all of you know who she is, though the older ones will remember that she famously took on Khrushchev and won..."

"... only because he let her," said a man who turned out to be Ferdyshchenko. "Oh but we do know who she is, don't we, and I have a nasty feeling that the conversation is going to pass from dull to outrageously tiresome and repetitive."

"Stay quiet, Ferdyshchenko, for once," Troyanskikonyev ordered. "Now in her nineties [Ferdyshchenko nodded furiously to ridicule such antiquity], Rahväema has a venerable curriculum of activities in the arts and politics which has won plaudits around the country and the world [Ferdyshchenko spluttered visibly], and is now very much engaged in the campaign to get food to those in our society who are struggling in the transition to a free market."

I stood up as though we were in political meeting, and I meant to take my opportunity whilst fully aware of its pointlessness. "I was never an uncritical supporter of the old regime, which in its seventy-four years inflicted many miseries on me and people close to me. In the last couple of decades, even those who ran the country didn't really believe in it, and the Moron stultified the country not with cruelty but with pettiness. Something had to happen, but what did happen was not inevitable. When the regime fell, I was pleased because I naively hoped that it would reform itself, by which I meant a more open society in which ideas could be discussed, but the fundamental values that worked in the regime's favour could be protected, because it was a society that delivered many important things: good education, good healthcare, full employment, a more relaxed atmosphere at work, considerable subvention of the arts without as much censorship as Western propaganda claimed – I'm talking of the later decades here – and a proper desire to look for artistic brilliance rather than financial gain through the lowest common denominator."

"Oh aren't they sweet, these communists," said Ferdyshchenko; "they sound so pious and then it turns out that they're just as elitist as the rest of us."

"I was never a communist, never a member of the party, but I suspect that you were, Ferdyshchenko, from when you were a young man or even a teenager."

"Oh nasty! You're showing your claws now, Rahväema, but so what! Of course I was in the party – for the very period you mention – but we have to move with the times, you know." And he looked at me condescendingly while everyone laughed. He loved those moments.

"The Birthmark's assistant," I continued, "said a very wise thing: that the greatest beneficiary of our Revolution was the Western working class. If that was right or even half right, then the Western working class is in for a rough ride. I think that it already is."

A professorial man with bifocals and a well-trimmed goatee who was staring at me with disdain decided to speak: "Have you never heard of the *trickle-down effect*[11]?"

"I'm afraid I *have* heard of that little bit of witchcraft people like you like to believe in, simply to salve your consciences, because you cannot be that stupid."

"How dare you?" shouted the man leaping out of his chair and turning red in the face. He tried to advance towards me but Troyanskikonyev and a woman, whom he was possibly married to, stopped him.

Troyanskikonyev turned to me angrily, "As I was the one who suggested that you should join in the conversion, I would like you to keep it polite – and I wasn't expecting the Communist Manifesto."

"Why is it that if I say something you don't want to hear," I said as firmly as I could, while conscious that I was on my own, "you accuse me of being a communist? Most of the Western parties of all colours didn't believe in such nonsense up until the eighties."

"Move with the times, dear Rahväema, move with the times," Ferdyshchenko was enjoying it as much as I was, because we both wanted to shake them up in different ways. "It's the only sensible way to behave, if you want to get on in the world. Why would we be parroting what Western parties said twenty or thirty years ago, just when it's much more profitable for us to be parroting what they're saying today. It's so bleeding obvious except to a child or someone struggling through second childhood."

"Ferdyshchenko, you're quite a performer, aren't you? Entertainer, I should say. And what people want most today is to be entertained."

---

11 *trickle-down effect*: English in the original.

"I agree, even children can see some things adults can't. But if that's what people want, why would you want to ruin their days – and evening and nights. And for what? Do you think that you're going to change anything with all your nonsense?"

"Nonsense is a word for what we disagree with. In other parts of our society, nothing of what I've said would be the least bit controversial. As I have said, I welcomed the fall of the old regime, but now I believe that it was a tragedy for the lands of the Triers and a tragedy for humanity as a whole. And why shouldn't countries be free to pursue different economic policies. The world is being redesigned in the interest of the so-called advanced economies, by which they mean the most destructive. We are going back to the policies of the nineteenth century, but in a more extreme form, and you call it modernisation. The rich will get richer and the poor will get poorer. The rich countries will get richer and the poor countries will get poorer. But this will not go on forever, as the planet cannot bear the weight of this load. I have no idea whether the next form of modernity will be better than this; in fact I doubt it. We are now putting our energy into handing out free meals, and I came tonight in the hope of getting more funding, but it is not the solution; it is no more than a palliative."

"Isn't this fun! Don't you think this is terribly nineteenth century? Thank God for that! It was a terrible bore pretending to love the workers! The poor are so unlovely. Always complaining and never happy with their lot."

"How strange Ferdyshchenko, I thought that it was the new middle classes that complain a lot. They never have enough."

"Rahväema," he said showing his teeth, "you're not that old woman I saw begging in the street, are you? – or was she selling her body? Who knows?" – and with that last question, he looked around with a sly grin to gather in the laughter, which was provided – "Let me take a closer look. Mmm, I think not, but the clothes are almost identical. Where did you get them? Your grandmother's, I presume. Hello granny," here he tried to hug me in a convivial and condescending way, but I stamped on his foot.

"Ouch, that hurt! They should keep you in a cage."

"Ferdyshchenko, don't ever try to touch me again. I've had enough of your coarse behaviour."

"You, Rahväema, are just a wrinkly leftover from the past. You should have been put away in a wooden box long ago. And deep into the ground – very deep because you're the awkward kind of witch who would take it into your head to come back and haunt us. Am I alone here or does anyone else think that Rahväema had used up her allotted span long ago? Tinkle, tinkle, tinkle, time's up. Could the old lady with the white hair report to reception? Her statutory euthanasia appointment has been booked and there are only ten minutes to go. Wouldn't that be great?"

Everyone smiled weakly and someone uttered, "Ferdyshchenko always overdoes it."

Ferdyshchenko smiled gleefully and danced a step or two, before saying even more loudly than usual, "But Ferdyshchenko is well known for being a terrible, terrible person, and he has no wit. None at all. Didn't you know that? But he is a very useful person. And do you want to know why?"

This time they were silent and each one of them exuded a different kind of glumness.

"Ha, ha," he laughed, and carried on shouting. "Ha, ha, trust Ferdyshchenko to put a damper on the evening. Terrible Ferdyshchenko. You're all speechless because I teased the old lady. Mrs Surelik, you might call her. Have you heard of the Surelikud? If you have, the fault is all hers. On and on dragging her carcass from one decade to another, repeating the same stuff over and over again: the Surelik culture, the Surelik language, the Surelikud do this, the Surelikud do that. Does anybody care? Did anybody care? But she didn't get the message. Even the Surelikud are tired of her, but she defies the laws of nature or physics or whichever ministry deals with these things, and just keeps going. Anyway, as none of you have asked for the answer to my question and none of you have said that I shouldn't provide it, I've tossed a coin and I'm afraid it says that I have to tell you."

"I didn't see you toss a coin," someone pointed out.

"Well that just shows who's the idiot in the room. The answer (and I'd better get it out before someone stops me) is that I say things that everyone else wants to say but doesn't because they're far too civilised. Don't you agree, Rahväema:"

"I do ..."

"Oh do you now? Did you hear that, everybody; she agrees with everything I said about her?"

"I was about to say that I do partly agree with your claim that you say the things that other people would like to say, but don't. However they don't keep quiet because they're civilised. Their being so nicely civilised is the reason they think those things they don't want to say."

"Hmm. Interesting, but why don't they say them then?"

"Because they know them to be foul. But don't worry, they'll soon lose their last remaining scruples, and they'll be chirping them away very cheerily. Think of this, Ferdyshchenko, you're what is now called an early adopter."

Ferdyshchenko's face crumpled into a mock pout. "Trust Rahväema to spoil the party by trying to be philosophical, just when we were all enjoying ourselves. But at least you've got a tongue in your mouth, which is more than can be said of this lot."

"Ferdyshchenko, shut your fucking trap!" came yet another voice in the crowd.

"That didn't sound very nineteenth century. Deary me, people used to be more offensive with – what shall I say? – a degree of panache. I think that what we've got here is a nineteenth century that is uncouth and ill-mannered. What do you say, Rahväema?"

"I would say that you have defined our current global situation very well – and also the way *you* speak."

Some people laughed, but others had had enough. "Get them both out of here. They're just a couple of bores."

"I will go," I announced, "but Ferdyshchenko should stay. He belongs in your company, not mine. He entertains you, but you should open your ears and listen, because there are some depressing truths beneath the frivolity – they are your future. I happen to know on a very good authority that Tallyrand said, 'The trick is not to follow slavishly the twists and turns of history, but to perceive what is about to happen and make it happen.' I thought about this when Ferdyshchenko was extolling the virtue of opportunism, and it seemed to me that you would also be very entertained by this authority who has been persecuting me for many decades. I would willingly gift him to you, but apparently it doesn't work like that. You need a conscience."

"Get her out!"

"She's as mad as Ferdyshchenko, but not in a good way."

"They make a fine couple. Ying and Yang."

Somebody pushed me, and Troyanskikonyev made no attempt to intervene. "I'm going; I said that I'm going." There was another push, and I was at the main door, with the party-goers following me, most not out of hostility but merely out of a desire not to miss any entertaining episodes. Then I was out on the sterile landing of the tasteful block of flats in the "best" part of Moscow. Progress had come full circle.

The scribe, the scribe again, she has lodged yet another complaint, but this is also an unusual one. Can I use the name of another writer's character? I think so. It is not that I have copied somebody else's text; what happened was that at this party in the capital during the nineties – the late nineties when people were going hungry (and I bet that the Western press didn't report on yet another one of capitalism's great achievements) – there was this man and I thought to myself that he was just like Ferdyshchenko in *The Idiot*, living proof that the right conditions had occurred for such a shallow performer to prosper. I could have given you his real name, but he has become immensely rich on the proceeds of his flippancy and he would probably have sued me. And won. Besides, I don't think that Dostoyevsky would mind; he was influenced by European writers. Of course I'm not improving on him, because that would be impossible. There was a literary dialogue between the Triers and the Europeans, and the Triers were always the improvers, belying the old lie of the Europeans that the Trier writers were "primitive". This is even more absurd than saying that the Surelikud are primitive, which unfortunately many Triers do. Moreover, my own infuriating Ferdyshchenko was not wrong about everything. And when he was wrong, he was so wrong that it hardly mattered. Or perhaps it did.

Homo Lupus Homini. Man is the wolf of men, or man hunts down other men like a wolf. Romans, it appears, had more self-awareness than modern empires. They would never have called their wars humanitarian, though they did call them "just". They didn't want to annihilate – perhaps because labour was such an important resource – they wanted to rule, enslave and impose their supposedly superior culture, brutally if necessary. Are humans naturally such feral animals? I don't think that the Surelikud are. It is not that we are innately different, I'm sure; it is that we were few, and our lands so boundless. Cruelty arises when we fight over limited resources. The question is can we ever remove the vicious germ of greed once it has pierced our epidermis. Is it a virus that lingers in our blood and occasionally reasserts itself as a full-blown illness? Is this why civilised man needs religion and through it seeks to return to his primordial state – an impossible task but one worth attempting? That is the Fall. That is the loss of innocence – not because of sex but property, which is the true source of insecurity. This gives rise to an insane desire to accumulate – to own, that crazy verb. To own land, rivers, buildings, livestock and ultimately other human beings. To every action there is an equal and opposite reaction, and out of this descent arise all the complexities of a moral world. Not moral because morality prevails, but rather because of its very noticeable absence. This gives people a strong desire to regain what they have lost, and the endless Manichaean struggle begins.

Troyanskikonyev did not want to see me for some time, and stopped donating which made me feel guilty. Where had the pragmatic politician gone? But I would eventually get back in touch, but before that I came across one of his friends. Halvatud and I along with some other campaigners were leafleting outside a warehouse which belonged to a company that was hoarding foodstuffs in order to increase prices, and out walked one of the other oligarchs he'd introduced me to. The man was as always in the company of a couple of bodyguards. It turned out that it was one of his many assets. I thought this could be a good opportunity to rekindle a relationship that barely existed, and I ran over shouting his name, but he looked at me blankly and sent over one of his men to stop me. As we would expect, the bodyguard was a big man of the new kind. He looked as though he worked out every morning after swallowing a handful of testosterone pills. The result was that smooth plasticky skin that appears to have been formed in a mould by some industrial process. I was no expert, but I felt sure that the grey suit that hung on his muscular body was of the highest quality – the latest European fashion.

"Lady, you've been insulting my employer and my employer doesn't like that kind of behaviour. He's a very powerful man and also fabulously rich."

The man's simplicity was almost disarming, and while I rummaged through my brain for a suitable answer, he continued in a more threatening vein. Halvatud eventually caught up with me and butted in, "And what is he going to do to a little woman and a cripple, this fabulously rich employer of yours? I don't think that you have to do all the weight-lifting just to deal with the two of us."

The man turned to him as though he hadn't notice him before, and said, "I can see that you weren't very lucky in the lottery of life, cripple, but today your last little bit of luck of has run out. I'm a very old-fashioned man, you know, and whatever my boss says, I don't like to hit a woman I'm not married to..." and with that he swung his fist so hard into Halvatud's face that he lifted the dear man off his feet, and he must have been dead before he hit the ground again. That fragile thread had been broken.

The thug was found guilty and condemned to twelve years in prison, but nobody believed that he spent more than two weeks there. I believe that Halvatud purposefully provoked the man's homicidal lust to deviate it from me, but his death left me completely alone.

Ah, the scribe is complaining that I'm not alone; I have her and the whole movement behind her. Yes, yes, of course. No offence was intended. I do appreciate her work and we're nearing the end, but I still don't fully understand why she does it. We don't agree on much, whilst Halvatud and I always agreed, even when we didn't. We belonged to the same time and place, and our disagreements only increased our mutual respect.

When Travel Teaches It Does So Most Powerfully – a Parable

Now I shall speak of a very unusual person: a Surelik seaman. The reader will mutter under his breath, "Who could be further from the sea than a Surelik?" There is some truth in that, but we must learn that the world is varied, and none of the categories humans invent could possibly encapsulate that variety. Besides, I'm in control here, and if I want my seaman to be Surelik, then so he shall be.

When he was fourteen just after the war, his family moved to Leningrad as it was then known, and there he was fascinated by the port and the docklands and watched with envy as the ships, large and small, glided through the calm waters of the harbour as though they were moved by some hypnotising spirit or supernatural power rather than a grubby diesel engine. He thought continually of exotic destinations, smoke-filled dockside bars where a man forever in movement could glide in and glide out. It would be hedonism without responsibilities. Light without dark. Laughter without tears.

It was no surprise then that as soon as he could, he signed up and started to travel the world. He found the smoke-filled bars, witnessed the fights and made love to women, some of whom he hadn't paid for. And it felt like hard work, and didn't by any measure or yardstick live up to his dreams. Most of the time was spent in cramped cabins, and even in moments of solitude, no privacy existed. This was slightly compensated for by the camaraderie that springs from working in harsh conditions in which each man relied upon the other, whatever differences they may have had.

He looked down on many of the peoples he met superficially on his travels. Like many Triers, he felt that European culture was superior, though he was misinformed. Like many Triers, he thought that the Triers weren't quite as good as those affluent Europeans, and so he also felt that as quasi-Europeans, Triers were at least superior to the rest of the world – two more beliefs that were entirely erroneous. Why, you ask, did he think like a Trier when he was a Surelik? Well, if you ask that question, you haven't understood the seductive nature of power and empire.

He studied the deathly, monstrous movements of the sea more carefully than the foreign ports he visited and where he greedily imbibed the sordid pleasures of reality that had substituted the sublime adventures of his youthful dreams. By now this was his trade and he had to practice it.

One day – a day like any other and of which he had no expectations – they came into a battered port where there had recently been a war between two so-called ethnicities. The war was not over because this war had been as inconclusive as all the previous wars. Its only result was the capture by one side of this port and a small town close by. The ship was bringing in aide from the Triers, but he'd taken little interest in such things after his first few trips at sea. What did it matter to our Surelik seafarer? And as soon as he was given leave to go ashore, he rushed off in search of a bar.

But there were no bars. Or should I say that there were no bars that were open for business. There were few people. Many had fled, and some in their panic, had left most of their possessions which were currently being looted by the victors, whose main concern was how to transport their plunder. The buildings which hadn't been destroyed were unchanged, but the human presence in the port was entirely different from the settled mechanisms of the week before, and it was unlikely that what had once appeared to be the way of things and the language most heard in the street along with its networks of friendships and rivalries would ever be restored.

Stupidly he started to wander the street and lanes of the town in the pointless search of a drink and a little music. Then he saw an old woman weeping. Her wind-scarred face could still express the desolation of an abandoned child. No one looked at her and quite possibly no one heard her. But our Surelik traveller – a soul lost in the harsh, clattering machinery of international trade – did look at her and did hear her cries of anguish, and like a hypnotised body he glided over and sat down and embraced her, almost in tears himself. She turned, and at the end of an arm barely covered in flesh and sagging skin, her sunburnt skeletal hand touched his cheek as though to verify the nature of this unexpected apparition. Suddenly, some dormant force within her sprang to life: she rose and beckoned him into the half-destroyed house, and they entered the part of it that still retained its roof. She led him into a small room barely illuminated through a small window by the evening sun, and on a bed lay a small child who was clearly – even in that fading light – extremely ill and perhaps on the point of death. The old woman was speaking in her own tongue and imploring with her hands as if praying to God, but when he spoke in the language of the Triers, she immediately understood something and gestured with the upturned palms of her hand that he had to wait there – exactly where he stood. She rushed from the room and he knew that he had to stay, but he didn't know what to do with the encumbrance of his body – so he did just as she had wanted: he didn't move an inch. He felt like an intruder but at the same time he felt small and unimportant in the face of tragedy. And stupidly guilty for having gone in search of some fun as though it were a human right.

After a while she returned with two men. They walked like those who have witnessed horrors, and thus could no longer be horrified by anything. They had the security of those who have reached the highest degree of insecurity, and thus feared nothing. The first had a serviceable knowledge of the Triers' language, and could therefore act as an interpreter, and he introduced the other man who was a doctor. First, they wanted to know who he was and what he was doing in their port. They seemed comfortable with his replies. The little girl was very ill, and she would die if she didn't get the right medicines. Did the ship have a pharmacy? Only the rudiments, as it was a cargo ship. They seemed to think that the rudiments would probably cover their needs. The doctor wrote the names of a number of medicines on a scrap of paper, and said that any one of these would do, but underlined his preferred option. He seemed distracted but it was probably lack of sleep. He, his friend, the old woman and her grand-child had been abandoned by those who rushed to save their lives. They all belonged to the ethnicity that had been driven out, and he had stayed behind because he knew that those who could not leave would be in need of him.

Our Surelik adventurer returned to his ship and spoke to the officer responsible for the pharmacy. He showed him the list of drugs and the man found one of the unpreferred ones which he placed on the counter in the surgery – a small room mainly consisting of cupboards. "I have to have a justifiable reason for handing these over," he said coldly. The Surelik Trier explained.

"She's not our responsibility," the officer said, "we can't get involved at a personal level. It's not our war."

"I don't care a damn," the seaman shouted at his officer. "I'm not leaving without this medicine."

The officer was shocked. "We'll see about this! I'll speak to the captain." He went off as though insubordination could bring civilisation crashing down, but he left the medicine on the counter – whether this was forgetfulness brought on by his outrage or quite possibly by an intentional ploy to avoid is own responsibility we shall never know. Our man of the seas grabbed it and ran off the ship – and continued to run until he reached the bombed-out house. The interpreter was still there and looked at the runner desperately attempting to catch his breath – so much so that he could hardly speak. The old woman was in a state of ecstasy and had taken possession of the medicine. For some time he and the interpreter argued over the meaning of the instructions, particularly the dosage. There was a smaller one for children, but in serious cases it had to be increased to the adult one. Eventually this was what they chose to do. The doctor wasn't there and the child was listless, silent and apparently no longer struggling to survive.

Our Surelik sailor never decided not to return to the ship; he simply knew that he couldn't leave until the girl was better – or died, but that was something he couldn't dwell on. The next day there was a small but discernible improvement: the girl's eyes had gained some life but her lips were trembling.

Over the next week, there was considerable improvement but she started feel agonising pain and occasionally she screamed. The doctor was called for, but it was two or three days before he came. He was busy, but he didn't move like a busy man. The Surelik was noticing these things in a way he never had before. For the first time he was observing foreign people in foreign ports. The doctor said that most cases he was dealing with were trauma. "There's little I can do with no functioning hospital and precious few drugs. The new regime is in no hurry to bring assistance." He looked at the child and didn't seem too bothered about the pain. The few pain-killers he had were for more serious cases. "Serious cases"? Had they got that wrong? The doctor said that the prognosis was now good, and the pain would subside and eventually she would regain her health entirely. He gave the old woman instructions for the child's diet. And he went with the same slow and regular steps he had come with. Like a sleepwalker. But no one was reassured because they had to listen to those screams. Doctors often get things wrong.

Overcome by emotion, the Surelik seaman wanted to stand out in the street for a while and calm his nerves. As he went he noticed a beam still ran across the main room without a roof or anything else above it, and a fan was hanging from it by its electric wire. For some reason this feature of destruc-tion fascinated him. Because the fan's base was detached from the beam, its awkward position - a broken limb - declared its uselessness and yet it carried a now melancholic history of endless use, which had once been taken for granted and almost ignored. Remembered only in the moment someone switched it on or off. He wanted to know if it still worked and, if so, what it would do in its fragile state. Giving it little thought, he switched it on and then off a few seconds later. It had started to jerk and spin absurdly, as though deranged in the deranged company of war's devastation. It too was frail and abandoned. Someone once had thought perhaps long and hard about it, bought it and carried it home as an investment for the future. We invest objects with emotions and attribute them with durability because this could reaffirm our own longevity, but they are as fragile or robust as we are: even our languages are fragile, as are our religions with their gods. Unlucky are those who pass their lives accumulating money and materials. Unlucky are those who think only of themselves, their own needs and their pleasures. More fortu-nate are those who seek to help others because the good they produce can outlive them. Nothing is forever, but some small deeds and their outcomes can last longer than the outcomes of renowned events chronicled with care by the famous or powerful. What deeds are these? A lesson taught, a tenderness perhaps or even a life saved. What else is there but kindnesses that somehow get through the sieve of civilisation.

One day the Trier Surelik asked the old lady through the interpreter where the child's parents were. "Father," she said and ran her index finger across her throat to indicate "killed". Then she held up the same finger to indicate "one death". "Mother," she said, followed by the same gestures but this time with two fingers for the count. "Uncle," she said. Three fingers. "Uncle," again and four fingers. "Aunt," with five fingers. Then she returned to the uncles with a different gesture: with arms hanging down she lifted them sideways in the same direction to indicate that they had fled. Using this elaborate semaphore, she informed him of the eight members of the family who had sought refuge elsewhere: two uncles, three aunts, two brothers and one sister. The siblings had been taken by the uncles and aunts along with their own children. The old woman, using the interpreter once more, told him that the surviving cousins numbered twenty-seven – orphans of the dead and children of the fugitives. "And your husband and the grandfather of the little girl?" the seafarer asked once more through the interpreter. The old woman genuflected and said, "Thank God that he died of a heart attack two years ago and never lived to see this day."

The child continued to improve and the pain went as the doctor had predicted. He came to visit and declared the girl to have been cured. Then the old woman wept, even as she smiled, laughed and shouted her delight. She hugged all three of them, starting with the sailor. He wept, the interpreter wept and even the doctor's eyes started to glisten – eyes that had seen great miseries. But the one who wept most was the Surelik seafarer. The doctor came over to him, and saying something in his own language, he put his hand on the foreigner's shoulder: "You have saved a human life. That's more than I have managed to do in these last few weeks." The man who had sailed most of the seven seas smiled through his tears and for the first time in his life he felt that he had done something significant, although however much he rummaged around his brain, he couldn't remember why he'd done it. In fact he could remember very little of what had happened since he first stepped foot in this port, except that he had discovered who he really was. That too was a mystery.

He gathered what few things he had, mainly clothes the old lady had given him, and he told them that he was leaving in spite of their protestations that his ship would have left. When he arrived at the harbour, he could not believe that the ship had sailed without him. There was a gap in the skyline because he'd never seen the harbour without his ship in it. He had done what a seaman must never do: he had jumped ship. And he had no choice but to return to the half-bombed-out house. They were overjoyed but unsurprised to see him, and the interpreter chose his words carefully from the Trier's vocabulary as he had processed them through the seafarer's second language, "You left so quickly that I had no chance to say what I wanted to say: we thank you even more than we would otherwise have done, because you are a foreigner. It seems such an incredible thing that we can hardly believe it." And the foreigner gave his reply, after which the doctor and the interpreter embraced him warmly and were lost for words. But I will not reveal it for the moment.

The youthful mariner would eventually find another Trier ship that would grudgingly take on a rogue seafarer who had jumped ship, because they had lost two seamen in an accident. Back home he would surprise his family by telling them that he would be going back to sea. And he would sail all seven of the seas, during the sixties and the seventies, long before the accountants of the new new regime got their hands on the whole seagoing business and ships could no longer linger in harbour. So for decades he would wander many ports, not stopping at bars but observing the people and places – and engaging with them. After fifteen years he would even return to that embattled port, still under the new ethnicity but smartened up and flourishing as though no death and destruction had occurred in its recent history. He would meet the doctor and the interpreter, who would be older but strangely unchanged, because when someone has discovered who they are, there is little need for change other than the marks age gradually inflicts. They would take him to see the girl who had grown up as the passing years demanded. She would have no memory of him, and would sit in silent embarrassment as the doctor and interpreter would tell every detail of the story. If a group of youngsters hadn't called on her, the middle-aged seafarer would never have known that she wasn't always this reserved. She would go to the door, hold them there in animated conversation and send them on their way, probably asking them to come back later. Then she would return to the sitting room – her sitting room – and adopt once more her demure manner. The doctor and the interpreter would continue the conversation. She would appear unable to understand the presence of the strange foreigner and saviour who would be standing before her. She would thank him, and he too would be embarrassed.

In the early eighties he would leave the sea, as it is a young man's profession. He would marry a Lithuanian woman and have three children. The God of the Triers is rarely kind to His own – as is probably true of all gods with or without the capital letter; for whatever overriding theological reason, gods are as fickle and erratic as judges. In the early nineties when the Drunkard would rule, they would be Triers for the Lithuanians and the Surelikud, and they would be a Sureliko-Lithuanian couple for the Triers. Still they would muddle through as would so many others.

So what did the seafaring man say in reply to the interpreter? The reader may well think that I've forgotten to tell them because I got carried away with what would happen in the rest of the man's life. But these words were so crucial to the idea of this parable that they must be its final ones. He said, "Not only am I no foreigner, but from the moment I saw this old lady enfeebled and weeping outside the front door of her seemingly roofless house, I lost all understanding of what we mean by 'foreign', a concept that is emboldened by flags and anthems and martial pomp and myths and jealousies and ancient hatreds and, quite frankly, the stupidity of the endless nationalisms which mistake a magnificent variety for fragmentation. We all belong to each other, and national greed causes war, an obscenity the Triers are well acquainted with because of the foul deeds of the Beer Cellars, as I learned as a child. But this is not about the Beer Cellars and the Triers, as all nations are capable of war. It is about being a human being. If I may say an unmanly and sentimental thing, it is about loving all humanity and every individual human being. It is about dreaming an impossible world and attempting in the meantime to perform every little act that could lead – however tentatively or feebly – towards a better world in which there is no war. I am not a Surelik and I am not a Trier. I am a human being, and you are not the one who should be thanking me, as I should be thanking you all for having taught me what I have to do with my life."

*

Inevitably the scribe is angry again. "Why have a Surelik who renounces his nationality? Why is that a good thing?" she says. "These ridiculous parables are not even parables."

What is the essence of a parable after all? The scribe thinks that it's a morality story, probably without thinking about it too much. I – as an outsider who is still on the outside – believe these Christian stories promote the idea that life is made up of encounters with reality which overturn an individual's understanding of his or her world. They can be interpreted in various ways or not at all. This is the exceptionalism of civilised life, because the real cause of these damascene moments is not the encounter itself, but the vacuity of the life that leads up to them. Adventures in civilisation derive from the fact that it is in the main so intolerably banal. If there are adventures in traditional Surelik life, then every day is an adventure. But adventure is not the word. Dangers exist but there is an acquired wisdom that allows us to overcome them, though success cannot always be guaranteed. It is not so much an endless struggle against nature as a constant cohabitation with it - or better inclusion within it. Because we are part of the environment rather than separated from it, we live in a way that barely evolves and thus allows us to enter into the cycle of the seasons and belong to them. This doesn't mean that we don't reflect on life and its paradoxes, because each generation in an oral society is called up to reinvent the wheel, but it is a wheel very similar to previous ones. As we age, we think thoughts that are similar to those of our parents when they were the age we have just achieved, or at least that is how I imagine it because I left traditional society at the age of six-teen, and when I did occasionally return to it, I carried the full weight of this civilised world I'd discovered.

So if it is the oppressive banality and the disconnect between who the civilised are forced to be and who they want to become that makes them suddenly rebel and take a leap of faith that leads them back to our primeval humanity, then this is the sole advantage of civilisation: the incentive for people to radically change their lives not in a direction that satisfies their desires but in a direction that leads them away from their selves and towards a consciousness of the whole, which under civilisation can be perceived in so many ways and such a privileged viewpoint. The self is a narrow cell that leads to depression and even insanity. The means to open the heavy prison door is not some magical key, but a perception. Fortunately not one single and unchanging perception, but one suited to the nature of their previous imprisonment in the self. This is the moment in which they see the world anew and are better able to deal with it. They have created an essence.

And this, dear scribe, is the only gift civilisation offers us, but it is a precious one and we should grasp it.

The scribe has looked at me with indescribable bafflement and simply said, "You talk a lot of nonsense." There speaks someone who doesn't feel the banality of civilised living to be oppressive. "It is not banal," she says with absolute certainty. I leave it to the reader to muse over which of us is speaking sense and which speaking nonsense.

People are not just symbols of nations; they are much more than that and primarily they are themselves. The story of the Surelik seaman says that not only is there no justice in this world for nations, there is none for any of us. I don't know if the Christians and Muslims are right about another life where there is justice, but justice most certainly has never existed in this life since the other life was thought of, nor will it in any future however distant. You cannot entirely undo the ravages of progress.

Now I'm going to reveal something I have never told anyone and it may finally silence the scribe: my detractors would often put out the story that I was going to bed with Halvatud, adding their own salacious imaginings about his crippled body, and this made me angry because it wasn't true or rather it wasn't true in the sense that they intended. I would have felt no shame if it had been true because he was the most attractive and charming man I ever met, even more than Osip or the unquestionably handsome Ilyudev.

One evening he asked me to come to bed with him, and I did. We both undressed and I saw for the first time the full extent of his body's fragility which contrasted with the vitality of his mind: his sunken twisted chest, the offset pelvis apparently only covered by skin and no flesh, his withered leg. He didn't hide his body, and his asymmetric face smiled at me before he climbed into bed. He was beautiful.

I would have made love to him, but he didn't want it. He just wanted to know that one woman would be willing to sleep with him for one night. One woman to know what he really looked like and to hold him. And, he said, what a woman he had found. I understood the magnitude of his love and how little he demanded in return. We slept in each other's arms, but he never wanted to repeat the experience, even though I suggested it. That one night appeared to have satisfied him and the bond between us grew even stronger. Of course he was full of love for everyone, and that is possibly why he didn't want sex or even to sleep together again. He may have felt that if all his love were to be channelled towards me, this would drain his tender heart which embraced everyone he knew and all humanity. His death made me rethink my nationalism. His death was his greatest statement. His death was the reason why I chose a Surelik man for my parable of the seaman's lost soul. It had finally taught me that we have to look to our own problems, and if they exist elsewhere, then in that land they must equally look to their own. He knew that idealising one's country is not loving it, but merely deluding it and encouraging the worst forms of petty nationalism. Every society can be bettered, and mostly this is achieved by the citizens of each one examining their own behaviours.

That night was an exciting encounter with fragility – the fragility of a sensitive and generous being who barely managed to be, and yet continued in spite of the harshness of humanity, nature and our century, like a spinning top that falters but never falls. A miracle of nature, which loves statistical exceptions or a miracle of anti-nature that defies that pitiless force with metaphysical stubbornness?

Perhaps it was my age. I was just over seventy years at the time, and my memories of handsome Ilusadev had faded – not even a glimmer of youthful vigour, his or mine. I'd felt joy at the tautness of his muscles that held him strongly to this world – apparently. His breath, his smell, his calm superiority, his tyrannical joy in me – the whole mechanism of his masculinity excited me. But did I know him? Did I think of what he may have gone through in the Civil War? What he'd done, and what he'd avoided? Surely he must have feared, even sensed the inevitability of an untimely death. Untimely? What an empty adjective to describe the tragic course of boldness in an age that rendered the courage of millions the only power on earth and yet a commodity that could be bought so cheaply.

Of course I loved Halvatud and I knew him well, though never quite enough. Whether or not it was a sexual love is hard to say; I never thought of it before we slept together. Many will question whether he really wanted it? But I believe that everyone needs love – all the different types of love, though possibly the beautiful and the charismatic don't, because they just take it for granted. Adversity can make people bitter or it can make people happy. He knew how to extract pleasure from the smallest things, and he was the wisest of men. He provoked the bodyguard because he was fearful of what might happen to me. How can I not weep after losing all that? After having witnessed Halvatud's death, how could I not dictate a parable of a man who finds a way to better himself through an encounter with violence on a massive and indiscriminate scale?

I do not fully know you, scribe, but I do know that I should be very thankful to you for all the work you do for me. In as much as I do know you, I think that I know where you're aiming, and those aims are not mine – or of my generation. They quite naturally belong to yours, and this is as it should be, but it irritates. Don't ask me to be more explicit about this; if you don't know what I mean, then you should do.

Now let me weep. No more for today.

Let me weep once more the tears of two women and not of one. That is what Halvatud deserves.

That night with Halvatud, scribe, I have to say something more about it. He came to me the next day and said, "Before last night I'd never looked at my body since I became an adult – never really studied it and never really thought about it and what it might look like to another person."

"But I love it," I said.

304

He smiled with a hint of condescension. "That is your sweet nature, Rahväemarmas, but I didn't. Last night when I undressed, I looked at it, I studied it and I thought about it. And well, I didn't love it. So this is what I've been lugging around all these years. It's barely a body. I wash it every few days, of course, but only see it fleetingly; I never look at it. Besides, there's not that much to wash."

"That's what is so fascinating, so beautiful. It expresses who you are: your courage, your wisdom and, most of all, your kindness which is the greatest human virtue of them all."

"That's not how I see it, and I would prefer to carry on ignoring it. Of course, with every step I take, I'm aware of it and its limitations. I fight with it and I never want to give in to the thing that disgusted my own mother."

"That makes no sense. This is only about companionship, as I understand it. Even if we only do it now and then."

"You don't understand. This is not friendship; this is love that longs to hold. So you think that this fragile frame deprived me of physical desires? Nature isn't that kind. We learn to live without things others take for granted. Of course we do. And we can be happier than those who have everything except perhaps pleasant spontaneous kindness to others - which you mentioned as the greatest virtue. I don't know about that, but it is the greatest pleasure for both the giver and the receiver. We live by giving and receiving, not for money or betterment, because those things are about survival which is very different but just as necessary in civilised societies."

"For you it is the greatest pleasure, Halvatud, for you ..."

"For me, for most. Unless, of course, this ageing new regime is replaced by one of state-sponsored avidity - the ridiculously misnamed 'free market', as though an abstraction could be free - which desiccates that most human humour."

"Halvatud," I hugged him, "you have a body as beautiful as your beautiful soul."

"You have a beautiful body made as it should be made. I certainly don't regret last night, and I shall hold it dear for the rest of my life, just as I shall always admire your beautiful but very troubled soul."

"Troubled soul," I cried with a hint of resentment.

"Rahväema, I know you very well, and I have dealt with the evils life has inflicted on me better than you have with yours. You have your own kind of courage – the courage that holds everything inside, and it is killing you."

"Well, it's not making a very good job of it; I'm as fit as the forest deer."

"Torturing you, then. That would be a better word. You're determined. Determined to change the world. But most people who do that, change it for the worse, either intentionally or unintentionally. But you want to change it for the better, and that's a difficult thing to do."

"Don't let's fight over our love," I kissed him and he smiled sadly. "So what are we going to do?" I asked.

"Just carry on as we always have."

"As though nothing happened?"

"No, something important has happened, which is why nothing must change."

He may have come to know me very well, and I think that he very probably did, but I never really got to know him. Did I ever actually try?

Rahväema's eulogy at Halvatud's funeral

Death comes to us all – to both the good and the bad, both the foolish and the wise, and of course both the rich and the poor, in order to make room for the following generations. But it doesn't do so indiscriminately, especially now we have a greater and more reliable knowledge of medical science and technology; it pursues the poor, the foolish and the good with greater alacrity. You could say that in the modern world of progress, death is less democratic and whatever the gains of medicine, they are counterbalanced by the efficiency of military technology. Surely with such injustice this side of death, there must be greater justice on the other side. Or so the God of the Triers would have us believe. And in this moment of pain in which I realise – perhaps for the first time – just how much Halvatud meant to me, I am susceptible – also for the first time perhaps – to this reasoning which is not reasoning but rather an unmerited consolation, because we live in a world that civilisation has reduced to a disorderly prison. We cry out for justice, but no visible sign that our cries of anguish have been heard has ever manifested itself in either heaven or hell. The vocal articulation of our grief is coldly carried away on the winds that circle this forsaken and yet beautiful, bustling planet.

> Unhappy boy to whom no father came
> to give advice, and whom
> no mother kissed or smiled at
> with loving pride, became
> a motivated man who only tried
> to help, and in helping
> disgusted others whom he'd helped.

The deceased came into the world deprived of most of what we call our birthright – those abilities that come with birth – and yet he did more, much more than most of us, and lived. Oh how he lived, our Halvatud! He travelled far, and wide was his knowledge of peoples diverse and human possibilities. He was my mentor, and how many held him so? Nature compensates; it takes away with one hand, and gives with the other. Where some have drive and haste, he had love and unhurried care for others. Where some display their wealth through elegant clothes and expensive things, he shambled through life uncaring of possessions. Shambled energetically, shambled heroically, I should say, because his every movement required great effort which somehow he disguised in calm effortlessness. It was what he did and did so well.

Halvatud was not unique, but he was a rarity. Exactly what he sought is hard to say, and I don't claim to know him well, though what I know suffices to know the virtue of the man.

There is no time or place that holds unchanging
To its past but heedless flows unthinking as it goes;
There is no language generously endowed
With words sublime and measured with a touch divine
That does not crumble into dusty fable
Besmirched with the coarseness yapping dogs display,
But always, however dull the times and harsh
The men of power, there shall be a Halvatud,
A human soul who flies to the heavens
Of human thoughts and ways of being.
This one has gone and left my dying soul
Bereft, but more shall come and always always
They will blossom on the dunghills of our rotten states.

He came from nowhere into my life, and had great hopes for me. I think that I failed him, but he never suggested this. The fight isn't over, but it will be harder without him.

He loved me
And I let him go
I loved him
And I didn't know

Because only when he died, did I fully understand the meaning of good and evil – an understanding civilised people had to learn because it surrounded them and entered the pores of their skin. Where money flows most freely, evil is called natural, whereas unfeeling nature knows nothing of good and evil, as everyone should know. Nature is the rule of survival, which language and emotion can free us from.

If God is, is He greater than the universe
Or just this small terrestrial hub
Of luscious green that feeds and fills
The timbered bounty of the forest floor
With life, its chatter and the constant grinding
Of cogs that drive the endless machinations
Of nature's blind but restless will
And the deep blue teeming surface warmth;
A separate world of equal abundance above
Blue deeps of a cold desert in liquid form
In which hermits live in darkness,
A dull reservoir, the cellar of the earth;
And bright purple that has no place
And is the colour of human imaginings,
Which, godlike, move and yet cannot be seen,
But are and change everything they touch
With their intangible hands?

If God is, is he the maker
Or the making of all this?
Or is He just the made,
The lumpy abstraction that is matter,
The potential rather than the seed of life?
I, the unbeliever, ask these questions
Because, if God is, then surely Halvatud
Was one of His most favoured creations,
His close disciple amongst so many,
Because God would not be
Parsimonious with goodness,
Would he now?

But still, a world bereft of Halvatud
Should be a colder place,
A deep sea in which a few ugly fish
Swim the darkness of loveless battle
For the substance of the earth,

And not a forest of exultant bustle.
For the forest dies and the purple fullness
Of our minds has gone too far
And strangled both the blue and the green.

I have never seen the sea and its blueness, except as an image
on TV. I have travelled to the capital and I came from the
forest. I have seen much more of the world than my parents
and grandparents would ever have dreamt of, but I have
seen little compared with Halvatud, who dragged his fragile
frame to every corner of the Triers' lands and those they had
acquired. I only speak Surelik and the language of the Triers,
as well as a working knowledge of the Little Noisy Musics',
whilst Halvatud spoke the first two and many others: Tuva,
Ossetian, Latvian and Armenian amongst them. Now many
of them are independent but they retain something of the
Triers', for empires – a great evil – do have the merit of mixing
peoples together and teaching them to coexist. He spoke of
them often and carried their wisdoms with our own. It taught
me that we have to honour our own cultures whilst learning
and liking the cultures of others – equally noble as they are,
and – thank God – diverse and so immense in themselves and
even more so in their number. Yet even Halvatud could only
scratch the sum of human knowledge and culture – but he
knew enough to be an excellent teacher.

One thing that I want to emphasise is that Halvatud may
have been a saint in his particular manner, but he was not
saintly. He loved life and its physicality. He felt privileged
to be in this world with all its beauty – and he never could
decide whether it was made for us and all the other animals
or whether we were made for it, which would have been the
more strictly Surelik way of looking at it. But he was of the
plain and adopted by the forest, just as I was of the forest
and was rejected by the forest. In spite of all the cruelties and
humiliations nature and humanity heaped upon him, he
loved them both as perhaps only a cripple can love. I call him

that because that was what he always called himself. Perhaps he said it with pride, and if so he would have been fully justified, though he never admired that state of mind. Perhaps he said it with boldness, which is what he had always used not only to get through life but also to enjoy it. Or perhaps he said it as a joke, because sardonic humour was another of the instruments he used to overcome adversities.

Whilst only cripples can understand the true meaning of love, it is also true that they can hate. Who knows when they make that choice, but for them it comes earlier in life, as they learn and thus mature more quickly. In a sense, all of us who have to live in this self-appointed civilised world are cripples – some visibly and some deep in their psyches. Civilisation, as I have said elsewhere, invented love and hate, just as it did good and evil. Halvatud embraced love as surely as any human being can: that is why he had to die, and that is why I'm sure that he would forgive his murderer. If they would ever meet in the other world the Triers believe in – but he and I never did – then he would sit him down and buy him a drink to demonstrate no hard feelings, always supposing that the Triers have taverns in their heaven. I'm sure they do!

So I'll end this eulogy with a few brief reflections on love – one of those elusive words we have to use often but only half understand – and you can tell me later if they don't describe Halvatud. But you won't because you'll find that they do:

> Love is a lonely thing
> That seeks out others
> To whom it gifts
> Its substance and, what's more,
> Its spirit
> And hope for things to come.

> Love is a lonely thing
> Whose company is company enough.
> It sweeps away the demons

Of the self,
And asks no questions
Of the hurts to come.

Love is a lonely thing
And is alone
Amongst all other things
In caring for them
More than for itself.

And that was the end of my eulogy. Some said that it went on for far too long, and some said it could not have been more appropriate to his tragic death. I cared nothing about their opinions; I cared only about his.

So then they came, the members of the West Siberian Surelik Cultural Committee, like so many sheep, to offer me the leadership again – the one they had removed on a previous occasion. There were quite a few members who had been at that last meeting, but Vladimir Paulusev was not; he had gone into early retirement exhausted by his career of doing nothing, having aged before his time. This time their eyes expressed not guilt and pleasure in what was making them feel guilty, as had occurred the last time, but relief as they were certain that I would accept. They probably were counting on what they considered to be my thirst for power, but there was little power left in the West Siberian Surelik Cultural Committee and besides I was no longer the same person. Two factors determined my decision to resume this role: I wanted to return to the lands of the Surelikud and when I looked at each of those dull bureaucratised faces, most of whom I was well acquainted with, I couldn't see one that inspired the least confidence in me. Ah yes, the scribe has pointed out that she was of the party, but that's exactly what I mean. By then she was already holding a prominent position. Although they didn't realise it, she was their only hope – consider the others! I know what they wanted: they wanted me to choose their successor because they were incapable of doing it themselves – all twenty-five of them. They thought that my death could not have been far off, and that in a year or two I would anoint one of them. How they must regret their decision! And how toe-curlingly servile they were – how complimentary. Not a word of the past, and not an admission that since they'd got rid of me the deterioration of the Surelik culture and language had accelerated rapidly. There were barely two hundred people maintaining the old lifestyle in the forest and all of them over fifty. The market abhors diversity, and even as people shout about its importance, the logic of "modernisation" and "economic laws" gradually turn us all into fragmented economic agents obliged to do the same things in the same way.

"I'll gladly accept your offer, since you have gone to all this trouble of coming here. I would not wish to let you down, and I can see that you have your problems," I said, and I cannot deny that I enjoyed my sarcasm. In my long life, I've suffered, it's true, but I have also had the pleasure of being proved right on many occasions even when I wasn't. Many who have lived better lives and made better decisions have not had such good luck.

I know what you're thinking: where's my humility? The typical memoir is full of faux humility, when it's not full of bitter resentment and recriminations obviously coupled with layer upon layer of self-justifications. Of course, humility – or call it meekness if you will – is a virtue. What is the opposite of humility? It's arrogance. If you raise arrogance to the status of a virtue, or even a necessary human trait, and you also want to save the planet, an overpopulated one at that – stuffed with human beings desperately fighting with each other for power and wealth and willing to do anything to achieve their 'rightful goal' – then you don't appear to have a well-thought-out morality or even a plan. You can have, I suppose, the arrogance of the few, which would mean the subjugation of the great majority who in their paucity of choice would be obliged to develop meek natures in order to hold onto life.

And this is what we've got today in the 2010s: a shrinking, absurdly wealthy elite, a layer of reasonably secure minders, minions and chancers, and below them the great mass of casual workers and the permanently excluded along with the gradual proletarianization of the traditional professionals and the highly skilled. Three layers of misery, and the luckiest is probably the bottom one, because they still have a society – or have they too been fragmented and plunged into dreams of impossible riches?

So humility is good. I'll agree with that, but if we're all nice and meek, then the first arrogant fool who comes along will take charge. What you need is someone who is both arrogant and enlightened, and that is what I am, or so I believe. There is a simple reason for this: having been born an uncivilised person, I have never developed an all-consuming craving for stuff, any stuff, big stuff like houses and cars, and little stuff like particular brands of skirts, dresses and scarfs, not to speak of completely unnecessary things like perfumes and makeup. I am driven by a desire to change the world by stopping people from changing it too much. In circumstances where they came back to me of their own volition and said, "Rahväema, do you want the leadership?" – what could I do but accept the offer for the good of us all.

Väikelinn once more! And how it had changed. More then ever before. I had to look at it hard before I could find the vague outline of the original modest town. In the centre, many buildings had been replaced by ugly modern blocks with garish shops selling the strangest of things at the ground floor. There were new hotels, because in the new economy people were in constant movement paid for by corporations. In fact prices in the centre were much higher than in the surrounding housing schemes built in the sixties and seventies. These fairly solid buildings were now in decay, and the poverty was striking. If Surelik was spoken at all, it was in these districts. I knew of the terrible damage that had been inflicted on the Surelikud of the forest since I'd left the region, but I wasn't prepared for the equally disastrous situation on the plain. Many speakers had left in search of work, and many Triers had moved in for the same reason. Since the late fifties people had been able to change jobs and move where they wanted but only now this process had accelerated in some areas, and the relationship between human beings and their region, though not destroyed, had been dramatically undermined. Without a change in policy, Surelik would die and all that would be left of the Surelikud would be a squalid, tacky museum visited by the occasional tourist on a wet day. Kurat's curse was having its cruel victory.

And obviously I barely knew a soul, other than the sheep from the West Siberian Surelik Cultural Committee. I envisaged a future of dragging my ancient bones from one dull, indecisive meeting to another, the arduous task of explaining the obvious to the terminally half-witted who are convinced of their own brilliance, and the difficulties in determining the sources of problems in an economic system as amorphous as the free market is. I thought long and hard, and almost resigned. But what was I to do with my remaining years, if not this quixotic rearguard campaign in which victories were merely the successful slowing-down of ineluctable forces? This would be an exercise in making use of most of threadbare resources whilst the sheep argued for the impossible and did nothing for the possible.

I gradually got down to work, and we had our little successes. I enjoyed the fact that my own language once more dominated my days, and I even started to have a fondness for the sheep – although sheep they remained. About six months after my return to Väikelinn, Troyanskikonyev got in touch with me, and said that he wanted to have a portrait of me painted. He had already commissioned a painter and I was to use the plane tickets he had sent me. "Why would you want a portrait of me?" I asked, and he replied as though this was a sufficient motive, "Because one day, Rahväema, you will be famous."

"For what?" I asked again, to which he just laughed and said, "Rahväema, you are priceless. Shall we say for upsetting people who need to be upset, including myself. I have resumed payments to your favourite charity, and I have thought a great deal about you since you left the capital."

"In the last six months you mean."

"Ha, you see what I mean. You always go straight to the point – like a child. You were an incumbrance in the capital, but now I wish you well."

Even though he had to deposit that innocent-Surelik cliché – a form of intellectual flatulence he could not resist – I had to admit that it was a gesture that could not have been motivated by self-interest, and therefore had to be accepted as an act of generosity. It would be a short break away from the losing battle, but he was wise enough to engage an artist who lived fifty kilometres from the capital's city limits in a small and exclusive community of wealthy artists and writers where I could do little harm. He greeted my acceptance with heart-warming gratitude.

The painter looked at me, as a potter looks at a lump of clay, or even as a butcher looks at a slab of meat that has to be cut down to its constituent parts and laid out in the display for public viewing. I was not a particularly prestigious commission for a portraitist who only dealt in prestige by enhancing the prestige of others. He lived in the rarefied banality of fame – of existences that are moulded by being known to people who cannot know them, such is the distance from which we view the famous in modern society.

Instinctively I returned his stare with a look of mild and slightly bemused disdain. That has become part of my nature, and I cannot remember when that happened. I do not even know if the process of change was sudden or evolved over decades. What was left of the submissive young Surelik woman who nevertheless had a strong sense of who she was and how to navigate an alien world? Perhaps not a single trait of character.

Little more than the vague outline of a physiognomy battered by years of suffering and success.

"You don't seem very relaxed," the painter opined without concealing his flaccid irritation. Ours would turn out to be a dialogue between the world-wearied.

"Quite relaxed, I can assure you," I said haughtily. "I have been interrogated by the NKVD, so I don't think that a *society* portraitist is going to upset my nerves."

He was shocked – and angry, no doubt. He believed himself to be a Titian or a Van Dyck, but not a Rembrandt whom he considered to be too invasive in his relationships with his subjects. "If you don't want this portrait, then we need go no further. I am in great demand and only took on this commission out of respect for your *benefactor*."

It was my turn to be shocked. That was how he saw me: a beneficiary, and this explained his attitude from the moment we met. I must have already understood this unconsciously, and this explained my prickliness.

"Oh yes, I want this portrait very much."

"Really," he smiled at last – the smile of superiority. "Of course, you'll be joining an elite group of people."

"Oh, not for that reason," I almost spat.

"Why then?" he asked, once more with the detached weariness of the successful who can maintain their success with little effort.

"I do not know myself. I feel that the life I've led has taken me far away from who I was. I'm hoping that your painting will reveal to myself some small aspect of myself that has eluded me."

"So many myselves."

"Of course you can't know me better than I do, because however much we don't know ourselves, we always know ourselves better than we know anyone else. We know our conscious thoughts, but we don't know anyone else's. All I expect of you is one small suggestion that I can build on."

He looked at me blankly, now trying to hide his irritation

or possible incomprehension. "Shall we get on with it? How about the pose?" He then came over to rearrange my arms and change the direction of my face. "A three-quarter view is best in your case," he added with unarguable professional certainty.

For some time we remained silent and gathered within the pleasant solitude of our own minds. He was at his work – absorbed and unaware of me, apart from my presence as an image to be transferred to his canvas. Then suddenly I felt bored and, struggling to repress my restlessness, I said, "We're attempting to suppress time."

He gave me one of his looks of incomprehension. It was infuriating that the image was now speaking, when it was supposed to let the painter work in peace.

"To suspend it with a likeness," I pursued him, determined to provoke a reaction.

"To suspend what?"

"Time."

"I haven't got time to talk about time."

"I'm suggesting that my portrait will freeze the way I'm perceived. The portrait artist has a lot of power."

He looked at me unimpressed by what I was saying, and then continued with his work, dabbing paint here and there, apparently following a methodology he had developed so long ago that he moved with confidence and almost with thoughtlessness.

Now I was the one to be irritated. "You'll probably steal my soul."

And then he smiled almost happily, as though something had suddenly been put into place and he no longer had to trouble his brain with it. "Yes, I imagine that native peoples do think like that."

I had walked into one of his stereotypes. We Surelikud have a word which often translates as "soul", but it isn't like the Triers' "soul". It can mean something akin to personality and also one's natural bent or energy. Perhaps as elusive as "soul", but not quite the same, because it has no religious connotations. We do not believe in the immortality of the soul. "No, it's not what you're thinking," I said. "Yes, I too may have heard of a people who believed that a camera could steal its subject's soul, but not all of us savages are the *same*, you know." I doubt that he perceived the irony in that word "savages". "In my opinion, it is the civilised peoples who have a tendency to become very similar to each other – to globalise, if you like. In any event, no Surelik would ever believe that."

"Then why did you say it?"

"Having heard perhaps the same urban myth. Sometimes we play the part of the savage – instinctively. For humorous effect. I was making conversation," I shrugged.

"Listen, I'm not here for a chat. If that's what you want, you should find a shrink – and get your benefactor to pay for it."

In that moment, mild aversion turned to intense dislike. After all these years that I've become as much a Trier as a Surelik, I am still not accepted. Or not accepted by some. There is that leader of the nationalist opposition who refers to Caucasians, Tuva, Surelikud and all the other minority peoples in the south as cockroaches. Special ones, he jokes, so that it is not enough simply to crush them under your boot; you have to use a gun. Unsurprisingly the Noisy Musics and the Little Noisy Musics have made a hero of him, because they want Siberia and its oil. And perhaps to build some more military bases to threaten the Wall-Builders. This painter could have been one of those who voted for that nationalist politician, but more likely his was mere ingrained prejudice that harboured no violence or even disdain that went beyond self-confidence nurtured by a sense of national superiority. He probably didn't want me dead or thrown out of the Triers' lands which include our own; he merely wanted me in my place, and that wasn't behind his easel, the subject of his talents. Why should he – a civilised man – paint someone brought up half-dressed in the forest? What had the world come to?

Computers, the Internet and Smartphones

The computer in some ways was like the printing press or going even further back the invention of writing, because all of these greatly enhanced humanity's ability to accumulate knowledge, which consequently became more accessible. The powerful both approved of its arrival because it gave them an advantage over competitors, as it didn't just change the way we write and move text around, it changed every form of economic and social activity. Also like the printing press, the computer frightened the powerful because the powerless could discover more information they were not supposed to know. Forms of censorship were invented, and more will be invented in the future. A brief period of greater transparency will be followed by mass surveillance and strict control of the flows of information, which could become more feasible online than it was with the printed word.

If the television entertained us into a state of catatonia, the computer and in particular those computers we use as phones started to erode the thing that most distinguishes our species: our ability to converse with each other in what we call a dialogue – a word which suggests that each utterance is a reaction to a previous one by someone else. Dialogue is a process of both speaking and listening by everyone involved, but in the age of the mobile phone and social media, we don't converse, we post whatever our fragmented brain wants us to, though usually it takes us to ourselves and all associated banalities. First we did this on the internet and then we started to do it our speech as well. The more we try to convince the world that we have the most interesting and fulfilling life, the more we sink into that quagmire of dissatisfaction where that image dissolves because we have failed to convince ourselves and have the unpleasant sensation that we're not convincing anyone else either. And what do we do? Instead of chucking the useless thing in the bin, we try even harder.

The scribe objects that I don't have a mobile phone, so

I have to accept that this is only my somewhat ill-informed observation, but sometimes it is easier to see things more clearly from the outside.

These things will not only change the way we think; they will change us into different animals. The feel of the world, the taste of the world, even the solidity of the world will be changed irreparably, as though some powerful genetic mutation had taken place which, just as a locust storm can be both constructive and destructive, highly organised and a bearer of overwhelming disorder driven by some obscure and unstoppable biological urge, previously unknown and yet half aware that it is strangling its own incomprehensible vitality. In plain language, it is a reality that will be the victim of its own success.

Then there are computer games: here we arrive at the complete deskilling of the human imagination. It's all done for us, and we don't have to add anything of our own – except our ability to react quickly. If we read a book, we have to reimagine everything and even if writers provide detailed descriptions, what we see will never be what they intended. With cinema and television, everything is more or less done for us, but good cinema requires careful interpretation of the images, and cinema is in some ways the most complete of the arts because it brings together the word, the moving image (with some directors, a painted canvas that constantly repaints itself) and music (or the lack of it). In any event, the purpose of great art is not to reassure but to unsettle, something that cannot be done with the computer game which is the quintessential entertainment that also symbolises who we have become.

The question I ask of progress and civilisation is this: is it wise to let technology rule alongside the market, its consort you love so much? Like the market, technology brings advantages of course, but it brings enormous social and ecological problems too. So if human beings were a rational animal – and I admit that if they are then they are only partially so – then surely they would take control of their lives and keep both technology and the market under control as well. If there's a bitter cold wind on the plain, you wouldn't just accept the situation; you would build a house and install a stove. It seems to me that modernity is utterly submissive to technology and the market in a way that it would never be to nature. The fact is that technology and the market are seen as a means to overcoming nature, which is the one force we can never do without, however cruel it may be.

Technology and the market are also the great forces that are deskilling our societies, and reducing human beings to consumers and domesticated animals entirely manipulated by outside forces that promote the contradictory idea that there are no longer any choices and yet progress is supposed to have created societies in which everyone is free to make their own choices. Nevertheless we do have choices but ones that require an act of will without which we are incapable of producing better societies. We have done so in the past, but like Halvatud they were fragile entities. Evil is ineradicable in a society based on private property, while good can only endure in a tenuous manner. All we can do is cling to goodness, even in the face of the ineluctable forces of capital. To give in to cynicism and despair would deprive our lives of all meaning, at least for someone like me, though I accept that people like my sister are better than me. Her protest was also an acceptance of her limited possibilities.

So what can we do? In the case of technology, we can always ask ourselves some very simple questions: do I really need this? If I do, are there any toxic outcomes for me, my family, my society, my species and my planet? As there are only twenty-four hours in the day, if I acquire or use this technology, will it obstruct the other things I want to do or need to do? These same questions should be asked by those who govern us – the corporations, governments, generals, state bodies and the like – but we can predict what their answers will be. If they did ask them, then we would have no nuclear weapons, but instead these blasphemous instruments of war will eventually be used if they continue to exist much longer. Here I am, a mother who abandoned her child, in order to lead a political campaign that proved incapable of securing our language and culture, and I ask myself what right I have to pontificate. My answer should be that precisely because I have lived long enough to see the complete destruction of my dreams, I am someone who is worth listening to even if you don't agree.

The problem is also one of risk which human beings are incredibly bad at assessing, both as individuals and as societies. It is also something observed by some Marxists – the ones who oversimplify almost everything – and they call it "the dialectic of partial gains". It is true that when a person, a class or a society achieves some kind of betterment in their condition, they tend to spend more time worrying about losing it than attempting to go on to better it further. Or to put it in language which most of us can chew on more easily, when people find themselves in a more secure situation, they become more risk-averse. If this process of increasing security carries on indefinitely, you end up with people who can barely go out of the house, with the exception of a small minority who feel so hemmed in that they go in search of danger to start living again. Risk is part of living, and yet it is also something we would rationally wish to minimise – but not too much. More important than eliminating risk completely, which would require a prison society, we should want to share out risk equitably through welfare services.

We also have to ask the question of what sort of risk. Risk of death is of course a serious one, but is the risk of mild discomfort a risk of great concern? Some people say that they can only drive expensive cars – usually manufactured by the Beer Cellars – because all the others don't have smooth suspension. The more we're pampered like a wealthy eighteen-century European landowner, the more we're incapable of living close to nature.

The Princess and the Pea

Long ago in the times that started with the Drunkard's rule, there lived a very rich man the origin of whose wealth no one really knew nor dared to ask. He had been a high-up official in the agency that made sure that no one took the old new regime's name in vain. This agency particularly disliked ideas that were similar to their own but not exactly the same. But this agency of scholastic dictatorship would eventually be the first to embrace the reforms that almost destroyed the country and also - it so happened - made them very rich.

I cannot remember where this rich man lived. Possibly it was in the east, possibly in the many-languaged mountains, possibly in the north-west or any part of the vast territories of the Triers. But it doesn't matter, because there were quite a number of rich men. And any one of them could have had a single, much adored child - a girl, it has to be said, if we are to follow the parameters of this ridiculous tale. What is important - very important - is that our Rich Man did have such a daughter, and she was not just the apple of his eye but a whole orchard in fruit. There was nothing very special about this little girl - at least not at the beginning - but she would be changed by her parents' wellspring of love, if that is the correct word to describe whatever flowed with such inexhaustible ardour.

Whatever she desired she was immediately given. She didn't even have to exercise her lungs by articulating a few solitary words in her own language which she hardly knew. It sufficed that she slowly and distractedly extended her arm and pointed a finger in a particular direction, always with an air of bestowing great beneficence on others - exactly on whom it was not clear, on society perhaps or the human race struggling as it was and as it should be.

It wasn't long before insomnia raised its ugly head. Usually the demon of old age or adults on the brink of some personal tragedy, this insomnia had no obvious cause, or at least not until a thorough examination of her bedroom had been carried out. It concerned a very small object. A ridiculously small object, which presupposes the existence of at least two mattresses before the offending object got to the place where it would cause such havoc. How it got there has never been explained and I can only speculate that it was the act of a malicious cook who secreted it somewhere on her body as she smuggled it into the bedroom of the unfortunate girl. But of course it was not discovered immediately. The only thing they could do was add another mattress to the bed in the hope that the child would be able to sleep. But however many they added, it was to no avail.

In the meantime the child who barely moved continued to point in various directions, and the parents would rush to placate her desires which seemed to have another wellspring of their own. Occasionally they would take her on shopping trips, initially in a pushchair but later four servants had to be engaged to carry her in a small, custom-built sedan chair which had its own computer screen to keep her entertained with films and TV programmes. She would be the cause of such enormous quantities of plastic being purchased that some evil tongues argued about how many factories in the Philippines survived on her consumption.

She was a plump little girl by now, and she looked out at the world from a blank but troubled face, as though she had lost something possibly of little importance, but the sense of that loss and the loss of her memory of it niggled. Still she stoically suffered in silence, and her parents could only sigh and admire her fortitude. Then quite unexpectedly when everyone had given up hope, the cause was discovered. There were now eighteen mattresses on the bed, and every now and then they had to be disassembled and taken out into the garden to have any dust beaten out of them. It was quite an operation, just as getting her into bed every night had involved a small army of designers, and skilled craftsmen had to be engaged to create the system of pulleys and platforms that raised not only the child but also the nanny who would tuck her safely into bed. How the offending object had managed to elude the attention of so many conscientious servants is difficult to understand, but there it was lying on the bottom mattress. It was a pea.

I know that this is testing the reader's credulity to its absolute limit, but this is what the sources say. How could anyone feel the presence of a pea under seventeen mattresses or, if they did manage to reach that herculean degree of fussiness, why would it bother them, let alone keep them awake at night? And in what kind of state was the pea after a period of years? Or was the malicious cook replacing it with another pea every time they dusted off the mattresses? And why didn't the malicious cook display even greater malice by increasing the number of torturous peas. Surely the Rich Man wasn't counting his peas every night.

You can tell that I have never been that convinced about the princess and the pea, and my scepticism was justified because in this case the disappearance of the pea did not improve the little girls sleeping patterns. But this too is of no importance, because here the story has an unusual twist, at least in this version. The problem with being a very rich man is that there is nearly always another very rich man who is richer and more powerful than you. And in a city nearby a very rich man had so consolidated his control over the local economy that he now had to go in search of the assets of another rich man, who happened to be our Rich Man. I say that he "had to" do this because it wasn't his decision; it was the market's. We should in fact now refer to the market as the Great Market because it has replaced god who has been pensioned off and lost his capitalised first letter in the process, and it is strange that this demotion should have happened in the land of the Triers precisely at the time that the atheist regime had died and a new regime had embraced the Church as the pillar on which the new new society would be built. Progress is erratic, but also intellectually incoherent.

First the rival bought the Rich Man's carpet factory and

vodka distillery, which the Rich Man didn't mind at all as liquidating a few assets is not necessarily a bad thing, and the sums offered for those assets were generous. But then it was a department store, a gym, a chain of supermarkets active in the whole oblast. Eventually the Rich Man declared that enough was enough and he wasn't selling anything else. He was then visited by four extremely musclebound individuals in James Bond suits and dark glasses. The intelligence of the Great Market is such that the richer the man, the more terrifying his thugs. Thugs come at different prices, and the wealthier the rival you want to scare, the more expensive the thugs that you'll have to buy. Perhaps it is understandable that some people perceive something divine in these perfect corollaries like the geometry of petals and sepals of a flower, which belong to mere nature rather than the pragmatic reality of the market economy. But I don't.

The Rich Man had to give in, even though the offer was far from generous, and after that the Great Market continued on its predictable course, which is even more cruel than nature's. In due and predictable course, the rival came after the Rich Man's personal assets, his homes, his cars, his paintings and his many symbols of wealth and success, but always he and his wife heroically defended the eighteen mattresses that supposedly assisted their delicate daughter to sleep. The rival and the Great Market, whose intelligence is as unfathomable as it is unerring, had no interest in the mattresses once the no longer Rich Man and his wife had moved them to a barn nearby, which they had rented from a farmer. There they continued to live, and I cannot say that they were happier or sadder, but there can be no doubt the parents were happier than the child. They had little time to reflect upon their misadventures, because they were too busy looking after their daughter and they had to dust off the mattresses themselves, more often because the barn had been used for storing hay. They had to cook for her and although they couldn't give her everything she wanted, they tried as hard as they could.

She, who had been brought up to think that love is expressed through a continuous flow of expensive gifts, could not recognise real love when it was set plainly before her. But then this is how humanity works: the lover is always happier than the loved one.

*

It is to be hoped that the scribe will have nothing to object to in this parable, given that the moral we can derive from it is so blatantly obvious and perhaps a little too moralistic. She sulks, as is her wont – as is her constant feeling of being unfairly mistreated in a world that she always considers to be fair, whatever the regime. Perhaps she's offended about what I had to say about religion. Ah no, she says that she's offended because my behaviour is offensive. But of course, what does she think that her role is in this project? Not that of a typist, although she does that too. I can get a shorthand typist anywhere, but I would have to look far and wide to find another easily offended, ambitious and not overly bright lieutenant. Her role, if we're going to write the job description, is to demonstrate that no career politician can get anywhere without being ruthless and occasionally even brutal. It is one of the prices I had to pay when I decided to put my struggle above everything else, even above whatever I considered myself to be. I have spent so much time fine-tuning my political persona that I cannot actually remember who I am – always supposing that the self actually exists. That's a little conceit that intellectuals invented shortly after I came to live in civilisation. The kind of thought that never worries the simple and innocent folk who haven't been civilised, and yet I have been corrupted enough to think that there is something in this conceit. Even if it is wrong about people in general, it's true of politicians – and perhaps actors who have to play so many parts, their selves have become just another part to play – part of the performance. And yet aren't "normal people" all people who have tried on various masks and then settled for one in particular, but it is no more than that: another mask.

The scribe has now got her head in her hands, and we'll have to go over this conversation again. I want it in, even if it doesn't paint me in a good light. I think that it is one of the reasons I wanted to write this memoir. Perhaps the only one. I am a conflicted person, I have to admit: I want to encourage people to be politically active, but not to do what I did and become a political leader. But why did I? So many reasons. My two husbands, who didn't consciously conspire towards this end, which they would never have imagined, but the sequence of our marriages, with their very different tragedies did by chance conspire to do just that, as did Halvatud's encouragement. But three more things were required: the birth of my son, Osip's terrible end and the despair that led to my hunger strike. I wanted something to happen or I wanted to die. Despair, I have to admit to it now after having been ashamed of it for so long, was the cause of my courage. I admire my own courage, just as I despise my lack of it, once I had gained a modicum of power. It's a cliché when describing so many political lives. A cliché, and is there a more condemnatory way to describe a life, particularly a political life, than to deprive it of its uniqueness. I speak with the bitterness of someone who has lived too long and seen their life's work unravel. Don't worry, scribe, I've never said anything to you that is even half as offensive as what I say to myself every day. I have been reduced to this: writing a memoir because my life's work cannot be read in its outcomes. They have disappeared.

The scribe looks up at me and says with an unexpectedly friendly smile, "In the end you didn't become a politician or even the leader of a political movement; you became an intellectual." It seems that this is supposed to excuse my bad behaviour.

"Have I become an intellectual?" I reply. "If I have, then I've become something there was never a word for in Surelik, and now we just use the Triers' word. And I must have become an intellectual when there is no longer any need of them. Who needs an intellectual when there's *entertainment*? - that equivocal word which is so real to advertisers but has no

329

more substance than our most absurd and futile daydreams. Fortunately in the lands of the Triers, some vestige of intellectualism survives because of their bookishness – the great success story of the old new regime.

"In the old new regime, there was the promise of its promise – a rational community that was neither rational nor a community, but could perhaps have become both of those things. Perhaps suffering was the price that had to be paid to be put on the road to that rational community. Is hope always delusory? Maybe, but there was dignity in standing up to the idiocies of people who built careers on inane loyalty to the policy of the day – and therefore the senseless disloyalty to values and beliefs once sincerely held.

"Somehow that seems better than the world we now live in, where everything can be bought and sold, even our bodies, even our meagre integrity, even the relationships we hold most dear. And have we got rid of the bureaucracies? Not at all, they flourish in all forms of progress and modernity, and once they have colonised another segment of our intimacy, there is no turning back. We accept and move on."

So my story is coming to its end. What? You think that exciting things can happen to an old woman of more than a hundred years? Getting out of bed is exciting – and exhausting. For me but not for the reader, I hope. I go to the office every weekday morning at about 11 o'clock. The few members of staff we still retain greet me with good-mornings and follow me with their eyes as I make my way slowly to my personal office. I shut the door behind me, sit down at my desk and smile with relief. I'm here and I'm alone. I'm here, I'm active and I'm *still* driven. Gone are the days – the heady days – of fighting against something that, although much stronger than me, for some reason feared me. Gone, gone, gone! Our current rulers don't even notice us; they're busy fighting amongst themselves, and their economy keeps us down all by itself. My fight is no longer a rearguard action; it is an attempt to salvage our dignity. The last shout of a defeated people. Defeated, I have to say, by forces beyond the borders of the Triers' lands.

Kurat's curse cuts deep, but I wouldn't cling to life if I didn't want to. I am so curious to know how all this will turn out, but I never will know the end of the disputed story we call history, because there isn't one, and besides my death cannot be far off. Perhaps I keep it at bay by keeping busy. It is just as much work to run a rundown or running-down outfit in a neglected part of the Triers' lands which is now more slighted than before it was created as an autonomous republic. In part this is because of threadbare resources now compared with then, but mostly it is the lack of that most powerful of humanity's innate propellants which we call hope. Before I make some fanciful attempt at a denouement, I will record a conversation I had recently with a Little-Noisy-Music journalist. I had some doubts about him so I insisted on meeting him in a café – the bigwigs' one that Osip went for, which is still the smartest in Vaikelinn even if we no longer have any bigwigs. They escaped like the rats they always were. I will keep to its more interesting parts because he was a tiresome fellow. After the pleasantries, we got round to the current nail implanted in my head – the idea that the empires are the source of all our planet's woes – and it started by chance from my admittance to never having seen the sea.

Journalist (smugly): I come from an island nation. It would be difficult for any one of us to have lived very long without seeing the sea.

Rahväema: I can imagine, but I can't imagine what I have lost.

Journalist: You have lost the chance to stand on the shore and watch the clocklike rhythm of the waves and marvel at the wondrous mechanisms of nature – or wonder at the endless repetition with carefully calibrated variations, which are dull, dull, dull. Our beautiful world is a gift from heaven or happenchance, or it is a gilded cage that suffocates our imaginations with the tedium of reality.

Rahväema: Do you really mean that you can't decide between the two?" (I said in anger and in admiration of such intellectual arrogance, which has always impressed me because it is alien to my nature and my culture). "Do you really live at such an altitude that you look on that dichotomy as though the two viewpoints were close together rather than at opposite ends of a very human spectrum?

Journalist: I am indifferent because I know that I cannot know, so why should I care and shouldn't I simply enjoy the mild tension between them?

Rahväema: Because yours is the rank cynicism of those who see humanity outside nature. One of the most important things I've learnt from your civilisation is that we cannot know anything with certainty. This was for me a bitter truth, as I came from a land of certainties and a modest eternity, but it does not lead me to your amoral disengagement. We can still look for relative truths from our human viewpoint circumscribed by callous nature against which we must struggle even as we admit that we belong to it like all other animals. This explains why evil is enduring and good is fragile and ephemeral.

Journalist: Someone like you will never understand the independence of the human intellect.

Rahväema: Someone like me...? A savage, you mean!

Journalist: Well, an educated savage, I'll give you that. But the intellectual limitations of the savage remain.

Rahväema: Really? There speaks a man with a single culture. I can understand more, because I can view reality from more than one viewpoint. You are alone with your arrogance and the certainty of your certainties even if you don't admit to them. You are somewhere I couldn't reach even if I wanted to. Nothing inspires me to that quixotic challenge. Stay where you are, because your approach – so typical of the West – will either whither or destroy us all.

Journalist: Oh, the West – the nasty West? Let's keep blaming it for all the miseries in the world. People in the Third World never make a mistake, I suppose.

Rahväema: There was a Little Noisy Music who said that imperialism consisted of a policeman and a soldier holding the "native" down, while a businessman goes through his pockets.

Journalist (sarcastically): Very wise for a Little Noisy Music.

Rahväema: What's more he went to the same school as my ex-husband. Apparently it was the most exclusive school in the land.

Journalist: But he wasn't your husband, was he? He can't be your ex-husband if he had never been your legal husband.

Rahväema: That's right – I don't know how you came to know that – but you're quite right. He was an evil bastard, if you want to know.

Journalist: But you fell for him.

Rahväema: And you want to rub it in. Well, of course I did. It was his self-belief, and you'll uncharitably think that I was a little woman looking for someone to help me through life. A protector? Far from it, I was attracted to his boyishness, even though he was older than me. There was something almost maternal in my feelings for him. "Feelings" I say, because

I have difficulty in thinking about that odious mistake. I was the one who wanted to protect him – that fully grown, overly confident, needy little boy. I who would abandon my own child was capable of those utterly stupid sentiments. I believe that the school must have been a factory producing intensely egocentric creatures terrified not only of poverty but also of anything less than fabulous and quite unnecessary wealth, and they must have been an elite whose voracious material and psychological needs the rest of the country had to feed. What unfortunate fellow citizens they must have been!

Journalist: But the wise one must have broken free.

Rahväema: You're right again. If you look at his photograph, you'll see a tall, thin man with a gaunt face who looks as though he were carrying the weight of the world's troubles on his shoulders. Which in a way he was.

Journalist: So how come he was so different from the selfish clones?

Rahväema: Something about an elephant he had to kill, I think. But that's the point: we're shaped by our environment, but not all of us turn out to be as convention dictates. Ultimately we have a choice; we can invent ourselves and rebel, even though we may always carry within ourselves something of the language, culture and mores we rebelled against.

Journalist: Are you talking of yourself?

Rahväema: Such hostility in your questions! Of course not! I didn't rebel against my own culture, but against the one I adopted in adulthood. I adopted that culture as a weapon to use against it. That, my friend, is something that *you'll* never comprehend.

Journalist: You know, I've read a few of your books – translated into the language of the Triers of course and I hope that you'll excuse me for not learning Surelik but life's too short for tiny languages – yes, yes, I've read your books and you could have been quite a good writer if you hadn't stuffed so much politics in your novels.

Rahväema: Is that right? You don't know much about my work then. I've also written books in the language of the Triers, although they're mainly about the Surelik language and society, or the history of the Surelikud in as much as we know it.

Journalist: Exactly! Why would I be interested in that. Whatever I might think of the Triers' lands and their politics, the importance of their literature is undeniable.

Rahväema: I don't think that a novel has to be either political or unpolitical, or that there's some golden mean of political content suited to it. A novel can be anything: it is the most chameleon-like of genres, because what differentiates it from the other forms of writing is that it doesn't tell people how it is – it allows the readers to interpret it in their own particular ways. There isn't one *Crime and Punishment* performed in one particular way, but as many *Crime and Punishment*s as there have been readers of it. Of readers who have performed it in their brains. The novel is the art form that requires the most of its reader-viewer-listener-spectator – or one of those ugly modern words, like the "consumer" or "end-user". I would call them co-performers, because no work of art can exist without its collaborator who understands it, delights in it, tires of it, is changed by it, is riled by it and above all doesn't value it in monetary terms – that's for the dull merchants who deal in it and thus objectify and commodify it. These soulless men are perhaps necessary – or rather are definitely obligatory in capitalist society in which everything has to be commodified – including our most intimate relationships. Is that political enough for you? I expect that it has filled your sensitive mouth with mud.

Journalist: A bit perhaps! But (he continued smoothly) I've been plying my trade for quite a few decades now, and I've heard it all. There's not an idiocy I haven't had to listen to, and there's nothing that can shock me.

Rahväema: If you've developed an inability to feel, you'd do well to change profession. But of course you will define that unhappy condition as urbanity. I'll speak no more idiocies to you, except this last one. You're a clever man and have learnt the Triers' language very well, in a manner untypical of your race – because you, like the bigamous husband I once had, probably think in terms of races – but you would have enriched yourself greatly if you had read the vast lands of the Triers like a novel, but instead you have read them like a history book in which everything in set in stone and perceived through the prejudices that brought you here in the first place. In other words, you came to teach and not to learn, and you'll return to your homeland unchanged and having gained nothing other than the urbanity that befits your age, or so you believe. In truth, it only shows how you've suppressed your creativity through all these years and missed a great opportunity.

Journalist: What opportunity would that be? (he spoke coldly to mask his irritation)

Rahväema: The opportunity to change and therefore to become yourself. Humans are social animals, so when as individuals they come into contact with another society with all its unfamiliar complexities, they are invited to assert their own individuality. Each individual will react in a different way. Society constrains us, and if we stay put, it is more difficult to be ourselves. Society does allow individualism, however great the cost, and conformity arises from our fear of exclusion, but the foreigner who arrives alone expects a degree of exclusion, and perhaps even seeks it out. And the cost can be lower in this case. It is a wondrous opportunity that can go in all sorts of directions, which you turned down for what? Your urbanity? Your world-weariness? Your attractive baritone voice of someone who has pissed in a lot of snow?

Journalist: Pissed in a lot of snow?

Rahväema: A Surelik expression. In our forest the snow comes every year, even though we are far south. It is because of our height above sea level. We didn't have lavatories, so we had to urinate outside. The snow changed every year and so it was different snow associated with different years. More snow, more years, more experience. An intuition that only an uncivilised people could come up with.

Journalist: Precisely! And I've had to put up with a lecture from a savage who in childhood never used a W.C.

Then he stood up and left, but not before adding, "I have more than enough material for this article." And I shouted after him, "My understanding of the language of the Little Noisy Musics is quite good. I hope that you'll send me a copy."
    I never thought he would, so I asked someone at the university to keep a look out for me, and eventually she sent me a photocopy. I will provide some extracts of the unflattering text:
    "I met Rahväema Ranavutavskaya in a decaying café probably built in the late thirties and it is doubtful than anyone has applied a lick of paint since the eighties. The atmosphere is provincial in the extreme, but unsurprising when it is immediately clear that the Sureliks are an indigenous people who have been unable to keep pace with the modernity. They show all the symptoms of such societies: an unhealthy reliance on funding

from central government, a tendency to alcoholism, the habit of blaming all their problems on others, and frankly a failure to understand that if you want a share in modern affluence you need to work for it. ... Ranavutavskaya is in fact fairly typical of the people she claims to represent. She is a wizened old lady who is very much a child of her time; in fact she reflects many of the myths and shibboleths of socialist regimes, in spite of her denials. She can speak quite good English, which must be to the credit of Sir Edwin Perkins, an old-Etonian and well-respected ethnologist whose painstaking studies of primitive peoples have quite unaccountably been eclipsed by smaller minds. He is supposed to have had some kind of amorous encounter with Ranavutavskaya during his field work in southern Siberia in the thirties. This is hard to imagine and there is no evidence to back it up, but she is very bitter about the whole thing, and if it is true, then this must be the cause of her contempt for our country and the way it ruled its empire, of which she has little understanding. It is the only evidence of an encounter of this kind, as I can think of no other reason for her irrational hatred of a people who have done her no harm. ... Ranavutavskaya is obsessed with her hatred of empire, particularly of the 'maritime' ones rather than the 'territorial' ones (her terminology, not mine). She has misinterpreted Orwell, when we all know that his criticisms were aimed exclusively at the empire in which she lived nearly all of her life. She thinks that Navalny, the anti-corruption campaigner, is a racist and a fascist, again without any evidence to back this up. ... Not only is Ranavutavskaya unable to understand what it means to live in a mature democracy like ours, but she also comes from the most backward of her tribe, the so-called forest Sureliks, and therefore struggles to keep up with events in the capital and the rest of the country."

Let readers make of that what they will. The Little-Noisy-Music journalist has created harmony between the me and my scribe, so he's not entirely a bad person – but almost. The irony is that the old new regime that died in 1991 had preserved the bourgeois culture of the nineteenth century, and yet was also innovative. Now we're like the West – no, not as bad as that, but slipping in that direction: the singers can't sing, the musicians can't play and the painters – well, they seem to have disappeared off the planet or to a place where they discuss concepts. Only the writers survive.

"Hold on," the scribe interrupts, "you can't believe that nostalgic claptrap. You'd be an embarrassment in Moscow – and even more so in any European capital."

"Very probably," I reply having noted that harmony was short-lived – and off we go. "What's that to me? I was forty before I really got a handle on those things. All my life I have been catching up. When I was a child, I didn't even know that paintings existed. I knew of cinema before I knew anything of that."

"Don't tell me that you admire all that square-jawed socialist realism! Please tell me you don't!"

"I do in a way. Admire? No, not that, but an admission that it served a purpose, yes."

"I knew it," said the scribe gleefully [yes, gleefully – get it down, scribe, get it down], "I knew that this is where you would end up."

Please note, reader, that at this stage in our conversation, I stared at the scribe in utter contempt at her stupidity – her inability to know me after all these years. "The first useful purpose of socialist realism was that it demonstrated how the state is incapable of creating great art. Of course, the state can be a good patron – one of the best, in fact – but it cannot dictate taste, not only because it lacks it, but also and above all, it lacks the ability to perceive what is only apparently not there. It is in the business of seeing things as they have always been seen, but great art is in the business of seeing things as they have never been seen. This is why socialist realism was a failure. It was insane of the Moustache to believe that he could command the necessary insanity of the artist – the terrible drive to distort in order to reveal, just as it is insane of the capitalist countries to believe that great art can be produced by the market – the mere ability to manipulate sales or demand through the tried and tested mechanisms of marketing, as though the insanity of the artist can perform to the tune of coins falling onto coins. Great art can be financially successful, as in the case of Dostoyevsky, Tolstoy and Shakespeare, but this cannot be the primary motivation which lies in the psyche of that particular individual."

"So it's all about genius," the scribe objects, "the generous, overflowing, Romantic mind glowing with genius."

"Not at all. Perhaps I led you astray with that talk of insanity. The dull insanity of the bureaucrat or market forces as against the explosive insanity of the human mind set free – a human plus something else: a hard-learned skill in the art in question. The principal madness of the artist is monomania, which is an inability to put aside an overwhelming passion to the point of near self-destruction. These are not things that a bureaucrat can understand, so when he recruits artists, he recruits other bureaucrats instead. Worthy people in many cases, but incapable of producing anything that pleases – or if it pleases, it only pleases other bureaucrats or the conventional people who are always drawn along in their wake. In other words, they produce for the day or even the minute, and fill the rubbish bins with the half-thoughts of the mediocre that resemble half-chewed cakes that looked tastier than they were."

"You're such an elitist," the scribe cries defiantly, and she's not entirely wrong.

"It's a wonderful world, if a Surelik woman from the forest who never went to school and was brought up in rags can be called that, but if you even stop to think about it, you'll find that the word 'elitist' has many meanings – as many as the people who utter it, and we always interpret it in our own way. Words are expansive, but the human ear is reductive.

"The second useful purpose of socialist realism concerns its actual output, which is often overlooked in the avalanche of scorn that envelopes it. We can agree that the great majority of it lacked artistic integrity, but we should also remember that all artistic movements create a few masterpieces and a mountain of dross. I'll concede that socialist realism produced more than many others, but are we saying that the statues in a Moscow underground station aren't great art just because they're of workers and peasants? When I first saw them, I wasn't that impressed but later I understood that they were being depicted like angels or warriors or men of power. It seemed that something was worth saving there; yes, in this case, something to admire. The existence of a unique culture – a civilisation perhaps – buried under the victors' prejudices."

And so we went on into the evening. We'll miss each other when this is all over – and that won't be long.

Listen, I should also speak more generally of how the Surelikud must behave. You'll have noticed how we Surelikud sit around and say, "This is how we Surelikud do it here; this is how we've always done it," as though this could justify anything and everything. And we smile to express the wisdom of our words, unaware of their emptiness.

Of course we would like to live in the world where our Surelik ways were solid, safe and as natural as dawn, dusk and the stars at night, and the forest was as unchanging as the mountains, but now even the mountains can be modified and holes drilled through them like a worm-eaten fruit.

Once, before the Triers came, things were different and perhaps in those days, we could glory in our good fortune and enjoy the tranquillity of our world. But no longer.

Sometimes, we are even more foolish, and say, "There will never be the like of us again." This is a more sophisticated folly, because it acknowledges the harsh and hostile reality we face, and even takes succour from the fact that we at least are Surelikud and can speak Surelik, and we should be proud of that because our children and grandchildren will never know the riches they'll have lost, as they become indistinguishable from the Triers. This fatalism is not wisdom, and is even more corrosive than the blindness of those who cannot see what is being destroyed before their eyes. I blame men and I blame chairs.

Men, because they're smug while women worry more about the generations to come starting with their own children, and chairs, because it's very difficult to think whilst sitting down, particularly in company. The Surelikud have always survived by keeping on the move. I myself am dictating this memoir whilst standing and pacing up and down. My seated scribe and I are anchored by her computer, but I will not succumb to the insidious and deceitful allure of the chair when I have to think.

The danger is real and we can survive only through change and cunning. We must move quickly on our feet and we must remain united. None of this is easy, and success is not guaranteed. The Triers and the Noisy Musics can sit around smugly, smiling inanities at a world they control, because they can make as many mistakes as they want and still survive. We don't have that luxury – that soporific luxury.

We must hold to our Surelik values, the greatest of which is our pacifism. This is not the pacifism of the submissive, but the pacifism of those who understand the technologic power of our enemies and their ability to listen to our every word and gauge our every thought; they would love us to rebel so that we could be obliterated from this world. Of course the moral argument is also strong and accepted in our culture, but now it is also pragmatic.

Many will say that the Surelikud are naturally an unwarlike and even cowardly people. Such critics do not understand the meaning of courage, but I will admit that we have never been warlike. Look at the Much-Languaged Mountains and how they have fought the Triers over the centuries. They are a pastoral, mountain people, war-hardened by their own internecine struggles, and for a long time their physical courage sufficed, but it is worthless now in this technologic, push-button age. There she goes again! My scribe always has some objection. Another silly name, she says, but this time she can't blame me; it's the name the Arabs used for what the Triers call the Caucasian Mountains, because the valleys were so deep and cut off from each other that they retained their pristine linguistic variety. At least until the Triers came and a long line of Great Caesars cast their avid eyes on that harsh terrain. Many, many triers met their death for that worthless piece of real estate over a period of sixty years. Worthless to the Triers, that is, for the Many-Languaged People loved to live on their steep inclines and look down to the small patch of fertility below and up to the cathedral heights above, carved by the greatest architect of them all – for, in spite of their divisions, they were all devout followers of God and his prophet Mohammed.

How many peoples there met the fate the Surelikud now could face? The complete annihilation of their language and culture. But unlike us, those who remain are still a bellicose people. I don't say that we're better than them, for what could they do? They had nowhere to run. They may have had their own forests to hide in and they did, but leaving their valleys was heavy going. Staying to fight was much easier, especially as these valleys were a cruel trap for those who did not know them – cemeteries for those obliged to follow orders.

The forests of the flatlands – or shall we call them the forests that conceal the plain and extend solidly in all directions – have made us who we are, and equally nature has made the Many-Languaged People who they are: a people of peoples, though less peoples now than before.

I call the Triers by this name because their world changes so many times and they still keep trying. I coined the term when their Great Experiment failed and the Noisy Musics came in like ghosts. They didn't invade like the Triers, though I hear that they do a lot of that in other parts of the world. They came to us through their customs and culture – and through their agents and advisors. Their food, their films, their television and their terrible music, of which they are so proud. It may have a few good songs but most of it sounds machine-produced, and no machine can emulate the skill and fevered intuition of the human mind. It also has an aggressive restlessness which we should take as a warning.

This is why I try to persuade people that the Noisy Musics are now our greatest threat and not the Triers. The danger of the Triers now is that they ignore us, having many problems of their own. But the invisible Noisy Musics want the whole world – every bit of it, including the Surelikud. If it's ear-piercing, then we'll pierce our ears, and if it's tattoos, then we'll turn our bodies into murals. Their hamburgers haven't reached us yet, more than quarter of a century after they took the capital by storm, but they will, even here in the back of the back of beyond. And our children will eat them in lurid interiors whilst listening to their noisy music and then go home to learn their colourless language from computers. We'll be colonised by machines and bad food, we'll be subjugated remotely and we'll be overrun by the ghosts of another people's thoughtlessness and prejudice.

When I explain this to seated men, they smile again, but this time with a little impatience, as though in the presence of a tiresome refractory mind which obliges them to repeat the obvious, the received wisdom they never challenge. "Your enemy's enemy is always your friend," they chorus as if it were the last word on everything.

"First you have to identify which is your enemy," I reply. And they laugh at the absurdity. They are trapped in the thinking of the past, and there's so much more to be said.

The learning and culture of the West is monumental and overpowering – sublime perhaps – but in old age it palls and looks like a series of set phrases full of doubtful premises; it has no heart, no beating pulse, no tear of pity, nor embrace of kindness.

Civilised people believe that goodness came after evil. That was how it had to be if you believe in progress: man was born like a baying animal, as cruel and cunning as they believe a wolf to be, but gifted with only a few inarticulate grunts that helped him in his endless life of hunting and killing. This absurdity is the ignorance of knowledge or the ability to know. We Surelikud believe that humanity was born solitary and thoughtful, and with a counterbalancing ability to sing, dance and enjoy each other's company, and First Man must have been First Woman, because no woman could be born of a man, but every man and woman has been born of a woman.

Europeans call fantasies "castles in the sky", but these are ambitious, egocentric imaginings. I didn't know what a castle was until I was in my forties. I may have seen one earlier but not recognised it as such. There are no castles in the Surelik lands, and no forts either. Then someone mentioned "castle" when I was entering a strange building and didn't know what it was. I was struck by the hard work and thought that had been put into it. Not in an aesthetic sense, as with a cathedral. No, here thought arose from distrust and hatred of other peoples – possibly quite justified. Its intricacies were imagined out of fear.

Civilised people think that we have no inventiveness, but they never ask why there are no castles and forts in the Surelik lands: well, obviously because the Triers had no fear of the Surelikud. Surely the paraphernalia of war cannot evolve out of the goodness of people, so why is it that evil are the primitive and the civilised are good and enlightened, when everything they do is generated ultimately from violence or the threat of violence. Of course our fantasies are not as grandiose as castles; we build shacks in the sky and paths that lead to stories and songs.

Civilised people forget that people like the Surelikud exist, if they can't see us. Then when they see us savages, they split into two opposing parties: those who find us repulsive and believe that we should be taken somewhere else – anywhere – or be disposed of, and those who find us quaint and think that we're on this planet to entertain them. The idea that we have just as much right to be here and would like to carry on living amongst ourselves just as we have for millennia never occurs to them.

My acquaintance with Western culture gave and took away, as I have said. It made me aware of how I had been thrown into existence, as we all are. Now I call it the disruption of life: we are born and have to adapt to a reality that is to us entirely unknown. We learn the shape of the world and its sounds, particularly the languages which enable us to communicate. I was born into a world that appeared to be the only world, and so it was universal and natural, though now I realise that it was unique and contingent. Modernity reveals the disruption because it reveals the great variety of human societies even as it attempts to homogenise them. If progress has its way, everything will be the same and the inability to imagine different worlds will return. Progress homogenises the moment geographically, but fractures the geography chronologically, because of its innate instability. The epochs become shorter and shorter. Will the moment when an epoch becomes no more than a second long be the moment of the apocalypse?

And you will ask, what does the disruption of being thrown into this world disrupt? Very possibly just non-existence. In our continuing ignorance, we can only wonder at the moment of impact. The interesting thing is that awareness of our original disruption is another disruption. It is the moment in which the substance of our existence – reality as we deludedly call it – feels as solid as an endless marshland where there's no hope of escaping its boggy grasp. And we have been stripped bare of the protective clothing – customs, mores and myths – that make existence bearable.

Some people are amazed at my adaptability: the way I have driven myself forward and learnt so much while retaining a strong sense of who I am and where my roots lie. When they kindly pay me this compliment, I feel that I am a fraud, but I am unable to deny the laurels I don't deserve. Why is that? Many things: vanity, most definitely; a desire not to offend those who have expressed how much they hold me in esteem, perhaps; my desire for the words to be true, undoubtedly; the fact that any negation would destroy the image I have carefully constructed over decades, very probably; a sense that I am entitled to the accolade after so much suffering and hard work, certainly.

However the opposite is true – or could be true. For surely I have been dragged through the twentieth century by history, and have not moulded my persona independently and taken on the world. I started, as the reader is now aware, with little more than a vague sense of what it meant to be a Surelik in the early part of the last century. My strong identity grew from my work as a lexicographer, because our professional lives are most powerful in shaping our characters. That was disturbed by the arrival of the weird and demented Little Noisy Music who unwittingly taught me so much about what humanity had become. During that period the old new regime not only taught me to love words and the writing and reading of them, but also instilled in me without my realising it a humanistic belief that was also universal. It stayed there like a seed in the desert and flowered with the arrival of the new new regime with its own concept of progress.

One thing that this new new regime has taught me is how little I have achieved. Halvatud was right: obligatory school-ing for the Surelikud would eventually destroy their relation-ship with the forest and therefore their language and culture. And I was the one who enforced it, simply to protect the autonomous-republic status, which would prove to have been doomed from the start.

The ecology of human culture is entrenched in the natu-ral ecology of the planet. It made no sense to concentrate solely on one small language – all small languages had to come together if their voices were to be heard. Paradoxically they would have had to use the dominant language in order to communicate with each other. So be it, if that is what has to be done, although I know how alluring those dominant lan-guages can be. We must always remember that all languages are defective in relation to each other, and yet each language is an incomparable masterpiece, a collective work of art that no writer, composer, musician, painter or sculptor can match. And whether it is carried in the heads of a hundred thousand or a hundred million is not of importance from an intellectual and artistic point of view.

Only under a particular economic system does it have any importance, but that short-sighted and soulless attitude is one we should be ashamed of, because humanity is much more than consumption and economic self-interest. Humanity becomes humanity when it believes in something beyond the instinctive needs of nature, however understandable they may be: justice, compassion, empathy, understanding and acceptance – all things that we could define as love. And these enhance relationships between people and between peoples, including their languages and cultures.

The difference between the Noisy Musics and the Triers before they exported their system to us was in how they perceived the individual in society – because all people, including those who deny the existence of society, could not exist without society. The Noisy Musics, often very religious people, believe in the soul which will go to heaven but don't feel in any way diminished by fighting as hard as they can to be rich. They have an irrational fear of being defined as suckers or losers, and this does not arise from any particular failing on their part, because it is inculcated by their society. But what do you do with money? You can only stash it or spend it. And if you spend it, what do you spend it on? Stuff. Bigger and bigger stuff. And what kind of society do you see out of your window? How content are you with your family, your town, your colleagues? Not much, because you've asked yourself the question and compared them with those in films and on the television, but you have to engender enthusiasm for them because you must convince yourself that you're not a loser. If you want to improve your skills, it is because you want to be considered the best, and your society delights in competition, but being the best is indefinable in most cases, so it is about self-promotion – incessant, untiring self-promotion that does eventually tire you. The idea that you could work hard to hone your skills solely because of the pleasure you derive from honing such intangible things would probably be looked on as "quaint" amongst the Noisy Musics, as one of their presidents defined the Geneva convention. And yet there was Meg, the heroic and neglected Meg whose lonely choice was to hone her knowledge of a neglected language and its shrinking society. The Noisy Musics are much more than my polemical dismissal of them, and some of their noisy music is in fact very good, but it doesn't have to absolutely everywhere as though no other music existed.

Popular movements rarely contain much tolerance. Like religions, despite tolerance being part of their credo. They draw sustenance and energy from core beliefs, even when these have been rejected by reality. The individual who objects, even concerning a relatively minor point of fact, is immediately condemned as a heretic and a distraction that could undermine the movement's momentum and coherence. This is the tragic condition of our species: we cannot find an intelligent way to use our ingenious technologies to benefit what humans are, partly because we have no real understanding of who we are, given our innate and chameleon-like flexibility. Vested interests are even more intolerant, but they use lies and distractions to make it seem that they are not the source of the violence.

I wouldn't call myself an activist and still less a militant. I'm a Surelik, and a true Surelikud would never call themselves anything as assertive as that. I am an advocate of the Surelik cause and in particular its language, without which we would cease to exist, even if they gave us an autonomous republic or independence. The young campaigners call themselves activists and militants, but they are much more submissive than I am to the centre and, worse, to the dictates of fashionable thinking – the insane economics of growth, steeped in the glutinous verbiage of evanescent progressiveness.

At this stage of a memoir, people are in the habit of saying that they have no regrets and that they did it their way, but I do have regrets, so many and they make me leap out of bed in the night, which is quite a thing for a one-hundred-and-fifteen-year-old woman. Regrets: things that were foolish and things that were bad. Foolishness can lead to evil being done to you, and evil being done to you can lead to you doing evil to others.

That is how our civilised lives work out. Messy. But I at least have one very particular moment in my life, and I suspect that the readers can guess it but I doubt that they can fully understand its magnitude, because they have never shared my hopes and ambitions. It is of course the moment in which the First Secretary spoke quietly into my ear, and gave me an autonomous republic ON A PLATE. It became easy to justify everything that came before because it came to that immense outcome, and all that came afterwards – but that slow unravelling of what had so fortuitously been gained has gradually destroyed that air of a fated life. They have cancelled each other out, but haven't quite taken us back to where we started, because I am no longer the same person. Kurat must have thought the pain inflicted by the near destruction of everything I had achieved would be greater than the pain I inflicted on those I loved or should have loved. He was right but not entirely: I have gained a wider understanding: the Surelikud's struggle to save their language and culture is part of a wider struggle to save similar languages and cultures around the world, and the struggle to defend the linguistic and cultural ecology is part of a wider struggle to save the ecology of the entire planet in all its incomprehensible complexity.

You know, I have often asked myself whether I'll ever understand the Triers' language and culture. I have studied it, internalised its every nuance, but I lack a Trier's childhood so I cannot smell, taste or feel the world as a Trier does. But have I lost the senses of smell, taste and touch of a genuine Surelik? Where is the Surelik girl who left the forest and fell in love with Pyotr Sergeyevich Ilusadev?

What does she say, my scribe? That I overanalyse things – that

I don't understand how society evolves – that the past is the past and you cannot let it haunt you. Hers, she says, is the luckiest generation ever. Ah, what does she know? What can she know? She considers the stupidity of modern ways to be good luck – to be happiness, whatever that is. I could weep at the dullness of youth – even if her youth must be in its mid-fifties by now. Not mine, my generation's real youth was monumental, grandiose; it was the titans attacking the gods and it was tragedy and sacrifice. So many died. So so many died that of course they haunt us; we want them to haunt us. To forget them would be to kill them twice over. And I am one of the last to understand. How can she? She is my foil, my friend and my chosen successor. The field was disappointingly sparse.

I've been living without a future for quarter of a century: when you get to ninety (or before), you know that death cannot be far off. There is little point in planning and of course you take life a day at a time. But then something else is triggered – something that is both eerie and liberating; it is a disconnect between the body and the mind – or is it the soul. Now everyone knows that *dusha*, the Surelik word for soul, came from the Triers' language and it is for us an alien concept. But quite possibly it is a useful one after all. We are talking here of a sense of being we all have and which seems real to us, even though it may be an illusion created by nature.

What does this mean? Well, it is very difficult to describe: a feeling – shall we call it that? – of no longer possessing one's body. It becomes no more than a useful carapace that you're obliged to drag around – similar in some ways to your clothes and your boots, except that it cannot be removed.

So when that chancer Ferdyshchenko started to insult me back in the capital during the nineties and go on about my advancing years, I was not offended. He had in fact spoken of me "dragging myself from one decade to another", and here too the buffoon touched upon an important truth. In old age we are weighed down by the failing machinery of our bodies, but we are also liberated from their neediness – or rather we should be liberated, because now in the West and increasingly amongst the wealthier Triers, the opposite is happening and the desire to defy old age with surgery, creams, special diets, hairdos and many other expensive subterfuges to delude others and above all themselves has become an epidemic of misery. Such people throw away the greatest advantage of old age.

The Scribe's Retort by Kiryutaya

I am the much abused "scribe" of this memoir. Although I was indeed Rahväema's secretary, I was also and still am a lecturer at the Surelik University in Väikelinn, and have a Ph.D. in Linguistics from Helsinki University which is considerably more than she can boast. On completion of the memoir's first draft, I was elected as the leader or general secretary of the West Siberian Surelik Cultural Committee, and to tell the truth, I felt the hand of history on my shoulder. I am not young but a middle-aged woman from a settled family outside the forest. Although educated in Russian, my family always spoke Surelik at home. We were literate in both languages.

Rahväema offered me this chance to set the record straight, and has promised not to edit it in any shape or form. I don't think that I'm saying anything the least controversial in arguing that she is not an easy person to work with. Stubborn and opinionated, she has probably caused more damage to the Surelik cause than she has furthered it. I am not going to criticise her in any way, because that is not my style. I am going to take this opportunity to be very positive about going forward. I genuinely believe that our struggle is one for democracy, prosperity and above all justice, as history shall demonstrate. As one of America's founding fathers said, "Those who deny justice to others do not deserve it for themselves."

Before looking at this memoir, its omissions and its self-regarding prose, not to mention how she campaigned, I would like to say a few things about Rahväema herself. For as long as I have known her, Rahväema has always had this smile. It is an ironic and somewhat superior smile. I have never been sure whether I am the cause of her disdainful merriment or whether it is merely this world of ours – or as she would probably term it with pronounced sarcasm, "this civilised world". A small woman clearly of East-Asian extraction, she had a great deal of charisma but it was not always used appropriately. To be fair to her, the prejudices of the twenties and thirties were difficult for her to throw off, and our decision to ask her to take on *temporarily* the position of General Secretary for a second time was a mistake.

People ask me why I put up with Rahväema for so long. Of course, she was a well-respected figure and had, at the height of her powers, achieved some important improvements in the status of the Surelikud. So to some extent, I was patient with her out of respect not just for her but also that whole pioneering generation.

Her career had many difficult moments: during the worst of the Stalin years, she hid in the forest and occasionally appeared at the settlements to say extraordinary things, such as "Wisdom is folly!" "Wealth of goods is poverty of spirit," or "Wealth of friendships and family is greatness of soul." There is some irony in this, because at the time she was without kin and without friendship, as the Surelikud of the forest mostly distrusted her. These were her years in the wilderness, when she was treated as a madwoman and feared. People had many more things to worry about than the future of Surelik culture.

Rahväema was certainly a most contradictory and occasionally exasperating woman. Although she became a highly educated autodidact, which she often attempted to hide from her followers, and she remained at one level the member of a distinctly backward society she had always been. Of course, some will accuse me of denigrating my own culture or at least condescension, but we have to face the facts: the forest Surelikud were a primitive people.

An example was her behaviour over a book she wanted to publish in the nineties, but withdrew when the publisher wanted to make some changes. You should know that she had published under communism and had accepted changes imposed by the censor. She may have complained vociferously but she accepted them in the end. When I challenged her on this inconsistency, she replied, "Censorship was intolerable, but at least it was predicated on a faith in the power of the written word – a shabby, distorted and bureaucratic faith, I admit. The free-market publisher, on the other hand, wanted to change the text to entertain the reader even at the cost of removing my essential arguments, which he possibly failed to understand. The catchpenny title he insisted on was an insult not just to me but to the whole Surelik people."

In other words, Rahväema was incapable of understanding the need to conform to the dictates of the market in a free society. She was unwilling to listen to expertise and adapt. We have to learn how to live with freedom.

I liked her idea of the world listening to the Surelikud and adopting their ways in order to save the world, but it is fantasy. I too was carried away by the sheer boldness of her ambition – weren't we all? But I am the voice of reason. For too long Rahväema has dominated our discourse with what should be and not what could be. She encouraged us with her dreams and her sacrifices, but no one dreams anymore and certainly no one wants to make sacrifices. She has outlived her epoch and now I have to educate the new Surelik middle classes about what the world has become and about how to have a stake in it. Moving forward, we need to build new strategic alliances and get the job done.

Rahväema's supposedly erudite outpourings show how far from the truth was her own invented history of being a nativist Surelik. She became a Russian intellectual, in spite of herself, and was increasingly integrated into the world she'd fought against, although she often directed the same accusation at me. Had she perhaps ceased to speak to her Surelik followers, and started to speak only to the world beyond? Was she actually dictating this memoir for translation? Something she often referred to. Was this an artful tactic or had she actually fallen in love with those she was supposed to be fighting against?

Rahväema seemed to be aware of this, as one day she said, "Civilisation – so-called – has trapped us within its meaningless comforts."

"Why 'trapped'?" I queried.

"'Trapped' because civilisation removes all choices by offering too many trivial ones."

I often felt that she said things solely to enjoy a rhetorical flourish, and on this occasion, I challenged her, "What is that supposed to mean? There's something empty in your extravagant claims you no doubt believe to be profound."

"Scribe," she sneered, "it depresses me that after all these years you still fail to understand a word I say. But in this particular deafness of yours, you provide a good example of what I have just said. In the comfort and security of civilisation you cannot understand anything, as you have become dependent on it."

Now let's examine the memoir itself. Rahväema claimed that she was born in 1900, but there is no proof of this. Births in the forest were not registered in those days. It couldn't have been much later, and the turn of the century was too close for her to ignore the opportunity. She became her carefully curated image. Who knows who she really was, or if she knew herself? So much work had been put into building a myth that coincided with history.

We quarrelled incessantly about the parables and all the other silliness. I told her to cut them out, but she smiled the superior smile that lifted her short stature high above me and said, "I have given up trying to explain some things to you. Both – the main text and the parables – are integral parts of the same work. And I have found that people like one or the other, but rarely both. This gives me much pleasure." She laughed, as though considering it a private joke.

However, there is an omission which is a much more serious matter. Before the fall of the Soviet Union, Rahväema often spoke of her three years in the Gulag, but afterwards she excised it wholly from her life story, most notably in this autobiography. She immediately shifted her hostility to the Americans, whilst becoming almost nostalgic for Soviet times. Consequently she decided not to reveal those years in the camps. She provided an explanation, but first I would like mention the little information she was willing to impart. It seems that not long after she had followed Halvatud back to the civilisation she sneered at, she was picked up by the Militsya for no apparent reason, and while she was in custody, it was found that she was wanted for vagrancy. Her trial was short, and she was not beaten. For them it was an open-and-shut case, and she was given ten years hard labour but the Thaw was not far off and the Gulag was shut down. She said that the conditions were so hard, that no setback or insult ever affects her much. If she had stayed longer, she would probably have been broken and become of no use to anyone, but this had apparently made her stronger.

So why did she leave out this important part of her lived experience? Let me make clear that she did not usually call me "scribe", but only during the dictation when she was "in character", as was the case here: "Scribe, why is it that with you I always have to spell things out?" she asked in that superior voice of hers. "The nightmare of the Moustache's years was over, and many writers have depicted the horrors of those times, and done it well. I prefer to concentrate on the new evils: poverty, never-ending wars, destruction of the environment – the wider global issues. Let the ghosts of those years rest in peace, but also in our minds. Those who lived through them will never forget. Besides Osip's death is enough for this book. Or did we delete it too?

"Listen, to dwell on one's own suffering is to make oneself a victim and draw all attention to oneself. You may object that this memoir is all about me – and again you are only half right: it is about me, but only Rahväema the political leader – the imagined person that I have become in the minds of my people. This is a very political book we're putting together, and even the parts that appear to be apolitical are indeed political – perhaps the most political."

I suppose that these words can in some way excuse the crazier parts of this book, such as the satanic Kurat who never ages. But she says "my people", an exaggerated claim over the Surelikud who are as divided and diverse as any other people. She did have prominence but this started to decline in the eighties, which explains her veiled affection for the old regime. She was, I believe, a very egocentric person. Nothing wrong with that. Now we are perfectly relaxed about such things, but egocentrism that meddles with history is inexcusable.

I challenged Rahväema about the existences of Kurat and Halvatud. Quite absurdly the first was unchanging and seemingly immortal, and the other surviving only by a miracle. And she replied in one of her more enigmatic moments, "You never fail to notice only the unimportant elements of a text. Where does that dullness come from? ... Oh, don't look offended. Being so easily offended only distracts you further. What you understood is not wrong; in fact it is patently obvious, but you must look further and away from yourself. Evil, in all its forms, is a constant presence, and even when it is pushed back, it awaits with certainty its forthcoming triumphs, but goodness is a delicate flower which blossoms in every child and is soon crushed in nearly all societies since the birth of civilisation. Where it thrives into adulthood, it is but passing evidence that humanity could organise itself better and more equitably, were it not for greed or 'covetousness' to use the Christian term most Christians wish to ignore. The tyranny of the desire to outperform others and humiliate others will always return, bold and disparaging of all who care about others and, most particularly, of 'do-gooders' whose very existence is an insult to the Kurats of this word."

"You'd better keep quiet about this," I countered, as I was and remain very sure of myself and my ability to confute her utterly ridiculous ideas, "and the defence of your characterisation only reveals your lack of ... sophistication. That is, unfortunately, the only word I can use for it."

Then she said the strangest thing, which I still don't fully understand: "It's odd that people like you who have been brought up in a fully literate society are unable to understand what literature is about." Then she adopted that arrogant pose of hers and marched out of the room without saying another word – the only time I genuinely managed to upset her. I felt uncertain and slightly lost, but eventually I just put it down to her little tricks. I doubt there was any real meaning to her words. She was, quite unusually, very offended and for many days she could barely speak to me. Work on this autobiography came to a complete halt, and in the end this must have been what brought her back to the dictation. It was as though she couldn't think unless I was in the same room as her – as though I were her mirror or her muse, in spite of her scornfulness.

Readers in other countries may wonder how Rahväema had such a hold over us. Even for me, it is a difficult question to answer. She drew her strength from her solitude, and even though she started her campaign in middle age, her longevity meant that we cannot remember a time when she wasn't dominant in Surelik affairs. Her ideas at times were unscientific or even fanciful, and her stories improbable or even impossible, and yet even modern rational minds like my own were partly drawn to them.

Clearly she lied or at least misled us by creating the myth of her Surelik purity, but she was purer than all of us, partly because of her age and partly because she was brought up in the forest and only learnt Russian in her late teens. She identified with that purity, but realised that she had to learn about the wider world.

Was her deceit vanity or a carefully calculated deception to further her political and cultural aims – to assist others and perhaps sacrifice herself? In recent times her interests genuinely went beyond the Surelik lands, and she saw all humanity as endangered as the Surelikud. This was where our paths diverged: I welcomed the fall of the Soviet Union as much as she regretted it. "The horrors of Soviet modernity," she would say, "were at least carried forward by good intentions, but now Russia is part of and also victim of a machine that is driven by humanity's base, petty and small-minded instincts that will sunder all the fragile, intricate and altruistic bonds that hold society together – bonds suggestive of something sublime, inexplicable and as necessary to us as the food we eat. This came from afar, from their millennial history, but they've now lost it and want to take us with them, and in the meantime the Surelikud have been obliged to run through that millennial history of suffering and loss of humanity in a mere century. The Triers' skin is thicker than ours; it carries generations of beatings, fears and Faustian pacts which were hopeless attempts to avoid the terrible suffering and humiliations of history. They think us to be innocent and naive, but I think them naive to think that we can live outside nature and even outside our own human nature – that contradictory vortex of desires, duties, empathies, cruelties, demands for power, and self-annulments. It is modernity and not primitive society that is the war of everyone against everyone else." In other words she had adopted a confused version of Russian Slavophilia which romanticised the peasantry!

You know, people ask me why I often revealed so many things about Rahväema's memoir, and criticised them openly during the dictation. They say that I have subverted the book I transcribed and worked so hard on. This is all very well, but I have a duty to the movement and this book will be a danger to it, unless it is put in its historical context. In spite of being in her fifties at the time, Rahväema was very much a child of the Thaw and never really developed her ideas much further after that time. "Peaceful coexistence" was what Khrushchev wanted, but both he and his protégé had no understanding of realpolitik. It was an existential struggle, and someone had to win. History has made its decision, and no responsible person would argue that the right side hadn't won. Capitalism has brought many choices which simply weren't open to us before. To survive in this exciting new reality, the Surelikud as individuals have to compete and show that we're as much part of the twenty-first century as anyone else.

I have told central government that, going forward, it is not really in the interests of the Surelikud to restore the autonomous republic. They have told me how much they appreciate my maturity as a politician and that they're ready for a strategic alliance – politely suggesting that this is a great improvement on Rahväema, and they tactfully avoided calling her deranged but implied something of the kind. We agreed, however, to involve all the stakeholders as soon as possible, and this is still our sincere intention.

I presented this commentary on her and her dictation to Rahväema herself and the first thing she said was: "Is this all?"

"Not everyone is as verbose as you are, Rahväema," I answered.

Then she skim-read it and returned it to me with her fist almost crumpling the paper, and she pressed it hard against my chest only to say, "Very good, Kiryutaya; it'll do nicely."

This was not what I had expected and as she walked away, I shouted, "Don't you want to make some changes?"

"No," she answered, "it's a view, and now it's an integral part of the book."

So I have her permission, and I'll make no more changes. We'll see what comes of it, and whether people will start to listen to me at last, because I have plans for the Surelikud.

Rahväema's Deathbed in 2017

We have set up a camera and a voice-recorder. We young Surelikud love technology which, like God, sees all, knows all and remembers all. But the old people disagree. They say, "Not at all. Not at all." They go silent and sigh before saying in a quiet voice, "Before the God of the Americans who brought us all this stuff, we could see all we needed to see, know all we needed to know and most significantly remember all we needed to remember, while also improving on it. We gave it mythical properties so that it could be handed down from one generation to another. Today nothing is handed down from one generation to another. The generations are like different planets in the firmament, each with its own orbit and purpose."

We young Surelikud laugh politely, and we know that one of the oldest old people probably agrees with us only on that point. Today we have set up a camera and a voice-recorder alongside her hospital bed where, according to her doctors, Rahväema Ranavutavskaya is dying although she seems to be as sprightly as ever – or nearly. There are twenty-seven of us crowded around her in a private ward, as well as Kiryutaya whose presence no one was sure of until the last minute. There is a feverish expectation and also a little unease, as is entirely normal in the presence of an imminent death – especially such an illustrious one as this. Or should I say illustrious amongst the shrinking population of the Surelikud.

Once we have introduced ourselves, and she smiles and nods to us benignly one by one, not without a degree of hauteur which adds a pleasant tension to the scene. Then there is silence. The longer it lasts, the more unsettled we become, and some of us feel that she is confused and does not know what to say, but I believe that her silence is calculated for effect.

She smiles as though some inner thought has amused her, and starts to speak: "As I have got older, I have started to fade, but this was not accompanied by a failing intellect as I had feared. Instead of death closing in, I found that my less urgent mind was connecting across vast spaces and cultures. I now feel the pain of others most fiercely, but I don't shout out for them to be avenged. I want an end to suffering and not its exacerbation. I started many years ago with the Surelik people, all of them – without exception or condition. You may call this love.

"We have been given time, but all we seek for in what we call life is security for ourselves. This is the progress I've been fighting against all my life – not to turn the clock back a hundred years or even some absurdly longer period about which we can, of necessity, know little. No, I fight against progress, because it has fragmented us, cheapened us, denied us creativity and instilled in us a desire for many more things than we need. We don't have to go back; we need to invent a new modernity that learns from the past and holds us together as a global people, and a planet whose physical resources are limited but whose intellectual resources and potential joys are infinite.

"I'm like a tree whose roots have suddenly learnt to sense – to hear perhaps – the rumours of this earth. Not a complete understanding but an awareness of its essence. Far beyond me, beyond the Surelikud and the vast lands and jurisdictions of the Russians to the lands of deserts and beleaguered equatorial forests dripping with warm dampness and luxuriance, I feel it all and wish to cry the sweet bitterness of an old woman's tears – no tears are so dense with meaning as these tears, and no tears are so neglected. They are dismissed as female foolishness bordering on insanity or even senility.

"No wonder that I have to keep up my facade of sternness and my aura of certainty, for the fate of the Surelikud depends on me and people like me, and perhaps so does the future of the world. The slightest sign of weakness, particularly in a woman, would be exploited by the powers that rule over us – the powers of modernity whose technologies enter our souls."

These words she now declares will later become so controversial. Some of us dismiss them as the ramblings of an old, old moribund woman. "Is her long life's work to be undone by a few minutes of words uttered from a confused mind," they ask sympathetically, "simply because of their chronology their position teetering at the end of a marvellous life giving them undue validity?"

Still others question her status as the "Mother of the Nation": "She was important once, but who is that frail woman at the time of her death? She belongs to another time, another century. In the digital age, the Surelikud can become a virtual people." Really, a virtual people? What could that diaphanous thing possibly be? And Rahväema was never frail, not even on her deathbed, as her ancient lungs pumped out those last fatal, fearful words, pronounced with all the prophetic zeal of a mind that has finally identified the endpoint of its life's struggle.

I was one of those who received her words as a revelation, a route that could put the Surelikud at the centre of the world and its history.

"There's one thing I have to say," she started very clearly after a pause, presumably for reflection. "We must not only be realistic in our aims, but also and more importantly we must perceive the moral imperatives of our times. It is no longer just about cultural autonomy or even political independence for the Surelik nation, but the survival of the Surelik nation within a viable world.

"I know that you don't want to hear this. You mutter and I cannot see all your faces. Sometimes, change or rather changing thoughts come out of arguments so complex that it is difficult to know where to start. So I have started at the most difficult point. I know that our dream was once a fully independent Surelik nation, something that had never existed before, because before the Triers came, we had no knowledge of nationhood, laws, police, armies and the written word, let alone the printed one. We lived as the birds do, free as the air and free of fear. Of course there were diseases, accidents, dangers and occasionally hunger, but there was no fear of subservience, malice and vertiginous power. This they call progress, and it has not only trampled us but also many peoples of the world. Though you don't want to hear this, hear it you will: many of those peoples have suffered much more than us."

"So when you went on hunger strike," one of us asks, "you were only a few years out of the labour camps, according to your 'scribe'. Had you not suffered enough?"

"That's correct, and it was Kiryutaya who revealed it. I was in the camps. When you've almost been broken at the wheel, you can stand up to anything because you no longer value life. But when the most powerful man in the country speaks into your ear softly and reverentially, and promises you everything you've been fighting for, you value life once more and some of that drug we call power starts to flow in your veins. You enjoy this and even believe some of the compliments that come with it, but then you age and you gradually perceive the emptiness of power. This is not a new perception, but it is from a different perspective. You no longer want to frequent the corridors of absurd hierarchies. You remember whence you came innocent and hopeful in search of knowledge whose contours you couldn't even have guessed at. You remember and you see the past in all its various colours; you wonder how you never noticed them before. But you couldn't have noticed them, because they encompassed your entire world, and now you remember them from a distant place, constructed out of ideas, passions, violence, hatreds, anger, so much suffering and then a touch of power itself. And that 'almost' is most important, because if I had been broken, then I could not have achieved anything, but the camps didn't quite break me, so they hardened me. And I was willing to take any risk. It turned out well for me, so I cannot complain too much. My pain was compensated not with money – which though useful never satisfies – but with joy. I speak of the joy that comes from a huge political victory, which can only be understood by a political activist, if that is what I was. The fact that it was gradually eroded does bring a little bitterness, but small nations, like humble people, do not seek power over others but simply for the load power places on their backs to be lessened or perhaps in some distant but happy moment to be removed altogether."

"Why didn't you mention the three years you were in a labour camp?"

"Wasn't my book long enough as it was?" Rahväema smiled.

"Rahväema, surely such an experience must have been life-changing as you've admitted? And therefore more important than many things you spoke of at length."

"What do you mean by important? Important in establishing myself as a victim, you mean. I am a political person – an activist driven by certain objectives. I'm deluded enough – arrogant, if you like – to think that I am capable of bringing about changes in our society – important changes. That is the aim that has been driving my life. It's true that in my distant youth, I lost a lot of time on relationships – most damagingly in the case of my ghastly bigamist husband – but eventually I got on with things by suppressing my own desires and needs. Who am I? I ask because we are created by our immediate relationships. The term 'social animal' has always belonged to our species and I mention it often. It is our inescapable essence and the source of our endless adaptability, but it is also the cause of our compromises and our unforgivable blindness to the realities and sufferings of those outside our group. A political activist of any worth and, even more so, anyone in pursuit of the truth must distance themselves from their contingent self to the extent that they no longer know who they are. They lose all interest in that, and this can also be liberating because it leaves pettiness behind. And is there anything that dulls life more than pettiness?

"Three years in a labour camp? Of course it changed me, as did so many other things, most of which can be found in my book, but what does that experience mean in the current context, when there are other battles to be fought? I reveal the evils of the Moustache's rule fully enough with the story of Osip Osipovich's judicial murder, which alone expresses my loathing for those unforgiving years. What more could be added? Besides Osip was a loyal communist. He understood that the Moustache was a malign despot and a destructive force, but he hoped that it would pass like a storm – as pitiless as nature itself. I cannot know how he met his death. Was he cursing the regime he loved or did he accept that the apparently random cruelty of those times had merely selected him along with so many other innocent victims? I believe that it was the latter, so why would I make a victim of myself, when so many others died, as did Osip. His was the story that eventually I most wanted to tell, but with some reservations; mine was a personal tragedy in which I didn't behave well, and I didn't want it to become a public one.

"We face other dangers now – more subtle and destructive ones, because they are so corrosive to the fundamental relationships that bind us together – which once occurred naturally but now have to be nurtured carefully in civilised society. The dangers now are existential – not only to ourselves but also to the future of our species and our planet. Everything in my autobiography leads up to that, and is written from the viewpoint of the final decades, which personally were less eventful."

Then suddenly I find myself saying, "Rahväema, I ask you this as a friend – and admirer – and I do so because this conversation is being recorded and final words often pass into posterity. By admitting this, are you not confessing to lying by omission? Your legacy is at stake."

Laughing weakly, she says, "Lying by omission: the twentieth century was full of it. People lied in this manner not only to others, but also to themselves. That is not my excuse, if an excuse is required, because you speak as one who never experienced the horrors of those years, and cannot understand. When I was in the camp, I could not survive by detesting it. To survive I had to accept it and slip into its demonic routine. But at the same time I had to fight to survive the next month, as without those months, the years would have been impossible. I did not waste energy on recording every little humiliation, and remember that every little humiliation was in fact enormous but overshadowed by every big humiliation – which were remembered because they have been engraved on my soul. Fortunately I was caught late and only served three years of my sentence. Many of my companions were there for much longer.

"And to survive my release, which in so many cases led to a psychological breakdown, I forgot everything except those most brutal humiliations, and those I closed up in a strongbox which I placed right at the back of my mind. Like most victims, I blamed myself. Above all, I saw my fate as justified, because I had abandoned my son to pursue a political career to defend my language and culture. You may object that such reasoning is absurd, but I have known many survivors and most of them have gone through similar experiences."

Another person says, "In the end we got to know about the camps anyway. Do you think that what Kiryutaya wrote at the end of your book was a betrayal?"

Before she can reply, the "scribe" breaks in and she's in tears: "Forgive me for all my criticisms of your names and parables and all those other things I said. I realise now that this was not 'silliness', as I put it, but your energy and poetic verve – your desire for a higher form of realism."

"My dear Kiryutaya, I may have had energy but I don't know about poetic verve, whatever that is, and I was not seeking a higher form of realism, something Dostoyevksy claimed in answer to a stupid question. He could only reply in a cleverly stupid fashion: never was there a writer who broke more rules in such a wonderfully creative manner. He was a gambler with money and a gambler with words.

"Nor did I seek absolute truth, something that eludes me – and eludes most people. In fact, you should be wary of anyone who claims to have found it. Which doesn't mean that it doesn't exist. It is a hidden treasure, which we may come close to as we stumble through life, but without ever realising it.

"I am just a Surelik woman who came out of the forest a long time ago and lived an extraordinary life. I can see that now, but that was not what I sought. That was not how I saw it at the time. I had no idea, and along the way I did wrong. I could blame the civilisation that ran on the concept of sin, but that would be dishonest. I am responsible for the hurts I inflicted on others.

"I wanted to tell the story – not of a victim but of someone powerless who found a way due to a quantity of good fortune to bring about some significant changes for a small people. I may not have saved the Surelik language, but I have at least prolonged its life.

"And in this you assisted me, dear Kiryutaya, in a way that you've probably never understood. You allowed me to deliver it as a monologue in the traditional Surelik form, and you allowed me to deliver it in part as a dialogue – the one between you and me – in the traditional form of one of the Greeks to whom Western Civilisation looks as though to another god – the god of patriarchy and contempt for barbarians – or savages, as they like to call us today. He was also the brilliant rhetorician who invented an anti-rhetoric whose false simplicity is the ultimate sophistry. This is why, I think, Europeans are convinced of their racial or cultural superiority; for them the Third World is populated by barbarians. It seems to me that Europeans have all the same ingredients – both good and bad – but in different proportions. And recent history has shown that even some European Jews can justify brutality on the same basis, which is something I find hard to understand because those of Osip's generation were never like that.

"You did all this for me, and I scorned you. Was I playing a part? Not really, because I chose you for your difference. We learn from misunderstanding – was there ever an engrossing dialogue between two people who agreed on everything? Of course not. Our differences were real, and therefore productive. I can only thank you, and you owe me no apology."

"It was a moment of madness," says Kiryutaya, "I think that my election to general secretary of the West Siberian Surelik Cultural Committee had gone to my head. You always said that every action comes out of a context."

"Exactly. And I don't suppose that you liked being called a 'scribe' either."

"No, I don't think that I did," replies Kiryutaya, gaining confidence, "but I never really understood what that was all about."

"Then I ask you to forgive me instead. But you have to understand that writing is a performance. The writer is no different from the actor, singer or comic. But no sensible person would be of the opinion that their performances were a reflection of their own personalities, because they obviously do things for effect. But for some reason they think that the writer – particularly the autobiographer – writes as if she were talking to her husband, child or even the cat. That's another of the reasons why I dictated it to you: I wanted to create spontaneous elements such as you'd find in a conversation between people of different opinions. And yet it was still spontaneity guided by art. We both know that we tweaked it quite a bit. The reader of my memoir – or our memoir, shall I call it – will know about the arguments we kept in the book, but not about the ones we cut out, which were perhaps the more interesting – or simply more interesting in their absence, because no work of art can be all-inclusive. It should only want to be. A human being is indeed an artful animal who attempts to project an image of itself for various reasons which are usually paltry and cheap. That's in everyday life, but in art the artful animal has to do everything she can to keep that image of her art. In everyday life this same animal filters all information received through human communication in the knowledge of this artfulness – with a proper scepticism and an unfortunate distrust. I say 'unfortunate' because that distrust makes of man the only social animal that is constantly alone. No wonder that we need art to escape from that and become ourselves once more.

"I speak of course of 'civilised persons' and damnably this is what I have become."

"All you had to do was tell the truth!" says Kiryutaya, who unconsciously is being carried along by the argument and has become forgetful of the mournful context which included a large group of people many of whom were Rahväema's admirers.

"You expect me to tell you the true story of my life? What is a life? It is an infinitely complex thing – a universe whose vague contours cannot be defined, and are always argued over. Most people think that their own lives are the narrative they want others to believe in, but others rarely do. Every human action, transaction, communication or emotion consists of a physical event, its intention and its interpretation unique to every individual but subdivided into infinite categories, starting with the distinction between those who know the person that action belongs to and those who don't. In that swirl of complexities often arising from the banal, we leave a trail of the indefinable – a mist of suggestions that we yearn to understand but can only simplify. Simplification allows us to produce a narrative as our brains are programmed to do, but not an understanding. The trouble is that when we have a narrative, we delude ourselves that an understanding is what we have – or maybe something even more extravagant: the truth you speak of.

"The physical event is surely the truth, you think, but even this superficial reality is subject to the unreliable senses of the actor and his or her observers, who may be more or less engaged. But the superficiality derives primarily from some-thing else: the observers know nothing of the real intentions of the actor, who in turn may not know much more than they do. And its interpretations? Well, this is a Milky Way in which all manner of prejudices, lacunae, linguistic differences, disparate etiquettes and social mores are at play.

"I also wanted spontaneity because I thought that it would allow me to skip all those uncertainties we encounter in our lives. I wanted to create a narrative in which I set off on a journey whose itinerary I had already sketched out. My successes would be my destiny and my failures mere obstacles for me to push aside. But dictation probably favoured honesty rather than a well-constructed narrative to present myself always as a leader in the making rather than a leader due to chance and a little quick-footedness. It is wrong to think that the company of our reason leads to honesty and detachment. To ponder is to have time to construct alibis and self-justification. Honesty, I now believe, comes from the human heart – from the conversational and not the literary. And all the time I had the inscrutable incomprehension of dearest Kiryutaya. I chose her well, but possibly for the wrong reason. It turned out well in the end."

"Still, I shouldn't have written all those horrible things about you."

"You had good reason, and besides, Kiryutaya, you're a civilised woman and you know there cannot be love without hate, or goodness without evil. As a Surelik from the forest, I had to learn that difficult lesson. In the forest it was possible to love without hate and to do good without knowing what it was, because the forest was vast and our needs small. If we wanted something, we could take it, and there was no need to take more than what we wanted plus a little extra for trading with the Russians. We had been conscious of their presence for many generations – or centuries – and we had relied on them for much of our clothing as well as knives and various other utensils, but our semi-nomadic existence limited our needs. Occasionally some rash person would purchase a watch during a negotiation with a Russian, but the proud owner would stop winding it up after a while. What purpose did it serve? It would take up room in his pouch or lie on a shelf in his tiny hut, valued as a piece of exotica – the symbol of a foreign culture, and yet no one would have envied him.

"Today, Kiryutaya, we live in a society where hatred is endemic, and you can be forgiven for occasionally hating just a little bit an awkward and unmannerly old woman like myself."

"Thank you, Rahväema. You taught me everything I know."

"Dear me, so little! I thought that you knew more than that." Some people laugh, and Kiryutaya blushes with discomfort in front of us youngsters.

"So you don't hate me after what I wrote?"

"Of course I don't hate you. I think that you're perhaps the best of a wretched, misled generation." This time there is more laughter and it was louder. "This is no laughing matter. Humans are social animals. They create their own individuality by interacting with others. Paradoxically the current economic system destroys the individuality it claims to promote by fragmenting them into consumers and wealth-seekers, each struggling in the same way to get on in life, yearning for the same bounty of riches and security. Some exploit and some are exploited but all are anxious and want the same things – neurotically so."

"Why shouldn't they seek wealth and security?" Kiryutaya asks.

"Why indeed? You're right to think that in previous societies people also desired those things. 'Why wouldn't they?' as you asked, but there is a difference now. In previous civilisations, people wanted those things, but ultimately understood that they could never be achieved. Illness, warfare, the violence of rivals, acts of God and any number of freak accidents preyed on their imaginations and they turned to religion, particularly in a crisis. They also understood that working as a community made life more secure, though still not entirely secure. But now wealth and security are believed in like a new religion, but nothing has changed. Those personal risks are undeniably lower, but the apocalyptic societal risks are greater, and yet the mirage of wealth and security persists.

"You see how important Kiryutaya is to me! I can rely on her to ask the right wrong question. Her inability to understand me is what drives me on. Without her assistance I could never have written my memoir. She is invaluable."

A silent youth steps forward and courageously puts Rahväema on the spot: "Why do you torture poor Kiryutaya so cruelly? She apologises and you distress her."

"Distress her? I'm dying, young man, so what do you want me to do in my last few weeks or days? Give up on doing what I have always done, and that's speak exactly what I think. You civilised people can disapprove of my behaviour, and then go behind Kiryutaya's back and speak ill of her. At least Kiryutaya knows exactly what I think about her, which is the most essential element of friendship. Distressing her? This is a distressing world, young man. Or have you failed to notice that as well? So many distressing things happened to me, but I was never distressed, because otherwise I would never have reached my current antiquity."

Then comes the inevitable question, possibly as an attempt to find a less contentious argument: "Rahväema, do you consider your life to have been a success or a failure, or a bit of both?"

"A bit of both, as is usually the case."

Perhaps disappointed by such brevity the questioner says, "Do you think that you've lost your radicalism in old age?"

"You *can* be radical in old age. In some ways it is easier in old age. It's true that old age is often fearful and self-pitying because so much time has slipped away, probably to little avail in the shadow of necessity or oppression. Old age often brings the obscene conservatism previously scorned in youth, and this conservatism is equally often construed as wisdom and pragmatism which supposedly come with experience, a word that conceals the most craven subservience. On the other hand the radicalism of youth is not universal and is often generational. The more radical the generation, such as the one that came of age in the West during the sixties, the more craven the subservience in old age. But old age does provide a particularly beneficial form of radicalism, because it removes ambition, which is the greatest incentive to compromise when compromise means complicity. Compromise where partial submission is traded for partial gains can be not only acceptable, but even the only way to avoid total defeat. Compromise that makes you complicit in immoral acts is however unforgivable."

Three days later Rahväema passed away quietly and calmly, as though she had at last said all that she had to say. The expression that she had carefully sketched on her mouth was the subject of some argument: was it a smile or was it a smirk?